Everything's
Still There

Also available by Kalyn Fogarty

What We Carry

Everything's Still There

♦ *A NOVEL* ♦

KALYN FOGARTY

alcove
press

Published in the United States by Alcove Press, an imprint of The Quick Brown Fox & Company LLC.

Alcove Press and its logo are trademarks of The Quick Brown Fox & Company LLC.

Library of Congress Catalog-in-Publication data available upon request.

ISBN (trade paperback): 978-1-63910-306-5
ISBN (ebook): 978-1-63910-310-2

Cover design by Sandra Chiu

Printed in the United States.

www.alcovepress.com

Alcove Press
34 West 27th St., 10th Floor
New York, NY 10001

First Edition: May 2023

10 9 8 7 6 5 4 3 2 1

Our Layla

Your soul was too gentle for this world. Eleven years of loving you wasn't long enough, but it never is with dogs like you. Your family will forever cherish the memories you gifted us with. I'd say rest easy, sweet girl, but we all know how much you loved to run fast. XOXO

Loved by the Fogarty family, December 2011–October 2022

◆ 1 ◆

BRYNN

Mid-May

The best advice I've ever gotten? Sleep when the baby sleeps. *Forget about the dishes and the laundry and the never-ending to-do list. It can all wait. Rest, Mama. You've earned it.*

—3BoysMamaMonty

"SLEEP WHEN THE BABY *sleeps.*"

That's what everyone keeps telling me. As if it's so simple. As if my mind could shut off the moment those blond lashes flutter closed against his cherubic cheeks. As if I won't lie paralyzed with fear that *this* will be the moment my baby stops breathing. Because who else will watch over him, monitoring every rise and fall of his little chest beneath the muslin swaddle, ensuring each breath is followed by another. Then another. Another.

"Sleep when the baby sleeps."

No, I won't be doing that. Instead, I force my heavy eyelids to stay open, blinking away the blur and burn of fatigue. I drink so many cups of coffee, my heart races, my pulse a live wire thrumming in my ear: *whoosh, whoosh, whoosh.* But no matter how on edge the caffeine makes me feel, my body is leaden with exhaustion, every step I take a chore that threatens to break me. I count the hours, then the minutes—seconds—until Kyle steps through the door each night. The promise of what comes next giving me the boost I need to make it through the meal.

After dinner comes my time of rest, the one hour a day I can relinquish my sacred watch over Cody while he plays with his daddy. One hour all to myself where my eyes don't just flutter closed, but cement shut, the weight of the day so heavy they can no longer bear it. When my alarm sounds, what seems like mere moments later, my body alerts me it's time to feed the baby. My next shift begins. The second half of my daily vigil that lasts long into the night.

No one warns you about this. While pregnant, I was given all the standard advice, both good and bad. I fully expected to not sleep, but I didn't take it quite as literally as it's proving to be. Between the unsolicited advice and all the books and blogs I poured over, I was naive enough to consider myself prepared for the trials and tribulations of motherhood: the exhaustion, difficulty breastfeeding, a gassy baby. Everyone promised it was all worth it. I was promised instant love and gummy smiles. They told me I'd be addicted to the sweet smell of my newborn's head. I fantasized about endless cuddles and the grip of a little hand around my finger. In short, I fell for all the bullshit they feed expectant mothers.

Why didn't they warn me I'd be terrified all the time? Not the nervous anxiety of a new parent. *That* I could have prepared for. Instead, I'm filled with the abject terror that something awful is going to happen at any given time. Everything is a source of distress or potential danger. Walking up the stairs? Frightening. What if I trip and drop him on his head or hit my own head and render myself incapable of caring for him? My solution is to shuffle like a toddler, both feet on each step before ascending to the next, all the while cradling Cody's head for dear life. Breastfeeding? Distressing. I'm scared he's not getting enough milk at every feeding, despite my engorged boobs and chaffed nipples. Cody's insistent cries before and after every meal seems proof enough that I'm inadequate, a failure. Does he cry because he's starved? Or is he too full? Sometimes he throws up after his meal, but I have no idea why. My only solution is to give him more. Always more. Until I'm sucked dry and bleeding, my baby still begging for something I can't give.

Kyle suggested formula so I could measure the bottle, give me peace of mind, but I'm assaulted with *"breast is best"* everywhere I look, so I resist this compromise. Everywhere I turn danger lurks, and no matter what path I try, I'm scared I'm doing it all wrong.

Kyle is back at work. The four weeks of parental leave his company offered flew by in a haze of dirty diapers and sleepless nights. Even though he wasn't commuting to the office each day, he was still preoccupied by dozens of emails and small fires it seemed only he could put out. His body was home with Cody and me, but his mind was often elsewhere. While I spend every second nervous about the minutia of life at home with a newborn, Kyle was anxious about all he was missing at work. He could barely hide his eagerness to button up his suit and get back to the office last week, kissing Cody and me goodbye at the door before skipping down the walkway to his car.

I don't blame him. His plush office offered something he might never find at home again—peace and quiet. Although he was helpful in his own ways, I was glad to see him go. It was a relief not to worry about him hovering over my shoulder all day, asking what he could do to help. I do miss showering more regularly. That task was much easier while I had a second set of hands available at midday.

For two weeks it's been just Cody and me for ten hours straight. Our morning routine remains the same. He wakes us at dawn with a blood-curdling scream that somehow has yet to wake Kyle. Maybe I should be angry at him, but I envy his ability to ignore these desperate pleas. One of us needs to rest, and either way, I know it won't be me. So, I spend a moment or two debating whether I should try to soothe Cody back to sleep. Generally, this is a waste of time and hardly worth the extraordinary effort for such little return. The twenty odd minutes of restless slumber don't serve either of us if I can even convince him to lie quietly for that long. Nine times out of ten, his gray eyes pop open and stare up at me, waiting for my next move, daring me to ignore him. If I don't rush to pick him up, his perfectly round cheeks puff out, his little brow furrowing before he digs deep, a shrill yell erupting from his tiny chest. This cry only gains in volume and anger the longer I leave him untouched. From there, his face turns first pink and then beet red, and my adorable little angel turns into a demon in the space of a breath. If I allow it to get to this point, there's no option left besides cradling him to my shoulder, where it will take at least thirty minutes of rocking and shushing before I convince him I haven't abandoned him forever.

Sometimes I try to vary this routine, but to no avail. I've swaddled him with a blanket with his arms in, his arms out, no swaddle at all. I've tried flat on his back, propped with a towel, perched on his DockATot. The only thing that works is holding him, and if I wait too long, the crying only quiets but doesn't stop completely. Too bad I can't stuff him back inside me like a kangaroo. I slept well while pregnant, comparatively speaking.

From four until seven, we snuggle on the couch or propped up in bed. He whimpers sporadically, and I shove a boob in his mouth to placate him, but this only works half the time. He thrashes left and right, smashing his pert nose against my chest and refusing to latch unless I hold his face over my nipple and force him to find purchase. At the hospital, the lactation specialist worried he might have a mild tongue-tie but never followed up after his initial evaluation. Another thing I should call the pediatrician about, even though the nurse constantly tells me not to worry. Each time she picks up I note the subtle exhalation followed by a brusque promise that *"Everything is normal,"* and she will see me at the next appointment, her manner of brushing me off as a hysterical mother both infuriating and embarrassing. Sure, I am a hysterical mother, but it would be nice if she'd at least pretend to care.

Around seven, I strap him into the BabyBjörn and make myself a pot of much-needed coffee before shoveling something quick and carb-y into my mouth. I haven't been grocery shopping since Kyle started back to work, and we're rapidly running out of food. Thankfully, he brings home takeout most nights, so dinner is taken care of. I rely on frozen bagels and dry cereal to get me through the days. As I stand at the counter, baby attached to me and crumbs falling to my shoulder, I worry I'm spoiling Cody by holding him so much. My mother said he was crying to manipulate me into picking him up, but I can't imagine he's old enough to wield such control over both of our emotions. Or is he? I vow to look it up, to hold him less, while also promising myself to eat healthier and to drink more water. *"You can't take care of a baby if you don't take care of yourself,"* the doctor reminded me at our first appointment. She gave me the whole spiel about putting your own oxygen mask on first, but I had to resist rolling my eyes. What mother wouldn't sacrifice her own mask to save her baby?

For the next few hours we both drift in and out of sleep, waking only long enough to fight through the feedings and the burpings. After each meal Cody writhes and screams in pain, his small body contorting like the child's in *The Exorcist*, while a burp or fart or poop explodes from one of his tiny orifices. Once this passes, he shrivels back down to his previous size and nestles in my arms, content until the next hunger pang wakes him with a vengeance. As afternoon rolls around, we watch television on the couch. The dishes are piling up and the laundry room is spilling over with clothes, but to get anything done I'd have to put Cody down, and the prospect of suffering through twenty minutes of rage screaming is too much for me to handle. So, I let it all go. I'll get to it, eventually. Maybe tomorrow it will be different.

Kyle gets home late most nights, carrying a different brown bag full of takeout: Chinese, Italian, Indian. The closest thing to world travel I'll be getting anytime soon. We eat together at the kitchen island, Kyle checking his phone while his laptop sits open in front of him. I relay the details of my day, and he smiles and nods, offering to take the baby from me. But Cody happily stares at his daddy, so I eat with my right hand and cradle him with my left, unwilling to risk upsetting him. After dinner, Kyle works in his study, desperate to catch up on all he missed those few weeks he was out of office. I watch more television.

Then my night watch starts, and I'm propped up with three pillows behind my back and one under each arm,

praying Cody doesn't fall from my chest, where he prefers
to sleep. Kyle snores peacefully beside me while I binge
Netflix until Cody dozes off. When I'm feeling brazen,
I lay him in his bassinet and roll onto my side, watching
him through the mesh netting, praying the sound of my
own breathing isn't loud enough to wake him. Regardless, we are up every hour or two. Sometimes less, sometimes more. It's all running together now. Awake, asleep,
in between. Who can even tell the difference anymore?

My eyes startle open as the clock reads 4:49 AM, the
numbers glaring bright red in the dark room. Cody
whimpers, the cries not yet spiteful. I woke up quickly
enough for him this time. He's slipped off my chest and is
wedged between my shoulder and armpit. Swaddled, he
resembles a baby burrito. I nudge him back into position
and fumble with the clasp of my nursing bra, my fingers
clumsy with fatigue. Whoever designed these things did
not consider sleep-deprived mothers trying to unfasten
them in the dark with a screaming infant in one arm.
Finally, it opens, and my engorged boob falls out. I cradle
Cody to my left breast and position his puckered mouth
in front of the nipple, but he shakes his head furiously,
refusing to eat. Kyle stirs and I hope this once he might
awaken. Ask if I need help. Instead, he sighs and rolls farther toward his side of the bed, oblivious. Leaning back
on my stack of pillows, I take a deep breath of my own,
willing Cody to cooperate. *"Hungry, tired or wet,"* common wisdom assures. Thank you, great parenting sage.

Still refusing to open his mouth except to scream,
I push the pillows aside and stand beside the bed, lifting Cody to my shoulder. Maybe he needs to burp, his
small tummy too full of gas to make room for his hunger. I push aside the bassinet, used so rarely in the last
six weeks, and stand facing the window overlooking our

backyard. A handful of stars dot the sky, but the moon is hiding some place out of sight. Rocking from side to side, I rub my son's back. Slowly he settles, but he's not asleep, merely waiting. Waiting for what, I haven't figured out. So I keep swaying, my frustration swelling.

Our yard stretches for more than half an acre behind the house. I stare through the sparse scattering of pine trees at the edge of our property and can make out the faint outlines of the houses in the distance, our neighbors on a parallel street. We moved here four years ago but still haven't met most of our neighbors, even though I always dreamed of living in a place where the people threw block parties and invited each other over for drinks and playdates with the kids, picnics in the park.

Flash flash flash. I blink, confused. *Flash flash flash.* Afraid I'm seeing things, I rub my eyes. *Flash flash flash.* A light directly behind our house flickers on and off three times in quick succession before breaking and repeating the pattern twice more. I keep my eyes open, waiting for it to happen again, but the woods stay pitch-black. Squinting, I study the space the light left behind, but it's even darker than before. 5:06 AM. It will soon be dawn, that time in the morning when the sun is just below the horizon and the promise of light is close at hand, but for now, the night is absolute. Whatever the flashing light is, it's done for now. I stare into the distance, wondering who else haunts this witching hour.

◆ 2 ◆

JOY

Mid-May

Lighthouses are endlessly suggestive signifiers of both human isolation and our ultimate connectedness to each other.
                              —Virginia Woolf, *To the Lighthouse*

I SOMETIMES FANCY MYSELF the modern-day caretaker of the Derby Wharf Lighthouse. In truth, the last caretaker's watch ended shortly after he abandoned his post to save his home from burning down during the Salem Fire of 1914. If rumors can be trusted, his wife ran from their house on nearby Summer Street to light the torch for him and was barely able to escape the wharf before the flames almost engulfed her too. William Osgood's watch officially ended when the lighthouse was converted to automatic operation in October of 1917. Whenever I make the short walk from my front porch here on Pickman Street to the end of the wharf, I think of old Willy's wife running through the streets while the town was ablaze around her, determined to maintain her husband's nightly vigil. I imagine I would've done the same in her shoes.

The lighthouse was built in 1871 and served as a beacon in Salem Harbor until it was snuffed out from 1977 until 1983. In 1983, the Friends of Salem Maritime, where I got my humble start, restored and relit the marker to aid in private navigation. Currently, a solar-powered optic light that flashes red every six seconds serves the purpose of guiding fishing and recreational boats to our harbor. She stands fourteen feet tall at lantern level, a square brick building painted red and marking the end of the Derby Wharf. My most favorite of the twelve historic structures making up the Salem Maritime National Historic Site that I dutifully oversee. The two other notable edifices are the Derby House, built by Captain Richard Derby, the first millionaire in the new world, as a wedding gift for his son; and the *Friendship of Salem,* a replica ship of the 1797 vessel called the East Indiaman. The other structures are all valuable pieces of Salem history, but far less impressive or visited, according to my log at the visitor's center and my own modest, yet educated, opinion.

Lighthouses have always enchanted me. Ever since reading Virginia Woolf's transformative novel during my sophomore year of high school, the romantic nature of the structures and all they represented struck me as nothing less than magical. To a young girl in the throes of adolescence, the lighthouse symbolized everything I dreamed of and feared most: longing, loneliness, desperation, and hope. The idea of a shining light guiding lost sailors to shore into the arms of lovers awaiting their safe arrival combined two of my favorite things—fairy tales and the ocean. I poured over history books and devoured stories of sailors drawn home by the light and others who crashed perilously into rocky shores when the light could not be seen.

Freddie and I moved to Salem in 1973. By this time, we'd been married for over a decade and had two children, the oldest not yet in kindergarten. Ready for a change, we traveled down the New England coastline in our old Jeep Wagoneer, the one with the charming wood paneling, leaving behind our families in Bangor but never losing our thick Maine accents. Though Salem was only two hundred miles south, it was like embarking for another universe. For the first year I spent my days crying to my mother, so lonely and out of place that I almost convinced Freddie we should hightail it back to Maine, where we belonged.

As the seasons changed, so did our fortunes, and Freddie's charter business picked up that first spring. By a combination of luck and happenstance, I stumbled on a part-time position at the Friends of Salem Maritime organization. I thank the gods for this group of women, for without them, the last fifty years might have unfolded much differently.

Loneliness and longing have always been woven together like a thick French braid in my relationship with Freddie. Ever since we first started courting in the summer of '59, I learned that Freddie was guided by the pull of the tides. The ocean called to him, luring him in with her ebbs and flow. Though he always comes home to me, I still experience the familiar stab of jealousy each time he pushes away from shore, leaving me behind. The Ocean is his mistress, her beauty matched only by her demanding nature. As a younger woman, I spent a good deal of energy harping over how much time I spent home alone with the children while he was unreachable, drifting somewhere offshore. He might as well have been on Mars. No matter how hard I cried or how loud I yelled, he still left, and eventually I succumbed to a life ruled by the water. Time and again Freddie promised that the kids and I were his priority, but in my heart, I knew the truth.

Once the kids were school aged, it was easier to fill the long hours while Freddie was gone. Baseball and ballet and school plays and carpooling ate up a good decade of my life. What little time I had left after caring for their every need was spent at the front desk of the visitor center at the Salem Museum, right smack in the center of Derby Square, across from the wharf. Every morning after the kids boarded the bus, I walked the fifteen minutes to my station, where I helped hundreds of visitors—even more in the fall months—by educating them about the history of our storied town. I specialized in the maritime history while my best friend, Gayle, took care of the more popular witch trials and Halloween lore.

Rubbing the last remnants of sleep from my eyes, I fumble with my left hand on the nightstand until I find my glasses and perch them on my nose before lifting my head from the pillow. I swing my legs from beneath the quilt without so much as rustling the right side of the bed. It's a motion practiced and perfected over the years, even if it gets a little slower every day.

I tiptoe five steps and I'm out the door and into the hallway landing, the soft rug warm under my bare feet, compared to the cold hardwood floor of the bedroom. Though it's spring, the mornings are chilly, and our old house has always been drafty. Four more steps and I'm at the top of the stairs. Grasping the railing, I ease down the twelve stairs, pausing on step eight, where the floorboard creaks and groans when you step too quickly. It's better to let your full weight down to absorb the sound. Lately I'm more aware of how narrow and steep our stairway is and I gingerly finish my descent, only letting go of the banister when both feet are set firmly on the bottom floor. Here the glow of a nightlight illuminates the landing, casting our front door in a pretty yellow glow. I turn right and squint my way through the dining room, careful to weave past the tight space between the serving table and the head chair so as not to stub my toe. Too many bleary mornings I've forgotten how narrow the room is, and end up wincing against the pain.

Finally, I'm in the kitchen. The waning crescent moon is making her final descent, and the room is lit by only the thinnest thread of her presence. We are heading into the new moon, a period of black nights every fisherman's wife bears with trepidation. The clock on the microwave tells me it's 5:06 AM.

I stand by the patio door and lay my hand on the light switch. I turn the light on and then off. Back on and off. Once more. Then I wait, counting. One. Two. Three. Four. Five. Six. After a slight pause, I turn it back on and off three more times in rapid succession. Count to six again. Flash the light, on then off, three more times before leaving the world in darkness once more.

Satisfied, I retrace my steps back up to the bedroom and slip unnoticed beneath the covers. Closing my eyes, I know I will doze peacefully until the first real rays of sunshine creep through the curtains.

♦ 3 ♦

BRYNN

Mid-May

A schedule defends from chaos and whims . . . but Chaos is a friend of mine.

—3BoysMamaMonty,
courtesy of Anne Dillard and Bob Dylan

NOTHING SATISFIES ME MORE than a well-executed schedule. An inspired theme with corresponding color scheme comes in at a close second. It's why I was drawn to event planning post college. After pledging Alpha Epsilon Phi at UMass Amherst, I was self-aware enough to recognize I'd never be the queen bee, an honor saved for the bubbly blondes who maintained their A averages while also keeping up their perfect bodies, nails, and tans. I was confident I'd be the most valuable worker bee in the hive, my brunette self the attractive— but not *too* attractive—sidekick, ready to buzz to the queen's aid. Whether it was organizing the Spring Fling, themed mixers, or a basic birthday party for one of my many sisters, I was the girl everyone turned to.

The Devil and Angel Party of 2006 was crowned best party *ever* thrown by ΑΕΦ, and it was all thanks to my meticulous planning. They say the devil is in the details, and not a single one escaped my careful scrutiny. I didn't mind that I spent most of the party scurrying behind the scenes, ensuring the kegs never kicked and the iPod playlist kept everyone bumping on the dance floor. It was my idea to insist every demon invite a cherub, so there was an almost equal amount of Heaven versus Hellions. Otherwise, I suspected every girl would show up in a red lace singlet and horns since UMass girls can't resist a chance to prance around in their raciest lingerie. My sisters joked I should have dressed as God herself since I orchestrated the night, but I was happy to wear a white slip dress and some silver makeup, the fairy godmother of the party.

Theme parties still excite me, although I've traded in keggers for Disney Princess parties and backyard October Fests. My first year after college, I worked as an executive assistant at a premier party consulting firm in Boston. At the time, I complained my boss was a type-A bitch who treated me like a glorified personal shopper or barista. This perspective changed after I struck out on my own a few years later. Although I resented the way my boss seemed to disregard my talents, I did recognize her extreme dedication to the events she managed. While she might have been cold and harsh toward me, she was always professional and charming with the clients. So even though she micromanaged my every move, her attention to detail was extraordinary, and her parties were an overwhelming success. Hindsight has shown me that it wasn't that she didn't trust me to do a good job, but that she didn't trust *anyone* to do the job as well as she could do it herself. Turns out, we share this trait.

As I rock Cody to sleep for the eighth time, I give up any hope of stealing a few minutes of rest myself. My mind drifts back to the last great party I threw, a theme new to me, which made it even more memorable. A local couple had called seeking help to celebrate their recent shift to "empty-nester" status now that their last child was off to college. There are two types of clients: those who retain some control over the details, insisting on being cc'ed on emails to vendors and on having the last say on all major decisions; and others, who let me handle it all, start to finish. This couple was thrilled to hand the reins to me, eager to flex their newfound freedom from such responsibilities. The party was a blast to plan, the unbridled ability to bring joy to a hundred guests like a drug to me. The Empty Nest party went off without a hitch, the partygoers reveling late into the night. The next day my Instagram feed was filled with snippets of the affair all carefully curated to fit my dynamic aesthetic, each picture racking up like after like. My inbox was filled with new clients, eager to obtain my services.

Scrolling through my phone Notepad I'm drawn to a list I made a few weeks prior to giving birth. Always a compulsive list maker, the prospect of checking off each item is usually enough to inspire me to get my ass in gear. As I read this terribly innocent list, I wince at how far off the mark I'd been. In my professional life, I was no stranger to the dilemma of reality not living up to expectation. I even took it as a personal challenge, setting out to create something shiny and bright from even the most mundane idea, with the goal of exceeding expectations. Once I would have classified this as my strong suit, my persistent optimism unfaltering. For some reason, I assumed this would translate into my life as a mother. *Wrong.*

★ ★ ★

Get baby on a three-hour eat-and-sleep schedule, I had written. *Easier said than done, Brynn.*

Pump after every feeding. Freeze enough so Kyle can take over one night bottle. I've saved a handful of baggies. I've no idea how long they last or if they even made it into the freezer. The pump is painful, and I'm pretty sure blood from my cracked nipples, mixed with the last bag I sealed. I joked with Kyle that it resembled strawberry milk before crying as I dumped the eight ounces down the drain.

Prioritize eating healthy and exercising thirty minutes a day. Log weight loss. My diet consists of coffee, carbs, and whatever takeout Kyle brings home. On a positive note, I log at least ten thousand steps from pacing back and forth, trying to get Cody to sleep. As for weight loss, I lost seven pounds, thirteen ounces in the hospital. I have a feeling I've gained it back, twofold. I'm too afraid to face the scale or my jeans to confirm or deny this suspicion.

The list goes on and on. Clicking out of the Notepad app, I thumb to my social media folder, where nothing reminds you of the stark differences between reality and expectation like a whole lot of face tuning and filters. My own Instagram feed hasn't been updated since the compulsory post-birth post, a shot of the happy family at the head of the operating table, our hair sheathed in blue bonnets and a drape protecting us from the view of my sliced-open midsection. Kyle smiles like a proud daddy, Cody is swaddled and screaming, and my eyes are closed against the pain and exhaustion. This photo seems to encapsulate the exact rhythm of our family life. I feel like we've existed in some form of this pose for the last six weeks. So different from the pictures leading up to the actual birth. Each week I diligently chronicled my pregnancy. A well-staged photo announced we were expecting. Cute bump pictures were posted every Thursday, my handy-dandy mini chalkboard reporting how far along I was, along with the appropriately sized fruits to mark the size of the fetus inside.

At twenty weeks we had an intimate gender reveal party, no blue and pink fireworks posing a fire hazard for us. It all culminated with an over-the-top maternity shoot, featuring me wearing an outrageous white dress while walking barefoot into the frigid March waters off the Salem shore. For each event I'd had my makeup expertly applied and hair blown out. The photos were edited to near perfection and captioned with short, witty phrases that racked up "like" upon "like." Saccharine-sweet comments and an abundance of heart emojis accompanied each one. *You're glowing! Beautiful! LIKE LIKE!*

My feed is missing all the photos I imagined posting after Cody was born. Always adventurous, Kyle and I used to love hiking and traveling, trying new things. For almost forty weeks I imagined strapping my baby into his ergonomically correct carrier. His chubby cheek would rest close to my heart, and I'd take him with us everywhere. We wouldn't be like *other* parents who lost themselves to their children. We'd be different, we promised. Our child would complement our life, adapting as though he was a piece of the puzzle we never knew was missing until he burst forth into this world, fitting snuggly in his place. Our baby would enhance the things we already loved. My *expectations* of motherhood were so high. Pre-baby Brynn enjoyed her stance up there on her high horse, looking down on the other mothers who clearly were doing something wrong, the ones she planned on being so different from.

The *reality* is nothing is going according to plan. Cody is always hungry but refuses to eat. He's constantly tired, but somehow neither of us can sleep. I expected to wake up every few hours to feed him. I expected the first few weeks to be tough. But I thought the time between feeding sessions would gradually lengthen until we were getting nice solid stretches of sleep each night. I thought Kyle would help with this, but he's proven incredibly resistant to the sound of his son crying only a few feet from where he lies. No matter how loud or long Cody screams, Kyle refuses to stir. Not that it matters. No amount of shushing, rocking, or swaying can harness my son's impassioned cries. It seems only a boob will suffice. As for my dreams of taking my baby everywhere. *Ha!* Hiking? Cody has traveled to and from the pediatrician three times and ventured into the backyard exactly once, and not even to the fence line. Just thinking about how much shit I'd need to pack to take him to the park, never mind into the wilderness, makes me exhausted. Imagining how often I'd have to stop to feed him, soothe him, change him . . . nope. Just nope. The realities of parenthood have proven infinitely harder than my Instagram-worthy vision for it. Like most social media, reality is a big letdown. Those Insta-mommies I follow who manage to dress their kids in matching outfits and get everyone to smile at the same time must know something I don't.

I stare at the feed belonging to 3BoysMamaMonty. All her photos fit a very specific orange and teal color palette, made popular a few years ago but still holding strong on this momfluencer's account. I'm sure she uses Facetune, but the editing is subtle enough to make one wonder if her skin is truly that smooth, her legs that long and shapely. Sparkly and bright blond, Montana Montgomery from South Dakota—not Montana, she laments, but maybe someday—has exactly one very handsome and famous husband, two pets (one dog and one cat), three boys under five years old, and four million followers and counting. She makes mothering look effortless. From her six-bedroom, four-bathroom modern ranch house, she shares photos of her family planting vegetables and herbs in their backyard garden, where they also raise their own chickens.

Somehow everyone and everything always looks glossy enough to be featured in a magazine spread, one of those *Country Living* shoots featuring a perfectly decorated farmhouse and a woman who brews her own sweet tea on her front porch. Monty is completely unattainable, yet relatable. The rational part of my brain tells me it's not real, but the part forever altered by postpartum hormones insists I keep scrolling, double-tapping this one and then that one. Commenting: *Aw, your boys are adorable!* It's like Montana is the mommy friend I share the everyday ups and downs with. *Like* on her newest post about how her fifteen-month-old son wouldn't sleep and woke up her three-year-old, who proceeded to climb into his brother's crib, effectively erasing all hope that the baby would fall back asleep. It ended with all three boys in bed with Monty and her husband. *Thank goodness for that California King mattress,* she jokes.

Off schedule, the boys were wild and moody. Chaos ensued. Unlike me, Monty is too cool to let this bring her down. Instead, she blasted a little Bob Dylan and let chaos consume her house until everyone ended up passed out on the playroom floor after lunch. *The only predictable thing about kids is that they are unpredictable,* she commented. Right on, sister.

The only predictable part of my night so far is Cody waking up at four thirty. By some miracle, he accepted my nipple and greedily sucks away, content for the time being. Without warning, he releases, wiggling his nose against my boob and grunts like a little piggy. I offer him more, but he headbutts me instead.

"What do you want?" I whisper, shifting him into a different position. He continues to mew, cute little noises that will only become more demanding. All the books promise I'll be able to decipher each cue, separate cries for hunger and dirty diapers, comfort and pain. They all still sound the same to me, like nails on a chalkboard.

"Please," I beg, swinging my legs over the side of the bed and wincing as I stub my toe against the leg of the bassinet. With my left hand I shove it out of the way. I might as well fold it up and store it in the basement with the other useless things we own. Maybe my little boy will be sleeping on his own by high school.

Cody furrows his brow, his pale blond eyebrows pinching together so he resembles a grumpy old man rather than a cherubic newborn. "Shh," I murmur, standing and swaying. Even in the rare moments when my son isn't in my arms, I find myself in this position, as though my body has reprogrammed itself in this short span of time, and my new normal is shifting side to side like a pendulum.

He whimpers and I change tactics, quickly flipping him onto his belly against my shoulder and rubbing his back softly, then harder, my fingers tracing frantic circles below his neck. He must need to burp. He can't possibly be hungry. I'm empty, drained, sucked dry.

Cody lets out a gurgled yelp. In the silence, it sounds louder than anything so small could possibly ever emit. I sneak a glance at Kyle, convinced this will be the time he's jolted awake. But his back is to me, and he sleeps soundly on his right side, oblivious of the battle ensuing on the far side of the bed. Maybe he's feigning sleep, squeezing his eyes shut and hoping I won't ask him for help.

"It's okay . . ." I plead, a desperate chant, my nightly mantra. "It's okay, it's okay, it's okay," I repeat, rocking side to side in time with my words. Cody settles and my fist unclenches against his back, my own breath starting to slow.

Outside the sky is so dark it's purple. Only a sliver last night, the moon has all but disappeared, casting the approaching morning in a hazy velvet blanket. Cody inhales and exhales gently, his weight subtly shifting. He's heaviest while asleep. My soft bed beckons, but before I allow myself the indulgence of lying down, a light outside catches my eyes. *Flash flash flash.* The same time as yesterday, just after five. My breath catches and I count the seconds. Six. *Flash flash flash.* My pulse races, my exhaustion forgotten. I count to six again and am rewarded with another *flash flash flash.* I wait, but the night remains dark and still. Cody stirs, his lips moving against an imaginary nipple, more peaceful in his dream feeding than in practice.

Closing my eyes, I debate crawling into bed beside my husband or heading downstairs to the couch and Netflix. I decide the silence is too good to last and spare one last glance at my pillows before tiptoeing from the room.

◆ 4 ◆

JOY

Mid-May

For nothing was simply one thing.
—Virginia Woolf, *To the Lighthouse*

A S A YOUNG WOMAN I was fascinated by the stories surrounding lighthouses. Beacons of safe harbor for ships and the sailors who captained them, they were a shining light in the darkness. But once upon a time, before automatic timers and LED bulbs, they were manned by a lone lighthouse keeper. Loneliness can breed desperation, and out of desperation many a romantic tale is told and retold, passed down until the truth is less important than the legend it inspired.

Many tales feature ghosts and other fantastical apparitions. Perhaps it was only the swell of the ocean hitting the rocks, its beautiful monotony so constant it drove the warden mad, tricking his ears into hearing the sweet notes of Beethoven's Piano Concerto No. 5 echoing against the stone walls. Or maybe he had heard one too many stories about the Seguin Island Lighthouse, his mind poised and ready to twist the circadian hums and clamors into something more nefarious. One of the earliest keepers of that torch was lucky enough to share his confines with his wife, a talented pianist. To break the silence—or drown out the sound of the waves—she'd play late into the night. Her husband, with no outlet of his own to cure his melancholy, was driven to insanity by the noise and murdered his wife with an axe before drowning himself in the waters he was so desperate to quiet. For years thereafter, it was said a piano could be heard as soon as the sun dipped below the horizon (despite the piano having been hauled away immediately after the subsequent keeper moved in.)

Freddie and I visited the lighthouse in 1984, a year before it was decommissioned. I strained to hear the music, but the only sound I heard was seagulls calling to each other amid the drowsy lull of the small waves lapping the shore. But I can imagine how one's ears might play tricks, eager to pick up the sound of something different among all that sameness.

A favorite anecdote centers around Boon Island Lighthouse. In the mid-1800s, a young woman named Katherine Bright married the lighthouse keeper and together they moved to Boon Island, right off the southern coast of Maine. How romantic to be secluded with your one true love, I'm sure the young woman thought. Although this story has many variations, all agree the weather took a turn for the worst after they moved to the island, with a deadly Nor'easter ravaging the coastline. Exhausted and physically ill from the toll of the storm, Lucas Bright knew he must still attend the light, so he tied a rope around his waist and traveled the short distance from the warmth of the house to the tower. Katherine watched from her window as a huge wave crashed against the rocks and engulfed her husband, pulling him into the deep waters. Somehow, she was able to grab hold of the rope and drag him back to shore. She tried desperately to revive him, but he succumbed to the cold ocean.

For five days (maybe six, maybe more, depending on the storyteller) Katherine climbed up and down the one hundred and sixty-eight stairs to tend the light while the storm continued to rage violently against the walls of the lighthouse. During this time, she hardly ate or slept. When the light was finally extinguished, the locals sent someone to look in on the young couple. To their dismay, if not surprise, they found the beautiful bride sitting on the bottom step of the tower, cradling the body of her dead husband. The townspeople rushed her back to the village, where she died shortly after, driven mad by grief and exhaustion. Since her death, there have been multiple sightings of a white apparition in the shape of a woman, and whenever the wind gusts, a terrible wail is said to resonate from the lighthouse, all her pain carried straight to shore on the crest of those great waves.

One keeper swears his dog chases an invisible entity around the island, and two others claim the lights turn on and off inside the tower when no one is around. The lighthouse is no longer open to the public, but Freddie and I visited the state park across from the lone island. Someday we'll get around to taking the shoreline cruise from York Beach. I'd love to see Katherine Bright.

The stories have driven me up and down the New England coast, dragging Freddie on tours by boat and on foot, eager to soak up the rich history and intrigue surrounding these special lighthouses. Over the years I've collected ghost stories like some women collect trinkets. No magnets or postcards for this old biddy. I prefer a good old-fashioned tale of mystery to honor the place. But like so many things in life, practicality has shadowed some of the romance. Although I'll always be partial to the legends and lore, Freddie convinced me to look beyond the supernatural and appreciate the magic of the structure itself. Everything from the height of the focal plane,

to the specific material used is all purposefully chosen to
withstand the harshest weather and maximize the efficiency in purpose. Every location encompasses a quixotic
history, but there's beauty in the ordinary details.

"Lovely day, isn't it, Spot?" I murmur. My distinctly
non-spotted black cat stares at me from his perch on the
wicker sofa, his bright green eyes inquisitive. Annoyed
at the interruption, he spares me a quick second glance
before continuing his previous pursuit of licking his
paws, first the left one and then the right.

"Maybe I'll tend to the weeding," I babble, more to
myself then the cat. He's ignoring me now, even though I
know he'll follow me to the edge of the garden and bask
in the warm spring sun while I pull weeds and prune
back the unruly rose bushes threatening to overtake the
perimeter fence. Freddie normally cuts them back after
the first frost, but he's been off fishing more often than
not this spring. It must've slipped his mind like so many
things do these days. I suppose it's my job now. You'd
think he'd have more time to putter in the yard now that
he's retired, but I swear he's around less.

Spot stands and stretches his long back, arching
toward the ceiling and letting out a deep mewl before
relaxing and jumping from the couch to the floor, where
he gracefully slips between my calves and rubs the soft
fur of his forehead against my knee. "Alright, alright,
breakfast first, then the garden," I promise.

I stand, careful not to step on his tail as he continues
to trace a figure eight between my slippered feet before
bolting in the direction of his food bowl.

Outside, the sun is starting to warm the day, and
the prospect of hours and hours of unscheduled time
stretches before me. It's only seven AM. Most people are
only waking now, but I've always risen early. The wife

of a fisherman, I'm accustomed to my day being ruled by the elements, and even though I'm no longer woken by Freddie's alarm, my body remembers, and I'm up before the dawn.

For now, I'll feed the cat and make myself a bowl of oatmeal. Start that letter to Katherine that I've been meaning to send. I could call, but I hate to bother her. She's always so busy these days, with her own kids both in high school and her demanding job. A nice, handwritten note from her mother will be a pleasant surprise. If she's compelled to call me back in return, all the better. I don't dare hope for a letter back. Kathy seems to think emails are interchangeable, but I beg to differ. No, a call would be just fine.

Spot leads me into the house in search of food. I nudge Freddie's favorite LL Bean boots out of the way. One of these days I'm going to trip right over them and break an ankle, I keep telling him. Always in the way, they are. As I pour the dry kitty kibble in the bowl, I start to formulate what I might say to Kathy. There's so much I wish to get onto the page. If only writing this letter were as easy as relaying one of my lighthouse stories.

Dear Kathy,

Remember when
I was thinking of visiting
How are the girls? Perhaps you all would like to come visit this summer fall?

The words won't come easily without another cup of tea and some breakfast, so I settle into boiling a kettle, deciding I'll sit down to write at lunch. Or maybe this evening, over a glass of wine.

◆ 5 ◆

BRYNN

May 23

Enjoy the season you're in, mamas! Everyone says little kids, little problems (big kids, bigger problems) but I say BS! All the seasons pose their own set of problems, but it's our job to capture the beauty in these moments. Take a minute to just BREATHE today. Happy Spring, everyone!

—3BoysMamaMonty

CODY SLEPT THROUGH HIS four thirty feeding, but my body jolts awake at quarter to five, poised and ready to empty my full and aching breasts. Previously a stomach sleeper, I've learned to sleep on my back. One clogged milk duct was enough to convert me.

Checking the clock, my first instinct is to panic. *Why isn't he awake?* But he's snoring peacefully against my chest, his chubby cheek smushed against my collarbone and a little trail of milk from our last feeding already dried on my shirt. Relieved, I marvel at how quickly a woman's internal clock changes in response to giving birth. Before Cody, I proudly declared myself a morning person to anyone who asked (and sometimes to those who didn't, I'm embarrassed to admit.) Every day I rose by six thirty AM and headed straight to the basement to watch the morning news while jogging for thirty minutes on the treadmill. After a quick shower and fifteen minutes to do my hair and makeup (I wasn't like *other* women, who needed an hour in the bathroom to prepare for the day—cue rolling your eyes), I was back at the kitchen island, sipping my morning coffee and scrolling through emails. The beauty of my job was that every day was a little different, and I was able to make my own schedule. A lazier woman might have slept in, skipped the exercise routine. But not me. I was motivated, a real self-starter. Back then I even limited myself to one cup of coffee, declaring caffeine was for the weak. I swore a little water with lemon was enough to jump-start the engine. Not going to lie: the current version of myself would really hate the before version.

When other mothers warned me I'd never sleep again, I always nodded sympathetically, but secretly I felt sorry for them. Their experience of motherhood seemed so depressing. They were always so resigned, crushed by their familial duties. For some reason I was convinced I'd be different. I had a *plan*. Once Cody and I settled into our rhythm, I hoped to schedule a final midnight feeding, after which Cody would sleep a nice long stretch until morning. Then we'd wake together and head down to the basement, where he would sit in his rocker while I resumed my normal, pre-baby routine.

Now what I wouldn't give to sleep in, even for one single day. I'd settle for seven o'clock. Seven would be glorious. Instead, my body snaps awake in fits and starts all night, my nerves tuned into every coo and whimper and rustle of the swaddle. On nights where Cody ends up, by some miracle, lying on his back in his bassinet, instead of on my chest, you'd think I'd sleep better. *Wrong.* Then I'm up all night, watching from the edge of the bed, my eyes glued to the rise and fall of his breath. Even though sleeping with him on top of me is maybe physically less comfortable (and probably less safe if you listen to the "experts"), it's easier. At least this way I can shove a boob in his mouth before the whimpers turn into full-throttled screams. My fantasy of waking together to get some exercise has been replaced with dreams of sleeping on my stomach with a pair of ear plugs, some blackout curtains, and a sound machine set to the loudest setting. And no baby in sight.

I should be sleeping right now. I should take advantage of the rare dawn that Cody decided to snore through. But I lie awake, even though my eyes are bleary with exhaustion and there's a vague throbbing in my temple, a sure sign of a migraine borne of dehydration and fatigue. And, of course, I need to pee. I thought my bladder would bounce right back to its pre-baby size, but it's yet another example of all that is permanently changed. Like my waistline and my ass.

Gently, I set Cody down on the vast expanse between my side of the bed and my husband's. Kyle rests peacefully, facing the opposite wall, the layer between us so thick that baby cries don't penetrate. Cody scrunches his forehead, his little nose wrinkling. I hold my breath, ready to place a hand to his chest, to soothe the beast lurking underneath his peaceful exterior. He resumes his heavy breathing and turns his cheek against the cool sheets, quiet again.

Flash flash flash.

5:08 today, a few minutes later. Somewhere across the woods, someone else can't sleep either. My bladder throbs, but I'm rooted in place, mesmerized by the spot where the flashing light shone. The space seems even darker than the rest of the forest, now that it's gone. My mind wanders into the darkness, into the ether. Maybe it's another new mother, feeding her baby at dawn, desperate for a little connection. Maybe it's a call for help, some sort of SOS I've been ignoring each night, safely cocooned in my big house. Maybe it's some sort of defect of electricity. A glitch. An anomaly in the circuit system. Maybe it's not even real, my mind playing tricks on me.

Six seconds later, the lights flash again in the same pattern. Another six count. Then they flash once more.

A message of some sort, meant for me. Blackness blankets the yard, heavy and final. I know it's over, but I count anyway. Hopeful. Six seconds pass. Seven . . . ten. Sighing, I turn from the window and tiptoe to the bathroom, but my bare feet aren't quiet enough, and Cody whimpers from the bed. Beckoning. Beseeching.

★ ★ ★

"Mommy's got this," I mutter, even though I most certainly don't have this. Cody stares at me from his reclined position in the car seat. Fifteen minutes after plopping him in here, and I've finally gotten him strapped in properly, even though it seems like the shoulder straps are impossibly placed and the chest clip keeps sliding down from his sternum (where it belongs) to his belly. According to the instructional YouTube video I've watched three times, both should be snug and secure. Theoretically, this makes sense, but I wonder if the woman in the video realizes how narrow a baby's shoulders are. No matter how tightly I pull, the straps refuse to stay put. As soon as I get the left one up and over the hump of his puffy jacket, the right one slips down.

Next obstacle: opening the stroller. Considering this was a luxury cruiser checking in at over fifteen hundred dollars, you'd think it would come with a remote control or a voice-activated system. The least it could do would be to snap open easily on its own, with minimal exertion. But no, it's large and cumbersome and much heavier than expected. None of the videos online show me how to unfold this monstrosity, and the instructions refer to it as *intuitive*, so I'm unsure if I'm simply stupid or this stroller is screwing with me.

After a few more minutes of wrestling with the beast, it pops open, and the handle smacks me straight in the chin. I've no idea how I'm supposed to lock the car seat itself in place and can only imagine there's some "intuitive" system I'm missing.

"We're gonna go for a little walk," I murmur. This elicits a smile from Cody. Or maybe it's gas—still hard to tell. "Just around the block," I continue. Obviously, he can't understand a word of what I'm saying, but all the books agree you should talk to your baby, explain what you are doing. It improves language development. Or maybe it helps you bond. It does something important.

A kernel of fear lodges itself in my chest as I lift the seat and struggle to lock it into place. We picked this Cadillac of strollers because it promised easy transfer of baby from car to stroller. This seemed very important when we considered all the adventures we planned. How naive I was to assume it would be so easy as to just click the seat in place and push the baby into my old life like he was some expensive accessory. Six weeks into this baby thing, and we haven't used this contraption once.

Hanging on the rack by the door is the designer diaper bag I registered for. A chic backpack, there are more pockets and compartments than I know what to do with.

Wasn't a diaper bag supposed to hold . . . diapers and wipes? *What else is essential to venturing outside of the safety of my home?* I wonder. Quickly, I google *diaper bag necessities*. Instantly, I'm bombarded with thousands of hits, each with a list that seems extensive, if not downright absurd. Half these lists were written by other moms, so they must be accurate, or else why would they bother to share?

Diapers, wipes, bottle, extra bottle, diaper crème, pacifier, plastic bags (what for?), *changing pad, hand sanitizer, sunblock, burp rag, swaddle, nursing cover-up, change of clothes, extra layers, toys, Band-Aids* . . . And the list goes on and on. Cody and I are only going around the corner. We can't possibly need this much stuff. But what if I do? Anything might happen once we walk out the front door. He could get hungry. It's not inconceivable that he might poop and need a change of clothes. It's sunny—the potential for a sunburn is high. Maybe we should just wait to take this trip another time. Tomorrow. Or the day after, even.

Cody lets out a loud wail, his face turning so red it's almost purple. He struggles against the straps of the car seat, stiffening his torso and stretching his legs before letting out a giant fart, followed by the inevitable sound of a huge diaper blowout, the type every mother dreads, the type that means yellow goo running up the back of the diaper and leaking from beneath the onesie all over the brand-new car seat cushion.

"Fuck my life," I mutter, plastering a smile on my face as I begin unstrapping Cody, since it's so important not to let him see my raging frustration. Careful not to get poop on my hands or on the pristine new backpack, I unfasten my baby. He lets out a satisfied coo, swinging his unsteady gaze in my direction and hitting me with a gummy smile. I know this smile should melt my heart, but I'm too tired. Maybe I'm wired wrong, my mommy gene misplaced. Or maybe I'm covered in shit and no amount of smiling, no matter how cute, makes that any more pleasant.

★ ★ ★

Take two. Both of us are changed, since, despite my best efforts, I'd noticed a smear of mustard-colored liquid smeared on the sleeve of my beige sweater. Cody looks like the cat that ate the canary. I wish something as simple as pooping could make me so happy. After struggling with the car seat again, my little bundle of joy (a few ounces lighter than before) is strapped securely in place, shoulder straps tight across either side and chest clip in the proper place. I'm aware we aren't getting into a moving vehicle, but God forbid I lose control of the stroller and he goes cascading into traffic, or we hit a speedbump and he gets jostled loose, his wobbly neck unable to support itself in such an event. At least he has this layer of protection, with its premiere safety rating. I shove two fingers between the straps and his jacket, testing the fit one last time.

As if on cue, a tightness runs across the front of my shirt and the familiar tug and pull of my milk letting down starts. I count back the hours since Cody last ate, sure it was only minutes ago—an hour, tops. But the clock on the microwave indicates I've been trying to leave for much longer. What was meant to be a quick stroll around the block has turned into an entire morning wasted in the foyer of the house. Cody stares up at me and wrinkles his nose. Even the baby is judging me.

"You hungry?" I ask. He blinks at me, lifts a finger to his cheek. Usually, he lets me know when he's hungry. Cody has never been coy about his appetite. As far as I can tell, he's perfectly content in his seat. Maybe the novelty of a new adventure outshines feeding time.

I contemplate my options: unstrap Cody and spend the next thirty minutes feeding him, or pump for a few minutes and pack a to-go bottle. The first almost guarantees we won't leave the house. Feedings are never quick or easy endeavors, and if I unstrap and undress him, I can confidently say I won't put us both through the whole ordeal again. In fact, the slight prospect of him falling asleep on my chest fills me with a little bit of glee. The possibility of closing my eyes for a few minutes dances in my brain and almost convinces me to abandon my mission. But I rally, reminding myself that Cody might not even latch and could end up red-faced and screaming, unable to burp after gorging himself on my boobs. Sleep is likely a pipe dream.

Pump it is. Although the flanges chafe my nipples so badly that no amount of ointment can ease the burn, at least I know milk comes out. Cody has only drunk from a bottle a handful of times. There hasn't been much need, since I'm always readily available. Initially, Kyle and I planned on sharing the burden of night feedings. Before Cody was born, we made a schedule that was intended to allow me some much-needed sleep in the first few weeks.

Cody had other ideas. He wanted his mommy and Kyle didn't have the same instinct for waking upon those first cries, often sleeping through his alarm and letting the quiet wails become inconsolable before stumbling to my side of the bed, where our baby would then refuse the bottle, insisting on the comfort of my chest. On these mornings, Kyle handed him over to me and promptly fell back to sleep, the unused bottle left to spoil on the nightstand.

Cody giggles, amused at my confusion. The longer the wait, the more likely he'll change his mind and

decide he needs a boob, now. I'll pump fast. We're only
going for a quick walk. A few ounces should be more
than enough. Who knows, maybe he'll even fall asleep
in the carriage, like so many other moms claim magically
happens. Maybe this walk will change everything.

★ ★ ★

Take three.

"Ready?" I ask while glancing once more at the clock.
Somewhere in all the hustle and bustle, morning became
late morning. No worries: I've nowhere else to be.

Cody smiles and I'm relieved he's still happy. Armed
with a diaper bag full of enough stuff to save myself and
baby in case of any potential emergency, I open the front
door and pull the massive carriage out behind me. The
sun assaults me, the early morning chill in the spring air
replaced with the first hint of summer. I immediately
regret my sweater and wish I'd thrown on one of the
sweat-wicking workout tops I'd favored while pregnant
but continue to wear, hoping they might inspire me to
work out. In the meantime, their stretchy material serves
to hide the mom pooch.

Squinting into the sky, I debate running inside to grab
my sunglasses. Cody watches me, his brow furrowed as
his fair blue eyes struggle against the bright glare. *What
is that yellow ball in the sky?* he's probably wondering.
He's only seen it a handful of times. I shake my head and
push the stroller down the walkway ahead of me. The
sidewalk is shady, and I've no clue where my glasses are
anyway. The thought of heaving the carriage back inside
is enough to convince me to brave the elements.

We make it to the edge of the driveway before my
chest constricts. At first, I worry I didn't pump long
enough. But it's not my milk. It's something worse.

Dread. It falls heavy to the pit of my stomach, leaving a long trail of acid from my mouth down my throat. My forehead is slick with sweat, and not because of the rising temperatures. I grip the handle of the stroller tighter, my knuckles white. It's like there's cement in my sneakers and I'm stuck in place, a statue of a mother. I try to take a deep breath, but it catches, and a low moan escapes my mouth instead. Cody tilts his head, his tiny mouth open.

"You can do this," I whisper, more to myself than Cody, who seems perfectly delighted with the situation.

Kyle thinks we do this every day. The stroller has been parked next to the door for six weeks, folded up and tucked behind the shoe bench. It's perfectly obvious that it has never been moved, but he was happy to play pretend. If you ask him what my morning routine consists of, he'd say Cody and I go for a nice long walk to the park after breakfast or head to the waterfront for coffee. Kyle would say I met up with a few local moms; he might even remember their names—he has a great brain for names: Tracy, the tall blond woman with the cute little girl, and Avery, the curly-haired brunette with the little boy a bit older than Cody. So easily these lies slip from my lips as we shovel lo mien and fried rice into our mouths, chatting about our days. He doesn't question my story, and why would he? As far as he's concerned, I have friends and a routine. It's enough for him—shouldn't it be enough for me?

"Let's go," I whisper, but my feet won't comply. Cody babbles, enough to jolt me into motion. A coo now might soon be a whimper, and a whimper can quickly turn into a wail, which is only a short trip to full-blown tantrum. Better to be moving.

I take a left onto the sidewalk. We're the second house from the corner, so it's only a few hundred feet to the stop sign. If we continue straight and walk a few blocks, we'll enter Salem Village. From there, a few more steps will lead us to the waterfront, one of our favorite places in my imaginary life. The park is in the opposite direction. But Cody and I go there enough—*every day, right Code-man?* I wonder if Tracy and Avery are there now, eating lunch with their littles—a bottle for the girl and some puffs and applesauce for the boy. Kyle's never asked the names of these imaginary kids, so they don't have names. Maybe they are picnicking and gossiping about the other moms in the area, specifically the strange woman from down the street who can't tell the difference between her baby's cries.

Instead of heading to the park—to my "friends"—I take another left at the stop sign. I push the stroller faster, my eyes straight ahead, wary of every bump in the pavement and each car that passes us. So far, only a single Jeep has driven by, but I know how many people drive distracted, weaving too close to the yellow lines on either side as they text and drive. The man in the Jeep lifted his hand from the wheel, waving politely at me and giving the stroller an extra wide berth before stopping for a full three seconds at the sign. A potential neighbor, I decide. Maybe it's Tracy's husband, a good dad, looking out for the families in the area. The quiet street and family-friendly atmosphere is a huge part of the reason we purchased our house. At least we got something right.

Each house sits on a large lot, none less than an acre. The back of our neighbor's house stretches expansively into the pine tree–filled woods, much like my own backyard. A simple wooden fence, more decorative than protective, separates the lot from the one directly behind it. High fencing isn't necessary when nature provides a perfectly adequate, and free, barrier. Thick trees covered

in ivy, along with all sorts of bushes, thorns and bram-
bles make crossing from one property to the next nearly
impossible.

I push faster. The next house comes into view. It's a
large Victorian style mansion, mostly redone. The ornate
towers on either side have been carefully repainted a deep
pink that I might have found offensive except for the chic
black trim on the door and the large shutters framing the
stately windows. The shrubbery is tasteful and obviously
professionally cared for, like most of the yards nearby.
I've no idea what the names of the plants gracing our
front walkway are, only that they are always carefully
trimmed, and something is always in bloom. A local
landscaping company handled the original planting a few
years ago and maintains it weekly. I wouldn't be surprised
if the company handles the whole neighborhood.

We pass in front of the pink house, a low fence whiz-
zing by my hip as I push the stroller faster and faster.
I squint through the trees and glimpse the back side
of my own house. That means it's the next house I'm
looking for. My backyard neighbor, my early morning
coconspirator.

It's a simple Cape Cod–style house with a rough dirt
driveway. A rusty Ford is parked out front, the back tires
on the grass and the front toeing the edge of the dirt.
Although weathered, the house has a loved-upon charm
emanating from the well-tended and bountiful flowers gracing the window boxes and hanging from hooks
along the edge of the newer looking porch that wraps
around the front of the house. Yellow paint is chipping
off the wooden shingles in places, but overall it's neatly
kept and quaint, although much smaller than most of
the other houses on this street, my own included. This
neighborhood is currently being bought up by families

drawn to the antique houses, but with grandiose plans to update, renovate, and enlarge. Kyle and I were no different. We loved our old salt box–style home, but this didn't stop us from knocking down a few walls to make an open-concept floor plan. Aside from this house's cute porch, the home looked original.

Standing at the end of the drive, I'm unsure of my motivation. I found the house. Now what? Suddenly my fascination with the owner seems silly. Part of me still wonders if the flashing lights are real or only a figment of my imagination, another Tracy and Avery, a story I tell myself to battle the loneliness threatening to drown me.

I rock the carriage back and forth, back and forth, a nervous tick in time with the ever-constant swaying my body has taken on. Cody is asleep, I notice, a few strands of tawny hair stuck to his damp forehead. Panicking, I wonder if he's overheating. I didn't think to take his coat off when we left the house, despite the change in temperature. Do babies get too hot? Is he sleeping or passed out?

"Don't wake a sleeping baby."

Dread threatens to overcome me again. *Congratulations, Brynn, you found the stupid house, checked it out. Now you can turn around and get back home, turn on a fan, draw a cool bath.* Is that a thing? I whip out my phone so I can google the best ways to cool a hot baby.

"Hi, there," a voice calls from the end of the driveway. I look up from my phone, in the direction of the source of the sweet sound, frozen in place. Part of me yearns to push my carriage away as fast as possible; the other part is unable to move. So much for my fight-or-flight response. I'm a silly deer stuck in the headlights. On the porch, an elderly woman pushes herself to standing from her seat on a wooden rocking chair. It's clear she's been there this whole time, watching me. My face burns red.

"I don't bite!" she says, laughing as she slowly makes her way to the doorway. "Come on up and say hi," she beckons.

Pulled by some invisible force, I push the stroller the rest of the way down the bumpy dirt driveway, drawn by the lightness in her voice.

◆ 6 ◆

JOY

May 23

Never did anybody look so sad. Bitter and back, halfway down, in the darkness, in the shaft which ran from the sunlight to the depths, perhaps a tear formed; a tear fell; the waves swayed this way and that, received it and were at rest. Never did anybody look so sad.

—Virginia Woolf, *To the Lighthouse*

"DON'T YOU LOOK AT me like that," I whisper, a smile touching the corner of my lips. Freddie always knew exactly what to do in these situations. It's no wonder he'd expect me to welcome the disheveled young woman into our house and offer her a glass of lemonade. It's also no wonder he'd make himself scarce during the encounter. Without a doubt, Freddie had a warm and welcoming heart. But actually entertaining new people . . . he left that to me. His eyes dance with amusement as I struggle to push myself to my feet. Getting down into the darn rocker was always a whole lot easier than getting back up.

"Well, don't bother yourself helping me or anything," I mumble. We both chuckle and I thrust my bottom all the way up from the flowered cushion. When I lift my chin up off my chest, Freddie is gone.

The girl can't be much older than thirty. She stands at the edge of my driveway, one expensive sneaker on the smooth pavement of Pickman Street, the other tentatively placed on the rocky dirt of my property. With one hand, she shakes the fancy-looking bassinet stroller back and forth, as if by sheer strength she might force the occupant to sleep. In her other, she holds an iPhone. It seems her generation comes with one of those glued to their palms.

Standing on the porch, I'm half hidden in shadows. The midday sun is directly overhead, the bright rays of May especially strong today. The girl squints in my direction, and I'm pretty sure if she could see me, she would've turned on her heel already. I wait, my left hand absently searching for my cane, propped up against the side of the house, and I watch her, afraid if I move too suddenly, she might disappear and prove to be some figment of my imagination. An apparition sent by the gods at high noon to quell an old woman's loneliness.

The woman looks down at her phone, releasing her clutch on the stroller, to shield the screen from the glare. She glances in my direction, but I sense her wavering, losing interest in whatever drew her here. I must act quickly.

Shuffling to the edge of the porch, my pesky slippers refusing to move at my desired speed, an unfortunate reality of age I'll never get used to, I lean against the porch railing. Freddie has been chastising me for this move ever since he built the porch over a decade ago, always warning me I'll end up toppling over the edge one of these times. But not today, I decide. The railing feels as strong and sturdy as ever, like my Freddie.

I lift my right hand in a wave, hoping my smile errs on the side of friendly rather than manic, as I feel. I'd hate to scare this young woman away, even though I suspect my apprehension is for naught. Desperation attracts desperation.

"Hi, there," I call out, my voice rusty from disuse. I cough, clearing my throat. "Beautiful day, aye?" *There we go—much better.* Clear, if not the same singsong sound of my youth. Freddie claims my voice could lure a sailor to the rocks. He called me his sweet Siren.

Even from this distance, I can see the panic in her eyes as they dart here and there, searching for the source of the voice. She opens her mouth but closes it so hard I worry she's bitten her tongue. Her limp brown hair falls across one eye, and she pushes it behind an ear, dropping her phone in the process.

"I don't bite!" I yell. "Come on up and say hi!" I move to the doorway, hoping this will encourage her to accept my invitation.

Instead of answering, she lets go of the carriage and bends to grab her phone. The stroller rolls a few inches, drawn by the slight downhill pitch of the road. It won't go far; she's far from the main road, and there's a curb at the edge of the sidewalk, but still, she lurches forward, in a panic to grab the wayward vehicle. A bit of gravel spins as she pulls the cart back to her side. A baby starts wailing, awoken by the rough handling of its floating bed.

I take a few more steps, both feet on the top stair. I want to assure her I'm only an elderly woman, not a threat to her or her baby. I don't dare descend to the yard.

"Would you like some lemonade?" I ask, noticing the sweat rings under either armpit of the woman's sweater. The day is already much hotter than expected. It appears this might be another spring that skips from the chill of winter straight to the heat and humidity of summer. Cool breezes and sweet spring rain, be damned.

The baby cries louder. The young woman takes a deep breath, and as she releases it, her shoulders sag as if the weight of the world lands straight across her slight frame. This girl is so different from my daughter, who always exudes an abundance of confidence, whose posture was ramrod straight, like a ballerina's, from the time she could walk, yet she shares something with my Kathy. When she looks up in my direction, I know what it is: something in the upward tilt of her chin, the slight defiance. Then her lip trembles and the resemblance is gone. Kathy never cried. My heart breaks for this lost girl, her sadness palpable.

"Come on up here, sweetie," I say, opening my arms. I pretend it's my daughter trudging up the walk, my daughter, who never once showed me such open weakness, who never needed me at all.

As if pulled by some invisible string, she turns the carriage and heads up the drive, the wheels spinning and bumping over the sharp chunks of rock sticking through the dirt, a phenomenon in New England that happens each spring after the erosion of all the dirt each winter. Freddie really needs to do something about it, lest we pop a tire on his old hunk of junk.

I wait patiently, standing as tall as my back and my cane allow. I'm reminded of my favorite stories, of the lighthouse keeper standing watch in his tower as errant ships sail toward shore, guided by the lights and sounds set forth from the safe harbor of the lighthouse. In some of these tales, the sailors were lost and desperate, driven mad by the sea. The never-ending swell of the waves with no horizon in sight, the constant motion of the ship—it's enough to push even the most stalwart sailor to the brink of insanity. Imagine craving stillness and solidity and finding only mayhem. No matter how hard these sailors wished for land, the only way through was through, counting the days, the minutes, the seconds until landfall. When these voyagers finally caught sight of land, or the promise of such reflected in the light of a beacon, they were too scared to feel relief, afraid it was just another trick of the waves, another joke of the sea, that cruel mistress so many others followed blindly, dragged in by the ebb and flow of her cycles.

But the sailors weren't the only ones driven mad. The keepers of the lighthouses watched the empty waves, convinced that the moment they let down their guard would be the moment they'd miss a ship in need of rescue. So they surveyed the horizon, that blue-gray spot in the distance where the water bleeds into the sky. Sometimes they swore they saw something, only to be fooled by a seagull or their own wishful thinking. Their tired eyes fell to the rocks and cliffs and insisted they saw the shape of a human, some poor soul thrown from a ship and swimming to shore, or to the sound of the mermaids and sirens who called them, drawing them to their doom on the rocky points of their station. The lighthouse keepers shone their beacons in the sailors' direction, in hopes of saving them, only to find that they were already gone.

I blink away the visions and focus on the young woman now standing before me at the bottom of the stairs. Her baby isn't crying anymore, but coos playfully from beneath the cover of the bassinet. Blinking again, I'm half sure she will bolt in the split second of darkness behind my closed lids, but she's still there when I open them. She looks up at me from lashes bare of any makeup, her own eyes bloodshot from a lack of sleep or crying. Maybe both.

I smile and reach out a hand, bidding her to join me. "I'm Joy," I say.

Like a sailor finally reaching shore, she stumbles the final step forward to take my hand. A tear falls down one cheek. "Brynn," she answers. "I'm Brynn."

◆ 7 ◆

BRYNN

May 23

Accept help from others—you aren't in this alone! #blessed with a supportive partner and the best little helpers a momma could ask for. Don't be afraid to ask—no, demand!—time for yourself. #selfcare is #momcare

—3BoysMamaMonty

JOY. FROM OUR BRIEF introduction, I can already tell her name is the perfect moniker. Everything about the sweet older woman exudes warmth and happiness, from the twinkle in her green eyes to the carefully stitched cat pattern on her navy cardigan. Turning her gently curved frame back toward the porch, she signals me to follow her. I push the stroller across the short distance separating us, eyeing the stairs warily. Breathing deeply, I debate the merits of unstrapping Cody and holding him versus wrangling the entire contraption up behind me. Cody gurgles and lifts both arms in my direction, wiggling his fingers my way. Thankfully, his demand for immediate attention has made the decision for me.

Parking at the bottom of the stoop, I bend and unclasp my bundle of joy from the safety of the car seat. Carefully cradling his head, I lift him to my shoulder and make my way up the stairs, stumbling on a large pair of black and tan LL Bean boots placed precariously to the right of the top step. Joy studies me, the wrinkles around her eyes deep and filled with nothing but kindness.

"Come, come . . . sit," Joy murmurs, using her cane to direct me to one of the two rockers pointed to face the street. A pitcher of lemonade rests on a wicker table between the seats. One glass is half full. A second stands next to it, as though Joy was waiting on the porch for me to join her.

"Thanks," I mumble, shuffling toward the rocker before landing heavily on the bright orange cushion.

Cody watches Joy as she settles onto her own rocker, a dent still in the cushion. I imagine she's been sitting here all morning, basking in the spring sunshine. She rests her cane against the faded yellow shingles before clasping both hands in her lap and looking at me from beneath her pearly spectacles. Some *before* part of me recognizes this is when I should engage in polite conversation, perhaps tell her a bit about myself and inquire as to how long she's lived in the neighborhood. Act like a normal human, capable of civilized interactions. Instead, a lump forms in my throat where the words should be, and I struggle to hold back the tears threatening to spill.

"Lemonade?" she offers. Not waiting for a response, she takes the glass pitcher in one shaky hand and pours a glass for me before refilling her own. "I made it this morning," she adds, her eyes dancing with a glimmer of the young woman she once was. My mother always said that your hands told your true age, and your eyes the age of your soul.

I envision Joy standing in her kitchen, squeezing the juice out of so many lemons before stirring sugar into the mix, tasting it along the way to get it to just the right level of sweet. *How many lemons, I ask myself, must it take to make this much lemonade? A dozen? More?* I find myself lost in the wonder of such a simple task and am only brought back to reality when Joy clears her throat.

"Before-Brynn" was good at this. Before-Brynn was charming and easy to get along with. I could walk into any event and fit in, no matter the occasion or crowd. It's why I was so good at my job. I was an expert at shedding my skin in favor of another; readjusting the mask as necessary. Somehow, I could be both unequivocally in charge while also able to fade into the background. How easily this identity slid away once the new one of *mother* took its place, leaving no room for the me I once was. Now I can hardly uphold my end of a conversation for more than a few moments, Cody constantly interrupting my train of thought, his needs overpowering everything. Now I only ever speak about the baby. I can't remember the last time I talked about something other than when he last ate, slept, or pooped.

Joy lifts her brow, patiently waiting for me. So lost in my mental chastising, I didn't even realize she'd asked a question.

"Sorry?" I worry she's already regretting pouring such a full glass of lemonade, and contemplate guzzling it down in one gulp so as to save the poor woman this awkward interaction.

Joy waves a hand at me, her gold wedding band catching the light. "No worries, my dear," she says, her voice slightly raspy at the edges. I wonder if it's with disuse or if it's always been her tone. Talking to Joy is like being wrapped in a soft cocoon, and I long to nestle close, curl up in its embrace. "I asked how old your little darling is?" she repeats.

Blinking a bit too hard, I promise to focus on the here and now, even as my eyes water, and the urge to settle back and keep them closed comes over me. *Focus.* This moment. This conversation. This cold glass of sugary heaven and the husky tenor of Joy's voice. "Almost seven weeks," I answer, forcing a smile. I can't wait until I can stop counting my son's age in weeks. It seems some mothers hold onto this measurement until their offspring are three hundred weeks old and entering kindergarten. "He was born early April." I brace myself for the inevitable response to my elaboration. Everyone always declares this is simply the *best* age (no matter my answer) and assures me he's *the most beautiful baby* (don't get me wrong—he is pretty cute, but I have a feeling they say this about all babies they meet) and then agrees that I'm the *luckiest* for getting to stay home with him (remind me of this when I'm changing my twelfth diaper of the day and wiping puke out of my unwashed hair.) They tell me to cherish these weeks because they'll be gone before I know it (*Promise?*).

But Joy surprises me.

"So little still," she muses. "I remember when mine were that little." Her eyes close as she loses herself in a memory. "So hard, that age." Not a question, but a simple statement of fact, one I whole heartedly agree with but have never spoken aloud. "My two are grown with children of their own now, but I remember how tough those early days can be."

Tears swim in my vision. Shrugging, I struggle to maintain my false smile, my teeth sinking into the fleshy skin of my bottom lip as I refuse to let it tremble. "Cody can be a bit difficult at times," I admit. The words feel like a small betrayal of my beautiful son. For all the hardships, I don't want anyone to think I'm not grateful for this blessing. I rush to walk back my complaint. "But I'm so thankful I get to spend every minute at home with him."

I *am* lucky. I've repeated these words to myself so many times in the last weeks, I almost always convince myself I believe them. Maternity leave is a luxury not all mothers are afforded, and the demands put on working moms offer a whole different set of trials and tribulations. When Kyle and I discussed our options, we mutually agreed I would stay home. Before Cody was even born, I felt guilty about sending him to daycare and only seeing him for dinner or bath time. It was more than I could bear, and I don't regret the choice. Most of the time.

Sometimes I imagine what it might be like, the other life. The thought of showering every morning and dressing in something other than yoga pants and milk-stained shirts before escaping the suffocating confines of my house might sound like heaven, but I'm sure the grass is always greener, and all that. Still, boozy lunches with clients while debating color themes and invitation calligraphy would be a welcome distraction from pumping and tummy time.

Joy chuckles, her stare unrelenting and knowing. If her own kids are grown with kids of their own, then she's a grandmother. I wonder how old she is. Sitting before me she's ageless. Wise beyond her years but with such youthful empathy she could be a contemporary, another mom at the park.

No matter her age, she's not too old to have forgotten the realities of motherhood. She nods, urging me to confide in her. I resist my initial impulse to keep my rose-colored glasses on, and decide I've nothing to lose by unburdening myself of all that I've bottled-up. Letting out the breath I've been holding since Cody was born, I begin talking, the words rushing out before I can tamp them down again. I talk and talk, pouring out my soul to this woman I've known all of ten minutes.

★ ★ ★

Buried somewhere beneath the half-truths and exaggerations is the real story, the one I can't bear even to tell myself. I don't tell Joy how I cry every morning while Cody sucks first from one breast, then the next, both nipples so chafed and raw that even his soft puckered lips cause bursts of pain so intense I force myself to bite my cheek so hard as to draw blood, to distract from the worst of it and keep me from screaming. Or worse. I neglect to share that each night I pray Kyle won't roll over and touch his hands to my soft midsection, his caress a question I've no desire to answer now, or maybe ever again. I hide from her the part of me that blames him for all of this. Once upon a time, we made love with the purpose of creating a baby. Now I resent the toll our actions have taken on my mind, body, and soul. I wish someone had warned me that, while it takes two to tango, it was *my* body that would be inhabited and ripped open, permanently changed, and *my* world that would be upended completely. In my limited experience, the majority of parental responsibility after that initial intercourse is distinctly maternal.

Instead of sharing the darker tidbits of my current reality, I channel my inner 3BoysMamaMonty. What would she say right now? *"Accept help from others—you aren't in this alone."* That was the gist of today's caption, positioned below a perfectly curated post featuring her three sons and their gorgeous father, dressed in matching black-and-white-checkered button-down shirts and bow ties. The boys were lined up, from oldest to youngest, and all looked up adoringly at their dad, who held one finger to his lips (*shh!*) and pointed with his other hand to Monty Montgomery, 3BoysMamaMonty herself, blurred (unquestionably still stunning) in the background. Monty appears to be taking a nap on the couch while their tabby cat, Beau, is curled atop her knee. The subtle filter matches the aesthetic of her feed, all the blues just a little bluer than is natural, the browns a little warmer than intended. The post is sponsored by a children's boutique, as prefaced in the caption. I double-tapped and hit up the link in the bio as instructed, unable to resist checking out how expensive those little bow ties were. Despite the fifty-dollar price tag, I ordered one for Cody.

As I studied her post, I searched for clues as to what her life might be like behind the lens. How easy to tell your followers to accept help when it's likely Monty has a staff of nannies on hand, maybe a housekeeper or two. I wouldn't be surprised if she had a personal assistant. Maybe she doesn't even come up with her own captions, the witty hashtags the design of some social media expert hired to create Monty's brand. Although her husband is often featured on her feed, I assume he's not doing the brunt of the parental or household duties. Brett Montgomery met Monty while they were undergrads, and married the same year he was signed to a major league baseball franchise. He was famous in his own right, and I find it hard to believe he's changing many diapers during his playing season. Perhaps he "helps" or "babysits" the kids, terms I bristle at every time I see a mother refer to her spouse in this way. When I'm with Cody I'm parenting and *doing my job*. The two times Kyle woke up to take care of Cody—the first while we were still in the hospital, when I couldn't stand because my C-section stitches were bleeding and infected; and the second, two weeks later, when I was so exhausted I threw up over the side of the bed—you'd have thought he was the prince in his very own fairy tale. He's yet to let me forget how he watched Cody *all by himself*, as if I should call the press or suggest a Hallmark movie be made in his honor, starring Kyle as super-daddy himself. Now I'm hesitant to ask for help for fear I may stab my husband with a butter knife the next time her refers to his few hours of baby duty after dinner as "daddy-daycare."

Cody fusses, sticking his tongue out and rooting around near my left breast. Immediately, my milk lets down, the sensation less urgent than normal thanks to the recent pumping session. Regardless, this is probably my cue to leave. The tug of disappointment is stronger than my desire to feed my baby, and shame courses over me. What is wrong with me that I'd rather sit here talking to a stranger than do the most natural thing in the world?

"Do you have a bottle?" Joy asks, her eyes flicking from Cody's face to my own.

Cody hardly ever accepts a bottle. It's unlikely he will drink from the one I've prepared, especially with the prospect of my boob so close at hand. But whipping out my boob on her porch might be too much, too soon. Joy and I shared a few stories and some lemonade, but I'm not sure we are ready for full frontal nudity yet.

Despite my misgivings, I nod before remembering that the diaper bag is still on the front lawn. Moving Cody while he's hungry and impatient will no doubt elicit a few wails. With every second that passes, I'm sure I should pack him up and push him the five minutes home.

"It's okay—I should go. He's a picky eater, and I don't want to torture you with his crying," I mumble, pushing myself to stand with my free arm.

Disappointment clouds Joy's face. "Oh, I see," she says, her shoulders sagging as she rests her lemonade on the table. "May I try?" she asks, holding her arms out in my direction.

Torn, I fear Cody will squirm in her frail arms and be too much for her to hold. But she's shown us so much kindness today, I would hate for her to think I don't trust her with my baby. In these moments, I wish my mommy intuition would kick in like Monty promises. I've been waiting nine months and change, and still—nothing.

What the hell.

"Sure," I say, holding Cody tight to my chest a second longer, willing him to cooperate. "I just need to grab his bottle from the diaper bag." My eyes dart to the stroller. Sensing my anxiety, Cody lets out a guttural cry. *Hungry. Scared. Needy.* This cry demands. I think. One of those cues, possibly all three.

Joy nods, holding her arms out again. "Here, let me take him while you get it," she says, her voice suddenly authoritative, leaving no room for argument. If only someone would speak like this all day, tell me exactly what to do then things might be easier. I bet this is what it would be like to have a nanny, my own Mary Poppins.

I transfer Cody into her outstretched arms, careful to hold his head until it settles on the soft cashmere of her sweater. But I needn't have worried. Joy expertly cradles him into the nook of her left arm and begins stroking his forehead with the pointer finger of her right hand. Instantly, he settles, looking up at her with his bright blue eyes, obviously curious as to who this new person holding him might be. Only a few people have held him since he was born, aside from his parents and the hospital staff. My fear of him having stranger danger was for nothing.

Afraid his contentment will be short-lived, I trip over the boots again in my hurry to grab his bottle. But my hustle is unnecessary. Cody is snuggled even deeper into Joy's embrace, his eyes closing as she rubs the space between his eyes softly, over and over.

Catching my stare, she smiles. "A little trick I used to do with my kids," she whispers. "Always makes their eyes flutter closed, especially when they are this small."

I take note of the gentle way she lets her finger trail the expanse of his forehead, tickling it rhythmically, stopping just short of the end of his nose. Mesmerized by the motion, my own eyes get heavy. I'll have to try this later when the little monster is raging before bed. Handing over the bottle, I remain standing in case Cody spits out the nipple upon realizing he's been tricked into eating some false version of breast milk while his neglectful mommy hangs out nearby, too lazy and selfish to offer the real deal.

Joy props Cody a little higher onto her left arm with a strength I couldn't have guessed she possessed. Cody opens his eyes and leisurely looks around. Instead of the red-faced fury he normally unleashes after awaking from a nap, he appears as though roused from the most pleasant of dreams. Joy presses the bottle to his lips but doesn't force it, holding it there until Cody decides he's ready. Once he moves to latch, she expertly tilts it upward, and he begins sucking, completely nonplussed that it's a bottle not a boob.

I watch in awe. This woman is enchanted. Or maybe she's a witch, luring tired moms to her porch with flashing lights and lemonade. We *are* in Salem, so it's not out of the question. It doesn't matter: I love her. I'll gladly play the role of Gretel if she can get Hansel to sleep.

"He's never taken a bottle that easily," I exclaim too loudly, before lowering my voice, afraid to break the spell.

Joy chuckles. "I have the magic touch, I guess." Some sort of magic must be in the air because I swear her face has changed since she began holding Cody. The years have melted away with every minute he's been in her arms, and she looks ten, twenty years more youthful. She glows with happiness.

Swallowing back any apprehension that lingers, I reclaim my seat across from Joy. After taking a sip of lemonade, I gather my courage and finally ask the question I came here to ask.

♦ 8 ♦

JOY

May 23

What is the meaning of life? That was all—a simple question: one that tended to close in on one with years, the great revelation had never come. The great revelation perhaps never did come. Instead, there were little daily miracles, illuminations, matches struck unexpectedly in the dark; here was one.
— Virginia Woolf, *To the Lighthouse*

"IT STARTED OUT AS a little inside joke between Freddie and me," I begin, settling Cody a little deeper into the crook of my elbow. Although he still suckles the nipple of his bottle, his eyes have fluttered closed, and a dribble of milk leaks down his chin. With one shaky knuckle, I wipe it away, and he smiles in his sleep, a dimple forming high on his left cheek. My Katherine has a similar dimple. I once told her it was an angel's fingerprint, left on only the most precious of babies. She never believed me and remained embarrassed by the mark until she finally accepted the peculiar quirk around the age of thirty.

Brynn looks back and forth between me and Cody, and I realize I've paused for too long, something that happens all too often with every passing year. Unlike my

own children, who are so easily annoyed by my wandering attention span, Brynn doesn't huff and puff or roll her
eyes at me.

"When we first moved down from Maine, Freddie
was out on charters all the time. When he wasn't out
early catching fish, he was taking tourists out on sunset
tours. It seemed like he was never on land, but constantly
riding out with the tides." I sigh, the old frustrations not
buried as deeply as one might expect after all these years.
"I was home alone with two small kids, one about to
start school and the other not much more than a baby. It
was lonely, and even though Freddie was more at home
on the sea than in our house, I still worried."

Brynn nods, a flash of understanding crossing her
unlined face. I resist the urge to reach out and take her
hands in my own, afraid to disturb the sleeping cherub
in my arms. Instead, I push on, thinking she might find
more solace in my story than in my embrace.

"Freddie and I always shared a love of lighthouses,
although I suspect his reason for loving them was much
different from my own. Before one particularly long trip,
he professed that *I* would always be his lighthouse, the
shining light in the darkness." I recall the moment so
vividly, his clean-shaven face permanently wind burnt
but decidedly less wrinkled than now, those blue eyes
sparkling like the ocean herself. His duffel bag was
packed and sitting by the door, his favorite denim jacket
folded across the top. The children stood on either side of
me, Katherine close to tears, as she always was whenever
he was set to leave, and Richard too young to understand
what was happening.

Brynn stares out at the street as a cyclist whizzes by, a
blur of red spandex and speed. I fear I'm losing her interest, this old story too personal and trivial to share with

a stranger. I've never shared it with anyone, not even Gayle. My kids know it only as an old woman's silly ritual. Just as I decide I should shift gears, offer the young lady a snack, she turns her gaze back to me and smiles, urging me to continue.

"I'm sorry this is such a roundabout way of answering your question," I apologize, offering Brynn an escape before I resume. I've never been accused of being straight to the point, and I imagine a young mother might be eager to get on with the rest of her day. Even though I'd understand if she decides to leave, I hope she stays.

She shakes her head, blinking furiously. "No, please, continue," she says, leaning forward in her seat, as though she's eager to hear the rest.

Pleased, I nod and lean back against the pillow, twisting my hip to one side. Too long in one position is the devil on my rear end.

"My daughter was beside herself that day. She thought Daddy was leaving forever every time he walked out that door for more than a day trip. As soon as she saw his bag packed, she'd be inconsolable. So, we made her a deal this time." I close my eyes and I'm back in the foyer of this house, wearing my favorite yellow dress, the one Freddie loved. I'm holding my two baby's hands and leading them to the back door. Back then, our yard had a few more trees and a wooden swing set, but otherwise it's mostly the same as it is now. "I led Freddie, Kathy, and Rich to the back of the house and made a big show of turning the lights on and off, three times in a row, real quick. Then I counted to six before flashing them three more times and then repeating the whole thing a third time," I say, chuckling to myself. "Rich was learning to count and could only make it to six, so it seemed like a good number, and three is *my* lucky number . . ."

The baby stirs and I stroke my finger against his cheek, settling him immediately. He lets out a tiny snore. "I promised that every night after sunset and every morning before the sun came up, we would flash the light like this, so Daddy would be able to see his way home to us." I swallow back the lump forming in my throat, all the memories bubbling to the surface, the past colliding with this moment. "Katherine was skeptical, always an intuitive little girl, but Richard was so excited, I think some of his enthusiasm managed to wear off on his big sister. From that day forward, whenever Freddie was out on a trip, we made a point of flashing those porch lights. By the time the kids were in junior high, they were so used to his comings and goings, the habit faded. When they began hanging out with friends and spending more time at sports practice and the mall, I found myself alone more and more. I started flashing those lights again."

Tears trickle down Brynn's cheek, and she brushes them away with the back of her thumb before letting her eyes stay closed. Always polite, I look away, pretending not to notice. "Anyway, that was years and years ago, but it's stuck for good. After the kids moved away, I gave up the night watch in favor of the sunrise session, and I flash those lights no matter where Freddie might be, out on the ocean or sound asleep in our bed. I'm an early riser, and it doesn't hurt anyone. I firmly believe it can only bring good fortune." Brynn's eyes are still shut, but a smile tugs at the corner of her mouth. "Who doesn't need a little good luck every morning?"

I wait for Brynn to look up. Cocking my head, I note the way her chest rises and falls, each breath a little deeper than the last. The tension I saw earlier in her jaw has relaxed; her cheeks are as smooth as Cody's. Her head lolls to one side, settling against the cushion of the rocker.

"Rest," I whisper, holding Cody a little tighter and brushing my lips against his cool forehead. "I'll watch over you."

★   ★   ★

On waking up, Brynn was so embarrassed that she knocked over her lemonade in her attempt to gather her things. Thankfully, it fell with a gentle thud on the wooden floor, and the glass didn't shatter, but the noise was enough to rouse Cody from his slumber. After assuring the poor girl that I'd handle the sticky mess, she burst into tears, causing her son to respond by also beginning to cry.

Torn between whom to comfort, I decided Brynn needed to feel the weight of her baby in her arms, a tiny anchor in her internal storm. Sometimes the line between yourself and your offspring is so blurry, it can seem you are one and the same, long after they have left the safety of first your belly and then your home. Brynn takes Cody into her embrace and begins rocking him back and forth, shushing into his ear. Together they calm down, Brynn still hiccupping back the tears.

I beg her to stay, offering to replace the lemonade with a cup of hot coffee or tea. Finally, I get her to laugh when I suggest a thimble of the brandy Freddie keeps hidden in the pantry behind the flour. She refuses the lot and thanks me for my kindness while hastily packing Cody and all her things into the fancy stroller at the bottom of the stairs. The whole while she sniffles back the tears that seem to fall without end.

"It was so nice to meet you, Joy," she says, shoving Cody's jacket and a dirty burp rag into the backpack. A few diapers spill onto the grass before she can manage to get the overfilled bag zipped. For a short trip around the block, she packed everything but the kitchen sink. "I'm so sorry I fell asleep." She shakes her head, the color still high on both cheeks. "I'm mortified," she admits without meeting my eye.

I wave and cluck my tongue. "You're welcome to nap here on my front porch whenever you like," I assure her. "I've fallen asleep more often than not while basking in the warm morning sun." Brynn smiles at me but continues to study her hands, her feet poised and ready to push away. "Seriously, though. With Freddie off fishing all the time, I'd love some company, and I think Cody's taken a shine to me." As if to prove my point, he stares in my direction and favors me with a gummy smile.

Brynn purses her lips, bouncing on the ball of those expensive Nikes. She opens her mouth to speak but closes it before a sound can escape. I wait. Over the years, I've found the best way to get someone talking is to keep quiet yourself. It's so tempting to try and fill the silence, to begin blabbering on and on so the other person forgets they ever had something to add. In my youth, I was too often guilty of this. Age has lent me a little wisdom. Freddie reminding me to listen more than I speak has helped too.

Both feet firmly on the ground now, she pulls Cody a little closer to her shoulder, cradling the back of his head with her right hand. "Sometimes I can't tell if he loves me," she whispers, her body swaying side to side a little faster. I remember the motion well, the constant rhythm of mothering young children. "I know I'm supposed to feel this unbreakable bond with him, but some days I look at him, and all I see is a little stranger staring back."

My heart breaks for this woman, hardly more than a girl herself, confessing the deepest shame of her own heart to someone she met only a few hours ago. Two answers come to mind and almost pass my lips, but I bite them back. *Of course, he loves you! You're his mother* is the first and most obvious response. *Your children will always be strangers* is the second, more honest answer. How many times have I looked at Katherine as a baby, then a surly teen, then a distant adult, and wondered who she was *really*? Richard wore his heart on his sleeve and always favored his mommy, but there are still days I wonder about the man he's become, and question who I am to him now, besides a burden who needs checking up on.

Cody stares up into his mom's eyes, a different color but the same shape and framed by the same dark lashes and stern brows. "I can tell he likes you," she continues, glancing up at me. "I can't tell if he smiles at me because he's happy or just has gas," she says, choking up again. She coughs to hide the break in her voice. "I should know these things." Shaking her head, she lets her shoulders fall before shrugging. "I don't know what the hell I'm doing."

None of us do. But I don't say this out loud. Brynn is too deep inside the throes to appreciate the levity in a sideways acknowledgment about the difficulty of life, even if it's the dead honest truth.

"Cody is a beautiful and happy baby. You might not be doing everything right all the time, but you are doing the best you can, and that is all you can do," I say instead. "You're his mommy. There isn't a doubt in my mind that he loves you most."

A tear falls down her cheek, but she doesn't rub it away. "He always cries," she moans, barely holding back a sob. "No matter what I do, he cries."

Unable to stop myself, I hobble down the three steps so that I'm face to face with her. I reach out a hand and brush the tear away before letting my palm rest against her cheek. A strand of hair falls against my finger, and I stroke it away gently, tucking it behind her ear. "He cries because you're his safe space. He knows you will listen. Think of it as a compliment," I kid. "He won't cry to me because he knows I'm just an old lady who won't be able to give him what he needs."

Brynn sniffles and giggles at the same time, a small smile lighting up her face. "Well, he must think I'm very safe then," she chuckles.

I cup her chin in my hand and squeeze lightly. Looking into her eyes for the first time since she spilled her lemonade, I see myself reflected in the watery depths. We nod at each other as she unlatches the brake and pushes the stroller down the drive, turning back once when she reaches the street, to wave, before heading in the direction of the corner, where she disappears.

★   ★   ★

My thoughts linger on Brynn long after she's passed out of sight. By now she must be home, or maybe she continued pushing Cody straight to the park to meet up with some of the other local moms I often see walking together, with strollers as big and fancy as the one my neighbor rolled up with. As much as I'd love to hope this for my new friend, I doubt this is where she ended up. I worry she's at home crying into Cody's hair, stressing about how she's doing it all wrong.

Times have changed drastically since I was a young mother home alone with my babies. Maybe I don't fully understand it, but I grasp that the pressure on modern moms is different from it was for my generation of women. Katherine has said as much to me as she struggled with two precocious girls of her own, complaining about the competitive nature of the private school her kids attend and the demands placed on parents to provide *more more more* for their children. Technology is partly to blame, the constant imposition causing us to compare ourselves to others. It's why I resisted Facebook for so long. I may be old, but even I can see how tempting it is to be envious of others posting about lavish vacations or even simple pictures of family events. Haven't I seethed as I "liked" a photo of my friend surrounded by grand-children and silently wished my own children loved me even half as much?

When I was Brynn's age, no one knew what went on behind closed doors. My friends and I would take turns hosting playdates where we'd drink wine in the kitchen while all the kids played together in the living room, only a gate and a few of the older kids around to make sure no one knocked over the furniture or choked on anything small. We moms would gossip and complain about how little our husbands did around the house, but it was all in jest. No one revealed the dirty secrets of their reality like it's so popular to do today. My friend Betty never told us her husband slapped her around if dinner wasn't on time, although we all assumed she wasn't as clumsy as she led us to believe. When Sharon drank two bottles of chardonnay all by herself, we didn't confront her or accuse her of being dependent on the stuff. No one staged an intervention. We each had our secrets and were happy to keep it that way. Women of this genera-tion would interfere, insert themselves in the messy lives of their friends and neighbors as if they not only had the right, but the moral *obligation*, to meddle. But that wasn't and still isn't my way.

Freddie's business began to take off when Katherine was four and Richard in that age between infant and tod-dler. That summer Freddie was off leading sunset booze cruises until nine PM. He'd drop the drunken tourists at the dock before turning back around for an overnight trip to catch tuna or whatever fish was in season. I still never know. Something people like to eat and that made us good money. His days were long, but mine were longer. I tried to be the good wife, the doting mother. The nights he made it home, I had a hearty supper on the table. Those mornings he rolled in tired and smelling like brine, I brewed a strong pot of coffee and served him scrambled eggs and bacon the way he liked. I did the laundry and the cleaning. I was with the kids all day, every day. We had no family nearby, I had no break.

The few days he was able to take off, he tended to the yard work and all the errands that piled up, the endless list of chores that got longer with every passing year. Some days he'd stop home for lunch and end up falling asleep on the couch with his clothes on, desperate for a nap. I'd kiss his forehead before untying his boots and tucking them beneath the couch, and resist the overwhelming urge to shake him awake, demand a nap of my own. Of course, I let him sleep, shoving my disgusting jealousy deep inside. I'd take Katherine and Rich outside, to let him rest, sometimes sneaking one of the Virginia Slims I kept hidden in the flatware drawer, when I thought the kids weren't looking.

Katherine was a moody baby, demanding and petulant one minute and then cute and content the next. It carried through into adulthood. After college she moved to Connecticut with her financer husband. I'm unsure of his title exactly—something with equities. Katherine only gets annoyed when I ask. She practices tax law at a private firm. We see each other twice a year when she visits with my two granddaughters in tow. She offers to host at her house, but I can tell it's an imposition. Since leaving, her life beyond Salem is hers alone. It is as if she didn't exist until she was gone. The life Freddie and I created here for her was never quite big enough.

Whenever I get off the phone with her, I wonder if I failed her as a mother. If *I* wasn't enough. Freddie reassures me her success as an adult is testament to the opposite. Our daughter thrived because of her upbringing. It makes me feel better, as he intends. For a while. Then the doubt creeps back in, and I wait another two or three weeks to hear from my distant daughter again, our song and dance well rehearsed, if not overplayed.

Brynn's fear of not being enough for Cody struck close to home, even a lifetime later. All the insecurities rushed back to the surface, even as I thought I'd overcome them years ago. Nothing better to do with my endless hours of free time, I begin analyzing all my regrets and disappointments as a parent, sipping my lemonade and watching the sun creep higher into the sky.

"Idle hands are the devil's tools," my own mother used to warn. What about idle thoughts, Mom? She never prepared me for those.

"Muffins," I announce, my dark musings evaporating into the ether, where they will wait to pounce in my next moment of weakness. Freddie looks up from beneath his bushy gray brows, and his hand stills, the pencil he uses to fill in an old crossword puzzle stopping mid-stroke. "I think that girl could use some homemade muffins." He chuckles and shakes his head. Baking is my solution to all of life's great mysteries. The precision and concentration required to get the recipe perfect always enough to push the rest of the troublesome thoughts far, far away.

Spot uncurls from his perch on the railing, lifting his back in a deep stretch. I envy his flexibility, longing for the days when I was so limber. Simply rising from this rocker gets harder and harder every day. I grab my cane and head for the door, nearly tripping on Freddie's boots. I shake my head and curse under my breath. No matter how many times I remind him, he refuses to put the damn things away.

BRYNN

Late May

Sometimes the strength of motherhood is greater than natural laws.—Barbara Kingsolver. So true, mamas! If you're doubting yourself, remember—YOU'VE GOT THIS!! Motherhood is our natural state, and our love is greater than any obstacle this world puts in our way. Take your babes outside today and enjoy the original Mother Nature and breathe deep.
> *—3BoysMamaMonty*

RIGHT FROM THE START, nothing went according to plan. After doing my due diligence, like any responsible mother-to-be with a slight (great) affinity for rules and schedules, I had created a meticulous birth plan for my big day. This plan was developed with the help of my midwife, OB/GYN, and copious amounts of online research. Since planning was my specialty, I obviously had a contingency plan, my "in case of emergency" plan B.

I also had a contingency for the contingency, but every star in the sky would need to misalign for this to come into play, or so I thought. Kyle talked me out of creating a plan D, assuring me there was absolutely no need to spiral down the rabbit hole that might take us to worry about such precautions.

Reluctantly, I agreed to plans A through C and typed each up, leaving a printed copy with all my various health-care providers along with two extra copies in my already-packed and ready-to-go hospital bag. Of course, I emailed a copy to both myself and Kyle. I was prepared. *Overprepared,* according to my midwife. The party planner in me begged to argue there was no such thing. Cody, on the other hand, had other plans.

Plan A was my ideal birth plan. Throughout my pregnancy, I had a few appointments with my midwife for all the important scans, but not as many as if I'd stayed with my OB/GYN practice. I wanted to limit my baby's exposure to any harmful rays associated with the imaging, even though I'm fairly certain they aren't dangerous. Either way, I clicked with the midwife at the practice and appreciated how supportive she was of my nonmedicated birth plan.

My pregnancy developed right on track, the baby meeting all the metrics and my body responding appropriately. I gained the proper amount of weight and passed every blood test with flying colors, even the test for gestational diabetes that involved the terrible-tasting orange liquid that I nearly vomited back up. In my fantasy birth, I'd stay at home as long as possible before delivery, letting my baby dictate when he was ready to enter the world. When I started feeling contractions, I planned on taking a light walk to keep my body moving, followed by a warm shower and a lower-back massage. My midwife suggested I cuddle with Kyle and watch our favorite movie to help keep my mind at ease and boost oxytocin. I even created a Spotify playlist of my favorite upbeat, yet soothing, songs to help me relax.

I debated the merits of a home birth but ultimately decided that I wanted to be in a hospital setting under the care of my midwife, in case there were any unexpected complications. Better safe than sorry, I reasoned. My OB/GYN would be on call (plan B), but my midwife was confident it would be a quick and easy labor. According to my plan, when I began having two to three surges within a ten-minute period, we would drive to the hospital (only a short eight-minute drive—nine if we hit every red light).

Once admitted to the private suite we'd already secured, Kyle would aid in setting the mood. We'd lower the lights and listen to my playlist. I'd begun practicing guided meditation and mindfulness even before I was pregnant, so I intended on putting this to use. My FitBall was on the list of things to take to the hospital, and I would take turns bouncing and rocking on the giant ball, helping to stimulate active labor. My prenatal yoga classes taught me some poses to help soothe any pain associated with labor, and I was a diligent student. My job was to stay hydrated, focused, and relaxed. My body would cue me into what it needed to do next. Everyone promised it would come naturally and told me to trust my body.

Kyle also had his list of tasks. His job was to help me visualize the birth. He was embarrassed to recite some of the mantras on his list, but I knew he would come in the clutch on the actual day. He was always good in a crisis, the calm and cool guy you want by your side in the big moments. I was confident he'd have my hand in his and follow his instructions to a tee.

Somewhere in all the planning and visualizations, I forgot that this wasn't about me, even if it was technically my body. It was about the tiny human I'd grown for nine months, who would decide exactly when he was ready to be free of his too-tight confines. My due date was April 28th, but my midwife and all common wisdom warned it might be a week on either side. Many first babies were late, the internet told me.

By this late point in my pregnancy, *everyone* had a birth story to share, the good, the bad, and the ugly. I was shocked at the detail some women felt compelled to go into in order to describe their experiences. Near strangers would tell me about their mucus plugs falling out or how they gave birth on the side of the road in the backseat of their husband's Dodge Ram. Early on, I found that there's something about a pregnant woman that inspires oversharing and that you were expected to reciprocate. I'm not sure I'll ever get over the bold questions people asked me or their willingness to touch, stroke, and probe my swollen stomach. Boundaries ceased to exist once the belly protruded.

April 8th wasn't much different from any other day, except the weather did one of those early spring shifts that left most Massachusetts residents with whiplash. March was brutal, a late snowstorm and ten days of below-twenty-degree temperatures kept even the most cold-loving individuals bundled up and indoors. At some point overnight, the temps began to rise. And rise. And rise some more. New England woke up to above-average temperatures, some forecasts predicting the high might reach fifty-two degrees. As people marveled at spring's early arrival, I worried I didn't have a light jacket to fit over my enormous belly. Armed with my errand list and an old windbreaker left unzipped over my maternity sweater, I set out for Target and the dry cleaner, annoyed my rain boots were so snug on my swollen feet. Last week's snow was melting steadily, and the world was left a damp and puddly mess.

When the first contraction hit, I was standing in the home goods section of Target. A sharp pain in my side, followed by a pulsating tightness that radiated through my uterus, stopped me in my tracks, and I clutched the cart with both hands to remain standing. The pain was gone as quickly as it started. Breathing deeply, I recited one of my mantras and assumed it was only a bad Braxton Hicks, since I'd had them sporadically over the last few weeks. Usually, they were worse when I sat, but my midwife warned they might also occur during exercise. Shopping wasn't exactly strenuous, but I did hop a few puddles in the parking lot.

The second came less than ten minutes later, stronger and longer than the first. Up until now, my false contractions hadn't been regular and didn't gain in intensity. If anything, they were more annoying than painful. Whatever was happening now was way past irritating and downright agonizing. I pushed my cart to the clothing section and sat on an empty bench near the changing rooms, hand on my belly and eyes on my iPhone, counting the minutes. Eight minutes later, another surge of pressure, followed by searing hot pain, ripped through my insides. When I closed my eyes, all I saw was blinding white, the excruciating ache in my side manifested into a burning orb so hot it lost all color.

With the last of my strength, I summoned a Target employee, a young woman who bent over me and placed a cautious hand on my shoulder before taking my phone into her other. In a moment of respite from the pain, I asked her to call Kyle, muttering the code to my locked screen. I didn't trust my shaky hands to dial. The girl winced before shaking her head, mouthing *voicemail*. This wasn't surprising since it was mid-morning on a Thursday. Kyle was diligent about only using his personal cell during his lunch break. It was unlikely he'd get this message for another hour, maybe two. The girl handed me the phone, still connected, and through gritted teeth I was able to leave a short message before another contraction slammed into my uterus like a freight train. *I'm in labor. Meet me at the hospital as soon as you can.* Hanging up the phone, I glanced down and saw a dark stain spread over the carpet beneath the bench. Before I could ask the employee to try Kyle's office, the bagel and cream cheese I'd eaten for breakfast came back up, spewing between my fingers as I struggled to hold the worst of the vomit in. The girl ran toward the front desk to get help, leaving me on the bench, with my head hanging between my knees, until the ambulance arrived.

★ ★ ★

Kyle got the message. An early lunch appointment meant he listened to the voicemail only fifteen minutes after the flustered Target employee handed me the phone. Around the same time the EMT closed the doors to the ambulance that would take me the short drive to Salem Hospital, Kyle was already in his car, racing up Route 1. Thanks to lighter than normal traffic, the drive that often took him over an hour took only forty minutes. Proving he was prepared for dad duty, he had the forethought to call our midwife and prepare her for my imminent arrival at the hospital.

When I arrived in Labor and Delivery, my contractions were less than five minutes apart, and each one gutted me from the inside out. Nausea and pain mingled uncomfortably, each contraction causing me to throw up so violently that my throat was raw and coated in a sticky bile, the food long gone from my system. Once I was settled into a wheelchair and carted up to my room, a nurse handed me a cup of ice chips to fight the nausea, but every drop of water triggered my gag reflex.

My midwife and a doula from her practice met me in
the labor suite. I'm embarrassed to admit I hoped they'd
insist on administering an epidural, the pain searing
through my body so intense that I couldn't imagine it
could get any worse without me dying. Instead, they
were calm and supportive, gently reminding me of my
careful birth plan and unfazed by my wild eyes and sickly
pallor.

I imagine they've seen just about everything in their
line of work, but at the time I was sure I was the worst
case of labor they'd ever encountered. Kyle ran into the
room as they were examining me, informing me I was
effaced but only dilated four centimeters. This sounded
like a lot to me, but I knew from all my reading that I
needed to be closer to ten to start pushing. The news was
devastating. How was it possible I was still sixty percent
away from getting this monster inside of me out? The
pressure on my back was growing and the desire to *push*
so strong I had no idea how I'd keep the baby inside a
second longer. It all seemed impossible.

Kyle held my hand and smoothed back my sweaty
hair. The contractions came faster and stronger, but my
body refused to dilate further. Every contraction weakened me, and every fiber in my body wanted the pain
to end so I could sleep. My midwife asked Kyle to play
the Spotify list, but since the speaker was tucked safely
in our hospital duffel, sitting uselessly in the nursery, it
only sounded lame coming from the phone speakers. Not
relaxing at all. I chastised myself for not having contingency bags in my SUV, Kyle's car. What a severe lapse in
planning judgment!

"I can't do it," I whispered to Kyle, to my midwife, to
anyone who'd listen. "Give me drugs," I begged. "Please.
Anything. Make it stop."

Kyle squeezed my hand, looking imploringly at the midwife, who shook her head, reminding us we both had insisted she refuse this request. We'd made her promise that no matter how much we begged, she wouldn't allow us to stray from the natural birth plan set in place. Now that I was lying there, I had changed my mind. I told her this, snapping at her, demanding she listen to me *now*. She smiled but continued to rub my lower back, maneuvering my hips this way and that, hoping to help my cervix to open.

Nothing worked. The doula carried a small yoga ball toward the bed and placed it between my legs. As she pulled my knees apart, a stab of pain worse than any so far caused me to scream. The alarms on the machine attached to my midsection wailed, followed by the heart monitor attached to my chest. All at once, the room started spinning and went dull, the fluorescent overhead lights dimming until my eyes fluttered closed.

The last thing I heard, as everything went black, was the midwife calling for a doctor and Kyle asking why there was so much blood.

★   ★   ★

In the end, everything was fine.

All the blood had been caused by a placental abruption, my placenta partly separating from the inner wall of my uterus. Since this put the baby at risk for oxygen loss and me at risk of severe hemorrhaging, my midwife and doula were replaced by the OB/GYN on call, and I was rushed into surgery for an emergency C-section. Let's call this Plan F, since a great deal more went wrong that I hadn't accounted for in earlier revisions. Since I opted out of the epidural, according to Plan A, I was forced to go under general anesthesia. My anger at this revelation was only surpassed by my terror. In hindsight, being knocked out and not remembering the entire ordeal isn't the worst thing in the world.

According to Kyle, the surgery took thirty minutes. Our baby boy was lifted from my womb, seven pounds thirteen ounces of gooey perfection. Since he was premature and had some fluid in his lungs, the doctor wanted to monitor him in the NICU for a few hours. Kyle agreed and followed our baby out the door, leaving me strapped to the table, to be stitched up. I'd lost a bit of blood, but nothing too serious. When I woke up, they wheeled me into Recovery. After being hooked up to a few IVs and debriefed by a brusque nurse, I was left alone to wait for Kyle and my baby.

I cried. And cried. And then I cried some more. I cried because I hadn't seen my baby yet. I cried because my carefully thought-out birth plan had gone to complete shit. I cried because my *after*-birth plan was useless. There was no skin-on-skin time for me and Cody, no time to nuzzle him to my breast and feel the invisible cord still connecting us outside the womb. I cried because I was convinced our relationship was doomed from the start, that breastfeeding would be impossible, motherhood would be impossible. I cried because by every indication so far, I sucked as a mother.

My midwife found me sobbing in the bed and tried to calm my fears. She promised everything would be fine, that Cody and I would simply readjust our plan and be stronger for the struggle. She said all the right things and I nodded, sniffing back the tears, and pretended I was indeed fine. Satisfied, she left me to wait for Kyle. But instead of my husband and son greeting me, yet another doctor entered and informed me that the fluid in Cody's lungs was a little worse than originally noted so he would spend the night in the NICU, two nights at the most. More tears ensued.

I struggled to heave myself from the bed, and with the help of a nurse I collapsed into a wheelchair, my recently sliced open midsection burning so badly I was convinced my organs would spill forth at any moment. Kyle finally made his way into the room, kissing my forehead before wheeling me to the NICU, so I could finally meet my baby through a layer of glass, where I watched his tiny chest rise and fall beneath a tangle of tubes and tape, the machines blipping away beside us.

Kyle rubbed my back, the space between my shoulder blades tender and sore. It felt like the time I pulled a muscle while rowing in college, but the nurse informed me it was only gas pain, one of the more common side effects of a C-section. He rubbed my back, and I cried into my hands, sobbing so hard that I prayed I would simply run out of tears, squeeze myself dry.

Kyle thought I cried because I was worried about Cody. But that's not the entire reason. No doubt I was terrified for my son. Completely and utterly scared out of my mind.

But as I looked in at him, his skin tinged slightly blue, I waited for the swell of love to wash over me. I waited for the surge of motherly instincts, the fierce desire to protect this little bundle with all my heart and soul. But it didn't come. I was looking in at a little stranger, one who looked more alien than human.

I cried harder. It was all wrong. It wasn't supposed to go like this. Shit like this happened to *other* people. I cried for the birth I envisioned, and the nine months spent looking forward to this day. I cried for everything I wanted to be feeling . . . but didn't feel.

★ ★ ★

This woman— it must be a woman, even though she's never shown her face, only her manicured fingernails, always a tasteful pink or glossy nude—removes the eggs from the carton, and like magic they are quickly arranged on top one another in a glass drawer before being tucked back onto the shelf. Dozens of eggs. More eggs than any single family could eat. The drawer slides onto the shelf with a satisfying swoosh, amplified by her savvy video skills. She moves onto the next drawer, emptying juice boxes and chocolate milks one by one and lining them up in a row— apple juice on the right, organic one percent milks on the left. Each carton lands with a small thud before she slides it back onto the shelf. Swoosh. Next are the apples, stacked in the crisper in what might appear a haphazard manner, but I know better. It's fruit Tetris, getting all those slightly odd-shaped orbs to fit just so in the drawer.

Scroll.

"Why put it down when you can just put it away . . ." The next creator chants, clapping her hands twice, and the laundry basket she carried with a pile of freshly folded T-shirts is now on the floor beside her dresser, a drawer open before her and the shirts magically inside. Beneath the video the hashtags mock me: *#momlife #organizingtiktok #momtok*

The door slams behind me, jolting me from my stupor. God knows how long I was sliding down the rabbit hole of TikTok. An hour can pass in mere minutes when organizational content catches you on your "for you" page.

"What the hell's going on?" Kyle says, his keys hitting the counter too hard. The sounds of the house come alive around me as I silence my phone.

The dishwasher hums, already on the rinse cycle. From the basement I hear something banging against the side of the dryer every few seconds, and I hope it's only some errant coins and not something that might burst out and stain things, like a lipstick. Then I remember I haven't used lipstick in months. Loudest of all is the incessant wail of Cody screaming from the Rock and Play, where he'd been peacefully napping only seconds before.

"I could hear him from the driveway," Kyle mumbles under his breath as he battles with the straps, his fingers eager to free our son and comfort him, but not familiar with the way the right side of the chest strap sticks.

Rolling my eyes, I drop the phone and nudge him aside. "Let me get it."

He hesitates, his fingers refusing to release the clasp as my own hands hover above his, ready to deftly unsnap the pesky clip like I do so many times each day. Reluctantly, he steps back, and I prove myself useful. Cody cries harder, his face more purple than red, like he's been crying for days, weeks. Sometimes it feels like he's done just that.

"He just woke up," I lie, even though I'm not sure exactly when he woke up. Surely it was not very long ago. I'd have heard him fuss. Unfortunately, my boy's cries can escalate dramatically in a very short time span.

Kyle opens his mouth to argue but bites his tongue. Instead, he places the brown paper bag next to his keys. "Penne alla vodka and Caesar salad," he says. "From Joanina's," he adds. "It needs to be heated up."

The sweet smell of the tomato sauce makes my stomach rumble, reminding me I haven't eaten anything since the frozen pizza at lunch. I'd give anything for a hot meal and a glass of red wine with my husband. But Cody's red-rimmed eyes implore me, his tear-stained cheeks ruddy with all the mixed emotions I'm sure are mirrored in my own pallid complexion. Fear, longing, love, and hate, all jumbled together and burning from the inside out.

"I need to feed Cody first," I start, my boobs already beginning to ache. The simple promise of release enough to kick-start the letdown.

Something akin to relief washes over Kyle's face. "Perfect. I need to send a few emails. Dinner in, like, forty-five minutes?"

My eye tics, the nerve pinching in time with my racing heart. I clutch Cody closer to my shoulder, shifting my weight, debating my next move. I glance at the clock on the microwave. It's already seven. I've been trying to put Cody down at seven forty-five since it takes me at least an hour to rock him to sleep. I'm desperate to get him on some sort of sleep schedule, but every night I'm thwarted by something as simple as eating dinner. Defeated, I nod.

"Sounds good," I chirp, smiling despite my desire to punch my husband in the face. Adding insult to injury, he smiles back and turns on his heel, eager to get back to his office. It's been a big night for Kyle. He almost lifted the baby from his rocker.

Since I couldn't hit my husband, I punch in 325 degrees on the oven and let it begin the preheating process. I suppose Kyle assumed since he picked up the food, the least I could do would be to heat it up.

Before Cody and I head to the couch, I grab my phone. My second favorite thing to scroll are recipes I'll never cook. As we settle in for first dinner, I search penne alla vodka and quickly fall down the mindless media hole. Who cares if I never organize my house or find time to cook a homemade meal again when I can watch all the better moms do it so efficiently in clips one minute or under on TikTok.

10

JOY

Late May

For now she need not think of anybody. She could be herself,
by herself. And that was what now she often felt the need
of—to think; well not even to think. To be silent; to be alone.
All the being and the doing, expansive, glittering, vocal,
evaporated; and one shrunk, with a sense of solemnity, to be
oneself, a wedge-shaped core of darkness, something invisible to
others . . . and this self having shed its attachments was free for
the strangest adventures.

— Virginia Woolf, *To the Lighthouse*

FOR SOME REASON I always envisioned getting older
would be different. Alas, it's more of the same. The
same laundry needing to be cleaned, folded, and *put away*.
The same dishes needing to be washed, dried, and *put*
away. The same groceries needing to be bought and
put away. So much of our lives is made up of putting
things away. Only difference is, now it's harder. The steps
down into the basement are a little steeper and trickier to
navigate with a full basket of dirty laundry, forcing me to
make two trips instead of one. The dishes might be a bit
easier after installing the fancy stainless steel appliance a

few years back but bending down to load and empty the darn thing is hell on my sciatica. Grocery shopping remains one of my favorite pastimes. Many women complain about such a mundane chore, but I've always enjoyed wandering the aisles, waiting for inspiration to strike. For this reason, I never make a list, instead letting the shelves and baskets of fresh produce speak to me.

Since I stopped driving, getting to and from the market has proven a bit more difficult, but Earl and I have a standing date every Friday at nine AM for him to pick me up in his shiny yellow taxi. For ten extra dollars, he waits in the parking lot, reading one of his mystery books while I shop. He always helps me with my bags, even though I insist I can manage on my own. But Earl's a gentleman, and who am I to deny him his chivalry?

Freddie oversees the other stuff. No doubt this would be grossly unfashionable in this day and age, but we're products of a different era. Katherine pokes fun at our marital split of duties, insisting our ways are old and outdated. She and her husband don't face the same challenges. Instead, they hire a cleaning person to handle the household chores. An au pair helps with the child rearing. A grocery service shops and delivers Katherine's weekly list. A landscaping crew keeps the exterior manicured and watered. On one of our last visits, Freddie admired the sparkling clean gutters and asked Samir how he managed to keep up with them. It was autumn in Connecticut, and the stately maple trees shading their Colonial were dropping leaves by the second. Samir laughed and shrugged, admitting to hiring a crew to clear away the debris once a week in the fall. Of course, Freddie was shocked another man would confess to what my husband saw as a weakness, but Samir was matter-of-fact, even proud. When we received their Christmas card that winter, featuring a beautiful family shot in front of an elaborately decorated front porch, Freddie joked that they probably paid someone to hang the lights. I didn't have the heart to break it to him: of course they did. So maybe Katherine laughs at us, but it's easy for her to extol feminism and knock the patriarchy when she's outsourcing the problems.

I'm standing before the open refrigerator door, the same off-white Whirlpool with the freezer on top that's been here since the kids were born, and take stock of what's inside. It's eight forty-five AM, and I'm dressed and ready in my favorite navy-blue trousers and white button-down. Freddie's denim jacket is draped over my purse, an expensive leather one Kathy got me for my birthday that caused poor Richard so much distress since they'd agreed not to go over-the-top crazy on presents that year. He'd given me a beautiful purple robe that I use way more than this extravagant purse, but he refused to be placated by my sincere thank-yous. I'd expected their sibling rivalry to die off as they grew older, but it had only intensified between my two hard-headed children.

The shelves are barren. A half gallon of milk nearing the expiration date, some apples, and a wedge of cheese are the only edible items in sight. Some wilting lettuce in the crisper is begging to be thrown out. Opening the freezer, I take note of plenty of frozen chicken and a few microwavable dinners. I know I have lots of potatoes and canned goods in the pantry, but I'm desperately in need of fresh vegetables. Some fish would be a nice change. Some cod or salmon, perhaps. It's been a while since I've eaten fish.

A horn beeps twice, startling me, even though I've been expecting the sound. I steady myself on the door before nudging it closed, my heart rate calming as I take a few deep breaths in and out. The handle wiggles beneath my palm, and I make a mental note to remind Freddie to tighten whatever needs tightening. I throw his jacket over my shoulders, to ward away the damp chill in the air, inhaling the fading scent of salt and Old Spice lingering on the collar. Grabbing my purse, I glance around the empty kitchen once more before nodding and heading out to meet my good friend Earl, who is standing beside the open rear door, ready to usher me to my errands.

★ ★ ★

Scrolling Facebook before bed has become as much a part of my routine as sipping a cup of chamomile tea and brushing my teeth. My granddaughters, Prisha and Myra, set up an Instagram account for me the last time they visited, but I hardly ever visit the page. They claimed it was best to use it on an application they installed on my phone, but it's hard for me to see the screen. I prefer to peruse Facebook on my computer, an old clunky desktop we keep in the spare room.

Richard wanted to get me a laptop so I could use it anywhere in the house, but I told him not to bother. Why would I carry a computer around with me when I had a perfectly comfortable chair and desk right here?

Richard has a new profile picture, and I click on his name. For as long as I can recall, he used a family photo of himself; his wife, Sarah; and their two sons, Johnny and Tyler, all wearing matching flannel shirts and jeans. The picture was a few years old now, the boys still in middle school. This new picture is of Richard, looking older and thinner, wearing a black winter hat and fishing gear, and holding a striped bass up by the lore as he beams into the camera. Tyler and Johnny, both as tall as their dad and wearing matching hats, stand on either side of him, pointing at the big fish. Sarah is nowhere in sight.

Neither of them outright told me they were having problems, but a mother's intuition is not often wrong. When I last spoke with Richard, he was evasive, but more than happy to talk about the boys. I learned that Johnny had passed his driving exam and had his permit. Richard laughed, warning everyone in Portsmouth to watch out, since the boy had a lead foot like his grandpa. I laughed right along with him. Freddie's penchant for driving too fast was now a common part of our family lore. Thankfully, our old Ford can't get much over thirty-five miles per hour before it begins to sputter, and the wheels start to shake.

Rich said Tyler was taking advanced placement chemistry and biology and was proving to have a real knack for the sciences. He was a high school freshman now, and I'd always known he'd be the bookworm of the family. His brother excelled in sports and loved the outdoors like his dad. I'm surprised Tyler still goes fishing with them, and suspect it's his only way to connect with my dear son, who has never pretended to understand Tyler's fascination with books and video games.

When I inquired after Sarah, his voice changed. A slight cough, a hesitation before telling me she was great and that she said hi. Usually, Sarah would jump on the line and take over the conversation. She loved to gab and was fiercely proud of her boys, always eager to share the daily minutia of their lives that I craved to hear and missed so dearly.

When the boys were small, Richard and Sarah had lived right around the corner, in a little two-bedroom cape. I saw them almost daily. But when the real estate market began to boom a while back, they got an offer they couldn't refuse and sold the house. It was immediately torn down and replaced by one of those modern

farmhouses you see on HGTV, boasting at least six bed-
rooms and a lot of windows. They moved to Portsmouth,
New Hampshire. Not that far, but not around the corner.
Since then, Sarah has been my lifeline to my grandkids.
And my son. But I hadn't heard from her since the abnor-
mally tense Christmas party at their house last year.

I continue to scroll his page. A few pictures of Johnny
and his baseball team, winning a game. Lots of comments
on those. *Good Luck at Semis! He looks just like you! Missed
you at the game—Johnny played great, as usual!*

I pause. Richard never misses a game. Richard was
the star player of his own high school. He used to coach
Johnny's little league. The Red Sox were his church. I
can't imagine any reason why he would not have been
there in person to see his son win the game.

My phone lies on the desk next to the keyboard, the
screen black. When I pick it up and touch the screen, a
picture of me with my four grandkids pops up. No pass-
word protection for me, I insisted. The phone hardly
leaves my house. Normally, I prefer to use my landline,
preferring the heft and weight of the handset over the
slippery square of an iPhone. Also, the volume on my cell
phone never gets loud enough. But I need to send a text.
I've been informed *no one* calls anymore, actual conversation another part of the bygone era I'm a remnant of.

I find Sarah in my favorites and open a new text message box.

*Good Evening, Dear! I miss our chats and hope we
can make time to talk soon. I was thinking about
you and wanted to check in.*

My finger rests near the "Delete" button. I'm not sure
if I'm overstepping my boundaries as a mother-in-law,
but I think this is okay. What I really want to ask is what

the heck is going on with her and my son, but I know that I'll only get an angry call from Richard, demanding that I stop butting in.

I look up and smile. "Should I send it?" I ask, eyes glancing back and forth to the doorway and then back to the phone.

He doesn't respond except to shake his head and shrug before carrying on his way. No one ever accused Freddie of butting in. He knew exactly where his butt belonged, he'd say.

Before I can second-guess myself, I hit "Send."

Give my love to Rich and the boys. Lots of kisses. Xoxo

I send the second message, proud of myself. Two texts in one night. Johnny and Tyler would be amazed at how hip their granny is.

Ready to close Facebook and follow Freddie to bed, I'm surprised by an alert on my phone. A new message from Sarah. Although I expected a response, she usually took a few hours to get back to me. Always busy with the boys, her hands were never idle enough to find the time to answer.

I miss you too. The boys are great and want to visit soon. You won't even recognize Tyler, he's grown a foot.

. . . I watch the three dots move as she continues her message.

I'm sorry I haven't been in touch. I've been waiting for Richard to call you, but I can see he still hasn't. I think you two should talk first. I really hope you are doing well, and I promise I'll call soon. Xoxo

I squint at the screen so hard my eyes cross. The first message filled my heart with happiness. But as soon as I saw those three dots rolling on the screen, I knew something was amiss. Mother's intuition. I debate calling Richard right now but decide it can wait until morning. Although it's not even nine and he's likely still awake, I need to figure out what I want to say. *"Sleep on it,"* Freddie would insist. I'm also going to assume Sarah is currently texting him, chastising him for keeping me in the dark over whatever it is we need to talk about. I wish I could pretend I didn't know what's going on, but that's a lie. A mother knows.

★ ★ ★

Sleep won't come. I lie in bed, worrying about Richard, obsessing over the text from his sweet wife, the mother of his children. When Richard first brought Sarah home to meet Freddie and me, I was convinced it would never last. The girl was beautiful—not a surprise because Richard was a good-looking man who never had any problem finding a pretty girl to date. Finding a girl worthy enough to meet his parents was an entirely different thing. After college my boy pursued an endless string of inappropriate women, since the idea of marriage and children and adulthood in general terrified hm.

The night he walked through the front door, hand gently on the lower back of a petite redhead with kind eyes and a disarming smile, I knew something was different. This girl charmed Freddie with her quick wit and insisted on helping me in the kitchen. A middle school math teacher, which put her right up there with the saints if you ask me, she was adored by her students and colleagues. I can't imagine a more difficult job then teaching numbers to hormonal teens, but she only laughed and said she loved the kids, mood swings and all. All night I kept waiting for the other shoe to drop, but it never did. Sarah was a sincerely good person who loved my son. Amazingly, he seemed to love her back.

Fast forward twenty years and two children later. Richard loves his family. Of this I'm sure. But he's never fully outgrown the petulant and spoiled mama's boy that he was when he was ten years old and demanding I buy him a baseball card *or else*. I'll never forget the temper tantrum he threw in the middle of the hobby store downtown. This was all because of a deal we'd struck. For every A on his report card, he could pick one card. When he sheepishly handed over the envelope containing that semester's grades, he hung his head in shame. Not a single A. This didn't bother me. Every student is different, and although my Kathy always did well in school and brought home good grades, Richard struggled in class. However, I always required he at least try. Beside each grade was a note from his teacher. *"Does not apply himself. Distracted in class. Hands in assignments late. Disrupts the class."* It was the comments that sealed his fate.

Yet he somehow convinced me to take him to the shop. To look. *"Only to look,"* he promised, batting his long lashes and hugging me tight around the waist. He claimed he wanted to see the cards so that he'd be motivated to try harder in school next semester. Obviously, I was being manipulated by my precocious ten-year-old, but I hoped maybe he would be determined to do better. Not surprisingly, this strategy backfired. A mothering misstep.

Standing before the card display, he pointed at his then-current favorite Red Sox player, Wade Boggs. He demanded I buy it for him. I reminded him we were only looking, but he planted his feet and doubled down his request, arms crossed before his chest and ready for a fight. At first, he simply begged and pleaded, arguing that I could hold onto the card until the next report card. With every word his voice got louder as he drew out every vowel, whined each syllable. He said it would be easier to have it ready at home as a reward for his accomplishment, so much easier than having to come all the way back to the store again.

As he stood before me, cheeks flushed red and brows knit tightly together, I realized that little boys like this grew up to be those lawyers on television, the kind I never liked so much, the ones who were always able to argue their way out of the sticky situations they were probably guilty of causing themselves. Refusing to be bullied by my own son, I put my foot down. I said no. My sweet boy turned from saccharine to acerbic in the blink of an eye. In a fit of rage, he swatted over a display of Legos, sending the blue and yellow blocks flying across the rug every which way. Other customers stared. The store owner stepped out from behind the register.

None of this bothered Richard, who looked me in the eye, still holding the Wade Boggs card, and ripped it straight down the center. He flicked the destroyed card in my direction and said I better pay for it, since Dad always said, *"If you break it, you buy it."*

Shaking my head against the memory, I roll onto my back, resigned to another sleepless night. Insomnia is yet another condition of aging, my body needing less and less rest with every year that passes. The clock reads three AM, still some time before my morning ritual. The minutes stretch longer than sixty seconds, each one cascading across the decades, bringing me back to the days when I was in the throes of motherhood. Strange how a lifetime can pass, yet individual moments can remain so fresh in your mind's eye, like you can reach in and grab them, hold them in the palm of your hand.

Horrified by Richard's despicable behavior, I apologized to the clerk and laid a five-dollar bill on the counter, more than the card was worth, but still not enough to excuse the mess and disruption my son had caused. Another mother pulled her daughter closer, shooting me a sympathetic look over her head, one of pity mixed with understanding. That look told me she'd been there too but was glad it was me and not her dragging her child from the toy store.

Richard ran across the parking lot and settled himself into our Jeep, his tears replaced by a stubborn silence. I suggested we go back inside and apologize, but he refused to speak, gripping the sides of the seat, and holding his breath until his face was beet red, full tantrum mode activated. Defeated, I buckled myself in behind the wheel and drove us home without so much as glancing in his direction.

When we got home, he ran straight to his room, slamming his door so hard the house shook. I threatened him with no supper and a spanking, promising Freddie's wrath when he got in and heard about the incident. About an hour later he came down the stairs, holding a picture he'd drawn of the two of us holding hands. In the corner he had scribbled, *I'm sorry. I'll get all A's next year.*

Clearly, he'd missed the message, but at least he was trying. That is what I told myself. He looked up at me with puppy-dog eyes and smiled, wrapping his arms around my neck and kissing me on the cheek. I tousled his shaggy hair and agreed to keep his outburst a secret from his dad. Somehow, he convinced me to order pizza for dinner. He was always so darned convincing, especially when guilty.

Parenting was both easier and harder in my day. After spending a few hours with Brynn from around the corner,

I can see so much has changed. Although I'd watched my own babies have babies of their own, who are now nearly ready to be out on their own, the world has turned even further on its axis. Being a mother fifty years ago is so different from twenty years ago, which is so different from five years ago, which is still different than it is today. Every year, the rules change, expectations shift. One generation of mothers is told to stay home and raise the babies. Another is told that you can have it all: work hard, play hard, mother hard. Today's moms are bombarded with the constant need for approval, social media blasting picture upon picture of perfectly matched families and birthday parties so elaborate they put my wedding to shame. Now everyone is always trying to outdo the last. I suppose this existed in my day. *"Keepin' up with the Joneses"* was one of my favorite expressions. But it was different. We only imagined what went on behind closed doors. Now you can watch it all on a live feed, family content for mass consumption. It's impossible not to compare yourself.

If a kid threw a tantrum in a toy shop now, it would be captured by another parent and uploaded to Facebook or that other video sight Prisha is always raving about and making up dances for. Hundreds and then thousands, maybe millions, of people would watch it and share. It would go *viral* as they say on the news, like it's a disease that is caught rather than a sick obsession that is learned. The mother wouldn't get sympathetic nods from other moms. Other moms would judge and leave their two cents in the comments, belittling the mother for raising an unruly child and offering unsolicited advice on how she could do better. A video of a bad day might follow that mother and child for the rest of their lives, nothing on the internet ever truly gone. People would label both the child and the mother as *bad*, and just like that, they would be *bad*. I'm thankful my bad day exists only in my memory and maybe on some long-forgotten VHS security footage from decades ago.

Squeezing my eyes shut, I tell myself for the millionth time that Richard's behavior that day was not an indication of a bigger problem, only a bad day. One of quite a few bad days over the years, but not something I need blame myself for. I did the best I could. Richard was a challenging baby, refusing to sleep and always colicky. His toddler years were better, his cherubic blond curls and dimples causing family and friends to treat him like a living doll, always doting on him. Katherine resented all the attention Richard garnered, pouting that he got away with everything. At the time, I denied this, but now I know it is true. Richard was my baby boy, and I coddled him. I allowed him to make mistake after mistake, and accepted a forced apology without ever making him pay the penance for his actions. I fear my gentle parenting created a spoiled man who expected the world to bend to his wishes, and when it didn't, he ripped it apart and ran.

Sighing, I swing my legs over the side of the bed, careful not to disturb the other side of the mattress. The room is dark, but I'm so practiced at navigating this space that I easily find my book on the nightstand and tuck it under my arm. With the other, I grab my robe from the chair and shrug my way into it, silent as a mouse.

"We did the best we could," I mumble into the darkness, knowing Freddie hears me, even if he doesn't respond. Either way, he'd never argue this point. In Freddie's eyes, I did better than the best. Maybe this is why I never did more for Richard. A cycle of complacency.

"Love you," I whisper, holding the book against my chest before tiptoeing from the room.

· 11 ·

BRYNN

Early June

Find your #momtribe and you'll never be alone. Nothing binds you to another woman like commiserating over the trials and tribulations of this crazy journey we call motherhood! Blessed to be surrounded by these beautiful, STRONG, mommas!

—3BoysMamaMonty

I WORRY A PART of me will always be stuck in middle school, forever awkward and desperately seeking the attention and, most importantly, the validation of the "popular" kids. Maybe everyone feels like this, some universal truth binding us all together with insecure tendencies. In any case, I'm going to keep telling myself this, that even cool girls like Monty Montgomery still fear they won't fit in or that their outfit is last season.

As I scroll through the comments on Monty's latest post, it appears that at least all *moms* are the same. We're all women struggling for acceptance, craving a chance to be understood during this trying season of our lives. Monty knows this. She gets it. Maybe her image is a little more polished than the average lady's in her comments, but beneath the filter and perfectly blown-out hair and artfully applied makeup, she's just like us. Like me. Those other women, two on either side of her, both holding up a glass of champagne so perfect I can practically see the individual bubbles rising from each long-stemmed crystal glass—they could be my friends. Monty smiles the widest as she looks to her left at a pretty brunette, who holds a hand to her mouth, so happy she's afraid her joy might overflow from her, spill forth like the orange bottle of Veuve sitting on the table behind them. In the caption, each woman is tagged, and I click on the brunette's profile, @TheRealCaraRae. Most of her photos are of her two-year old daughter, Violet. Cara doesn't have nearly as many followers as her good friend Monty, but enough to rack up hundreds of "likes" on each photo.

I backtrack a few months and pause on a makeup-free Cara holding an ultrasound picture. The caption reads: *Our hearts are broken. Today our beautiful angel baby had no heartbeat Although he was only in my belly for nine weeks, he will be in our hearts forever. #1in4 #miscarriageawareness.*

Settling back on the park bench, I click my phone off and toss it in the diaper bag. Enough Instagram for now. Even the shiniest lives have their dark spots. In a way, it makes me feel better. A little less alone. Undoubtedly, this was the effect Cara was going for. Sharing our stories, even on the internet, should connect us. Invisible threads looping from one account to the next, tying around our eagerly scrolling thumbs and attaching to our hearts and minds, binding us to one another. So I'm not sure why I suddenly feel so empty. Reading about Cara's pain feels distant and surreal. It's hard to wrap my mind around Monty's joyous post existing in the same space as a post about something as serious as baby loss. It's like emotional whiplash, and the skeptical part of my brain wonders if it's all only to elicit "likes."

Cody snoozes peacefully in the stroller. After scouring the mommy forums, I was thoroughly chastised for strapping him into the car seat with a jacket on. I learned from some very helpful, bordering on condescending, mothers that it was extremely dangerous for that extra layer to exist between the baby's chest and the straps and in the event of an accident the baby might be thrown from the seat entirely. Honestly, if the accident was bad enough for anyone to fly anywhere, I would debate that it was because of a half inch of fabric, but I will admit Cody is much more comfortable sans jacket.

Since our visit to Joy's a few days ago, we've gone twice to the park and once all the way to Main Street. An unfortunate diaper blowout prevented us from entering any stores, but I dare hope to grab a cappuccino the next time we venture that far. Baby steps.

The bench near the swing set is occupied by three women, each with a stroller parked within arm's length of her. The woman in the center is clearly the leader of the little mom tribe gathered here today. Two toddlers chase each other around the slide, one older than the other. The older boy keeps racing up the steps and sliding down the ladder, causing the younger girl to giggle with delight each time he explodes from the green tunnel. I imagine the blond girl belongs to the woman on the left, her own hair a slightly darker version of her daughter's. *Tracy,* I imagine. The woman on the right edge of the bench is a little older than the other two, older than me. I'd say mid- to late thirties. Her dark hair is expertly curled and held back with a velvet headband. A string of dainty pearls is wrapped around her neck, and I can see her sparkling wedding ring from across the park. I thought *my* princess-cut diamond was a little ostentatious, but the one weighing down Avery's finger is comically large. If I didn't know better, I'd assume it was a piece of costume jewelry, but Avery would never wear a fake. Each time she rocks the stroller, the ring catches the sun, shooting blinding rays in every direction. I hope her baby is wearing sunglasses.

Holding center court is the queen bee of the park: a tall blonde wearing a cream-colored cashmere sweater and suede pants; each article of clothing looks tailor made for her. The confidence she must have to wear something so decadent around small children! Does she not ever spill milk on herself? Her little boy is a bit older, likely not attached to a bottle any longer. But boys are messy. Dirty hands and the constant snack crumbs. So many perilous things ready to stain those beautiful pants. *Monty,* I decide. She's the Monty of Salem Park.

Cody stirs and I rock him a little harder, willing him to stay asleep. The tittering laugh of the mom tribe trickles across the space between us. I watch, wishing they would look my way, catch my eye and smile in my direction, wave me over. I give in to this daydream, envision myself smiling back as though I hadn't noticed them before. I'd confidently stride over to them, for once able to unlock the brake on the stroller without a struggle, and park Cody beside Avery's sleeping baby. I'd reach my hand out to introduce myself—to Monty first, of course. She would then tell me each of their names, then their children's. We'd chat for a few minutes. Conversation would bring us to where we each lived, and I'd tell them my address, knowing they would all be very aware of how much every house in the neighborhood cost, knowing they were weighing and assessing everything about me. We'd exchange numbers, promise to have a playdate soon. I'd beg off, using Cody as an excuse. But really I didn't want to be the only mom standing. Bowing away gracefully and leaving them wanting more is the right play. Next time I'll get to the park first, claim the seat to the right of Monty, forcing one of the other women to stand.

"Is anyone sitting here?" A voice startles me from my daydream, and my arm jerks. Cody fusses, a few soft mews escaping from the seat. They will only become louder, more insistent. Damn this stranger for interrupting me and waking my son.

"No," I snap, harsher than intended. The woman is about my age and wears a baseball cap over a frizzy blond ponytail, the hairs around her ears sticking out at odd angles, a halo of curls backlit by the bright June sun.

She flinches as though I've slapped her, and I wish I could take it back, start over. First impressions are everything. This is ingrained in me from my years planning parties. Strapped to the front of her is a toddler who looks entirely too large to be carried in a BabyBjörn.

"Thanks," she mumbles, stumbling backward, awkwardly holding her baby across his chest as she straddles the edge of the bench, as far from me as possible. She plops a fashionable diaper bag on the expanse between us. "Little guy is getting heavy," she mutters, more to herself than me.

I smile, nodding in her direction, unsure what to say next. Before Cody, I never struggled with conversation or polite interactions. It was part of my job, a part I quite enjoyed. Now I wonder if I should apologize or simply ignore my bad manners and ask her about herself, her baby. Neither seems very interesting to me, so I remain silent, hoping Cody hushes himself in his stroller.

The woman unstraps the baby from his holder and sets him on the grass in front of her feet, where he stands on wobbly legs. Toddling forward, he almost falls but rights himself before stepping in my direction, using one hand on the bench for balance. Cody rustles from beneath the blankets, lifting a socked foot and kicking his beloved rubber giraffe, Sophie, to the ground. Instantly, the toddler makes a mad dash for the teething toy, snatching it from the ground and shoving the squeaky favorite into his own mouth.

"*NO!*" Without thinking, I reach out and grab the giraffe from the boy's hands, pulling it from his gummy mouth. As my fingers connect with one spotted leg, some part of my brain screams at me to *stop*, to release the toy and step away from the child. But it's too late. The boy falls to the grass. He stares up at me with wide eyes, then closes them tightly, his lips quivering before he begins crying, tears streaming down his chubby cheeks.

As I grip the giraffe in my right hand, the weight of a thousand stares presses down on my shoulders. Not only is the boy's mother looking at me in outraged silence, but the tribe of moms across the way are all openly glaring in my direction. To my horror, Avery holds up her phone, the bedazzled case glittering in the sun beside her obnoxious ring.

"Oh my God," I say, dropping Sophie on the bench and reaching down toward the fallen toddler, who is still on the grass, screaming even louder. Tears bubble from both eyes, but he looks more shocked than hurt, thank God.

"Don't you *dare* touch him," the woman hisses, shouldering past my arms and scooping her child into her own, pulling him tightly to her chest. She brushes a kiss on his forehead and shushes into his blond curls.

But the little boy is inconsolable. The tighter his mom holds him, the more he seems to cry, each wail louder than the last as he grips her sweatshirt in his grubby fingers, his tears staining the gray jersey knit.

As if on cue, Cody begins screaming, the combination of being awoken from a nap and hunger coming together to form the perfect storm. Thrashing around wildly, he kicks the blanket from the stroller, puffing his chest against the straps and punching the airs as he gasps, choking on his sobs.

I'm paralyzed. Panic has settled over me, and it's impossible to move, impossible to think. My motherly instinct to comfort Cody is in direct conflict with my social instinct to apologize to this stranger, and rather than picking one, I do nothing. Out of the corner of my eye, I notice the camera still pointed in our direction. I make eye contact with the woman holding it. She sneers.

"I'm sorry," I mumble, my flight instinct finally overriding all else, firmly pushing my body into motion. *Escape,* it screams. "I don't know why I did that," I whisper under my breath as I grab my backpack from the bench, shoving the wicked Sophie in a side pocket. In my rush, I knock the other mother's bag from its perch, a bottle and an assortment of odds and ends spilling across the grass. I bend to pick them up.

"Leave it," she growls, using the toe of her tennis sneaker to nudge the bag closer to her. Kneeling in her shadow, I feel like a stray dog being kicked while it's already down. I drop a blue Binky to the grass and rise, stumbling back on my heels to give her space. My hip bumps the stroller, causing Cody to howl with outrage again. My pulse pounds in my ear, beating in time with the surges in my son's wails.

Lifting my chin, I brace both palms on the handle of the stroller. With the toe of my right foot, I disengage the brake, clicking it three times before the damn thing unsticks. Free from the lock, it lurches forward, slipping on the dewy grass. I chase it by taking a giant step, refusing to stagger away with my tail between my legs.

Squeak! The high-pitched cry of none other than Sophie the giraffe announces my departure as I step on the errant teething toy that must have fallen from my bag in all the commotion. Without looking back, I kick it once more, eliciting a small yelp of pain from the lost toy, and I inwardly cringe, recognizing my walk of shame as a meme in the making.

★ ★ ★

My college roommate and best friend, Ali, got married right after graduation. Although we stayed in touch for a few years, the trajectories of our lives set us on two very different paths. Sitting together in the dorms, and later in our sorority house at UMass, we promised we'd be besties forever. Of course, I would be Ali's maid of honor at her wedding to her college sweetheart, and without a doubt she'd be mine when I married the man I'd yet to meet at that point.

Unfortunately, life had other plans for us. Fast-forward to my wedding. Ali found out she was pregnant after I'd already booked the venue and sent out the save-the-date cards, and no matter which way we did the math, she'd be close to popping by the time I walked down the aisle.

Looking back now, I'm embarrassed by my behavior, which was nothing short of the worst sort of bridezilla. As crazy as it now seems, I was angry at Ali for getting pregnant and stealing the show. I was furious her thirty-eight-week baby bump would be vying for attention in every wedding photo, and I spent way too much time searching for dresses that might hide the bulge, going as far as suggesting maternity Spanx. Things were tense between us in the weeks leading up to my big day, and I wonder if the stress I'd caused her might have been one factor in her going into early labor.

Ali didn't make it to the wedding. She delivered her sweet baby girl, Willow Jayne, about the same time that I was raging on about my rehearsal dinner plans being ruined. Of course, it wasn't Ali's fault. I know that now. Hell, I knew it then but was so self-involved in the biggest party of my life that I couldn't see the forest for the trees. After the dust settled, I met Willow a handful of times. Ali never asked me to be her godmother, another promise broken. We exchange holiday cards and the occasional text, but once Ali decided to move to Colorado to be closer to her husband's family, the time between talks became fewer and farther between. Now we are barely more than social media friends, resigned to following the other's life in bits and pieces online, tiny snippets that would never add up to even a portion of the whole friendship we once shared.

After Willow was born, Ali created an account just for the baby. At the time, this was a very trendy thing to do, even though I found it a bit creepy to be reading captions supposedly written from the perspective of an infant. Each month Ali updated the feed, telling all Willow's followers about her growth progress, favorite things to do, and foods she liked to eat. I followed because that's all I have left of my best friend, and I "liked" every post, even though I often wondered if I should call Ali and make sure she was okay. Sometimes the posts read a bit unhinged, a desperate plea for help. I never called. Sitting here scrolling through the feed, updated much less frequently now that Willow is in school, I know I should have. These were the posts of a lonely mom shouting into the void, hoping someone might hear her. I'm thankful for the comments by other friends, other moms who recognized what @WillowJayneIam really was.

Today is my six-month birthday!! Mommy and Daddy surprised me with a trip to the petting zoo, where I got to meet goats, sheep, and my favorite thing yet—a pony!! There were some ducks and geese, but I didn't like them as much—their flapping wings scared me a bit.

I'm very curious about everything and especially love grabbing for my mommy's phone and the remote control. But anything I can reach is fair game! Although I can't crawl yet, I'm rocking back and forth on my hands and knees, and I think I'll be on the move any day now. Look out world!!

I just started eating some solid foods, and so far I love avocado, hate oatmeal, and am not so sure about applesauce. Mommy's milk is still my favorite thing, but I'm open to trying new foods.

Sleep? What's sleep? I was getting pretty good at sleeping all night, but Daddy thinks I'm a night owl in the making because I'd much rather hang out with my parents then go to sleep all by myself. I don't want to miss a thing!

Looking forward to our next big adventure next month when we visit Granny and Grampy in Colorado. This will be my first airplane ride. Stay tuned for what I think about flying!

Xoxo, Willow Jayne

The caption sits below a carousel of pictures of Willow in an assortment of outfits, along with one of her snuggling a small pony's face at the petting zoo. At the time, I probably just glanced at the photos and hit "like."

Now I read it over and over, fascinated at what might have compelled my friend—the friend who was voted most serious in our sorority—to write such a whimsical and fantastical diary entry from the perspective of a six-month-old. I'm at a loss.

Cody is propped up on my breastfeeding pillow beside me on the couch. After suffering through a torturous five minutes of tummy time, he reluctantly accepted my breast and managed to only throw up once this time. He watches me with interested eyes, and I wonder what he's thinking. If Cody were to write his own posts, what might he say about his mommy and daddy and all the fun adventures he's had these two months?

Hi! My name is Cody Mitchell, and I'm almost two months old. So far I've had a pretty boring life. Mostly I eat, sleep, and poop, although I prefer the first and the last. Sleep is overrated. I don't always love to eat either, but spitting up in mommy's hair and refusing a bottle can sometimes be a fun game. Nothing bad to say about pooping. Pooping is the best.

My mommy hasn't quite figured out how to take me many places yet, so I've mostly stayed in the house and watched her scroll on her phone. The few times we've left the house have ended in disaster—either Mom falls asleep on some stranger's porch, or she winds up yelling and stealing toys from babies. In any case, it always ends with me screaming and Mom crying.

I loved my teething toy, Sophie, but mom left her in the park on the ground. I refuse to take a Binky and none of the other stuffies make me as happy

*as that giraffe did. RIP Sophie, darling. Mom tried
to give me one of your cousins, but I know it isn't
you.*

*Daddy plays with me at night, and I always love
this time, since I only see him about an hour a day.
But it's my favorite hour! I wish I saw Daddy all day
and Mommy for only one hour. Then my life would
be wayyyy more fun!*

*Nothing new is planned for next month. I'm get-
ting bigger and bigger, but Mom keeps forgetting
to take my monthly photos like she promised she
would. Before you know it, I'll be all grown, and
there will be no record of my growth. Good thing
I learned how to keep a diary on Instagram all by
myself—obviously we can't trust Mommy to do it!*

Xoxo, Cody

But which photo to add? Clicking open the camera
on my phone, I peruse the pictures. Most of them are of
Cody sleeping. Despite my son's criticism, I did manage
to take some shots of him a few days after his one-month
birthday. Somewhere there's a handy-dandy month-by-
month mat meant just for the purpose of milestone photos. I contemplate digging it out of the basement. No one
will know if I fudge the dates here and there.

Cody gurgles next to me, and I lift my eyes from the
screen. He smiles up at me, his lips rimmed with chunky
white dribble. So much for keeping all the milk down.
Sighing, I plug my phone into the charger, deciding to
forgo the photo shoot and take Cody out for another
walk to clear our heads. Kyle won't be home for a few
more hours, and that's a lot of time to kill. Maybe I'll call

Ali. Or at least think of something to text her. I miss my friend. Maybe it's not too late to reach out. Better late than never. Who knows, maybe Ali will be my mom tribe, a more experienced mom ready to take a fledgling under her wing. Cody gurgles again, the vomit landing on the couch, a few drops spattering to the carpet. Sighing, I wipe up the mess and decide Ali probably doesn't want to commiserate with me when she's already been there, done that, and—worse—done it without me.

12

JOY

Early June

Such she often felt herself—struggling against terrific odds to maintain her courage; to say "But this is what I see; this is what I see."

—Virginia Woolf, *To the Lighthouse*

WHEN SHE KNOCKS ON the door, I've finally settled down on the couch to watch an episode—or two—of *Grace and Frankie*, my most recent guilty pleasure. For years I resisted all these streaming services, maintaining there wasn't anything worth watching that couldn't be seen on network TV. I finally gave in, and I wish I hadn't been such a stubborn old mule for so long. The ability to watch as many episodes as my heart desires all at once is such a luxury. I'm amazed at how I ever survived waiting a week to see the next show. And no commercials. Wonders, be.

Somehow, I know its Brynn. The front door is closed, not that I can see it from the living room anyway. Something about the tentative two knocks, followed by three sharp ones, each a little harder than the last, echoes the young mother's timid-on-the-surface demeanor.

Women like Brynn are the reason expressions like *"Still waters run deep"* resonate. Using the clicker to pause my show—yet another miracle I'll marvel at till the day I die—I gingerly push myself up from my spot and navigate around Freddie's recliner, currently void of my husband, therefore the perfect place to rest my cane for easy access.

"Coming," I call out to the visitor, who I'm certain is my neighbor. I shuffle a little quicker to the door, afraid she will leave if no one answers it immediately.

My trip to the grocery store feels a million years ago, but it was only a few days in the past, so the fridge is stocked with a bit of food, although I might have purchased some more nibbles if I'd know I'd be having company. I chastise myself for not making a pitcher of lemonade straight away this morning, like I normally do. The lure of Netflix was too strong. An hour on the couch was too tempting, and the lemons remain in the crisper. Thankfully there's a few cold diet colas on the shelf. Not all is lost.

Opening the door, I'm not surprised to see my new friend—I dare call her a "friend," since I believe our last conversation sailed us out of neighbor territory. Brynn holds a red-faced Cody to her shoulder, absently patting his back with the tips of her fingers. Pat pat pat, pat pat pat. Cody doesn't seem to particularly like this motion, arching his body against the pressure and kicking his legs into her ribs. She continues to smile at me; her straight white teeth could be on a poster for the benefits of proper orthodontic care. But something in her eyes is unsettled, wild. She's looking at me but also past me. Through me. Her pupils dart left and right in time with the patting on Cody's back. Left, right, left. Right, left, right.

"Joy, hi," she exclaims too brightly, as if we had a scheduled visit, and she wasn't showing up at my door unannounced. Not that I mind. The benefit of Netflix is I can watch my show whenever I want. I'm in no place to be denying myself real company. "I'm not interrupting you, am I?" she adds, worry creasing her face.

I shake my head and chuckle. "Only saving me from myself," I kid. She cocks her head in confusion. "I was about to watch too much television and waste the rest of this beautiful day inside," I clarify.

She nods, knowingly. "I'm guilty of binging Netflix way too often," she says, finally settling her hand against Cody. He appears to appreciate the end of the tapping.

"Binge?" I ask, testing the word in my mouth. My granddaughters have thrown the term about, but I've never understood the context. They always talk so fast, ping-ponging from one topic to the next so that I can't get in a word edgewise, never mind bother to ask them a question.

She tilts her head, considering. "Like when you watch fifteen episodes in a row without moving except to get more snacks or maybe pee," she says, laughing to herself. "When Cody can't sleep, I go downstairs and end up watching entire seasons of bad reality shows before breakfast. I think it's a disease."

I nod, since I've likened it to exactly that: an awful disease, or at least a terrible addiction.

"You're welcome to come watch my show with me," I offer, warming to the idea of the company of a friend to laugh over Jane Fonda and Lily Tomlin's verbal sparring. But I note the slight fall in Brynn's face at the prospect and change course. "Or we can sit out on the porch and chat for a bit?" She nods eagerly, and my heart lifts.

I open the door wider, propping it open with the brass ship statue that sits by the door for this very purpose. "You go ahead and get yourself and that little angel seated. Would you like anything to drink? I've no lemonade made, but I do have soda."

Brynn collapses into the same seat as her last visit, resting Cody on her lap, nestled into the crook of her elbow. "Would it be too much trouble for a cup of coffee?" she asks, her voice suddenly weary.

"No trouble at all, dear," I say. "Be back in a jiffy." The cool breeze follows me into the foyer and to the kitchen, the curtains rustling. Dust bunnies dance across the stream of light, and I vow to vacuum soon, air out the house. I blame Netflix for the neglect.

★   ★   ★

I memorize the way Brynn takes her coffee: light with two sugars. To be safe, I brought out cream, sugar, honey, Sweet'N Low and a nondairy creamer, although I assume she would've warned me if she was lactose intolerant. Nowadays it seems like everyone is afraid of good old-fashioned cow's milk. I add a pink packet to my own mug and stir in a heavy pour of cream, then sip before adding a touch more to cool it down.

"Thank you," she murmurs, blowing on the edge of the cup before taking a second sip. "It was a long morning," she snorts, lifting her brows and glancing down at her babe, who dozes in her arms, his lids fluttering and mouth puckering against an imaginary nipple.

I reflect on my own long morning, those protracted minutes before dawn, each lasting a lifetime. My days were no longer filled with the hustle and bustle of new motherhood, but the painful emptiness of nothing to do and nowhere to be. "Do anything interesting?" I ask, hoping I might live vicariously through Brynn, if only for the afternoon. I consider trading a cup of coffee for a glimpse into the outside world a fair exchange.

A cloud passes over Brynn's face as she stares down
into her coffee cup, but it's gone by the time she looks
up again, the tightness in her jaw suddenly replaced by
that same, too-white smile she had plastered on when she
knocked on the door. But her eyes tell a different tale. "I
met up with a few friends over at Salem Park," she says,
her voice higher than normal and a touch too loud. "We
meet up twice a week and let the little ones play." She giggles, the hand holding the mug shaking so a few drops spill
over the edge and dribble down her thumb, leaving a caramel trail down into the wrist of her light-colored sweater.
"Well, Cody doesn't play, *obviously*. But I chat with the
other moms, and we watch the older kids run around."

Her cheeks are flushed pink, and a few beads of sweat
bubble along her hairline, despite the cool breeze that's
picked up since the sun moved behind the trees. If she
were my daughter, I'd be tempted to hold the back of my
palm to her forehead and check for a fever. But she's not
my daughter, I remind myself, and resist the urge. "That
sounds lovely," I muse, testing my coffee again. Finally
cool enough to sip. "These other moms live locally?" I
ask, thinking of the women I always see pushing baby
carriages in their tight workout pants and brightly colored jackets.

Brynn nods, her smile unwavering. "Yes, all from
right around here. It's great," she says, her eyes wide and
unblinking, the feverish glaze having moved onto her
pupils, which are black and watery. Unwell. "It's why
Kyle and I moved to this neighborhood. For the family
atmosphere." An errant piece of hair falls from her ponytail across her cheek and she brushes it away with her free
hand. More coffee spills from the cup. A few drops land
on Cody's head, and he stirs. Unsettled, I can only hope
the liquid is as cooled as my own.

"How lucky for you both," I say, my eyes glued to the coffee sliding down Cody's ear as it disappears inside the collar of his blue onesie. "I cherished my friends when my kids were small."

She catches my eye and glances down. Noting the spill, she uses a thumb to wipe away the wet spot in his blond curls before shooting me a sheepish smile. "They're the best," she sighs. "We call ourselves the Salem mom tribe." Her voice changes once again, an octave too high, unnatural. Her eyes dart toward the street, and I follow her gaze, but there's nothing in the distance.

"There's Monty," she starts, now looking past me, through me. "She's so beautiful and *such* an inspiration. She has three little boys and somehow manages to do it all. I don't know how she does it," she says, her words spilling too fast from her mouth, the syllables twisting and spinning together. "Then there's Avery. She works from home but is super successful. Interior design," she swoons. "Her son is two, so he'll be ahead of Cody in school, but I imagine they will be great friends." She strokes her son's cheek, and he opens one eye. I swear he pulls away from her touch. "Tracy is a stay-at-home mom too. Her daughter is a year old and looks just like her mommy. Tracy and I have so much in common. We might start going to yoga together," she whispers, her breath ragged, like she'd run a marathon rather than explained to me the dynamics of her friend group.

Brynn stares at me with wild eyes, waiting for my response. I've no idea what to say. She's lying. I might be not much more than a stranger, but I'd bet my bottom dollar that not one word that rushed from her lips was the truth. This much I know is true. What I don't know is *why* she would lie. Either way, the story she spun is as false as the smile she's had glued to her face this whole time. Normally, I'd never tolerate a liar. I always told my children that lies were a temporary solution to a permanent problem. Freddie liked to say he was a kind man, not a stupid man, whenever Richard would try and pull a fast one on him. Perhaps it's my advanced age or simply my desire to hear a good story that isn't being broadcast from the tube, but I don't send her packing from my porch. Not yet, anyway.

"Well, if they do geriatric yoga at this studio then count me in too," I joke. The color drains from her cheeks. I wait a beat before the punchline. "I'm kidding. These hips aren't meant for downward dog anymore."

She laughs right along, the tinny sound of someone convincing themselves something is funny. Or maybe she's convincing herself something is true. My neighbor is proving more a mystery with every minute.

"Two wrongs don't make a right." My mother taught me this, and I passed along this age-old wisdom to my own kids. But what's the harm in a little innocent fibbing? Not all lies are created equally. Some are only the stretching of the facts, twisting the fabric of reality, offering an *alternate* truth. Clearly, Brynn is not troubled by a bit of hyperbole. Some say truth is stranger than fiction, but in my recent experience this is not the case. Truth can be mundane. Truth is often boring. Sometimes the truth needs a little *embellishment*. A little fib can shine so much brighter than the lackluster *truth*.

"Your mom tribe sounds a lot like my group of friends at the historical society," I say, allowing myself the pleasure of remembering busy days at the front desk of the museum and tourist center. Closing my eyes, I envision the steady stream of visitors passing through the doors year-round and the long lines wrapping around the front steps at Halloween, Salem's favorite holiday.

Brynn sets her nearly empty coffee cup on the table between us and rests her head back on the chair. "Do you see them often?" she asks, lifting her brow. The wild look in her eyes is gone, leaving behind the red-rimmed tinge of exhaustion. The purple rings below each lash-line are more severe than at our last visit. I wonder if she's been sleeping. Probably not.

Biting my lip, I debate my response. Noting the hopeful glint in her gaze, I choose to tell her the truth as I wish it to be, even if reality falls a bit shy.

"All the time," I say, smiling widely. Maybe your mouth stretches a little further with every lie you tell, further and further to help hide the deception. The Cheshire Cat comes to mind. "My best friend, Gayle, volunteers with me. We used to work every day but dropped down to a few times a week as we got older," I say without even the slightest hesitation, amazed at how easily the story slips from my mouth. In truth, I haven't seen Gayle since Christmas, although we do speak on the phone every Friday. She jokes it's to check in to make sure the other hasn't dropped dead. Morbid, but that's Gayle's humor. "Harsh realist" would be the way I'd describe my best friend.

"Dorothy is the third member of our little group," I continue. "She's the youngster of the group, only seventy-two. She still works every day, mostly handling the bookkeeping and such. She says she's never going to retire, but who knows?" I chuckle. Dorothy's face comes to mind, her tightly cropped curls that are always set exactly in place, a matching strand of pearls wrapped around her neck and in either ear. Dorothy is the youngest of us, but she has an old soul. I think Brynn and Dorothy would get along.

"Are all your husbands fishermen?" Brynn asks.

The last time I saw Dorothy was at the funeral, her tear-stained face pinched beneath her wrinkles, trying so hard not to let her composure crumple. An image of her reaching her arms out and holding me tight to her shoulder flashes before me, the way she wrapped me in her embrace, even though she's at least five inches shorter than me. She's such a small woman, and I'll forever be amazed at her strength, especially in the wake of all that grief.

"No, just my Freddie," I say, my chest tightening. "Dorothy lost her husband a while back to cancer. Gayle's husband is—was—a lawyer. He retired some time ago."

Brynn frowns. "I'm sorry," she mumbles. "It's lucky you have each other," she says, her voice catching and sending a spark of anguish through my own heart.

She's right. How lucky I am to have such friends. How foolish I've been for letting the time get away from me, letting our friendship languish. Too easy it's been to blame ailing partners and age for the distance between us. An excuse, and a lazy one at that. Once we saw each other daily, and it was not enough. Now we settle for every few months, allowing phone calls and letters to do the heavy lifting that should come from face-to-face interaction. I itch to call my two friends now, invite them for dinner. But it's an itch I won't scratch. Sometimes the truth is not only boring but too painful to bear.

Spot jumps onto my lap and curls into a tight ball. He rests his chin on his paws as I stroke the soft black fur along his back, feeling the steady vibrations of his purring beneath my palm, reverberating up my arm and into the deepest parts of me.

"Did I tell you why I named him Spot?" I ask, even though I know I haven't. But it's a story I've told many times over, and it always gets a good chuckle. No one can resist a nice heart-warming tale about cats and light-houses, told by a kind old lady. Now that I think of it, maybe the laughs are more out of pity than anything else. I shake my head. No. It's a charming story, and I'm a charming storyteller. No harm leaning into one's strengths.

Brynn shakes her head and murmurs a soft *no* under her breath. Her cheek rests on the crown of Cody's head. Her eyelids droop, but she looks more relaxed than she did earlier in our visit, the weight of her lies no longer balancing on her shoulders.

"Owl's Head Lighthouse in Maine is one of my favorite places, right off the coast near St. George. Freddie and I often camped in the park," I begin, settling into the familiar rhythm of the tale. "When we were much younger, of course. The last time we visited was eighteen years ago, to celebrate our anniversary." The memories drift over me, covering me like a muslin blanket, airy and almost see-through, but not quite. "We spent this last time in a cabin instead of a tent, both agreeing we were long past the time when sleeping on the ground was romantic." I remember the cabin well, the buffalo plaid pillowcases and homespun quilts on every surface, the big stone hearth and leather sofa. It wasn't much, but it was enough.

"We loved St. George because it sat smack dab in the middle of the trifecta of Maine lighthouses—at Owl's Head, Whitehead Island, and Marshall Point." I pause, noting Brynn's eyelids flutter before they jerk open, and she yawns. I decide to skip a few beats, get to the good part. No one has ever accused me of being concise. "Back in the day, the Owl Head keeper's daughter had a springer spaniel named Spot. That dog loved to watch the shore, and whenever he saw a ship, he'd bark furiously and tug

at the fog bell with his teeth until the ringing broadcast over the sound, In return, he was rewarded with the
whistle of the ship, causing his to rush down to the rocky
shoreline below and bark some more. One stormy, snowy
night, a worried wife of a sailor called the keeper when
her husband was running a few hours late. Tales of Spot's
ability to hear a boat whistle were legend by now, so the
wife hoped Spot might be able to heed the call. At first,
there was nothing. But later that same night, Spot rose
on his haunches and began barking to be let out. Unable
to get to the bell, now covered in snow, Spot ran to the
highest point on the cliff and barked like mad. Following
his trail, the keeper finally heard the boat's whistle. Spot
kept howling, alerting the boat to where the lighthouse
was. The boat sounded three sharp whistles, a sign that
they were now able to chart a course home. Spot saved
that ship from disaster," I exclaim, chills running down
my forearms, setting the hairs standing up, like every
other time I'd told this story.

"What an amazing story," Brynn says, a smile crossing her face. A sincere smile.

"One of my favorites," I admit, even though I have
so many to choose from, some not quite as happy as this
one. "After visiting the lighthouse, we headed back to our
little cabin for dinner. It was a foggy night—you could
barely see your own hand in front of you. As we sat down
to eat, we heard a scratching at the door. Freddie got up
to investigate, but there was nothing on the porch. This
happened three, four times before Freddie finally went
outside." The image of Freddie, his duck boots untied
and a winter cap perched atop his head as he stares out
into the fog is so vivid I can feel the damp breath of that
night on my cheek. He was still so handsome. "When
Freddie finally looked up, he saw smoke. Lots of it. He

came rushing into the house and ran to the kitchen, where there was an old wood-burning stove. When he opened the door, black smoke ballooned into the room, sending him gasping and choking for air. We rushed around the room, opening all the windows and doors, desperate to air the cabin out. Once he could finally see, he discovered the flue was closed, and the pressure from the fog sent all that smoke back into the house."

Brynn lifts her head from the back of the chair, sitting a little straighter. On the edge of her seat, I'm pleased to note. "What happened?"

I pet Spot behind his collar, the bell attached to the front jingling once. "A scrawny black cat jumped up into the open windowsill of the kitchen and meowed in our direction. It proceeded to leap from the counter and saunter gracefully into the living room before climbing up onto the leather couch and snuggling up against a pillow," I say. Spot opens his green eyes and stares up at me. Clearly this is his favorite part of the story. "As we finished waving the smoke from the kitchen, he moved from his place on the sofa to the kitchen table, where he helped himself to some of the salmon Freddie had made for dinner. I'm pretty sure he lapped up a few sips of beer before curling up to sleep in front of the fire."

"Spot?" Brynn asks, nodding down at my old feline friend, who has resumed his nap on my lap.

"The one and only." I smile, catapulting through eighteen years of time and then back to this moment. "After saving us from potentially setting the whole cabin on fire, he refused to leave us alone. He didn't have a collar and was desperately in need of a few square meals, so we decided not to fight him, and packed him up with the rest of our things and brought him back home to Salem. Black cats are a prerequisite in this neck of the woods," I joke, although I think it might actually be the truth. "So, that's how we ended up with a cat, without any spots, named after a dog."

"Amazing," Brynn whispers, her lips brushing the side of her son's head with a soft kiss. "What an amazing story."

"One of many," I say, pushing off the porch with my slippered toes, sending my chair rocking. "Let me tell you another."

And this is how we spent the next hour on the porch. I spin happy tales of lovers brought to shore while Brynn falls asleep to the soothing sound of my voice, calmed by the ebb and flow of my stories. I keep talking, one eye firmly on Cody to be sure he doesn't slip from his mom's grasp. I keep talking—to myself, to Spot, to the porch—remembering things I thought I'd long forgotten. As I talk, I wonder how much these stories have been stretched and twisted and embellished over the tellings, and decide I don't much care. I love them anyway. As I talk, I make note to ask Freddie to drag that old bassinet up from the basement so next time we can lay that little boy down and give his mom a proper nap.

◆ 13 ◆

BRYNN

Mid-June

Unpopular opinion here: My husband doesn't HELP *with the kids. My husband doesn't* BABYSIT. *My husband doesn't get a gold star when he makes dinner or changes a diaper. No. My husband* PARENTS *his kids. My husband is an equal partner in this journey called parenthood. Let's all stop glorifying the dads who do the bare minimum. We—YOU— deserve better. #equalpartners #notthe1950sanymore*
                                                    —3BoysMamaMonty

"I'LL BE BACK BEFORE you know it," Kyle says as he spirals a forkful of spaghetti against his spoon before shoving the sauce drenched bite into his mouth. A red dollop of tomato sticks to the corner of his lip, caught in his three-day-old stubble. In our dating days, I might have pressed my own mouth against his, whispering something seductive against his cheek before kissing him deeper, making him forget about the meal in front of him, and urging him to devour me instead. Now I'm only tempted to smudge it away and tie a bib around his neck, his messy face another thing for me to clean up.

I grimace, swallowing the last of my dinner before tossing the napkin from my lap onto the empty plate. Unconsciously, I tally up the calorie and carb count netted in this Italian feast Kyle brought home, and guilt washes over me. If I keep eating like this, I'm bound to gain more weight. Sighing, I vow to start my diet. Tomorrow.

"What?" Kyle asks, his brow furrowed. His shoulders sag, and I notice his eyes already drifting to his leather work bag hanging from the back of the stool. He's itching to finish dinner—and this conversation—and head to his office. I can't blame him. How I long to escape from the untidy business of dishes and uncomfortable small talk.

"Nothing," I say quickly, forcing a smile that will excuse Kyle from asking any more questions. Passive deflection is for both of our benefit. Cody has been napping almost twenty-five minutes in the swing and will likely wake up soon. I'd rather not be mid-argument with Kyle over his much-anticipated trip when I'm beckoned away by hunger cries from the living room. I've known about the big West Coast tech conference for almost a year. Kyle has been planning on attending since well before Cody was born. Back when I was still pregnant, I had no problem with the idea of him leaving. Back then I was excited for him. Back then I'd been thrilled at the prospect of ten days alone with my new baby. It sounded blissful. Long strolls in the park, lots of photo shoots to capture all the milestones, a long uninterrupted stretch of time for me and my son to bond.

Oh, to be in the *back then*.

"You sighed," Kyle says, letting out a long sigh of his own. He crosses his arms over his chest and leans his weight against the back of his chair, fixing me with a frown that says nothing but also everything.

He looks at me in this way more and more recently. He thinks I don't notice when he comes home and immediately begins taking inventory of the status of the house, his eyes darting across the kitchen island and noting the dishes I've failed to clear away or the stack of unopened mail I'm collecting in the corner. He thinks I don't notice when his nose wrinkles up after he kisses my forehead, as though he's caught a whiff of my four-day unwashed hair, hanging limp from my scrunchie. He thinks I don't notice how rarely his hands linger on the soft skin of my midsection when he hugs me before bed. Even though sex is the furthest thing from my mind, it would be nice if he at least *pretended* to still want me. Instead, his fingers trace their way up my spine, away from the extra inches on my hips and the flab around the waistband of my cotton panties.

"I didn't sigh," I say, resisting the urge to do exactly that. Clenching my jaw, I count to three and slowly exhale. I smile. "Time got away from me, that's all." I wish it was only time that has gotten away from me.

Kyle nods, his shoulders visibly relaxing. "I'm sorry, I know things have been hectic lately. After this trip it will be less crazy at work, I promise," he says, his hands idly tearing away at the corner of his red-stained paper napkin. "I hate that you're home alone so much." A few pieces flutter to the counter. Soon there will be a little mound of paper snow, a habit he's had since we met.

Not in the mood to discuss the unfair allotment of parental duties, I stand and push away from the counter, the legs of my stool catching on the tile and groaning in frustration. "It's fine," I say too brightly. I begin clearing the counter, stacking the silverware on the plates. We hardly touched the Greek salad but had no trouble finishing the fresh loaf of bread and butter that came with the meal. I debate saving the salad, but it's already dressed. In the trash it goes. "Seriously, I have more than enough to catch up on around here, and the weather is supposed to be beautiful all week. Cody and I will have plenty to do."

He smiles, clearly relieved. Anger boils close to the surface, but I bite my tongue against the truth. Nothing good will come from blowing up now. Kyle is leaving either way, and sending him off with the image of his crazy wife screaming at him isn't the vibe I'm going for. But it would be nice if he'd recognize that I'm obviously lying to him. I've never had a good poker face, and post-partum hormones only make every emotion more visible in my face. He's chosen to play along and pretend all is well and good, to suit his needs.

"Don't be mad . . ." he starts, handing me his plate instead of standing to clear it himself. A nerve twitches in my eye. I envision swatting it from his hand, the tomato-stained ceramic shattering to the floor, sharp pieces scattering in every direction, his handsome face frozen with shock. Shaking the image from my head, I take his plate and place it gently in the sink with the rest of the day's dishes.

Turning toward him, I hope my face doesn't betray my increasing annoyance. "Nothing good ever comes after that statement." I chuckle, even though I don't find anything about the situation particularly funny. Kyle shoots me a wry grin, one that used to melt my heart. But not tonight. Tonight, I wish he would hurry up and get to the point so I can have a shot at running the dish-washer before Cody needs to be fed again.

As he stares at me with his stupid grin, I realize I never emptied the dishwasher after running it yesterday. Or maybe it was the day before. The days are all running together, and another wave of irritation bristles over me.

I yearn for a glass of wine, something to take the edge off the stress headache brewing behind my eyes, but I've been trying to cut back, hoping to save a few hundred calories each night. *Fuck it,* I decide. What's another hundred calories after a meal like that? My ass isn't getting any smaller by tomorrow.

"Wine?" I ask over my shoulder before pulling a chilled bottle of chardonnay from the wine cooler custom built into our island. It was a luxury I initially scoffed at but find myself appreciating more and more with every passing day.

Kyle shakes his head. "I invited your mom to come stay while I'm gone," he says, his words racing together as though he's been working up the courage to say them and knows the only way to get them out is as fast as he can. He looks up at me from beneath his long lashes and bites his lip. At once I know exactly how my son will one day look at me when he's trying to weasel his way out of something.

Somehow, I don't drop the bottle of wine. At first, I'm sure I've misheard him, but as I replay the words over again, there isn't much room for misinterpretation. Yet it's an impossible collection of letters and syllables, all forming a statement that makes no sense. Kyle knows my relationship with my mother is only bearable when we limit exposure to biyearly visits and monthly phone calls. Distance really does make the heart grow fonder, in our case. After Cody was born, I agreed to increasing the calls to weekly FaceTime chats so she can see him grow. I have already begun to reevaluate this decision since she spends much of the call irritated that Cody is asleep or not interested in looking at her.

"Excuse me?" I muster, placing a wineglass on the counter and filling it halfway. Then I add a little more.

"When?" My mind races, unable to process this information. Kyle invited my mom to stay. Kyle invited my mom
to stay *while he was away*. At least with him here as a buffer, things might be tolerable. Why in the world would
he ever think this would be a happy surprise?

"While I'm gone," he repeats. "I thought you could
use the extra help, and it might be nice for Sandy to get
some quality time with Cody, give you a little break here
and there."

I take a long gulp of the chilled wine, the liquid both
fruity and oaky at the same time. My favorite blend.
Another sip. Maybe if I drink enough, this conversation
will prove to be a bad joke.

"Brynn?"

Lifting my gaze over the rim of the glass, I notice
the concern on Kyle's face, his emotions so obvious as he
works through my response. First confusion, then annoyance, and finally frustration flash across his features—the
slow blinking of his eyes, the corner of his mouth turning down in a frown, the licking of his lips. He's quiet,
debating what to say next. I'm sure he's considering how
best to diffuse the situation, to calm his ungrateful wife.
Not once will he wonder if he did something wrong. He
honestly thinks calling my mother is doing me a favor
and that I should be thanking him instead of silently
reproaching him. Never will he question why he didn't
ask my permission or even my opinion. It won't occur to
him that he felt compelled to arrange this visit in secret,
not because he wanted to surprise me, but because he
knew I would never agree. If Kyle thought any of these
things, then he'd know he'd made a terrible mistake, and
none of this was for my benefit, or even Cody's. No, this
is his desperate and misguided attempt to alleviate his
guilt for leaving. It's not about me at all.

"When does she get here?" I ask, resigned to the reality that my mother is coming. She may very well be on her way already. Knowing Kyle, she's sitting in the driveway right now, awaiting her cue to make her grand entrance.

"Tomorrow morning," he says, still frowning. "Are you mad? I thought this could be a good thing . . ."

When we first started dating, Kyle always told me how he loved that I always rolled with the punches. Brynn never gets angry or argues or nags, he told his friends and family. Brynn is *cool*.

Over the years, this became more and more a part of our couple dynamic. No matter what, I never got mad. Being the chill girlfriend and later chill wife became my whole persona. So much so that if I ever became *mad*, it was so out of character that Kyle didn't know how to react. He could not fathom that I might have a strong visceral reaction to something because I'd made a point to always remain cool. So, I learned to reframe my anger into something else more digestible. Disappointed. Frustrated. Overwhelmed. Never mad. Mad bordered crazy, and no one wanted to be the *crazy* chick.

Strangely enough, I've always wondered why when men are mad, it's not considered an emotional response, not even an emotion at all. Only sensitive females are plagued with the unsavory emotionality of anger or rage. When I read *Gone Girl* after college, I was terrified at how much I related to the main character and her effort to maintain her cool girl status. I never told Kyle this, fearing he might start sleeping with one eye open.

"I'm not mad," I say, exasperation coloring my cheeks and my tone. *Not mad, I'm furious. Livid. Outrageously angry. Irate. Full of hot rage.* "I'm surprised, that's all. I wasn't expecting a visitor, so I'm going to have to change some plans around. You know how I am with my schedule," I kid, finishing the last sip of wine and replacing it with another heavy pour. As far as Kyle knows, my strict adherence to a schedule is still true. He has no idea that my schedule went to shit about eight weeks ago.

Instantly he brightens, reassured I'm not *mad*. Surprise is something manageable, malleable. "I'm sure your mom will be happy to watch Cody so you can have some alone time," he says confidently. "You can get a manicure or a massage, treat yourself." In Kyle's mind, those are the pillars of every woman's self-care fantasies. Pre-baby I had my nails done twice a month, and my hair was always freshly highlighted and fashionably cut. I didn't need massages because my life was blissfully free of stress. I'm sure he doesn't mean this comment as a dig to the current state of my ragged cuticles and lifeless locks, but it stings just the same.

I smile. Sip. Smile. Sip. Repeat.

★   ★   ★

Maybe it won't be so bad. Maybe Mom will embrace her new role as grandma. New name, new identity. It's not like she was the worst mother ever. She was fine. Mom and Dad did the best they could. I never wanted for anything. We had a nice home, lots of *things*. In lieu of love, we had an overabundance of stuff. Our family was normal from the outside, idyllic even. But I was always the cause of discourse between my parents. It's like by being born I interrupted their amazing life together, and with every passing year they took their resentment out on each other.

A few weeks after I graduated high school, they split up in what I now recognize as a remarkably amicable divorce. They claimed they didn't stay together for my sake, but the timing was dubious. A coincidence, they claimed. I left for college and my parents went their separate ways. My mom wasted no time in pursuing the life she missed out on while being a stay-at-home mother to her only child. Single and unattached suited my mom, whose favorite pastime is talking about herself to anyone willing to listen.

"I'll get him," Kyle says, eagerly pushing away from the counter. The room falls back into focus, and the quiet whimpering of our son stirring, fills my ears. "Hey, big guy, you hungry?" Kyle whispers, unstrapping him and lifting him to his shoulder. Cody settles and smiles his gummy smiles at his daddy.

Most days they only see each other for a few minutes in the morning before Kyle leaves for the office. By the time my husband descends the stairs, freshly showered and smelling like Tom Ford cologne and toothpaste, Cody and I have been awake for hours. Sometimes I'll have the baby strapped in his carrier while I attempt to clean up and make a pot of coffee, but usually we are planted on the couch, watching Netflix. Kyle is chronically late, so he generally only has time for a quick kiss and cuddle before he's backing out of the drive and racing south toward Boston and his plush office filled with other adults and intellectual conversation. For ten days we won't even get the quick goodbye. It'll be my mother invading my space.

"I think he wants something I can't give him," Kyle jokes, holding Cody close while our son kneads his knuckles into the firm expanse of his chest. His mouth puckers as he roots around Kyle's nipple area. He hasn't begun crying yet, but it's coming. My breasts tighten and bloat before the familiar tug and tingle of my milk letting down relieves the pressure. I should've agreed to formula feed. Then I wouldn't be experiencing this primal pain, and Kyle could warm a bottle with his left hand and hold Cody with his other, practice what so many mothers are forced to master: the art of doing two things at once. Resisting the urge to roll my eyes, I hold my arms wide and cradle Cody close, his dinner waiting.

Kyle follows eagerly on my heels as I head to my spot on the couch, where I stretch my legs out on the ottoman in front of me. He watches me unstrap my nursing bra, and I'm still embarrassed by the pure awe on his face. If I were a different sort of woman, I'd wield my maternal body with pride, embrace the swell and blossom of my engorged bosom. But I'm not that woman, and I shy away from his gaze, wishing I had a swaddle to cover myself—my exposed boob vulnerable beneath his intense scrutiny.

"I got him," I say, desperate for him to leave me in peace. If I've any hope of Kyle viewing me as a desirable creature again, I think it's necessary to maintain some separation between my boobs as sexy versus snack-y. "Go finish packing," I suggest, knowing my husband well enough to guess he hasn't begun the process. "Maybe we can have a glass of wine once he goes down," I offer, even though the two glasses I chugged have left me more sleepy than anything else.

He smiles down at me and kisses my forehead. "When I get back, I promise to help out extra," he says without even a hint of irony. He squeezes my shoulder and I recoil from his touch. Although I'm sure he means well, I can't help but bristle at his implication. I resolve to start sending Kyle some of Monty's Instagram posts. It wouldn't hurt for him to follow a few parental accounts since I'm pretty sure his feed is filled with cars, fish, and stupid jokes. Maybe he would be inspired to know that

Monty's famous husband never *helped out*, but was an equal partner in their parenting journey. I let out a little snort.

"What?" he asks, his eyes crinkling at the corners. He exudes love; it radiates off him in waves.

I look into those eyes, so similar to his son's, and reward him with exactly what he wants. "Nothing," I say, forcing a smile. "Everything's perfect."

★   ★   ★

This may be the longest consecutive stretch of time I've spent with my mother since college. Part of me wondered if things would be better now that I was not a moody young adult, eager to make my way in the world. Summers between semesters had been the worst. I'd split the months between Mom's and Dad's houses, neither ever feeling quite like home. Both of them mostly ignored me, a quality my friends envied in comparison to their overly intrusive parents. Despite my desire for independence, I secretly craved something more. Like maybe *this* summer Mom would take an interest in me or *this* summer Dad would ask me about my future. They never did. Instead, they offered to find me my own apartment when I graduated, and agreed to pay for it until I got my feet on the ground.

Kyle left at dawn. I was already awake with Cody when he tiptoed down the stairs. I've been trying to read the same novel since before I gave birth but, at the rate I'm going, might finish around the time Cody graduates kindergarten. Frustrated, I laid it down on the sofa beside me and kissed Kyle goodbye. His excitement was palpable, and I was sincere when I told him to have a good time. In another life, I would've suggested packing Cody up and making a vacation of the whole thing.

Mom's Volvo pulled into the drive a few minutes shy of eight AM. Mom's a lot of things, but late is not one of them. One of our only shared qualities is our punctuality and respect for a proper schedule. From my spot at the kitchen island, I watched her unload a ridiculous amount of luggage from the trunk: a large roller bag, two duffels, and what appeared to be a hat bag. Not exactly sure where she thinks we will be going while she's here, but she has an outfit for any potential scenario.

We spent most of the weekend inside. The forecast before her arrival was for sporadic showers and overcast skies. This transformed into terrible thunderstorms and no sun in sight for two full days. My mother hates the rain and was happy to stay indoors until the world dried itself off. Along with the clouds, the temperatures plummeted, doubly ensuring we would have no reason to venture forth from the house. Three days of rom-coms from the nineties, reruns of *Project Runway*, and a variety of takeout made the visit almost enjoyable. Almost.

"Rise and shine, sleepyhead," my mother croons. She's standing in front of the coffee maker, staring at the complicated control system of our combination espresso maker and coffee grinder. "What magic words must I say to conjure up a pot of coffee from this fancy contraption?" she says, her tone light despite the implied dig. Since I married Kyle, she's always commenting on any outward display of wealth, as though buying anything more advanced than a Mr. Coffee coffeemaker was ostentatious. Never mind that I also made fun of Kyle for purchasing this café-grade machine, especially as I was still learning how to use it. It's only okay when I poke fun.

"I'll make a pot after I put Cody down . . . unless you want a latte?" I ask. I've decided to ignore the fact that my mom seems to think Cody and I slept in until seven thirty this morning. Kyle was right in putting her up in the downstairs guest suite. Cody's dreadful wails at two AM and again at five thirty must not have traveled all the way to the far end of the hall. Lucky lady.

She grimaces and lifts her brow. "No fancy latte for me, dear. Just a regular old cup of joe." She watches as I struggle to latch Cody into the swing. Color rushes to my cheeks, but I refuse to let her get a rise out of me this early. Not before I have my own cup of joe.

Cody smiles as I clip the strap across his chest, and my heart surges. He stares at me with those big blue eyes, the actual color becoming more defined by the day, rather than the dark blue all babies are born with, and I smile back, pursing my lips and making the kissy noise that always makes him smile. But instead of another smile, his cheeks puff out, and his eyes roll back before shutting completely. Alarmed, I bend to readjust the harness, afraid I've tightened it too much. Fumbling again, I look up just in time for Cody to let out a small burp followed by more vomit than someone his size should be able to produce. Milky liquid spews from his open mouth directly onto my face, and I fight the urge to immediately throw up myself. Cody sucks in a few breaths, but he's not done. His lips part, and the last remnants of his breakfast end up splattered across the neckline of my lightweight sweatshirt and stick to the strands of my hair, still loose around my shoulders, since my mother commented on how I would damage the ends if I kept wrapping it up in a messy bun.

Emptied out, Cody resumes smiling in my direction. I bite back the bile forming in the back of my throat and attempt to wipe the puke from my cheeks, the slimy white liquid leaving a film along the back of my hand. Cody managed to spray most of the mess on his mommy, so his onesie only has a small stain. Of course he finds this spot immediately and begins rubbing the sticky fluid between his fingers.

"Oh, honey, you know how I am with vomit," my mom's voice says from behind me. I glance back and note that she does look a little green as she holds her hand up to her lips like she's about to gag. "I'm sorry—I'll give you a minute."

And just like that, my mother abandons her daughter and only grandchild to clean up all alone. It's not as though I expected her to be much help while Kyle was away. Growing up, Mom was always queasy about bodily fluids. The sight of blood causes her to faint, and she left cleaning the bathrooms to my dad or our once-a-week cleaning lady. I've always suspected it must have been Dad who did most of the diaper changes and burping when I was a baby, and this moment confirms my suspicion. I wonder if a lack of maternal instinct is hereditary.

Sighing, I debate how to tackle the mess. Cody seems perfectly content playing in his own spit. If anything, he looks happier than ever. I guess violently emptying his tummy of the milk he gorged earlier is one way to improve his mood. Grabbing a burp rag from the counter, I wipe his mouth and hands before scooping up a particularly chunky pile of spittle collecting around the chest clip of the swing. Satisfied that he's as clean as he's going to get without a full bath, I wipe my own face and neck and carefully pull my sweatshirt over my head, afraid to move too fast lest I add more mess to my hair or risk spreading the droplets of puke framing my forehead. Standing in the kitchen in my flesh-colored nursing bra and maternity jeans, the weight of everything crashes down on me. This happens more and more lately. I long for a nap and a hot shower. The smell of sour milk permeates the room. No doubt it will linger all day.

"Maybe if I make your grandma a coffee, I can convince her to watch you while Mommy hops in the tubby," I say to Cody, causing him to smile and stretch his arm in my direction. I'm almost tempted to reach over and grab his fingers, but this ended poorly for me the last time.

Instead, I pick up my phone and text my mom. I doubt she'd hear me call to her across the house, even if I yell.

Coffee is brewing. You're safe to come back.

The distant ping of her phone sounds a few seconds before her footsteps can be heard, approaching briskly from down the hall. My mother insists on heels, always.

"Goodness, Brynn. Go take a shower before you stink up the whole house," she exclaims, shaking her head in disgust and waving me away. "And maybe dress in something you wouldn't mind leaving the house in," she adds, her brows lifting as her gaze travels the length of my body.

My cheeks color despite my best effort to check my embarrassment. I should've known Sandy would not approve of my recent love of athleisurewear as all-day everyday wear. I thought I was safe by wearing jeans, even if they were stretchy and didn't have a button or zipper. But my mom has always dressed each day as though she may bump into an arch nemesis from high school: full makeup, accessories, and her signature cardigan set and slim-fit trousers with heels.

"Sure thing," I mutter, grabbing my dirty sweatshirt and burp rag to toss in the laundry bin. "Thanks for watching him." I nod toward Cody, who is smiling at us from his seat, blue eyes bouncing from one of us to the other.

Mom startles but recovers quickly, so quick it's almost easy to believe she hadn't forgotten about her grandson sitting in the kitchen.

Waving me away, she smiles at Cody. "I'm his grandmother," she says. "What else would I do?"

★   ★   ★

Mom and Cody aren't in the kitchen when I return, my hair still wet, but thankfully not smelling like rotten milk anymore. I opted to skip the blow-dryer in favor of swiping on two coats of mascara and adding some tinted moisturizer. A dollop of pink gloss on my lips finished the look. Finding a Sandy-appropriate outfit in my closet was another story. Most of my pre-baby pants are eagerly awaiting the reappearance of my pre-baby body, so I changed into a pair of black jeans with a little extra give and swapped my sweatshirt for a peasant blouse that was forgiving in the midsection while also quite pretty. Although I wasn't entirely satisfied with my reflection in the full-length mirror, it was better than before, if still far from *before*. Maybe Mom will approve.

"Well, that's certainly an improvement," Mom chirps from her spot on the couch in the den. The television volume is low, but the familiar sounds of a home renovation show fade into the background.

"Thanks," I mumble, eager to pour myself a cup of that coffee I brewed earlier. My stomach grumbles, and I realize I've yet to eat today despite feeding Cody three times since waking. They say breastfeeding causes the weight to fall right off new moms, but I've yet to see the proof. My baby boy is basically attached to my boobs, so you'd think I'd be invisible by now, my body evaporating the more he takes, takes, takes. But every bagel I consume refuses to convert into milk, preferring to settle squarely on my hips, while each cookie I sneak finds a home on my ass. The blogs said breastfeeding moms should consume a few extra hundred calories a day to ensure high milk production. Maybe only salads and fruit turn to breast milk, not all calories consumed, in fact, equal. This would explain the skinny moms.

Mom places Cody on the soft play mat laid on top of the rug, and instantly I feel guilty for the meager few minutes a day he spends practicing tummy time. Each time I place him on his chubby little belly, his whole face turns beet red, and he wails, offended that I've sentenced him to this torturous position. The doctor said it was important for Cody to develop his neck and arm muscles, but my son seems determined to remain a little jellyfish, all squishy limbs and floppy joints. If we make it five minutes, we are lucky. For the entire time, he insists on resting his cheek firmly against the mat, his tears collecting on the happy teddy bear emblazoned beneath him.

Mom doesn't attempt tummy time, leaving him on his back to stare up at the assortment of woodland creatures hanging from an arch suspended from one side of the mat to the other. Before standing, she rattles a squirrel holding a shiny acorn, and the whole thing sways and spins, much to Cody's delight.

Even with my back turned, I can sense her impatient energy. Refusing to engage, I slowly stir cream into my coffee, watching it swirl from black to brown, to the perfect khaki color. Her eyes bore holes in my back as she waits for me to finish adding two spoonfuls of sugar. I've cut back from three but can't give it up. I decided I needed the caffeine, and couldn't bear to drink it black. She begins gently tapping her foot against the tile as I lift the mug to my lips, testing the sweetness. Just right.

"I can handle Cody if you've got something to do
. . ." I say, still facing the coffeepot. Even though it's still
early, she's already showered and ready for the day. I'm
pretty sure she's even curled her hair. This would explain
the plethora of luggage she dragged in here the other day.
I'm certain there isn't a curling wand in the guest bath.

She taps her long fingernails on the counter, and I
clench my teeth. Closing my eyes, I take one more sip
of coffee and let the hot liquid calm my nerves. Forcing a smile, I turn to face her. First thing I notice are
her bright pink nails, perfectly shaped and glossed, a far
cry from my own ragged stubs. The last time I had a
manicure, I was pregnant, and the fumes made me lightheaded. I ended up leaving the salon with only my left
hand painted, minus the thumb.

"I thought we could do something today," she says,
ceasing the annoying cacophony of her nails on the
quartz. "We've been cooped up all weekend. Let's go for
a walk. You could use the exercise," she notes.

I open my mouth to protest, but there's no point.
This statement wasn't made from malice. Sandy's from
the generation who believed Slim Fast and Weight
Watchers were staples in every women's diet and were
sold on the belief that females only mattered if they were
thin. When I was thirteen (and weighted a hearty eighty-
seven pounds), Mom convinced me to follow the grape-
fruit diet with her. She was "concerned" I was gaining
too much weight during puberty. She survived on a strict
twelve-hundred-calorie-a-day diet and was never heavy
a day in her life, and the thought of her daughter being
hefty terrified her.

Soon after I got my first period, she taught me how
to track my calories, buying me, for my own backpack, a
tiny notebook like the one she kept in her purse. I wonder

what was more important to her after giving birth to me: caring for a newborn or losing the baby weight? I'd bet it was a close race. Since her arrival, she's reminded me no less than four times how she's weighed exactly one hundred and twelve pounds since her wedding day and only gained twenty-two pounds in her entire pregnancy. If she says this again, I may have to literally pat her on the back or give her a gold star. Clearly, she needs more than I'm giving.

"Cody and I go to the park almost every day, Mom," I say, hoping to regain some of her faith in me. On the one hand, I could give two shits what she thinks of my parenting and exercise schedule. On the other, I'm still the pitiful little girl desperately seeking her mommy's approval. Our dynamic refuses to shift; our relationship so predictable it's pathetic. "It was only the weather that kept us in," I remind her.

She nods, eager to agree. "Of course, of course. But it's beautiful today, and I'm going stir-crazy in here. I'm not sure how you do it . . ."

Biting my lip, I shrug and sip my coffee. What is she so unsure of? How I stay inside all weekend? Raise an infant? Generally, exist?

In an instant my resolve deflates. My willpower for dealing with my mother (and life in general—go figure) dissolves, and I long to drift back upstairs and crawl under the blankets. If we had a different bond, I might tell her this. Another mother might wrap me in her arms and tell me she knows it's hard and that's why she's here. Another mother might send me to bed and promise to take care of things while I rest. Another mother might not judge. Another mother, but not my mother.

Unsure whether these thoughts make me indignant or only sad, I decide to test my theory since I've always been a glutton for punishment when it came to Sandy. "Actually, it's been really hard," I admit. Saying the words out loud releases a small bit of tension I'd been holding in my neck. However, seeing Mom's eyes widen before she inhales loudly causes it to come right back, twofold. Defeated, I push on. "I'm exhausted."

Neither of us speak for a moment. Even though she often acts clueless, I know my mother is as smart as a whip. She knows what she *should* say right now, and it's strange to observe as she internally debates how to react to my brutal truth. Another mother would offer to help. Another mother would try and alleviate some of the load I confess to struggle with. She opens her mouth, and for one instant I wonder if she's finally going to be *that* mother.

"Having a newborn is hard work," she concedes. Lifting her chin, she sets her shoulders back and stands a little straighter, a pose I remember all too well from childhood. "The only way through it is through it, and this time really does go by so fast. Before you know it, Cody will be all grown up and won't need you anymore, and you're going to miss these days."

Inside, I scream. Inside, I rage. If one more person tells me I'm *lucky* to struggle and will in fact miss these trying times, I might go crazy. *"Cherish this time,"* everyone says. People make this comment on Monty's Instagram all the time. She always responds with a yellow heart emoji, as if there was any doubt that she was actively cherishing all the moments. As if. *"The days are long, but the years are short."* Another favorite euphemism. I'm pretty sure Monty used this one in a recent caption.

"Brynn?" Mom repeats.

Blinking, I remember she's still spouting motherly wisdom at me, and it is my daughterly duty to hang on her every word. My mistake, of course.

"Yep," I mutter, nodding manically while wishing she would shut up, shut up, *shut up*.

"You do look a bit tired, dear," she whispers, glancing toward the den, where Cody now swats at a hanging racoon. Satisfied he didn't hear that his horrible mother is something as horrible as *tired*, she looks back to me.

Shrugging, I abandon all feeble hope of motherhood uniting us. She failed my test, as I knew she would. Somehow, I'm more disappointed than I'd anticipated. It still amazes me how I continue to be surprised by her failure. "I'm fine. He didn't sleep well, that's all."

Mom brightens, clearly relieved I'm finished sharing the dirty details of new motherhood. A baby not sleeping is normal. Neutral territory for us to regain our footing. "Don't worry. This too shall pass. You were a terrible sleeper until about three months. Then you slept in your crib straight through the night. Such a good baby," she muses.

My jaw hurts from how hard I've been clenching it. I chug the last bit of lukewarm coffee before setting the mug down on the island. From the den, Cody's sounds have shifted from those of a content baby to something else. Bored and hungry baby, perhaps. Or maybe he misses me.

Mom follows close on my heels, awkwardly standing behind me as I lift Cody from the mat and press him to my shoulder, rubbing the small of his back as if it's the most natural response in the world.

"I need to feed him again," I say, mentally calculating how long it's been since his last meal. Less than three hours, but considering he ejected most of the last one, it's not surprising that he's hungry so soon. I fumble with the strap of my bra, wishing I had one of my versatile nursing sweatshirts with the nearly invisible lip under my chest where a boob can stealthily slip out undetected. I'm going to need to completely disengage my arm from this blouse—the price of wearing something pretty.

Mom's face blanches. Clearly our biyearly visits are not enough to warrant a proper level of comfort for my exposed nipples.

"I'll give you some privacy," she says, shifting her gaze to the TV, which has moved onto a house-flipping show. "Why don't you go get your nails done later?" she offers. "I'm sure he'll be ready for a nap soon, and I can watch him while you do something for yourself."

My heart softens a bit. It's as likely to be a dig at my bad hygiene as an olive branch, but it's something.

"Just make sure you remember to burp him this time," she chastises, clucking her tongue. "We don't want a repeat of this morning's mess, do we now?"

★ ★ ★

Leaving the house was no easy feat. I can count on one hand how many times I've been out without Cody since giving birth. Two were for postpartum checkups with my OB/GYN and the third was to pick up a prescription multivitamin with vitamin D. Kyle stayed home with Cody on those few occasions, armed with a bottle full of pumped milk he never needed to use and enough toys and gadgets for an army of babies. It was all for naught, since Cody slept peacefully in his rocker for the short span of time I was gone. Of course, he woke up immediately upon me reentering the house each time.

Mom isn't as chill as Kyle, who simply waved me away, one eye on the baby, the other on his laptop or phone. She insisted I show her exactly where the bottle warmer lived and how to use it, even though I told her it was highly unlikely Cody would be hungry anytime soon, or even want a bottle from her. I joked that if she convinced him to start using the bottle, I'd throw a party and hire her full-time as the nanny. She didn't find this funny. After our crash course on bottle warming, she made me write a list of emergency contacts on the pad in the kitchen, although I assured her she had all the important numbers already stored in her phone. *"Just in case,"* she maintained. *"What if my phone dies?"* Showing her the charging station didn't alleviate this worry. A tour of the nursery, in which I pointed to the extra binkies, onesies, diapers, and a multitude of random things she imagined she might need in the hour—two hours max—that I'd be gone, was the last requirement.

This all took about an hour, and I began to fear that Cody would in fact grow hungry before I returned. Out of an abundance of caution, I slipped out a boob one last time and force-fed my hungry little hippo from the left side only until his eyes fluttered closed against my nipple. Mom gently lifted him from my embrace, eyes averted to prevent catching sight of any skin, and settled herself into the love seat. After strapping myself back in place, I set the remote control and a cup of coffee within easy reach on the side table.

"Go! Enjoy yourself. Take as long as you need," she whispers, one hand stroking the back of Cody's blond head. "Maybe one of your girlfriends is free for lunch?"

"Thanks, Mom," I say, backing from the room.

Before I can second-guess anything, I grab my keys and purse from the foyer and rush to the car, afraid my sudden fit of crippling anxiety will stop me dead in my tracks if I cease forward motion. I should be thrilled to escape the house. Instead, I'm filled with dread.

★   ★   ★

I sit in the parking lot of Glamour Nails for ten minutes before reversing and heading downtown to the best diner in Salem, MaryJo's. My nails are in desperate condition, but who cares about a fresh manicure when all my hands will do is change poopy diapers all day? For a second, I consider heading to the mall to buy some new clothes but decide that's only admitting defeat. Although close, I'm not quite ready to throw in the towel on one day fitting into my size four jeans again.

While idling in the lot, the hunger pangs get the best of me, and since I'd expended approximately a thousand calories feeding an infant already, food was the obvious destination. Tapping my pitiful nails on the steering wheel in rhythm to the eighties pop song playing on satellite radio, I debate calling a friend before remembering I don't have any. All my pre-baby friends are MIA since the shower (my fault as much as theirs), and I'm guessing Tracy and Avery are still pissed about the incident in the park (ha!) No doubt Monty is too busy for such a last-minute invite. There's Joy . . . but I don't have her number. I make a mental note to add it to my contacts next time I stroll by. Joy would appreciate a lunch call.

I order pancake and eggs. A side of bacon. I wash it down with two glasses of orange juice and a steaming mug of coffee with cream and three sugars. I finish with dessert, fresh baked apple pie with whipped cream and caramel. I eat it all, every last bite. I'd lick the plate if I weren't in public. Disgusted with myself, but pleasantly full, I leave a generous tip. Checking my watch, sure I've been out for at least two hours, I'm disappointed to see I've been gone only fifty-two minutes.

To kill time, I park down by the lighthouse and watch the tourists mill about, taking pictures of the shoreline and strolling the boardwalk. Even though there aren't many people around, it's still early for the summer people, and October is really Salem's month to shine, it's nice to feel like a part of civilization again.

At 11:20, I reverse out of the spot and head the five minutes home. Being out in the world has me craving the quiet space inside my home; the quiet space inside my home that only exists when I don't have a house guest.

★   ★   ★

"I thought you were getting your nails done?" Mom asks in lieu of a greeting. She's sitting at the kitchen island, stabbing a piece of cantaloupe with a fork. On arrival, she took one look inside my refrigerator and insisted on grocery shopping. She returned with an assortment of fruit, cottage cheese, and yogurts—her daily diet since I was a teen.

Ignoring the question, I ball my hands up into fists at my side to hide the ragged cuticles and naked beds that are so offensive to my mother, my husband, society. "Where's Cody?" His rocker is empty, and the house silent.

She gestures toward the den and I tiptoe to the doorway. My son is asleep on his stomach on the play mat, one hand resting beneath his cheek and the other splayed out to the side. The same way Kyle sleeps.

"He fell asleep about five minutes into tummy time," Mom says from behind me, as if this wasn't a big deal, as though my son spontaneously falls asleep anywhere aside from my arms all the time. Irrationally, my eyes fill with tears. For some reason, I never imagined my own mother would be better with Cody than I am. More evidence that something is wrong with me.

I swallow, biting the edge of my cheek to hide the tremble in my voice. "Mom," I start, unsure what to say. On the car ride home, I wracked my brain to think of an excuse that might incite her to volunteer to leave. Kyle was coming home early. I felt sick. A tornado was heading straight for Salem. Telling her I didn't want her around anymore seemed both cruel and not entirely the truth. By the time I pulled into the drive, I had nothing. "I've loved having you here." I swallow again, my resolve withering under her intense gaze. She holds a piece of fruit near her mouth but doesn't eat, waiting for me to finish. Clearing my throat, I continue, "Cody and I are so thankful you've been here to help . . ."

"But?" she says, cocking her head. She lifts one thin, perfectly arched brow, urging me to continue. Patience has never been her strongest suit.

The only way through it is through it. Taking a page out of mom's playbook, I decide the truth is the only way forward. At least some version of the truth. "I feel guilty for keeping you from your life for so long. I've already stolen almost five days of your time. I don't want you to feel as if you need to babysit me for five more."

Mom frowns, toying with the piece of cantaloupe and my words. Long ago I learned that if I reframed things so Sandy's needs were front and center, I was always more successful in getting what I wanted. In high school she'd allow me to sleep over at a friend's house on a school night because I convinced her she needed a night to herself or a morning to sleep in. Paying for a SAT tutor was going to *save* her money since I'd get a scholarship with higher scores. It wasn't a lie, per se. Subtle twist in the truth.

"I'm so glad Kyle arranged this," I add, the white-hot rage I'd experienced after he told me the plans, not forgotten. Surprisingly, the visit had not been all bad or as bad as expected. *Yet.* Five more days is a long time, and

I fear Mom will overstay her welcome given the chance. I'm saving us both a bad memory. "I don't want you to feel obligated to stay. Cody and I are good," I promise.

She nods, laying her fork on her plate. Her shoulders fall back, and her face relaxes, the frown replaced by something I can't immediately discern. At first, I think it's disappointment, and a wave of regret passes over me. But then the corner of her mouth lifts in a half smile, and I recognize the look for what it is. Relief.

"You do seem to have a pretty good system here," she agrees, smiling in my direction. Her eyes drift past me, and I can tell the wheels are already spinning and her mind is elsewhere, probably making plans for the weekend that don't involve forcing me out of the house or criticizing my self-care routine. "You're so lucky you don't have to go to work," she says. "It's so nice Kyle makes enough for you to stay home and be with Cody. I missed so much when you were a baby."

Inhale, exhale. Inhale, exhale. Repeat. Don't scream, don't scream. Smile. Smile. For one brief instant, I was sorry I asked her to leave. Just as fast I know I made the right decision. I'm pretty sure if she stays one more day, our relationship might break beyond repair. Comments like this are why I only see Mom a few times a year. Of course, she assumes it's Kyle's decision for me to stay home, like some old-fashioned couple where the man brings home the bacon and the woman raises the baby, barefoot in the kitchen. She forgets our conversation from *two days ago*, where I told her this was *my* choice and that I was simply putting my career on hold, not forever. She's never taken me seriously, referring to my business as if it were a hobby, like I planned parties for my own pleasure. As for all she missed as a working mother . . . bullshit. She was the secretary at Dad's insurance agency, which he owned.

It's not like she couldn't have called in sick whenever she felt like it or, hell, taken extended maternity leave. Pretty sure Dad wouldn't have fired her for staying home with their daughter. *Mom, you didn't want to stay home with me, which is all fine and dandy, but don't pretend like you didn't have the choice.*

"I am lucky," I agree. Arguing will get me nowhere, fast. Worst case, she decides to stay and make things right.

She pats my hand before pushing the stool back from the island and standing. "I'll go pack up while the little guy sleeps," she says. Her energy is barely containable. "This way I can see him before I leave. Heck, I might be able to make pottery class with the ladies tonight."

A small flicker of jealousy pinches my chest. I've no desire to attend pottery class, but once upon a time I used to do things with my friends. Drinks downtown. Coffee after yoga. Target runs. Once Mom leaves, I vow to text a few friends to catch up. It's been far too long.

"Sounds fun," I say, lifting her dish from the counter and emptying the wilted melon pieces into the garbage. She hasn't cleared even one dish this entire weekend. A small thing, but one on the long list of reasons I'm happy to see her off.

"Brynn?" She's paused at the edge of the room, one foot in the hallway leading to the guest suite. Looking up, I wait for her to continue. "I'm going to leave some eye cream for you in the guest bathroom." She lifts a pink fingertip to the small lines around her own eyes. "It's never too early to start taking care of those wrinkles."

Inhale, exhale, don't scream, smile. "Thanks, Mom." *Repeat.*

◆ 14 ◆

JOY

Mid-June

There it was before her - life. Life: she thought but she did not finish her thought. She took a look at life, for she had a clear sense of it there, something real, something private, which she shared neither with her children nor with her husband.
—Virginia Woolf, *To the Lighthouse*

"IT MUST'VE BEEN THE spring of 1975," I begin, my mind wandering back in time, peeling apart the curtains between memories not quite forgotten, but packed away in the far corners of my conscience, hidden beneath the happier thoughts placed on top that weighed down the bad ones. "Katherine wasn't in school full time, and Richard was a toddler. To say I had my hands full was an understatement."

Kathy with her dirty-blond ponytails, front tooth missing. Overnight she morphed from my chubby baby girl to a mini adult, her legs lengthening and thinning out, the shape of her face changing from round to its current heart shape. I remember the smoothness of her skin against my palm as if it were yesterday.

"It was a rough winter and cold spring. Not as bad as what hit us in seventy-eight, but right up there. Fishing in the winter months slows down to a near halt, so Freddie took odd jobs around town to make ends meet and get us through until the spring thaw. Usually by this point, things had picked up, but not that year. The fish weren't biting. Still too cold for them, I suppose. Either way, Freddie was out of sorts worrying over the bills, even though I told him we were scraping by," I say, chuckling. "Freddie might've brought home the money, but it was me who handled all the household expenses. Not sure my Fred could tell you how much a gallon of milk cost, never mind how much to fuel a house."

Brynn sips from the glass of lemonade, her head resting squarely on the back of the rocker. When she knocked on the door this morning, I was hardly surprised. Last week she told me her husband had a big work trip scheduled, so I stocked the fridge with some of her favorites in case she stopped by with Cody. She's already eaten three of those almond cookies she liked so well last time.

"Freddie agreed to a deep-sea charter for some executives from Boston who were referred to him by a previous customer. By this point, he was desperate to grow this part of the business. *'It's where the money's at, Joyous,'* he promised." I shake my head, all those arguments over money clanking around and clouding the better parts of these memories. Freddie always wanted more for us. I only wanted more Freddie. The argument had rattled on and on.

Cody mews from his bassinet. The old wooden crib was tricky to navigate up the narrow staircase from the basement, but somehow, I managed. *Lucky you didn't fall and break your neck,* Freddie chastised when he noticed it set beside Brynn's chair on the front porch. She reaches out and pulls the edge closer to her, setting it rocking back and forth, the hinges moaning and begging for a little oil. The soothing creaking noise quiets Cody.

"There was a storm in the forecast, but it was still a way off, Freddie said. He didn't think it would hit us but that it would head south around the Cape instead, missing the North Shore, like so many storms did. My Freddie believed he could wish a storm away by sheer force of will. He intended on making this trip, making this money. No weather was getting in his way."

The Thursday before he left was picture-perfect: bright yellow sun set against a robin-blue sky, without a cloud in sight, and a warm spring breeze hinting at summer. One of those tricky May days that has you forgetting what a terrible winter you survived only a few weeks past. It's a phenomenon of New England, a necessary ruse to keep the residents fooled into dwelling in such a dreadfully fickle climate. His trip was scheduled to leave early the next day, and the newsman promised three more days of sun. Freddie was elated. On Friday I woke at dawn with Richard, who was cutting teeth and up at all hours, and spotted the sun beginning to rise over the horizon. With dread, I watched not the bright yellow orb of the previous day but a giant ball of fire climbing the tree line and creeping toward the heavens like the mercury in a thermometer rising with fever.

"'Red sky in morning, sailors take warning,'" I mumble. Brynn furrows her brow, and I realize I've only said part of the story out loud. Too many days alone has weakened my storytelling bone.

"The old expression sounds too simple to be true, but only a fool doesn't heed such a humble warning. Freddie wasn't a fool," I say, shaking my head against the familiar lump rising in my throat. "But sometimes I think he only pretended to be color-blind." Our joke in happy times, a bitter dispute in the bad times. At thirty-two, Freddie was deemed color-blind after a lifetime of being unable to discern between red and green. It was his excuse for running the yellow light and for sailing into dangerous waters. *Red means go, right?* he'd kid, his blue eyes twinkling, the left corner of his mouth upturned so the dimple high up on his cheek deepened so far, I fell right into it. Devilishly handsome and foolhardy. My mother warned me to beware of boys like Freddie. Suppose I was blind to some things too.

"I begged him to stay home, to cancel the bloody trip. When that failed, I insisted he reschedule, a literal rain check. We yelled, hurling words at each other we couldn't take back. It wasn't like Freddie to ignore me, but he firmly believed this was his big break. A little storm cloud wasn't going to stop him."

Katherine creeping down the stairs and peeking around the corner, her startled expression when I threw the vase of tulips, the glass shattering into a thousand pieces on the dining room floor. Richard hiding behind my legs, watching it all. Freddie hollering at me to go to bed and quit making a scene in front of the children, as though I was fighting all alone, a crazy woman. Guilt runs slow and deep, a steady trickle in my old veins. My anger, however, is still red-hot, a flash flood. Mad after all this time.

"I never hated Freddie so much as I did that morning," I admit, confessing one of my heart's most guarded secrets. "I refused to flash the porch light that night. As he walked out the front door, I told him I didn't care whether he ever made it back to shore, that he deserved the sea, that mistress I'd turned a blind eye to our entire marriage." I pause, my chest heaving as it did that day. "I told him I hoped the Ocean wanted him, because I sure as hell didn't anymore."

Swallowing against the pain, as raw as that stormy morning, I remember a different trip. Then another. Different year, different season, different weather, different words, but mostly the same fight, the same love and hate wrapped together so tight I lost sight of where one emotion started and the other ended. I remember the hurt in his tired eyes, the blue faded by the decades, every line and crease in the corner as familiar to me as those on my own face. This time he shook his head, running his hand through what was left of his hair before slipping on his favorite ball cap. Another time he sighed and opened his arms, his tanned forearms bare because it was the dead of summer, his full head of hair buzzed to the scalp to fight the heat. Oh, how I longed to stumble into him, let him enclose me in a hug that might force him to reconsider, to *stay*—just this once—to choose *me*. Each time I was too scared to go to him, too scared he'd choose wrong. Both of us too stubborn to give an inch, so we pulled back a mile, then a mile more, until we were oceans apart.

"Those were the last words I yelled at him before he walked out the door forever," I say. There was a time I might not have been able to tell this story without tears falling down my cheeks, but I'm dried out, a hollow pit of regret.

Brynn leans so far forward on the rocker, I fear she will topple over. She places a hand gently on my knee, startling me straight back to the present time.

"But he came back, right?" she asks, the crease between her eyes deep and full of hope.

I've forgotten why I began this story in the first place. Closing my eyes, I try to capture each errant thought, settle my rattled brain. Freddie looking back over his shoulder before closing the front door flashes to the forefront, and I choke on the image. I wish I could step back in time and kick myself in the behind, set my anger aside and call after him. Tell him I loved him, prove to him I needed him more than the Ocean, show him I was stronger than the tides that pulled him away from his family, tough enough to save him when his own strength failed.

But that was a different story. I think.

"He came home," I whisper to Brynn, who's staring at me with increasing concern. Her eyes are red rimmed with exhaustion and something else. Something I think is understanding. "The storm raged all night. The kids and I stayed up late, watching *Robin Hood*, and they fell asleep on the couch. I waited up while the wind whipped rain sideways against the shutters so hard the whole house shook. By dawn it had passed. The forecast called for a glorious spring day." I shake my head. Why didn't he simply delay the trip one day, save us all the heartache? One day would've made all the difference.

"The kids woke up and I made breakfast. I refused to let them see me worry over their father, so we went about our business as usual. Noon rolled around, and when Freddie still hadn't walked through that door, I began to fret. Another hour passed, then another. At three, I packed the kids up into the Jeep, tricking them into thinking we were getting a sweet treat in town. But I drove us straight to the dock, unsure what we might find."

Cody stirs, unsettled by the story. Brynn lifts him from the bassinet and nimbly unhooks the left side of her bra while lifting a flap on the front of her shirt, a fancy top that lets her nurse the baby without anyone hardly noticing. It's the first time she's felt comfortable enough to feed Cody in front of me rather than rushing the five minutes home. Averting my eyes, I continue.

"The *Maine Runner* was tied in her usual spot, and Freddie's truck was in the lot. As soon as I saw that boat, every emotion hit me at once. Relief. Happiness. Annoyance. Anger came last. All the same things I felt before the storm . . . everything was still there. If Freddie was back safe and sound, where the hell was he?"

Katherine in the back seat, informing me we'd passed the ice cream shop and confused as to why we didn't stop. Smart as a whip, she wouldn't let me trick her out of her treat. Richard whined that he needed to pee. Meanwhile, I clutched the steering wheel, desperate for them to shut up and give me a moment to *think*. One or the other always wanted something from me. The needs of children consume you when you're a mother. Your own needs come second or third, probably fourth. Your children's needs are your needs now. You're no longer a self, but split off into tiny, needy pieces of yourself, each adding up to both more and less than the whole.

"I pulled alongside the dock house and left the car to idle. Freddie would've been furious to find me checking up on him, but I needed an answer. I hadn't slept a wink for all my worrying, and to find his boat and truck there . . . well, I was a woman on a mission. I left that car running, with the kids in the back, and marched right up to the young man sitting at the desk. I'm pretty sure I scared the bejeezus out of that poor boy when I demanded to know the whereabouts of Fred McGregor," I chuckle, remembering the way he stuttered his answer. Back then the boys covered for the boys, some secret code protecting their own. When this kid looked at me, he decided Freddie was the lesser of the two evils he faced.

"Freddie was down at Derby's Bar with his partner, Jim, and the men from the charter," I finish, clucking my tongue with long-held resentment. "Whether they were celebrating all the big fish they'd caught or celebrating surviving the worst spring squall in a decade, I'm not sure, and I didn't bother asking." Disappointment in my husband and in myself for being the desperate wife wash over me. "Either way, I held my head high as I heaved myself back into the Wagoneer and headed to the sweet shoppe. Freddie sauntered through the front door a few hours later, all smiles and smelling of Miller Light. I'm still not sure whether that boy from the dock told him I'd been by checking up on him.

Brynn frowns, shifting Cody a little closer to her armpit and using her right hand to cradle his head. "Then what?" she asks.

I shrug. "That's it. We never fought about him leaving on a trip again," I say, the lie burning my mouth as it passes my lips, reddening my cheeks. Not a total lie, but not the truth either. I only learned not to try and stop him from going about his work. It was only asking for more heartache.

"Oh," she murmurs, clearly disappointed. She probably wanted to hear Freddie changed his mind after this storm and decided his family would always come first. Maybe she hoped I'd prove to be a stronger woman, the type that was unwilling to let a man dictate her life. Any other ending was likely more satisfying than the reality. That's the true cruelty of reality: it never quite lives up to the hype.

"Freddie wasn't a bad husband or a bad dad. In fact, he was amazing at both," I start. "Things were different then. Freddie loved the water—there's no denying that. Fishing and then the chartering, he truly loved it. But it was more. It was what he did to provide for his family, and he didn't take this duty lightly. To him *staying* would've betrayed his oath to me and the kids. It took me a while to see it from his perspective," I admit. It took many years of hiding my resentment (or not quite hiding it) and holding my tongue (or not quite holding it) but it was a lesson I learned the hard way. "Freddie left because he loved us," I say confidently. "And he always came back."

Until he didn't.

* ★ *

Brynn finished the sleeve of almond cookies and listened to two more of my stories before sharing the real reason for her visit. I sat patiently while she recounted every detail of her mom's visit, only pausing to sip her lemonade and shush Cody. When she was finished, both mother and child looked ready for a nap.

"Am I being ungrateful?" she asked, leaning her head back and sighing.

I consider everything she's said and try and put myself in her mom's shoes. Slowly, I shake my head. "Not at all," I decide. Brynn's mom reminds me of my mother-in-law when I first married Fred. Every offer came with a condition. Each backhanded compliment tinged with ill intent. She was exhausting to navigate. Nevertheless, she was family, and as insufferable as she may have been, I tolerated her in small doses because I had to. Over the years, we settled into a rhythm that worked for us. By the time she passed away, we were almost close to friends.

"It's nice you were able to visit, and I'm sure she enjoyed her time with her grandson," I start, carefully choosing my next words, "but the purpose of her stay was to help you out and give you a chance to rest. It sounds like it had the opposite effect, and it's best you cut the visit short, for your own sake."

Brynn smiles, clearly relieved I didn't lecture her on how grandparents deserve time with their grand-kids. As a devoted grandma myself, I believe this is true but that it is a right earned, not demanded, or taken for granted.

"Thanks for saying that," she whispers. She brushes a piece of hair behind her ear. "I'm afraid to tell Kyle . . ."

I wave a hand at her. "In my experience, a husband doesn't need to know everything about the relationship between a daughter and her mother." Freddie certainly didn't understand the fraught connection between Katherine and me after she left home. That was between us girls.

She looks at me doubtfully, and I can't help but laugh. "I'm not suggesting you tell him the visit was so wonderful that he makes the mistake of asking her again!" Brynn laughs with me. "But you can tell him you're thankful for the gesture, but next time you've got it under control."

"Next time?" she repeats, face falling.

Not for the first time, I long to reach out and hold her, hug her close and tell her everything will be okay, that these are both the longest and shortest years of her life. But I never wanted to hear the comfort in that statement, as true as it has proven to be. So I smile at her and deflect, something I've always excelled at if you ask my own daughter.

"Freddie and I are planning a trip in the fall," I say, the words escaping in a breathless rush before I can stop them. "It's for our sixtieth anniversary, since we missed out last year." *For so many reasons.*

Brynn shakes her head as if she's shaking away a storm cloud, and her face lights up. "That sounds fun," she exclaims. "Where to?"

"The Fanad Head Lighthouse in Ireland," I say. The name sends shivers up my spine. It's one of the most beautiful lighthouses in the world, and I've been begging Freddie to take the trip since we were newlyweds.

It was always too far, too expensive, too time consuming. Work was always too busy, the kids too needy. The excuses stacked on top of excuses. After he retired, there shouldn't have been any excuses left, but we still didn't make it. "I'll show you pictures next time you come over," I promise. It's been a while since I've poured over the guidebooks stacked in my living room, and even longer since I've had anyone to share the beauty with. "Would you mind feeding Spot and watering the flowers while we're gone, dear?" The trip is still a few months away, but it's never too early to make plans. Making plans makes it all the more real.

Brynn doesn't hesitate. "Of course," she says. Cody opens his eyes, and a soft cry escapes his lips. She shushes him. "I'd love to help you plan the trip," she says, murmuring into the baby's soft curls. "I love to plan."

Looking down at my hands, I see they are wrinkled with age and blotted with new dark spots I swear didn't exist yesterday. When I look back up, she's already begun packing up her things, ready to take Cody home for a proper feeding and nap. Thankfully, she doesn't notice the tears trailing down my cheeks. "I'd love that," I whisper before wiping them away, relishing the happy warmth they leave on my fingertips.

◆ 15 ◆

BRYNN

Late June

Truth: I'm scared all the time. Being a mother is scary. But every day we wake up and do it: feed the baby, take the kids to school, help with the homework, cheer from the sidelines. We do it and we are made stronger. Our perseverance and love are greater than the fear, but the fear only makes us MORE powerful.

#warriors #momstrength #youdontscareme

—3BoysMamaMonty

"HOW ARE YOU DOING with the breastfeeding?" Dr. Felix asks. She holds my file open in front of her, the details of my pregnancy, birth, and current postpartum health outlined in the pages of notes and hospital discharge forms paper clipped together.

My hand lifts to my chest inadvertently, as if the mere mention of my breasts might cause them to swell and leak. This has happened all too often, some primal instinct kicking into gear so that my body changes from my own autonomous vessel to one designed purely to sustain another. A beautiful phenomenon when it works and insanely frustrating when it doesn't.

When Cody struggled to latch properly, Kyle could not understand my exasperation. To him, my body was this amazing thing that grew a life and continued to support that life. Kyle said he wished his body could make such a transformation. It was a nice sentiment, but easy to say while knowing it's not possible. While I agree it's cool what my body can do, somedays I want possession back. It's strange how something that should be your own can feel like it belongs to someone else completely.

I shrug. "It's fine," I say without much conviction. She glances up from my file, the slim black frames of her glasses slipping down her nose. Lifting her brow, she waits for me to say more. Everyone always wanting more. "I'm not sure I'm producing enough milk," I admit, the shame of inadequacy rushing to my cheeks. "Cody had a real hard time latching at the hospital and still fumbles sometimes."

She nods and scribbles this down. I try to read her writing, but it's chicken scratch and upside down—gibberish. I wonder if I'm failing this test.

"Did you see a lactation consultant?" she asks, biting the cap of her pen.

Panic sets in. Was it my responsibility to schedule this? Wasn't that her job?

"They mentioned something about a possible tongue-tie at the hospital?" I say, hating the question in my tone. Clearing my throat, I slow my breathing, will myself to sound more confident than I feel, eager to prove myself a competent mother and not some bumbling idiot who can't even feed her baby right. "But then he latched, and we never followed up with a consultant."

"I see," she says, noting the failure on my chart. "How is he sleeping?"

I laugh. "Sleep? What's that?" I joke, hoping my light tone might trick her into thinking I've got it all under control. Only a mother who's doing it all right would be able to kid about such things. Like Monty and Avery and their breezy way of acknowledging the hardships while also letting us all know they've got it down pat.

Dr. Felix smiles and waits. Waits for *more*.

I swallow, my heart thundering in my chest. Beads of sweat collect around my hairline, and I long for a glass of water, some fresh air. Doctor's offices are either freezing cold or boiling hot. "He sleeps for a few hours at a time. He prefers to nap when I'm holding him." We both glance to Cody, sleeping peacefully in his car seat on the floor next to my leg, making a liar out of me.

More scribbling. "Have you tried different swaddles?" she asks. "He should still be sleeping on his back, but transitioning to a bassinet or crib is really the safest place for him. No blankets or pillows yet, but there are a ton of great swaddle options on the market that might get him to sleep somewhere other than your chest." I wish I could tell if her smile was one of kindness or condescension. My emotional filter is off-kilter.

"Thanks," I stammer. "I'll look some up when I get home." She smiles again. Kindness. I think.

"How about *you*?" she asks, eyeing me up and down. I imagine what she sees. Young woman with purple circles beneath her eyes, greasy hair piled in a messy bun on top of her head, and about thirty pounds too many stuck to her increasingly wide hips. My file must list my pre-baby height and weight, a healthy one hundred and thirty-five pounds and five feet five. Not overly skinny or fit, but *svelte*. Back then I liked my body. I worked out every day and tried to eat healthy. I long to explain this to her, to show this doctor I'm not the woman she sees sitting in front of her. I'm someone else. I don't know *this* woman anymore.

The postpartum questionnaire asked if I felt happy "all the time," "most of the time," "not very often," or "not at all." Of course, I picked "all the time." Is anyone truthful on these? If I'm honest, I would check all the boxes because I've no idea what happiness even is anymore. Before-Brynn would not consider my current state "happy," but post-baby Brynn? Her happiness gauge is broken.

> *Have you been able to laugh and see the funny side of things?*
> *Have you blamed yourself unnecessarily when things go wrong?*
> *Have you felt scared or panicky for no very good reason?*

I've always been good at tests, especially multiple choice. The correct answer to these questions:

Of course, I can laugh and see the funny side of things as much as ever.

I've never blamed myself for things that go wrong.

I'm not panicky or scared, no, not at all.

I check the boxes I'm supposed to, eager to get an A on this test since I'm pretty sure I failed all the others. My own mental state is something I can control, but Cody's sleep cycle and my breast milk and weight loss are another story.

Dr. Felix skims the questionnaire and frowns. "Brynn," she says, before pushing her glasses back on her head, her long blond hair framing either side of her delicate face. On the shelves behind her desk, I notice a framed photo of her three daughters, all blond and elf-like, just like mommy.

"Yes?" I ask, my voice quiet. Suddenly I feel like I've been called into the principal's office. It only ever

happened to me once, in fifth grade. I was caught looking over the shoulder of the girl in front of me during
a social studies test. I wasn't cheating, per se. I simply
wanted to check that we had the same answer to one of
the questions. We did. I didn't change my answer or anything. I explained this to the principal, and after lectur-
ing me on keeping my eyes to myself and the importance
of answering test questions honestly for the sake of my
education, he sent me off with a lollipop and a pat on the
shoulder. This feels weirdly similar.

Before the doctor can answer, Cody blinks his eyes
open and looks around the room. Once he realizes he's
no longer in the car or in my arms, he does his favorite thing. Scream. He writhes against the chest strap, his
cheeks puffing out as he closes his eyes, his cheeks first
pink, then red, then violet. Dr. Felix and I stand at the
same time. "I'm sorry," I stammer, eager to quiet Cody
but knowing the only way is to whip out a boob, ASAP.
"He's probably hungry," I say and immediately regret the
weak *probably*. I want the doctor to see I know my baby's
cries. "He is," I mumble. "Hungry. He's hungry."

Dr. Felix places my folder on the counter beside the
speculum and lube. Ironically, I think a pelvic exam
would've been less invasive than this thorough exam of
my mothering skills.

"Don't worry," she says, squeezing some antibac-
terial lotion onto her hands before vigorously rubbing
them together. "You're doing a great job, I promise."
She pushes her glasses in place. "I'm going to leave some
pamphlets with the receptionist while you pack up here. I
want to see you back in two months. I think you're about
due for your yearly physical."

I nod, desperate for Cody to settle. I'm sure the entire
office thinks I'm awful for letting him cry this long. But

they don't know my son. He won't stop until we are out of this office.

"Thanks," I mutter. Cody's wails echo in the small space after the door clicks shut. Fumbling to gather my jean jacket and purse in one arm, I attempt to scoop up the car seat and diaper bag with the other. In my rush, the unzipped diaper bag tips and spills some random odds and ends to the floor.

"Fuck!"

The door swings open. "Sorry," Dr. Felix says, smile intact. "Meant to remind you to use birth control now that you can be intimate again. A lot of moms think they can't get pregnant while breastfeeding, but that's a myth." She laughs, shaking her head. "You have no idea how many women end up accidentally with child again."

I force a smile, struggling to shove an errant Binky back into the bag without dropping my purse or, worse, the baby. I don't divulge to the doctor that I've no need for birth control. Like they taught us in Sunday school, abstinence is the best policy.

"Anyway, we can discuss long-term options like an IUD at your physical, if you're interested."

Standing up, my arms straining under the weight of all I carry, I feel the sweat trickling down my back and yearn to get the hell out of this furnace and into the car, where I can blast the AC and radio, drown out the cries, and feed Cody in relative peace.

"Thanks again," I say, hoping she will at least hold the door open while I make my escape.

"Here are your pamphlets," she says, eying my full hands and tucking them into the side pocket of my diaper bag.

She steps aside and I hurry from the exam room into reception, every eye whipping in my direction as Cody

screams with increased force, a warning to all the expecting mothers clutching their stomachs, sure they will *never*
be like me.

★   ★   ★

With one arm I attempt to latch my baby to my right
boob, his second favorite. Early on he made it quite clear
he preferred the left side. Since I tend to find it easier to
maneuver on that side as well, it's usually dried up by
midday and we're both forced to make do with what's
available. Cody thrashes against me, smushing his nose
into the side of my swollen breast, refusing to open his
mouth against my chafed nipple, which is beginning to
resemble a fresh strawberry that's been gnawed away by
a squirrel.

Our familiar song and dance follows, me chasing
his lips with the tip of my nipple and Cody playing coy.
With my free hand I slide the seat back a few inches to
give us some room before he smacks his head against the
cool leather of the steering wheel.

"Eat, baby," I beg, clenching my jaw so hard I fear my
teeth will evaporate right out of my mouth, like in one
of those Freudian nightmares. "It's right there," I moan,
flicking the nipple left, then right. Finally, he gives in
and begins to suck as though he's starving. It's been four
hours, so maybe he is.

Relief floods over me and spills down my cheeks. The
tears run hot and fast, dripping down my face and into
my mouth. I don't wipe them away, knowing I can't keep
up with the stream, and I don't want to risk disturbing
Cody, anyway. From the control on the steering wheel, I
turn up the volume, Matchbox Twenty's "Unwell" filling the space of the car but unable to fill up the empty
void inside of me. I turn it up louder.

Family and Friends Can Help
*Postpartum depression is a real illness and not a
sign that the new mom is weak or not working
hard enough to get better. Father, family, and
friends can provide help.*

Is it the "Baby Blues" or something more?

POSTPARTUM DEPRESSION & ANXIETY
SUPPORT GROUP
Mondays, 1–2:30 PM
$25 per group
*You are not alone! We are here to support you
and help you find happiness and balance in
motherhood!*

Clearly, I didn't do as good a job of fooling Dr. Felix
as I thought. She saw right through my false smiles and
carefully answered multiple-choice questions. I throw
the stack of pamphlets to the floor of the passenger seat,
where they land on top of a few Starbucks cups and granola bar wrappers that may or may not have been there
since before I gave birth. I assumed the milky smell in the
car was me or Cody. Turns out, it's likely rotten soy milk
from the last chai latte I ordered.

I'm a lot of things, but depressed isn't one of them.
I'm tired. Overwhelmed. Overstimulated and over-
touched. But what new mother isn't those things?
WWMD? I ask myself while fumbling in my purse for
my phone. I accidentally jostle Cody, and he loses purchase on my nipple, the hard nubs of his gums biting
against the already shredded areola. I wince, the sharp
sting of physical pain a welcome respite from the churning inside my brain.

Sniffing back the last of the tears, I wait for the pleasant hollowness that usually follows a good cry, like a cool morning after a spring rain. It doesn't come. There's a compression inside my chest and no number of tears seems to release the pressure. With my left hand I pull up Instagram and scroll until I find the post I liked earlier. *Truth: I'm scared all the time. Being a mother is scary.* Truth: I'd "like" this again if I could. But since one "like" is all the internet allots us, I thumb through the comments, all one hundred and fifty-four of them. This post has been a hit. Four hundred thousand likes and only posted four hours ago. Four hundred thousand mothers read this caption and felt heard, seen.

Hitting the little white bubble, the empty void inside is suddenly filled with butterflies. It feels like the first time I picked up my home phone and dialed the seven digits the cool girl from math class wrote in my agenda notebook. Amelia Brooks, the most popular girl in seventh grade. Dialing those numbers filled me with the same mixture of anticipation and excitement I feel now.

> *Thank you for sharing. Knowing such an amazing mother is also afraid makes me feel less alone. <3 <3*
>   Post.

Perfection is the enemy of happiness, or so they say. Monty has shown me how to combat the multitudes of contradictions motherhood places on women. Be a doting wife and mother, but make time for yourself. Work hard, but not so hard that you don't make time for your family. Motherhood is messy but be sure to frame the mess in a way that is digestible for the masses. Monty does all this with grace and a sense of humor. If only I could be a little more Monty, a little less Brynn. Then I'd have motherhood all figured out. Then, even if I'm not perfect, I might be happy.

Desperate for more connection, but not desperate enough to comment twice on a single post, I clutch my phone and contemplate texting my bestie in Salem, Charlotte. Anxiety threads its way back into the void and I decide to read through our messages, the last few exchanged in the days following Cody's birth. Charlotte congratulating me and asking how I was feeling. My first responses were those of a glowing new mother, words of thanks sent in a haze of hormones and exhaustion. When I got home, I sent her a picture of Cody wearing the onesie she gifted us at the baby shower. After this back and forth, Charlotte asked if I wanted to meet for lunch. I declined since Cody didn't have his vaccines then. She asked if I could escape for coffee. I declined; it was Cody's nap time. She asked if she could bring bagels to the house. I declined—Cody was cranky, and I'd been up all night. Her last message: *I miss you. Let me know if there's a time I can stop by and meet the little guy. Xoxo*

I never responded.

The joy I felt moments ago deflates. This message was from May 18th, more than a month ago. I could text her back now, claim I missed the message. But Charlotte knows me too well and would see straight through it. I could be honest; tell her I'm drowning and in desperate need of a shoulder to cry on and about thirty cups of coffee. Or glasses of wine. But Charlotte is still childless. She and her husband have been trying to conceive for over a year. Complaining about the minutia of motherhood would be cruel when I'm sure Charlotte would kill to have a baby of her own to complain about.

I close my phone and toss it in the console. I hope Charlotte knows in her heart this isn't about her. A better friend would call and tell her that. I'm not the better friend anymore.

Cody looks up at me, his big eyes shining cobalt in the late morning sun. I smile down at him, pleased his eyes have only turned a more brilliant blue than when he was a newborn.

"Time to go home," I murmur, closing the flap on my nursing tee and resting him against my shoulder to burp. He lets out a little roar, a few dribbles of spit up sticking to my hair. I don't bother wiping it away.

★   ★   ★

Leaving the house with a newborn is exhausting even under the best circumstances. Every parenting article I read warned me of this. I guess I assumed they meant physical exhaustion. I wasn't prepared for the extreme mental fatigue that accompanies even the shortest trip.

Even when I was nine months pregnant, my ankles swollen and the Braxton Hicks making sleep a distant joke, my trips to the OB were not as bad as this two-month follow-up. Sure, I was tired and uncomfortable, but it was nothing compared to the emotional drain and stress I feel at this moment.

Cody must agree. Somehow, he fell back asleep during the twelve-minute drive home. Using my ample butt, I bump the car door shut as quietly as possible, praying he doesn't wake up in the twenty-foot walk from the driveway. Fumbling with my keys, I manage to unlock the door and maneuver us through the foyer without him moving a muscle. The universe is taking pity on me.

I set his carrier on the rug beside the couch before facing the mess that is my kitchen. The island is littered with mail I've been meaning to sort, mixed with various breast-pumping paraphernalia—a bottle here, a phalange there. I find it easiest to pump while perched on a bar-stool, my boobs about even with the countertop. The area around the setup is sticky with spilt milk I always mean to clean up immediately but end up forgetting to wipe down after being interrupted by Cody crying and cutting my twenty-minute session short. The hazy off-white stain against the gray-and-white-swirled marble is gross and crusty. Disgusting, really. Two bins of laundry sit beside the basement door, one clean and in need of folding, the other a pile of Kyle's I never got around to throwing in this morning. Downstairs, there's a wet load of baby onesies and burp cloths probably starting to go stale since I forgot to switch it over to the drier before bed last night.

Every surface calls to me, beckoning me to get off my lazy ass and finish the task I started. I know I should take this rare moment of peace and tiptoe downstairs, out of Cody's hearing, and catch up on all the laundry. My eyes shift to the built-in desk along the far wall. Next to my laptop there is a stack of thank-you cards, a picture from the disastrous newborn photo shoot gracing the front of each one.

The photographer claimed it was best to do the shoot the week after birth since the baby would be sleepy and easy to pose. This was not our experience. Cody refused to cooperate, screaming bloody murder every time the poor girl tried to rearrange his outfit or move his arm. He even peed on her in protest. We managed to get a few cute shots out of the bunch, but if you look closely, you can tell he wasn't sleeping as peacefully as pretended. I keep meaning to write them out, but this requires two hands, and I'm often only able to sacrifice the one, and never for more than a few minutes at a stretch. If only

I could send out a mass email: *Thanks for the baby shit!* I'm sure Kyle's mom would be scandalized. Hell, Before-Brynn would be horrified.

Before-Brynn would sit down and jot down a quick list, prioritizing the tasks at hand while efficiently deducing which options held the least potential for waking the sleeping cherub in the next room. Before-Brynn loved lists. Kyle joked I could save myself the five minutes and start doing things, but I found a list ultimately saved me much more time than it cost. A list was a challenge, a test. Before-Brynn loved a good test.

Post-baby Brynn takes another look around, and as the pressure inside her chest balloons, decides there's a zero percent chance she can get it all done before Cody wakes up. Instead of picking a manageable goal, she opts to leave it all for later. It's been a stressful morning, and the dishes and dirty counter can wait. The sheer quantity of stuff to do is overwhelming. Impossible.

"I deserve a nap too," I say to myself, whispering into the empty kitchen. "Sleep when the baby sleeps," I mumble as I kick off my sneakers. The imminent promise of sleep reminds me how truly exhausted I am. The shades in the den are drawn against the midday sun, only a few slivers of light sneaking past, stripes of light against the carpet. I choose the darkest section of the couch and pull a cozy throw blanket from the ladder rack against the wall. Lying on my side, I debate setting an alarm. If I close my eyes, I could sleep forever. But who am I kidding? My luck, Cody will sleep another fifteen minutes before demanding my attention. I tuck the phone under the pillow, and my eyes flutter shut. Even though it might be a short nap, even a few minutes of blissful oblivion is welcome.

★ ★ ★

I struggle to the surface, eyes open and studying the rip-
pling layer separating me from the rest of the world, from
the air I desperately need. My chest is ready to explode,
my muscles ache with exertion. I kick and kick, but my
strength fades and the surface only gets farther away, no
matter how hard I push myself. Lifting my arms over
my head, I grasp the space above me, but I can't pull
myself to the top. I'm sinking. The sound of my heartbeat
whooshes in my ears, the beat louder with every second
I'm underwater, even as it starts to slow down, the space
between the sounds growing wider, stretching. Closing
my eyes, I give in. I go limp, dropping my head back so
my hair floats behind me, tendrils extending in all directions like an auburn halo. The pounding in my head quiets until it's almost silent. Beautiful silence.

Buzz.

Buzz.

I burst through the surface, gasping for air, only to be
greeted by the relentless vibrations in my ear. Blinking,
I realize I'm no longer under water. The buzzing gets
louder. *Your phone,* my brain signals beneath the fog of
sleep. My mouth is painfully dry and my ears ache, the
sensation of pressure so heavy I want to lift the blanket
back over my head and make it all go away.

Buzz.

My phone demands I listen. Through half-closed
eyes I glance at the screen. I don't recognize the number
and hit "End" before noticing the time. 1:13 PM. That
can't be right. There's no way I slept over an hour.

Panic rouses me from the couch, and I catch a toe in
the wide knit fabric of the blanket, almost toppling to the
rug face-first.

Cody stares blankly at me from his car seat, his big
blue eyes open but glassy and dull. The front of his onesie

and car seat are covered in milky vomit, some already beginning to curdle.

"Cody!" I yell, the sight of his lifeless face freezing me in place. "Baby," I moan.

One second. Two. Three. Infinity in the space of almost no time at all.

He blinks and every synapse in my body fires at once. With shaking hands, I begin unbuckling the slimy chest strap. Cody lifts his chin weakly and tries to swallow, gagging on the remnants of breakfast stuck in his cheeks. My fingers slip in the cold vomit, but I get him unclasped and lift him to my chest. The movement causes his head to loll back, his neck not strong enough to hold it up. He throws up again against my shoulder, a hot stream of fluid that's more bile than milk. By the amount of puke everywhere, he can't have much left inside.

"I'm so sorry," I whisper, carefully cradling his head and brushing the mess off my sweater and away from his face. His arms are limp at his sides, a little rag doll. His cheek feels cool and clammy against my palm.

"It's okay, baby," I murmur, scanning the room for my phone. It was just on the couch cushion but must've fallen between the cushions. With one hand I rip aside all the pillows and blankets. "Fuck!"

Before-Brynn was great in a crisis. When a bride spilled red wine on her white dress at a bridal shower, I knew exactly how to get the stain out before it set. Good as new. When the caterer forgot to load the box of wine onto the truck, I knew exactly who to call to get that party liquored up, ASAP, so no one was the wiser. There wasn't a problem I couldn't fix. I was dumb enough to think this quality would lend itself to parenting. Out of an abundance of caution, I'd taken the baby CPR classes, read all the books, prepared myself for it all. I knew I'd be as cool as a cucumber in a baby crisis. Before-Brynn was an overconfident asshole, I decide.

Call 911. Except my phone is missing, and I never plugged in the landline we installed with the cable upon moving to Salem. *Find your fucking phone.* Tried and failed—next. *Clean him off.* This I can do. My brain activates my legs, and we hustle up the stairs to the nursery. Placing Cody on the changing table, I notice his lips are tinged blue. I pull the wet onesie over his head and pull a fleece sleep suit from the drawers next to the crib. *Take his temperature.* How? Ear . . . forehead . . . rectal? I'm frozen in place. Cody whimpers, the saddest sound in the whole world. I abandon the idea of taking his temperature. *Hospital.*

I zip him up, wishing he would cry, scream, something. But he stays quiet, his liquid eyes staring at me, accusing me. *You failed me,* they say. Grabbing a few burp rags from the bin, I rush back downstairs and proceed to wipe the worst of the puke from his car seat. The hospital is fifteen minutes away, thirteen if I speed. But I won't speed. Not with Cody in the car. Never with Cody in the car. Fifteen minutes and everything will be okay. Everything will be okay. It's all okay.

· 16 ·

JOY

Late June

Was there no safety? No learning by heart of the ways of the world? No guide, no shelter, but all was miracle, and leaping from the pinnacle of a tower into the air? Could it be, even for elderly people, that this was life?—startling, unexpected, unknown?

—Virginia Woolf, *To the Lighthouse*

"REFLUX . . ." BRYNN SAYS, shaking her head. "The doctor looked at me like I was a moron," she confesses, dropping her eyes to her hands. She spins the band with the big sparkly diamond around and around her left finger.

Cody snoozes happily in the bassinet. When the white Lexus SUV pulled up the drive, idling besides Freddie's truck for a few minutes before cutting the engine, I couldn't guess who might be behind the wheel. I can't remember the last time a car that wasn't Earl in his yellow taxi had come calling. A few minutes before the mysterious stranger arrived, a late afternoon shower passed through the area, forcing me off the porch and back inside.

Considering I spent two hours this morning watching Netflix, I decided to park myself on the love seat in the living room, *To the Lighthouse* open in my lap. Whenever I need to unwind, I turn to my favorite novel. But reading the familiar words often makes distraction easier, and every few pages I found my attention drifting out the window to the raging rain and wind. That's when the fancy car crept up the drive, and my book is currently abandoned on the arm of my chair.

"I'm sure that isn't true," I reassure her. "How were you to know it wasn't something more serious? That's what doctors are for."

Brynn shrugs, letting out a long exhale. "I guess," she mumbles, biting the corner of her lip. "He was so cold and limp," she repeats, physically shaking the memory from her mind. "I didn't know what else to do, and I couldn't find my phone . . ."

"You did the right thing," I say again. After I shuffled Brynn and the baby inside and offered the soaking wet girl a cup of tea and a towel, she told me the whole story. If I were in her shoes, I would have done the same exact thing, and I told her as much. I'm not sure why she won't cut herself a break.

Opening her mouth, she begins to speak, but snaps it shut so hard I fear she's bitten her own tongue. She glances at Cody, her lips trembling. "If I hadn't fallen asleep, it wouldn't have happened," she whispers, eyes watering. "I never should have left him in the car seat like that," she spits, chastising herself with every word. "The doctor said sleeping while sitting up makes reflux worse."

Nothing I say is going to convince Brynn to stop blaming herself for the scare this morning, but I still wish to comfort her. If only babies came with step-by-step instructions. Mothering would be far easier if that were the case. But they didn't have such guidance back when I was raising kids, and despite all the advances in technology and medicine, they still don't have one. Google and the internet have changed things, surely. But not always for the better. Katherine constantly researched things rather than asking her doctor, or—God forbid—her own mother for advice. As if I could possibly know anything about babies even after keeping two alive myself.

"You didn't do anything wrong," I firmly repeat. "Any mother would have left a perfectly content baby sleeping in their carrier. Anyone who says differently is a sanctimonious liar," I say, earning a small smile from Brynn. "And shame on that doctor for making you feel otherwise. It wasn't like you were going to leave him there all night! For goodness sake."

She sighs and shrugs again. The purple half-moons beneath her eyes are darker than the other day. Full moons now. Obviously, she isn't sleeping enough. Brynn constantly worries she isn't taking care of Cody well enough, but she forgets to take care of herself. Who worries about Brynn?

"I know you're right," she agrees, brow furrowing. "Still, I should have put him down in his crib." Her smile doesn't reach her eyes, but she's trying. "I'm not sure how I'll ever sleep again," she muses, but her tone gives me pause. It's understandable that she might be hesitant to nap while he's in his car seat, but I hope she realizes she can't watch him sleep forever.

Picking up my novel, she thumbs through a few pages before setting it back down. Cody rustles in the bassinet, and her face pinches with irritation she tries hard to hide.

Before she can get up, I wave her back down. "Let me watch him a while," I offer, reaching out a hand to gently rock the bassinet back and forth. Cody quiets but doesn't fall back asleep. His tiny hand reaches up toward the mobile hanging across the top. "You can run some errands or do whatever you need to do."

She hesitates, her eyes darting from me to the baby and back again. I know what she sees. A feeble old woman who can hardly get herself up off her chair, never mind care for a newborn. I don't blame her hesitation.

"Just for a bit," I add, gathering my strength and standing as if every muscle wasn't screaming at me to slow down. "I was going to bake some cookies. Why don't you feed him quick while I get the ingredients out. Then you can leave him for an hour. He can help me bake," I say, realizing I'm babbling but unable to stop myself. My desire to help Brynn in some small way today is so great I will say anything to get her to agree. She spins that ring, the square edges catching the soft glow from the lamp and sparkling against the ceiling. She wavers. "When was the last time you took a hot bath?" I ask.

She snorts, covering her mouth with her hand in embarrassment. "I haven't been able to take a five-minute shower in days, never mind a bath," she laughs. Lifting her fingers to her stringy hair, she pulls at a strand and winces. "Vomit is a great deep conditioner, I hear," she kids, letting the piece fall to her cheek.

"Go home and take a long, hot shower. By the time you get back, we'll have a dozen chocolate chip cookies cooling on the rack," I promise.

She exhales slowly, nodding. "Okay," she agrees, a little light coming into her eyes. "I'll be fast, I swear," she says, already lifting Cody from the bassinet, ready to feed him. "You're *sure* it's okay?"

I grab my cane from its perch, even though I suddenly feel as light as air. "I'm more than okay, dear."

"Thank you," she says, holding my gaze. "You're a lifesaver."

I grin and head to the kitchen. If only she knew hers wasn't the only life being saved here.

★ ★ ★

Cody watches as I knead the dough, my hands cramping as I work it between my fingers, ensuring every ingredient is mixed and buttery soft before I roll it into balls to place on the baking sheet. He's perched in a bouncer seat that Brynn set on top of the kitchen table. After feeding and burping him, she realized I only had the bassinet and car seat available for him to sit in. Since he didn't like to linger in the bassinet while awake, she insisted on running home to bring me one of his rocker seats so he could be propped up and comfortable. I didn't try and stop her, knowing she would only leave him if he was happily secured in a safe spot. Much to my delight, she said she'd leave the seat here for when she visits, since she has multiples at home.

"Then you roll it like this," I say, showing Cody the ball of dough before plopping it on the sheet. I repeat twelve more times, a perfect baker's dozen.

"Chocolate chip cookies were my Richard's favorite," I tell him, wiping my hands on my apron.

Freddie looks up from beneath his wireless spectacles, the one's he was so embarrassed to start wearing after he turned seventy-five. Only for reading, never outside the house. *National Fisherman* is open in front of him. Cody chirps from his seat, and Freddie nudges the rocker with his fist, sending it bouncing.

"Forgive me, both Richard and Freddie's favorite," I remedy, smiling in their direction. Freddie resumes reading his magazine but can't help himself from casting looks at the baby every few minutes.

Humming to myself as I wait for the oven to preheat, I start rinsing the dishes. I could load the dishwasher, but it takes so long to fill a proper load, it seems wasteful these days. Adding the ingredients without measuring cups, I don't have much to wash. I've always added the flour and butter by memory and feel, mixing it together until the texture comes alive in my hands. This used to drive my precise daughter crazy. Katherine wanted to know exactly how much of each to add and didn't believe I could *feel* the right amount. I told her it felt like love in sugar form, earning myself a hearty scoff and eye roll. Inevitably, she'd complain the cookies were too sweet or too chewy and claim it was because we didn't follow a proper recipe. Needless to say, my love of baking didn't get passed along to Katherine. Richard always offered to help, but he preferred eating the raw dough to learning the process of creating a finished product. Maybe Brynn will want to help make cookies with me sometime.

The oven beeps and I slide the sheet inside, checking the clock on the microwave. Nine minutes until I peek back inside, but I've found eleven minutes in my old stove is the magic number.

"Remember when we used to make a wish whenever the clock struck 11:11?" I say, smiling to myself. Each morning the kids and I would stop and count down the seconds until that charmed number appeared on the clock, all three of us closing our eyes and sending our wishes out into the universe. Even Katherine enjoyed this ritual. Until she reached those wretched preteen years where everything I did was lame and deemed offensively uncool.

"Richard always wished for more baseball cards, and I'm pretty sure Kathy was hoping for world domination, or at least acceptance into Harvard," I joke. My children in a nutshell: Richard always chasing material things and Katherine always chasing perfection.

Freddie takes the spectacles off and cocks his head at me. After all these years, no words need to be exchanged. We can read each other like books.

"Me?" I flush. No one's ever asked what I wished for in all those years. Without hesitation, I tell the truth. "I always wished you'd get home safe."

Cody swats at the mobile, sends the stars and moon cascading into each other. I'm transported back. Richard smiling at me for the first time, his chubby cheeks ruddy. I blow kisses his way, and he rewards me with another. The whole time I wish Freddie was home to see it, but he was working. Always working. Katherine notices my attention is on the new baby and hurls her sippy cup across the room. The top falls off, and what's left of the apple juice splatters against the wall, dripping into the new shag carpet.

"Kathy!" I yell, exhaustion and frustration ruining the moment. Richard startles at my raised voice, and his face crumples, his grin turned to pure angst. He begins to wail, and Katherine bends to pick up the cup, shooting a triumphant smirk in my direction.

"I'm sawry," she says. Her new favorite expression. I'm pretty sure she does naughty things so she can apologize in her sweet little soprano. Freddie finds it charming. Me, not so much.

I lift Richard to my shoulder and shush into his ear, rubbing his back. Now I need to steam the carpet. We've been thinking about selling our little ranch house and moving down the coast, to somewhere in Massachusetts. Freddie has big dreams and claims that's where they will all come true for us. Massachusetts doesn't seem all that different from Maine, but his conviction is contagious.

I've been trusting that man since the first day I met him. Not going to stop trusting him now.

"Shush," Katherine says, holding a finger to her mouth and scowling at her baby brother. Her other favorite thing to do. Shush him when he cries and shake him when he's asleep. *"I want to wake him up to play,"* she says, shrugging when I ask her why she would do such a thing. Once he's awake, she walks away, leaving me to deal with the consequences. I know she's only little more than a baby herself, but she already knows how to push my buttons. Every single one of them.

All our family lives here. Both sets of grandparents live nearby, and they have already been so helpful with watching the children while I run errands, take care of the things that would be impossible with two babies attached to my hip and breast. The only time I get any peace and quiet is when Evelyn and John stop by, or my own parents.

We won't know anyone in Massachusetts aside from one of Freddie's fishing buddies. They want to start something together, some chartering business. Freddie's whole face lights up when he talks about it, which is every other minute lately. When I bring up my concerns, he argues I'll make new friends. He promises our family will come visit—it's only a few hours' drive. *"This is our dream, baby,"* he says, so earnestly. *"Our dream,"* he always calls it. He says it so often, I'm starting to believe it. My own dreams fade into the background, replaced by *our dream*, and then Katherine's and Richard's.

"No, it was our dream," I remind myself. He closes the magazine, arms crossed over his chest, waiting for me in staunch silence.

"Don't be getting all huffy," I mutter before checking the cookies. Two more minutes. "We built a beautiful life."

I'm not ungrateful. Our dreams did come true. In the beginning, it wasn't easy. But I learned to love our new home, and eventually I made new friends. The children thrived. Freddie's business blossomed. Our life together was as perfect as any life might be.

He nods and rises from the seat, grinning down at Cody, who coos and reaches out to him. Freddie blows him a kiss and then one in my direction, winking at me.

Eleven minutes pass, and I pull the cookies from the oven, perfectly golden brown on the edges and gooey and soft in the middle. It's not 11:11, but I make a wish anyway. The seat beside Cody remains empty, no footsteps traveling back down the hall in my direction. Freddie never had a sweet tooth.

Sighing, I pick up the spatula and transfer the cookies to the cooling rack. "You can't eat these yet," I say, my voice cracking against the heavy quiet in the kitchen. "But someday I bet you're going to love my chocolate chip cookies."

Cody's eyes flutter closed before popping open once more as he fights off the sleep threatening to overcome him.

"It's okay," I whisper, Cody's lashes grazing his cheeks now. My eyes trail down the hall. "You can go, now."

★   ★   ★

Forty-five minutes after leaving Cody and me alone, Brynn's headlights illuminate the front room. Cody is asleep in the bassinet, his arms over his head and legs splayed out to either side, a baby starfish. Brynn warned me he had trouble transitioning from the rocker to crib, but he only protested for a few minutes. I rubbed his chest and softly sang the only song I could think of—"Country

Road"—until his breathing settled and he drifted back to sleep. I've been flipping through the most recent issue of O Magazine to pass the time ever since.

Before she can speak, I lift a finger to my lips and nod toward the bassinet. Her eyes widen in surprise, and I can't help but smile. I'm glad I exceeded her expectations. As quietly as possible, I lift myself from the sofa and meet her in the foyer as she gently clicks the front door shut behind her. Together we tiptoe-shuffle down the hall toward the kitchen. Cody doesn't stir.

Her hair is slicked back in a bun, still wet from her shower, and her face is bare of any makeup, but somehow she looks five years younger, revitalized.

"How was he?" she asks, clearly bracing for the worst despite evidence to the contrary.

"A total angel," I reassure her. She cocks a brow at me, and I chuckle. "Truly! We baked some cookies, and then he promptly fell asleep. He's been out for nearly twenty minutes already."

She lets out a relieved breath. "Thank goodness. I was so worried he'd scream the whole time and you'd never want to watch him again," she admits before taking Freddie's seat at the table. Inhaling deeply, she grins. "My God, these smell amazing!" As if on cue, her stomach rumbles loudly and her cheeks redden. "My tummy clearly agrees," she kids.

"Have you eaten today?" I ask, realizing I missed lunch and it's nearly eight. The evening escaped us both. Most nights I'm sipping my tea and preparing for bed by this time, dinner long since finished.

She shakes her head. "No, but it's probably for the best." She points at her midsection, which looks neat and trim to my eyes. "Maybe if I miss a few meals I'll finally be rid of the mommy pooch."

I roll my eyes and cluck my tongue, a habit Katherine finds irritating yet also inherited from me. "That mommy pooch grew an entire human being," I remind her. "I think you earned yourself cookies for dinner after the day you've had." Without waiting for her response, I busy myself placing the still-warm cookies onto a porcelain plate and sliding them in her direction.

"Aren't you going to sit and enjoy these with me?" she asks, her eyes sparkling in a way I haven't yet seen. As she looks up at me from beneath her bare lashes, I can see the girl she once was, before the tired blanket of motherhood covered her up.

"I sure am," I say, stepping to the cabinet beside the fridge, where Freddie keeps his not-so-secret stash. "I think we've earned a nightcap to go with these cookies," I add, winking at her as I pull a bottle of Johnny Walker Blue onto the counter and pour three fingers into two jelly glasses.

Before sitting, I push the bouncy chair to the side and settle in across from her, my normal seat. "Cheers," I exclaim, holding my drink across the table. She lifts and clinks her cup against mine.

"Cheers," she echoes, holding her arm out a beat too long and smiling before taking a small sip. She winces as the liquor hits her lips and then takes another long swallow. "This might be the best night I've had in a long time," she whispers.

Closing my eyes, I savor the delicious burn of the whiskey. "For me too, dear. No doubt in my mind."

$$\bullet \quad 17 \quad \bullet$$

BRYNN

Late June

*#hotdad alert! Even after almost eight years of marital bliss,
I still get butterflies every time my hubby walks into the room
(never mind when I see him in his #5 jersey and a backwards
ball cap—swoon!)*
What does YOUR man do that leaves you breathless?
—3BoysMamaMonty

For Kyle's thirtieth birthday I spared no expense.
Never one to need an excuse to throw a huge soiree,
since parties were *literally* my job, I was pumped to have
a legitimate reason to go all out. My husband's big 3-0
was the perfect opportunity to flex my party-planning
muscles. It was even more exciting that I would get to
enjoy the fruits of my labor for this one and not be stuck
behind the scenes.

A true Cancer, Kyle has always been a homebody
who hated being the center of attention. He also hates
surprises. As a result, I controlled my initial instinct to
throw a huge surprise bash, knowing I had to dig deeper
to balance my husband's introverted nature with my own
desire to shower him with all the love and affection on

such a milestone occasion. I spent months brainstorming, jotting down ideas on my phone notebook, only to erase them after further thought. For help, I emailed back and forth with his mom to discuss his favorite parties as a child. After serious consideration, I ended up scratching the dinosaur go-cart themed thirtieth from contention but decided I could tailor the *concept* to his current interests.

Thirty was a big year for Kyle. He'd just been promoted to a senior director level at his technology firm, and our life suddenly felt much more serious than it had only a year or two before. In an instant we went from twenty-somethings out drinking on the weekends (and many weekdays) and renting an apartment in Boston to *adults* searching for a house in the suburbs and fulfilling our dream of starting a family. This birthday party needed to mirror this major shift in our lives, and I'd finally found the perfect theme to accomplish just that.

Kyle's *Aged to Perfection* thirtieth was party perfection. Respecting his disdain for surprises, I'd designed a special invitation for him, requesting the honor of his presence. I had similar invites mailed to thirty of our closest friends and family. For the big night, I rented a cool warehouse space that had been recently converted into a swanky event venue. The owner gave me a discounted rate since I'd hosted a few corporate events there recently and had already secured the spot for an upcoming bat mitzvah I was planning. Since I'd specified cocktail attire on the invites, I spent the afternoon before the party getting myself pampered—manicure, pedicure, hair blowout, and makeup. The stylist even added fake lashes and some extensions to put a little oomph to my half-up, half-down hair-do. A photographer friend agreed to capture the evening, and I wanted to look picture-perfect.

Kyle wore a cobalt blue suit and the TAG Heuer watch I gifted him (in bed because I knew he'd hate opening presents in public.)

The night was a happy blur. On one side of the room there was a whiskey tasting station. Outside in the garden there was a cigar bar. For dinner, we had an assortment of steaks—filet, ribeye, skirt—and a carving station. Dessert was Kyle's favorite, red velvet cake served with bourbon or an after-dinner wine. Kyle loved his party, and I loved throwing it for him. The picture strip of us laughing and kissing in the photobooth is one of my most "liked" on Instagram. A photo of us smoking a cigar in the garden is still my profile picture. That night we made love like it was the first time, and as we lay in bed, our limbs tangled up in a heap of sheets, I told him not to expect such a grand gesture each year. But parties were in my blood, and I couldn't help myself—Kyle's birthday became a *thing*.

He skips into the kitchen this morning, sliding across the cool tiles in his socked feet. I've already been awake for three hours, changed four dirty diapers, breastfed twice, and am working on my first pumping session of the day. He lifts my chin and dips to kiss me, and I pull away, clutching the pump to my breast.

"I haven't brushed yet," I mutter, licking my dry lips and running my tongue over my grimy teeth, the sour taste of stale coffee coating everything.

He stands before me like an eager puppy. If he had a tail, it would be manically waving back and forth, back and forth. *Pet me. Pay attention to me. Tell me I'm a good boy.* I wait for him to bark, or at least say something, but he remains silent and continues to grin at me.

Irritated, I switch the pump off and shield my exposed side with my right arm while wiping the errant drops of milk from my chest. No matter how careful I am, I always manage to spill the golden liquid down the front of my shirt. The first time I knocked over a full three-ounce bottle I almost wept, the expression *"Don't cry over spilt milk"* suddenly making sense. The time and energy required to produce such a tiny amount hardly seems worth it sometimes.

"What?" I stammer, flustered beneath his insistent gaze.

His body sags. My excited puppy looks like I just kicked him.

"What's wrong?" I ask again, hoping I sound less annoyed than I feel. Cody is finally napping after a rough night and rougher morning. My mental list included wiping down the kitchen, switching the laundry, and attempting to online-order a grocery delivery service. It took a few months, but my body is finally sick of take-out, and as much as I love carbs, I'm craving vegetables. Hauling Cody to the supermarket is not a task I'm ready to tackle. Virtual shopping seemed a viable option. In her story this morning, Monty plugged the company she uses.

Kyle frowns and shrugs like a petulant child. I imagine Cody will look quite similar in about ten years.

"Nothing," he mutters, hesitating a second longer in front of me before heading to the coffee maker. He lifts the pot from the warmer and shakes it. "No coffee left," he states.

"Sorry, it's been a long morning," I snap back. Never mind that I'm the one who makes coffee every damn day except the occasional Sunday. The least he can do is make himself another pot. I'm pretty sure his assistant gets him Starbucks every morning anyway.

He drops it back into place a little harder than necessary and busies himself pouring beans into the grinder.

More than a couple fall to the counter before bouncing and scattering to the floor, hiding beneath the lip of the cupboards. Obviously, he doesn't bend to pick any up.

A bean settles under the edge of the mat at the base of the sink, and I know it will remain there until I vacuum, one more chore to add to my never-ending list. My face burns hot and a flush creeps from my cheeks all the way down my exposed chest. Irrational fury blisters beneath the surface, ready to burst forth and set the whole place on fire.

"What the fuck is your problem today?" I demand, my voice a quiet warning. I'm only able to temper my desire to scream because I refuse to wake the baby.

Kyle doesn't turn to face me. Instead, he drops the scoop, a sharp clatter against the quartz counter and then a delayed clang as it hits the tile floor. I stare at the back of his head, his broad shoulders hunched forward. If my eyes could shoot daggers, he'd be dead.

"Nothing," he mumbles, shaking his head. Straightening up, he proceeds to add water to the reservoir before starting the grinder, the noise aggressive in the silent kitchen. My pulse races as my brain fights to understand what the hell is going on, why my normally passive and loving husband is so eager for a fight.

Cody cries from the den, a single sharp plea for attention that will be followed by many, many more if I don't attend to him immediately. Shooting Kyle a nasty look from across the room, I expect him to look ashamed for waking the baby. He only looks sad. Defeated, even. Somehow, I've managed to fail both my husband and son before eight AM.

After a quick diaper change and a five-minute boob snack, I return to the kitchen with Cody in tow. Kyle stands in front of the island, to-go mug in one hand and a half-eaten granola bar in the other.

"Say goodbye to Daddy," I say, holding Cody out so Kyle can kiss him on the forehead, an olive branch in adorable baby form. For some reason I feel the need to apologize, even though I've no idea what I should be sorry for.

Dutifully he lays a quick peck on his head, not meeting my eye. "Love you my little Code-man," he says, tickling his tummy before kissing him one more time and letting Cody grab at his fingers.

"Have a good day," I say, lifting my brow, trying to get him to look at me. It would be nice to at least send him off on a good note. I smile, turning my cheek so he can kiss me like every other morning.

He nods, releasing Cody's hand and picking up his leather work bag from the stool. "You too," he says, walking across the kitchen and out the front door, leaving me breathless and confused in the middle of the room.

"What the *actual* fuck," I say to myself, bouncing Cody on my hip. Kyle isn't easily disturbed. I've no idea what caused such an abrupt one-hundred-and-eighty-degree rotational shift in his mood, from the happy-go-lucky Kyle who'd walked down the stairs to the pissed off man who stormed out of the house a few seconds ago.

We walk to the fridge so I can pour a glass of water. Pumping leaves me desperately dehydrated, and in my latest effort to be healthier, I vowed to drink at least a gallon a day. Monty swears to her followers that this is the cause of her glowing skin and seemingly endless energy and vitality. I suspect quality makeup and discreet fillers don't hurt, but one step at a time. Water first, Botox and collagen later.

Sipping from my cup I replay the morning as if I were rewinding an old video, pausing at every scene, convinced it was something I said. On the front of the fridge is the family calendar. Back when I had some control over my life, I was a diligent schedule keeper and preferred to keep track of all the major events on paper, always afraid they would get lost in the digital cloud. A date is circled in red sharpie. Today's date. June 27th. *No.* Not only have I forgotten to plan a party for my husband's thirty-fifth birthday—*that* might be forgivable. *Oh, it's so much worse.* I've completely forgotten it was his birthday at all.

★　★　★

The hours drag on without a single text from Kyle. Normally this wouldn't concern me. He wasn't one to chat idly while at work. But after this morning's tense goodbye, I hoped he would reach out. Between all the feedings and tidying up the nursery, switching out Cody's newborn-sized clothes for the roomier one-to-three-month options, I kept checking my phone, the knot in the pit of my stomach growing with every passing minute.

Lunch rolled around. Kyle's a self-proclaimed workaholic and usually has his assistant grab him something he can eat at his desk. But this is also when he sends me a message, a small reminder that, despite his hectic schedule, he's thinking about me and the baby. In response, I'll send him a selfie of Cody sleeping on my shoulder, careful to always smile brightly into the camera as though snuggling on the couch midday with my bundle of joy is the best part of my day. Because it was. It *is.* Those little moments when he breathes deeply against my ear and the silence in the house is absolute, I meditate on how lucky I am. As he snores, I consider all that is beautiful in my life, the advantages I have been granted. Monty constantly implores her followers—the mom tribe—to check their privilege regularly to take stock of how fortunate (#blessed) we are to be mothers, to be responsible for such a tiny treasure.

As Cody naps, nestled against my breast, I close my eyes and say thanks for all I have. Thanks that I can stay home and care for my son while my abundant life is well provided for. Thanks that I don't have to worry about money or bills or work or the pesky details of life outside these four walls. I smile as I say thanks, the muscles in my jaw tense with stress and fatigue. I smile wider, say thank you harder. My eyes close tighter, my throat constricts. I smile so hard that tears fall down my cheeks and the pressure in my chest expands so far that I fear my heart might shrink right away.

Bite the bullet and send the first message. A voice, long forgotten, calls to me from somewhere deep inside. Before-Brynn tries to push her way to the forefront. Before-Brynn, who was so strong and confident and oh-so-sure of herself. Before-Brynn, who never doubted Kyle's love or her place in his life. Before-Brynn would've laughed this off and flipped the whole script. Before-Brynn could do better than making lemonade out of lemons. Before-Brynn would shake it up and make a gin fizz.

I pick up the phone, which has been turned upside-down on the couch next to me, my pathetic attempt to prevent myself from checking the screen every fourteen seconds. Still nothing. Kyle isn't normally this stubborn, but it's also been a while since we've had this type of disagreement. Honestly, I can't remember the last time we properly fought over something. My life has been so wrapped up in the day-to-day chore of keeping Cody alive and maintaining some semblance of sanity, there was never time to argue with Kyle. It was easier to peacefully coexist, one less thing to worry about.

Maybe this is the problem, Before-Brynn chimes in. I can picture her smug face, her (perfectly waxed) brows lifted (she used to have time for a beauty regime) and her head cocked to one side, her curtain bangs falling across one eye (she had a fashionable haircut, once.) Before-Brynn loved to be right. People found this quality both charming and annoying in equal doses. Between Kyle's job and my duty to Cody, there hasn't been any time left for our marriage. The fault lies with us both. Kyle comes home from work and escapes to the quiet of his office. I know I've been less than welcoming when it comes to any romantic overtures. By the end of the day, I'm all touched out, done with being *needed* since I'm never off the clock. Cody always needs me, is always demanding my attention, even when he's sleeping. I know this should feel different than Kyle *wanting* me, but it's a thin line. Want and need require the same thing from me: *give, give, give.* It's hard to keep giving when there's nothing left of me.

Resentment floats to the surface, mixing with the guilt and frustration. I stew in it, the emotions thick and ready to boil over. On the one hand, I'm horrified and ashamed I've forgotten my husband's birthday. On the other, I'm annoyed that a grown man is making such a fuss about the oversight. Sure, I'm the one who made his birthday a big deal. I've set the precedent high. But maybe I get a pass this year, considering the tiny human I shoved forth from my loins was distracting my attention.

Clearly, it's *my* fault. I've done such a good job pretending to Kyle that taking care of the baby is so easy, he must think I'm sitting at home all day with nothing to do besides plan elaborate celebrations, my party planning always nothing more than a silly hobby in his mind.

You can't have it both ways, Before-Brynn chides in her best know-it-all tone.

Even though I roll my eyes at my former self, I tend to agree. My options here are limited. I can either keep up the ruse of amazing stay-at-home mom or I can admit to Kyle that I can't do it. I refuse to be a failure.

> *I'm sorry. You know your birthday is my favorite day of the year. It was a tough night with Cody, and I forgot which way was up and down this morning. Please forgive me ☺ I promise to make it up to you tonight. Love you lots.*

I hit "Send," the hollow pit of my stomach suddenly filled with the fluttering of butterflies. Before I can throw the phone back onto the couch, there is the immediate ping of a response.

> *No, I'm sorry. I'm an asshole. You've been nothing less than superwoman, and I acted like a big baby. Looking forward to celebrating tonight. I'll bring home Greek. Love you most.*

I can breathe again. Some of the weight lifts off my shoulders, and I realize just how much tension I'd been holding since Kyle slammed the door this morning. *I'll bring home Greek.* As relieved as I am, a new worry burrows in its place. Back when we lived in our tiny apartment in the Back Bay, the one with the kitchen the size of a coat closet, we rarely cooked. Whenever Kyle or I was *in the mood*, we joked that we needed to eat light, and this always meant Greek takeout from our favorite Mediterranean spot, Calypso's. I'm not surprised he remembers our little inside joke.

Cody rustles against my breast but stays sleeping. I wish we could stay like this for the rest of the afternoon, but my brain is already buzzing with all the things I must do to prepare for Kyle's impromptu surprise party. When I made my mental list this morning, laundry and dishes were high up in the order of things. I scratch them both off and replace them with an emergency full-body makeover, a task that didn't even make the top ten (or twenty) up until this moment. I can't recall the last time I shaved my legs, never mind any other part. List: shower, shave, makeup, and hair. What the hell will I wear? Before-Brynn would bake a cake, from scratch, no doubt. This version is going to settle for ordering one to pick up. Better than nothing. As if sensing my sudden anxiety, Cody stirs, but this time his eyes open and immediately bore into my own. *What next?* He seems to ask. *How will you do this while also keeping me happy?*

"I don't know," I whisper, my earlier relief forgotten. "I don't know."

★   ★   ★

Not only did he bring home Greek, but he even special ordered it from Calypso's. I doubt he made the trip from his office to pick it up, but it's the thought that counts. It was more delicious than I remembered, the falafel perfectly crispy on the outside and soft and spicy on the inside. I'd often joked I could drink their tahini sauce, and it didn't disappoint. Still, I'm careful to not eat too much, even though I'm starved. I know I can't magically shrink my tummy, but I can ensure it doesn't further expand to accommodate a food baby.

Cody watches us eat, completely content to suck on his Binky and swat at the mobile as the seat bounces to the tune of "Twinkle, Twinkle Little Star." I finish my salad, letting Kyle pour me a generous glass of Chianti. Considering the giant leap we might be taking tonight, I know I'll need a little liquid courage to help loosen me up. The whole bottle may not be enough, but then I'd have to deal with the messy business of pumping and dumping anyway, so I savor each sip and hope my post-baby tolerance is still low.

Always skilled at reading the room, Kyle glances back and forth between me and the baby. "Let me clean this up while you get him settled to bed," he says. I resist the urge to chuckle at the nonchalant way he assumes putting Cody to sleep will be as easy as feeding and laying him down. Instead, I nod and carry my glass of wine to the couch and place it on the side table. All the books claim the best time to drink is while actively breastfeeding. It seems odd, but I suppose it makes sense. By the time the booze hits my system, the baby should be full, burped, and ready for bed.

Kyle busies himself throwing out the empty containers and stacking the dishes in the dishwasher. He must really want to get laid. Normally he leaves them in the sink, that one extra step of opening the dishwasher door one step too many. Not tonight. Tonight, he's pulling out all the stops. How far we've traveled from our rowdy pre-marriage days, when we would've made love pressed up against the counter, not caring what spilt. Now foreplay comes in the form of a clean kitchen. It should turn me on, but the mom guilt surges. That's my job.

"I'll do that, babe," I call out. In order to have better access to my glass, the one with the silly inscription "Mommy Juice," engraved across the side, I start Cody on my right boob. He fusses, pissed at me for giving him the "bad" boob. I hold my nipple against his mouth, and he reluctantly latches, chomping down extra hard with his toothless gums. A mini punishment. Taking a deep breath, I refuse to let this chore break the mood. "Go take a shower and I'll meet you upstairs," I offer, hoping Kyle takes the hint and gives me a few minutes of privacy. And silence. He's like an elephant in the kitchen.

"You got it," he agrees, ducking his head inside the darkened living room and blowing me a kiss before scurrying up the stairs, his eagerness palpable. I wish it were contagious. I wish the thought of touching Kyle and being touched was enticing. I wish I wanted to kiss him and claw at his back and wrap my legs around him, losing myself in the bliss of sex with my husband. Once upon a time, I enjoyed it. More than enjoyed it. Our sex life was healthy, better than most of our friends'. I keep sipping my wine, hoping with every swallow I'll feel the tug of desire. But each sip makes me feel a little lightheaded and more sleepy than sexy. My lust for a good night's rest is insatiable.

More guilt. I do want this. I want to reconnect with Kyle. But the websites all agree that it's completely normal to be nervous to have sex for the first time after birth. I'm not crazy. It's probably going to hurt a little, they warn. It might take a bit longer to "warm up." I wonder what my beautiful park friends would advise me if I texted them now. I imagine myself on a group chat, a mommy-tribe text chain where we share everything, all the little details of our lives right down to the nitty-gritty sexual minu- tiae only the best of friends disclose to each other.

Avery is the dominant one in her relationship. With her powerful job and no-nonsense attitude, she not only schedules sex into her daily calendar but prioritizes it. Sex is a release for Avery, not a chore. I need to channel my inner Avery. Tracy is more like me. We are softer, more passive in our appetites. Not in a way that makes us weak or submissive, of course. Never that. Tracy never calls it *sex*. In our chats she refers to it as *lovemaking*. Avery pokes fun at her, but we all love this about her. Tracy maintains she needs to be in the mood to fully engage with this part of herself. Candles, lavender massage oil and a sexy but sophisticated playlist are key to her practice. She loves lingerie, claims it makes her feel powerful.

What should I wear to hide the belly and enhance "the girls?" I might text, adding a string of emojis.

Tracy would respond instantly: *Stop! Your body is perfect!!* Always body positive and supportive, even if she's lying.

Pragmatic Avery: *Baby-doll teddy, all the way. Purple, it's your color.* Purple is my color, always has been.

Monty is not as active on our group chat, but none of us mind. She's so busy. When she does chime in, it's extra special. Like now: *Candle on the dresser, lights off. Necklace and nothing else. Nothing takes focus away from the flaws like nothing at all . . .* Her message gives me goose bumps, the first sparks of arousal coursing through me. I sip the remainder of my wine before noticing Cody has fallen asleep. Looks like his least favorite booby filled him up after all.

Go time. My plan is to carefully transfer Cody to the nursery. Risky move, considering his room has been used as storage for his clothes and assorted baby paraphernalia, but I rolled his bassinet into the center of the rug earlier and even convinced him to nap there for fifty minutes. I didn't dare attempt the crib. Baby steps. Either way, fifty minutes should be more than ample time for Kyle's big not-so-surprise birthday present. I doubt we will need more than twenty. The baby monitor is propped up on the changing station, tested and ready to go. A white noise machine set to gentle waves is the final trick. If everything works, Cody will be down within a few minutes.

Before standing, I text Kyle:

Cody about to go down! Need a few minutes to get myself ready . . .

Kyle knows me well enough to read between the words and will head to his office and give me the bedroom. I hear the door click shut as I head down the hallway to the nursery. Gently laying Cody down, I hold my breath, not sure if I'm hoping he starts screaming, saving me from what comes next, or if I want him to remain sleeping. He doesn't stir. The waves crash peacefully as I back from the room.

With the help of my friends, I've opted to go with a purple satin slip that accentuates my boobs. Pre-baby I was an average 34B that passed as a nice C with a good push-up bra. Post-baby, I'm a solid and perky D. I'd love to get the rest of my body back into Before-Brynn shape, but I wouldn't mind keeping these. I follow Monty's advice and clasp the diamond necklace Kyle bought me for my thirtieth around my neck. The delicate gold chain and three round gems draws attention to my collarbone, away from the trouble zones on my lower half. A few spritzes of my favorite perfume on my wrists and nape of my neck. A dab of lavender moisturizer on my elbows and knees. A final brush through my hair, my locks longer than normal and falling to cover either breast. I glance in the mirror. I look pretty. Sexy. I channel my inner Aphrodite.

I light two candles and place them on the dresser before dimming the overhead fixture.

Ready.

I wish I'd poured another glass of wine before heading upstairs. My buzz is blurring the edges of the room, so I lie back on the bed, propping myself up on the throw pillows, angling my hip to lengthen my legs. I've forgotten what drunk feels like. The closest I've gotten recently is being so overtired that the room spins, but it's not like this. This is sparkly and sweet. This feels magical. I don't want it to end.

Kyle peeks his head into the room. Clearly, he's been preparing too. He wears a pair of black boxer briefs and nothing else. I study his body. The familiar rise of his toned chest, a sprinkling of blond hair. Trim waist tucked into the tight waistband of his boxers leading to powerful thighs, strong from running. A flash of envy at his ability to consistently work out, his body never forced to swell and bend and break to make way for fatherhood.

But then he smiles at me, the wrinkles around each eye a little deeper than last year. He's changed too. Only differently. I pull back the bed sheet.

"Happy Birthday, old man," I kid, a joke as old as our relationship. He's only three years older, but I'll never let him forget it.

He tiptoes across the room, his eyes twinkling as he looks me up and down. Channeling Monty, I lift my chin and meet his gaze, forcing myself to rise above my own insecurities. Kyle isn't looking at the stretch marks and cellulite. He's looking deeper. I feel him search straight into my heart and I open my arms to him, letting the sheet fall.

"You're beautiful," he whispers, gently laying me back against the pillows, his strong arms on either side of me.

My pulse races. My body remembers this, and I'm stunned to realize I do *want*. I more than want. I *need*.

"I know this isn't a big party," I murmur, sighing as he traces his finger from my cheek down my shoulder, tracing over my collarbone and tickling my chest. I bite the corner of my lip, the other side curling into a smile. "But I think this might even be better . . ." I gasp as he kisses the hollow of my neck, nibbles his way to my ear.

He breathes deeply and rises above me before resting his forehead against my own, so our faces are mere inches apart. "I've missed you," he says before pressing his mouth hungrily against mine, catching my breath in his own until we are one again.

★   ★   ★

I fall back against the mattress, clutching my arms to my chest. Mortified, I desperately attempt to cover the warm, wet spot spreading across the purple satin of my left breast but it's impossible. The stain bleeds and bleeds, turning the fabric black. The liquid runs hot and furious, covering my face and my chin. Everywhere.

"Babe, seriously, it's okay," Kyle says, resting on one elbow to face me. His brows furrow in concern, and he wipes my cheek with the edge of his palm. It's not milk on my face. I'm crying.

I sniffle back the tears, pressing a hand to my heart to steady my breathing. My voice is gone, lost, so I shake my head and turn away from my husband, who is being nothing but kind and understanding. This man saw me give birth, held my hand when I was most vulnerable. But this is worse.

"Brynn," he murmurs, gently grasping my shoulder and turning me toward him. "It's no big deal," he says, chuckling. "It's kind of funny, if you think about it."

Snapping my head back to face him, anger replaces my shame. "Funny?" I hiss, dropping my arms and exposing the ugly proof dripping down my ribcage. "It's disgusting."

Everything had been perfect. Better than I'd expected. Kyle was gentle, patient in getting me ready, his hands and mouth exploring territory lost to us both for some time. I allowed desire to consume me. For the first time since giving birth, I didn't think about Cody or what anybody else needed. Only myself.

In the heat of passion, Kyle lifted his lips to my breast. I was afraid it would be weird, but my fears were misplaced. This was a very different sensation. I liked it. I enjoyed being touched in that way. I wasn't self-conscious. I felt sexy and powerful. But then the monitor came to life. The tiniest whine, hardly even a cry. The sound he makes sometimes when he turns from side to side. But it was enough. My left breast, which I neglected to empty in my rush to put Cody to sleep, tingled and tightened with something other than desire. My overproducer of a boob, Cody's favorite snack, had heard the dinner bell. I grabbed at my nipple as though I might staunch the primal instinct, but it was futile. The prickling of the milk letting down began instantly, and milk began pouring forth. Not a dribble or a drop. A faucet. My exposed boob exploded all over the pillows, the mattress, Kyle's face before I could hastily shove it back inside the purple slip to help stem some of the flow.

Kyle caresses my arm. "It's not, I promise," he murmurs. "It's natural," he says. I doubt he even recognizes that mansplaining the event will not win him any favors.

"If you fucking call it beautiful, I'll punch you," I mutter, wiping my cheeks. Mascara mixes with my tears and what I can only imagine is diluted milk. Minutes ago, I felt pretty. Now I'm literally a wet mop of milk and sad girl tears.

He looks at me, his puppy dog eyes hopeful, as if I might wipe off the spilt milk and go for round two. I'm not sure if I should be flattered he still wants to have sex with me or take pity on the poor guy. Either way, it's a no go for me.

"I'm sorry," I sigh, swinging my legs over the side of the bed and effectively ending our session. The weight of his stare is heavy. "I can't."

He exhales, his optimism deflating. "I get it," he says, even though I'm pretty sure he doesn't get it at all. I don't think he could ever understand how it feels to lose complete control of your bodily function like this. I glance down at my chest, the cause of all this distress. My breasts haven't been my own for some time. For years, they were there for Kyle's pleasure (although, I admit I shared in this pleasure.) Now they belong to Cody. Some might argue that their current role was their original intent. I guess I never had any control over them at all. The thought unmoors me. All the wine I've drunk washes over me, the taste sour in my mouth. The fuzzy feeling of being drunk isn't pleasant anymore.

Cody wails from down the hall, the sound echoing on the baby monitor. Each wail becomes two before bouncing into four. Eight.

"I'll get him," Kyle offers, standing naked across the room as he searches the floor for his boxers.

Pulling the slip over my head, I replace it with one of his shirts thrown over a chair. "It's fine," I insist, grabbing a pair of panties from the top drawer of my dresser. "He's probably hungry."

Kyle laughs. I spin to stare at him, incredulous that he refuses to acknowledge the gravity of the situation. "What?" I demand, my hands on my hips.

He drops his gaze, holding his hands across his unprotected groin as though he's afraid my look alone might wound him. "Nothing," he mumbles, bending quickly to snatch his underwear from its hiding spot beneath the duvet. He looks up at me and sheepishly adds, "Was just going to say he's probably shit out of luck . . ."

I roll my eyes at him, unable to repress the snicker that bubbles from my mouth. Unable to help myself, I smile. Maybe tonight wasn't a *complete* loss.

"Maybe I can wring out my nighty," I kid, kicking the ruined negligee in his direction.

"Meet you downstairs?" he asks, lifting a brow. "One more drink to toast thirty-five?"

I shrug, wishing I could be as positive as Kyle, even for one day. "Sure," I say, before heading to the nursery, where the wails are increasing in volume and force by the second.

What would Monty do? I wonder, opening the door so I can comfort my screaming baby. *This would never happen to Monty Montgomery.* I grab my son and lift him to my breast, unsure how the hell I'm supposed to feed him from this empty vessel.

◆ 18 ◆

JOY

July 4

A light here required a shadow there.
—Virginia Woolf, *To the Lighthouse*

BRYNN SNEAKS UP ON me as I'm in the middle of
dead-heading the roses. This should've been done
weeks ago, before the inevitable dry spell that hits in
the middle of July, but I mistakenly hoped I had a little
extra time. But it's been uncharacteristically arid and hot.
Even though the air is heavy with the threat of a storm
and my knees ache every time I stand, the skies remain
stubbornly clear, the forecast hot and humid as far as the
meteorologist can tell.

Not that I trust Henry the weatherman from Channel
17 much. He's a handsome devil, but he predicted a cold
and snowy winter that only yielded about four inches and
the thermometer never dipped below 15 degrees. Henry's
a self-proclaimed *Florida-boy* so I suspect he truly believed
these stats a cold and snowy winter made. So, I forgave
him his terrible predictions. Plus, he looks a bit like my
Richard and lord knows I've always had a soft spot for
sweet boys with crooked smiles.

I'm not sure how long she stood behind me as I bent over Rosalee, my favorite of my bushes. She always blooms the brightest. As I clipped back her dry edges, I felt more and more guilty for neglecting my pruning for so long. Even Rosalee looked withered and sad, the bright sun no longer her friend but a fierce competitor for the spotlight.

"Joy?" her soft voice startles me from my reverie. My right arm jumps, my reflexes not as sharp as they once were, and I snip too close to a bud. I wince, sure I've cost Rosalee a child because of my carelessness. Petting her flower, I promise to make it up to her with some extra fertilizer.

Pushing the large brim of my straw hat back to the crown of my head, I wipe my forehead with the sleeve of my linen shirt. "Brynn, dear," I exclaim, my disappointment in hurting my flowers forgotten at the sight of my neighbor and son. I only began gardening later in life as a hobby to fight off the loneliness of getting older. Rosalee won't begrudge me the company.

Brynn smiles, but I can't see her eyes behind the large frames of her sunglasses. They cover nearly half her face and have a fancy logo on either wing. No wonder she hardly has any wrinkles. The sun doesn't stand a chance against such a shield.

"I didn't mean to creep up on you," she says, her right hand absently rocking the stroller back and forth. The reflective sunshade is drawn down over the seat, but I can tell by his scissoring little legs that Cody is awake.

I wave a gloved hand at her, but my heart continues to race a bit faster than I like. Freddie keeps saying I ought to have my hearing checked, but I keep putting it off. What does it matter if I need to turn the television up a few notches higher than I used to? His hearing is worse than mine, so now we can simply yell at each other in peace, neither of us concerned about being too loud.

Brynn probably didn't sneak up on me. Pushing the big carriage across the patchy lawn couldn't have been easy or quiet. The gentle heaving of her chest and the beads of sweat dripping down toward her eyebrows indicate it may have been a loud arrival, even if I was too caught up in Rosalee to notice.

"Lost in my thoughts, is all," I murmur, my heart settling with each breath. "I'm actually ready to go in and get a drink and a snack," I lie. In truth, I planned on finishing Rosalee and starting her neighbor, Juliet, before the sun rose too high in the sky and forced me inside. "Care to join me?"

She nods eagerly, using the toe of her sandal to unlock the brake. Pulling off my gloves, I shove them in my apron pocket before following her back across the lawn, my joints protesting every step. Perhaps a nice sit down in my rocker is exactly what the doctor ordered this morning. Juliet will certainly understand.

By the time I reach the top of the steps, Brynn has already pulled the bassinet out on to the porch and is settling Cody inside. I love how she makes herself at home so easily. I'm not sure Katherine ever felt so comfortable when visiting with the girls when they were younger. She was always complaining about the lack of central air or critical about the sharp edges and exposed electrical outlets.

"I never know what to dress him in when it's this hot," she mutters over her shoulder. "Long sleeves seem too warm, but with short sleeves there's the risk of sunburn . . ." her voice trails off as she stands, the blue bonnet Cody wore now gripped in one hand. Facing me, she shrugs. "No matter what I do, I feel like I'm doing it wrong."

I watch her push the silly sunglasses up on her face, using them like a headband to hold back the loose hair falling out of her ponytail. When her shoulders sag, she looks twice her age. Defeat is written across her pretty face, etched in the tight pinch of her mouth and the deep furrow of her brow, the despondent stare that always seems on the verge of tears.

My instinct is always to comfort Brynn. Since the day she showed up at the end of my driveway and every visit since, I've been compelled to nurture her, hold her close to my bosom and stroke her hair, vow that everything will be okay. Something about her inspires empathy. For this reason, I gravitate to this woman so unlike my biological daughter. Katherine never failed, even when she was actively failing. She was confident to a fault, so sure of herself that even in the worst of times she rejected compassion and refused to show even an ounce of weakness. Where Brynn is fragile and soft, Katherine was always steadfast and hard.

Oh, how I longed for a daughter who might enjoy staying up late to gossip about boys and clothes. When teenaged Kathy had no interest in this relationship, my friends promised we would get there as adults. So, I waited. And waited. I still dream of the day Katherine comes to visit and sits on the front porch with a glass of lemonade in her left hand and holds my hand in her right. How I hope I don't have to wait until my waiting days are done.

Cody coos from his spot in the bassinet. My heart melts, but Brynn doesn't flinch. If he cries, she'll be on him in an instant. The happy moments are lost on her.

"He looks exactly the right temperature to me," I declare, attempting to raise her spirits. But she doesn't even crack a smile. My body begs to sit down, but I hush it back. This girl needs the type of help I can only give while standing. Rolling my shoulders back and fixing her with a stare that always made Richard come clean, I double down. "What's the matter?" I ask, firm but not aggressive, the finest of lines when dealing with a delicate creature. If you're too easy, they shrug you away. Too forceful, they retreat inward. Either way, you end up closed out.

Brynn sighs, biting her lip. I resist the urge to ask again. Sometimes the best way to get someone talking is to stay quiet. Eventually, someone will step up to fill the silence. We stare at each other, her green eyes glassy. When she looks away, I know I've won.

"Did you ever feel like you were bad at everything?" she asks, shaking her head before laughing to herself. But it's not a nice laugh. The sound breaks my heart. When I don't respond, she continues. "Some days I feel like I can't do anything right." She pauses again, waiting for me to do what I've always done, fill the silence with compassionate words. But I realize my kindness has been nothing more than a Band-Aid on a gaping wound. As hard as it is, I remain silent and hope my open heart can be more comforting than my empty words.

Cody whimpers, distracting us both for a moment. Brynn pushes to her feet, eager to attend to something physical. But he settles easily. I can tell she's almost disappointed he didn't require *more*. She lets out a deep breath and I'm afraid I've lost her, that tenuous connection extinguished. But she falls back to her seat and rests her forehead in her hands.

"I don't know how to do it," she murmurs. "How do other people manage to be perfect mothers and wives and somehow make time for themselves?" She looks up at me, her face naked of all emotion. A lost girl. "I thought it would be so much easier," she snorts, swallowing back her pride. "But by all objective markers, I completely suck at this." She leans back, looks to the ceiling. Looks anywhere but at me. "Some days I feel like nothing more than a shadow of the woman I used to be," she starts. "But that's not even a good metaphor. A shadow is still attached to a self and I feel so far removed from myself that I can't even remember what I was like *before*. I'm untethered," she continues, her voice hollow and low, so unlike her normal cadence and tone. She clasps her hands in her lap, begins twisting that big diamond. "Maybe I'm a ghost," she wonders aloud. "Some ghoulish version of myself. Some days I feel invisible. Others I don't recognize myself in the mirror."

Usually, I'm of the mind that a cold drink and some cookies can fix anything. This might be one of the few times where I'm pretty sure no amount of comfort food can cure these blues.

I hobble past Cody who is currently entertaining himself by sucking on a Binky while simultaneously pulling his right sock off. The left is already removed.

Settling down on my seat, I pivot so I'm facing Brynn. I reach both hands out and she instantly grabs my palms, her sweaty fingers interlocking around my arthritic knuckles. I choose my words carefully. It would be so easy to assure her she was doing everything right and promise everything would be okay. So easy are all the things I've said to Brynn up until now.

"What made you think it would be easy?" I whisper, my words no longer a placation but an invitation. An invitation that is eagerly accepted.

★ ★ ★

She didn't ask, but I decide to tell her anyway. The girl is drowning. Sometimes the only way to save someone is to dive into the deep and hope you are strong enough to save you both.

"I had Katherine when I was thirty-two," I begin, staring out at the quiet street. Only a few cars have passed all morning, everyone already at the beach or heading to BBQs later today. For now, it is only us. "I know that might not sound old according to today's standards, but back then women had babies a lot younger." I swallow, the pain of these long-ago memories as fresh as if it happened yesterday. One of the many reasons I keep this story locked inside.

"Kathy was my first baby, but I'd been pregnant six times before then. Freddie and I married when I was twenty-four and we started trying for a family straight-away. All our friends were married, and it seemed like they were all pregnant or already carrying around infants. We were late to start." Images of my younger self float to the forefront of my mind. Maybe I wasn't so naïve that I believed babies were delivered on the beak of a stork, but I did think some magic occurred around one's honeymoon that ended in pregnancy. So, when the weeks turned into months and then more months and still nothing, I began worrying something was wrong. Maybe the magic was lost on us.

"A year later I finally got pregnant. This was not for a lack of trying. Freddie was keen on that part," I laugh, remembering our newlywed bliss and wanton desire for one another. "I lost the baby early, at only six weeks. The doctors assured me it happened to a lot of women and since I was young and fertile, I should get back up on the horse and try again. Nothing to worry about," I repeat the words I heard over and over.

Brynn doesn't turn to face me, keeping her gaze fixed on the street, same as mine. But she reaches out her right hand and lays it on top of mine, squeezing lightly.

"Of course, we followed the doctor's orders. I was sad, but I believed what he said, that I shouldn't worry. It was an anomaly." Old anger simmers to the surface but I put a lid on it, force it down for now. "A few months later, I was pregnant again. This time I made it until ten weeks." I shake my head, trying to erase the sensation of hot blood trailing down my thigh and the cramps in my belly that caused me to double over in pain while stirring the applesauce I made to serve with the pork tenderloin in the oven.

"The doctor didn't have a better explanation. We didn't have all the fancy ultrasounds and testing you have today. He did prescribe me a pill that was supposed to help support pregnancy," I say, wishing I could rewrite my history into one where I made Freddie take me to another doctor. I didn't like the man, but he was the same doctor who delivered Freddie and his brother so there was a familial loyalty that a wife didn't dare defy. "DES, it was called. It was taken off the market a few years later after it was proven to be dangerous. Thankfully, I only took it for a short period of time, although the side effects were dreadful." I shake my head. Had Google existed, imagine how much pain and suffering my family might have been saved. *If only.*

I could carry on and on, but I've come to peace with the way my fertility was mishandled. Brynn doesn't need my entire sob story; just a hand to clutch in the depths.

"My next pregnancy was the following year: 10 weeks again. Then two the next year, one ended at 8 weeks and the second made it all the way to the second trimester. That one destroyed me. After losing that one, I decided I didn't want children. I couldn't face another loss. The hope and fear were constantly battling one another, and each baby stole a piece of my heart when it left my body.

Freddie was desperate to keep trying. I'm not sure if he wanted the baby for himself or me. He thought the baby might save me. But I wasn't so sure. I was in a very dark place."

Brynn squeezes my hand again, confusing me as to who is saving who here.

"I pushed Freddie away. I lost all interest in sex. All my friends had multiple children by now, so I kept to myself. The pity in their eyes was too much to bear. A big part of me wished to leave," I confess, another hidden secret of my soul. "I loved Freddie with all my heart, but every time he looked at me there was a glint of something new in his eyes, something I grew to loathe. I fantasized about walking out my front door and catching a Greyhound to anywhere else."

I pause, catching my breath. The truth is liberating, even though every word feels like a betrayal of my husband.

"Of course, I never did it," I clarify, wanting to be sure Brynn didn't think me the type of woman to give up. "We fought a lot and Freddie was gone more and more. Ultimately it was our mutual stubbornness that led us to try again. I lost two more babies, twins this time."

Brynn shifts to face me. "I'm so sorry," she whispers, tightening her grip on my shaky hand. "You don't have to continue if it's too much."

I shake my head. I want to finish. Need to finish.

"By now I was thirty, an old maid in terms of motherhood if you asked any doctor. I'd finally come to terms with a life made up of Freddie and me. Maybe we'd get a dog. We considered adoption, but never followed through. Instead, we settled into our life, no longer under the constant storm cloud my pregnancies created." I smile. This is the part of the story I've told many times before. Normally, this is where I begin the tale, leaving out the multiple losses. Being an old spinster garnered enough sympathy on its own. "As soon as we stopped worrying about conceiving, we got pregnant with Katherine. This time, it stuck. Katherine Grace was born a little early, but completely healthy at 38 weeks. Three years later, Richard Francis was born to term."

Over the years, I've discovered you can learn a lot about someone based on their response to my "miracle" babies. Religious people claim it was God's plan all along. My rational friends tend to believe I got pregnant because I stopped worrying, blaming stress as the top contributor to loss and infertility. Those who tend to be more spiritual vs religious remind me that every loss brought me to exactly where the universe intended me to be: the mother to Katherine and Richard, my true children. This reasoning always gives me pause. By this logic, if I didn't lose my first baby, or the second or any of the next, then my real children would never exist. Maybe in some other life I have three kids, all girls. In another, a set of twins. Perhaps in some alternate reality I'm divorced and living alone in Arizona with only a few cats for company. The possibilities are infinite.

Brynn surprises me. I'm not entirely sure which reaction I expected. More apologies, maybe.

"When you were going through all that, did you ever wonder if you just weren't meant to be a mother?" she asks. A white Range Rover cruises down the street and we both turn to watch, the faint thrumming of the too-loud stereo trailing in its wake.

No one has ever asked me this before. If it were someone else, I might be offended. If this were thirty years ago, I would have walked away without answering. Today, the question makes sense. It's the question she should ask.

"All the time," I answer, without hesitation. "After each loss, I convinced myself that fate or destiny was speaking. Motherhood wasn't in the cards for me. As we struggled, I convinced myself it wasn't easy because it wasn't meant to be."

I turn to look at her. She pulls her gaze from the safety of the street to meet my eyes.

"Even after I had Katherine, I wondered if it was all a mistake." I clear my throat, hoping I'd somehow come around to the point I'd been trying to make all along. I've never been short on words, Freddie always said. My arguments tended to chase their own tails before catching anything. "When I finally held my crying baby in my arms I vowed to prove to the world, God, Freddie . . . that stupid imbecile doctor, *everybody*, that I deserved to be a mother and that this wasn't some mix-up, that this was my fate all along."

Brynn starts to smile, but I shake my head. I'm not finished.

"I thought getting pregnant and staying pregnant was going to be the hardest part. How could I think otherwise, after all the misery I'd been through? But it didn't get easier, only harder. Kathy was a difficult baby and a stubborn child. With a little hindsight, I realize I pinned all my hopes and dreams of motherhood on this poor kid. As a result, she pushed me away. She's brilliant and driven, but deep down, I think she resents the pressure I unintentionally placed on her. Instead of learning from my mistakes, I tried to 'fix' them with Richie. Turns out, coddling a child and giving in to their every whim will create a very spoiled and petulant adult."

Releasing Brynn's hand, I wipe away a few tears from my watery eyes. The truth hurts worse when spoken aloud. I haven't revealed anything I haven't thought to myself a million times. I've just never shared it until now.

"What I'm trying to say," I say, forcing a weak smile. "Mothering isn't easy. From conception to birth, straight through the baby years and all the stages into adulthood, every step of the way challenges you. It will try and break you." A tear strolls down Brynn's cheek but she doesn't wipe it away, letting another follow the salty track down her jaw. "You won't do everything right and you won't do everything wrong. You will worry and fret, but that only shows you're a good mom. Bad moms don't worry whether they are bad or not," I assure her, nodding my head confidently. "And you won't break," I add, smiling for real this time. "Motherhood bends you all sorts of ways, but I promise—*you will not break*."

★   ★   ★

Brynn begged off before noon, claiming she had a lunch date with a few friends from the neighborhood. Something rings false each time she mentions these women, this Avery and Tracy and the one she idolizes, Monty. I can't put my finger on exactly what it is, but it reminds me of when Katherine was in high school and tried out for the cheer squad. Never much of a dancer and more comfortable at the library than on a sports field, my Kathy was fighting against her true nature—as teenagers often do— and trying on different personas until the proper one fit. I suspect Brynn is testing out where she fits in the pecking order of young motherhood, so I can't fault her for trying. Sitting and chatting all day with an old lady can't be the most exciting connection, even if we do get on quite well. I only hope her new friends appreciate her sweet soul and help her work through her insecurities. I know Brynn's not a teenager, but girls can be mean, at any age.

Brynn inspires me to venture outside my own comfort zone. Maybe it's the electricity in the air, thick with the promise of turbulence. More likely, it's seeing myself reflected in her shifty eyes as she packed up her diaper bag and tucked Cody into the stroller, her flip flops echoing on the sidewalk as she headed toward the park. Or wherever she was going. After she rounded the corner, I shuffled inside and phoned Earl. I'm not sure who's more surprised by my request to head downtown, my trusted taxi driver or myself.

Forty-five minutes later I'm looking out the window at Salem Common buzzing with activity. The swing sets are packed with children and the picnic tables are brimming with families eating lunch while watching their kids run around the perimeter of the park. Earl takes a right onto Essex before waiting at the busy intersection to cross over to Hawthorne. My heart races as he flicks on the blinker as we approach our final stop, Derby Street. Back when I used to walk to work, I took the more direct track straight down Orange off Essex. The slightly more circuitous route is a nice change. I haven't been this way in ages. Everything is the same, but different in that way things tend to change when you aren't actively in them anymore.

"Want me to wait?" Earl asks after pulling into the only spot open in the Maritime Historical building lot.

Now that I've arrived, I'm unsure of my plan. There are so many people. A few sit on the stairs leading up to the museum. Everyone looks like they belong.

I meet Earl's eye in the rearview mirror. His face is the same as always, open and kind. Patient.

"No, thanks," I say, not wanting to keep him from his other fares, especially since I've no idea how long I'll be and I'm sure he's charging more for holiday rides. I clutch my purse in my lap, realizing I don't have my cellphone with me. The kids insisted on giving me an iPhone last Christmas, but I hardly use it. Mostly it sits on its charger in the kitchen, waiting for the infrequent FaceTime calls from my grandchildren. So eager to leave the house earlier, I neglected to even leave a note for Freddie. No one has any clue where I am.

"Will you come back in, say, one hour?" I ask, the guarantee of a set pickup time filling me with relief.

"Sure thing, Miss Joy," he says, unbuckling his seat belt. "I'll meet you right back in this spot in one hour, exactly," he reassures me.

I nod, afraid to speak lest he hear the trepidation in my voice. This is the first time I've ever asked him to bring me anywhere other than the grocery store or the post office. I can tell by the slight hesitation in his movements, that he's nervous to leave me alone.

He opens the door for me and I take his hand, allowing him to lift me from the lowered back seat. Like the gentleman he is, he bends and retrieves my cane and ensures I'm steady on my feet before getting back behind the wheel. I wave, lifting my chin in the direction of my destination. Only after I've taken a few steps toward the doorway and ascended the first three steps does he return my wave and back from his spot, leaving me for my one hour of adventure.

★ ★ ★

Terry, her name and face vaguely familiar, informs me neither Gayle nor Dorothy are working today. In fact, Dorothy only comes in one Sunday a month during the summer but will be back to every Sunday in the fall. Halloween has always been her favorite time of year, so it makes sense she'd save her energy for the busy season.

Gayle, Terry tells me, gave up her position in the back room at the end of winter. Apparently, she's spending the summer at her son's ranch in Wyoming. Although I'm sad I don't get to see my friend, I am happy to hear she's finally realized that dream. She's been eagerly waiting for her husband to step down at his law firm, retirement always still *one year away*, she would complain. It seems he's finally taken the plunge. I wish the fact that she didn't call to tell me the news didn't hurt my heart, but I'd be lying. We used to tell each other everything, gossiping among the stacks in the basement or chatting over coffee in reception. Maybe it's been a while since we properly visited, but I thought I was a close enough friend to warrant telling such a monumental thing. The idea that it might be because Gayle and I aren't close anymore stings.

"I can leave a message for Dottie, if you'd like," Terry offers, her hands busy searching for a pen and paper on the messy front desk. When I manned the station, there was a place for everything and everything in its place. The chaos before me infuriates me. Does she have no pride in her job?

"No, thank you," I respond curtly. Her eyebrows raise slightly, and she drops the pen, not stopping it from rolling into a clutter of paperclips and thumbtacks. She settles back in the chair, her mouth set in a thin line. Looking at her, I wonder if Terry and I might have been friends if we'd worked her together. It's possible I would've been the one in charge of training her. Had that been the case, I would have insisted she keep the desk tidy and always organized. But I don't work here any longer and neither do my friends. All that's left is for me to leave Terry to her mess. "Thank you for your help," I add, hoping to make up some for my impoliteness. She allows a small smile in my direction before setting her sights on the young couple walking toward her, the mother holding a baby around Cody's age.

Glancing at my watch I note I have forty minutes remaining until Earl returns. I wander to the back corner of the room where the community cork board covers a generous portion of the wall. Flyers advertise everything from pet sitting to guitar lessons, everything pinned haphazardly together creating a smorgasbord of opportunity and vibrancy, all available at your fingertips. Before the internet, there were corkboards. My eyes drift from one leaflet to the next, the ones printed on brightly colored sheets of paper catching my attention and taking me on a roundabout journey from one end to the next.

On the biggest sheet of posterboard in the center of it all is an announcement for the annual Fourth of July fireworks spectacular. According to the red, white and blue banner, the best place to view the show is at The House of Seven Gables, located across the way from the museum. It's also Nathaniel Hawthorne's birthday, the caption says, and what better place to celebrate then at the place dedicated to one of his famous novels. Freddie will be eager to go, even though he will argue *The Scarlet Letter* is in fact Hawthorne's masterpiece. I disagree. I look forward to spending the afternoon arguing the validity of each point while sipping lemonade and enjoying the firework show from our own backyard, the sparklers just visible over the tree line in the direction of the water.

But Freddie will want to take the boat out and watch the show from the water like he suggests every other year. *Best view in the house,* he insists. Our kids loved this tradition when they were little, before they got invited to pool parties and BBQs at the beach. Even I enjoyed the festivity for some time, even though I've never liked the ocean at night. But at some point, it all changed. Freddie and Jim rented the charter out to tourists, eager for the *best view*. Fireworks on the bay became a business venture and I was left to watch the show alone, waiting for the kids to get home from their friend's houses.

"I'll ask Brynn what she's doing tonight," I mumble, causing the man beside me to glance at me out of the corner of one eye. He grabs the tiny piece of paper with a phone number for a fishing trip off one of the flyers. I'm tempted to give him Freddie's number, but I let him go. Freddie's busy enough as it is.

Thirty-two more minutes to kill. I sigh and head back to the front door. A nice walk along the dock will be fun, check out some of the new boats Freddie covets. Terry lifts a hand to wave as I leave and I wave back, resting my weight on my cane as I struggle to push open the heavy door.

Earl is parked in the same spot as before, his car idling. I'm sure he's blasting the AC to fight the brutal heat. As I watch, his head bops up and down as he dances to the radio, probably Tom Petty or one of those rock bands Richard always favored. My heart swells with gratitude.

On seeing me, he jumps out to help me in. He doesn't say a word about why he's there a half an hour early and neither do I.

"Enjoy your visit?" he asks. Without waiting for an answer, "Where to next, Miss Joy?"

I close my eyes, relieved to be within the safe confines of the taxi, out of the brutal humidity and away from the disappointment of a place I no longer know. "I appreciate you, Earl," I say, something I don't say nearly enough. Gently, I rest my hand on his shoulder. "You can take me home now."

Nodding once, he puts the taxi into reverse and heads back to Pickman. As we weave through Salem on our

five-minute drive, I realize I don't know Brynn's number. There's no way for me to call and invite her to the
show later. It was a silly idea, anyway. I'm sure she has
plans with her mom friends from the park. How awkward for her to explain to them why she's dragging along
her elderly neighbor.

Earl escorts me all the way up the stairs. I'm exhausted,
today much busier than I'm accustomed to. A long afternoon nap is in order. When I wake up, I'll ring Dorothy
and find out the scoop on Gayle. No doubt she will have
the number to the ranch. I want to take advantage of the
spark in the air, use them to ignite my long-neglected
relationships. After a nap, that is.

◆ 19 ◆

BRYNN

July 8

*I've been holding out on sharing the big news, but I can't
wait any longer . . . The Montgomery clan will be adding
a little baby sister to the mix this December! Our hearts are
so full and the boys are SOOO excited to add a girl to their
crew. Safe to say this lil' one will be the princess of the family!
3BoysMontyMama needs a new handle, poll in my stories!*
                                              —3BoysMamaMonty

I DOUBLE TAP, ONE of three hundred thousand to have
done so already. Monty is pregnant. I do the math
and conclude she must be at least twenty weeks. Scrolling back through her feed, I find her last pregnancy
announcement. She was only thirteen weeks when she
told her followers she was due with her third boy.

The comments are mostly the same. Lots of pink heart
emojis and *congrats!!* followed by kissy faces and too many
exclamation points, as if each person is trying to outdo
the last. Pinned to the top of the feed are comments from
other mom influencers, Monty's online mom tribe.

*So happy for you. You're the strongest Momma I know.
XoXo.—WFHMommyX2*

A rainbow emoji is tucked at the end. Mirabelle, aka WFHMommyX2 is a frequent contributor to Monty's page. The redheaded beauty works from home (as indicated by her handle) and chronicles the trials and tribulations of mothering her twin girls while running her successful interior design consultation business. While she doesn't hide the fact that she takes advantage of the help of a live-in nanny, she implies most of the workload—both home and career—falls to her alone.

There's an angel watching over your beautiful family. ILYSM <3—TheRealCaraRae. Another rainbow, this time from Cara Rae. Monty's pretty brunette friend recently shared that she lost a baby in a sad post that garnered lots of likes. There's a blue checkmark next to her name. I'm pretty sure she wasn't verified that last time I clicked through her profile. Cara's status as elite influencer has been cemented. Her very public friendship with the more popular Monty has been instrumental in her fan base. As if on cue, a reply to this comment pops up in real time:

> *Thinking of you. I know your rainbow is coming. XO.* —3BoysMamaMonty

I long to text Tracy and Avery, see what they think about this announcement. Something's up, I'm sure of it. Someone like Monty wouldn't wait one second longer than necessary to share such exciting news with her followers unless there was a specific reason to wait. If only I could decipher these cryptic messages among the mom tribe. Their words are both cagey and obvious at the same time, and I hate that I'm not in the loop.

Cody naps on his Boppy beside me, a new and welcome development. For the first few months, he hated the pillow, refusing to remain sleeping with the slight incline. Last week I lay him down so I could reclasp my bra, and to my amazement, he closed his eyes and stayed asleep for nearly an hour. After our scare in the car seat, I've been hesitant to leave him resting upright for so long, but we've had no problems. Two free hands during nap time is a gift in itself, even if I spend most of my time using them to scroll through my phone the entire time.

A quick Google search gives me the answer. Instantly, I feel guilty for assuming Monty was hiding anything from us. A rainbow baby is a baby born after loss, I learn. This explains the many rainbow emojis and the private— yet very public—exchange between friends. Somewhere between baby boy Marcus and this pastel pink post, Monty miscarried. In a very uncharacteristic move, she withheld this information from her followers. I'm both irritated she broke her own rule of full transparency and proud of her for protecting something so deeply personal. The push and pull of social media tugs at my mind and heart, the two at odds with one another, and I struggle to untangle the reality from the glamorized fiction. This suggestion of pain is a reminder that beneath the shiny surface is a murky underbelly only shared after it's been wiped clean and fed through the appropriate filter.

I wouldn't be surprised if Monty one day gathers up her courage and shares the story of her loss, the photo and caption chosen specifically for the purpose of eliciting maximum effect: empathy, compassion, strength. She'd be lauded for using her platform to connect with others who share in this pain while also being persecuted for posting for attention. Push and pull.

"Everything all right down here?" Kyle asks, popping his head into the den. His hair is still wet, and the top two buttons of his pale blue shirt are undone. His spicy cologne wafts in my direction.

Looking up from my phone, I smile. "My friend is pregnant," I tell him before closing the app and laying the phone facedown next to my leg.

"Do I know her?" he asks, crossing the room to brush a quick kiss on my forehead.

"No, just one of the local moms," I answer, butterflies twisting in my stomach as I fib.

Kyle lifts his brow, considering. "The blonde or brunette?" he asks, pursing his lips. "Tracy?" he guesses. His open face gives me pause. I'm surprised he remembers her name.

"Not Tracy, but she is blond," I say, swallowing back the ever-increasing guilt. "It's Monty. She's having a little girl, finally. She has three boys already," I add, unsure why I need to continue to embellish my story, deepen the lie. Everyone says it's the details that get you caught.

"We should invite the whole crew over for a barbecue before summer is over," he suggests, then clucks his tongue. "Three boys? Must have their hands full," he murmurs before heading back to the kitchen. I hear him lift the coffeepot from the warmer and pour a mug.

"Definitely," I agree, raising my voice a little louder. "They are all eager to meet you."

A moment later he peeks back in on me. "I'm going to be a little late tonight," he says, only one button left undone now. His steel travel mug is in his right hand. "I promised Alex I'd get a drink to celebrate his promotion."

Before Cody, I would've met them at the bar for this drink. One drink would turn into two, then four, then maybe dancing at Venu. Alex and his wife, Shanti, lived right near our old apartment. We were couple friends. Then we moved to Salem, disrupting the ecosystem of our relationship. Shanti and I became Facebook friends who sometimes texted. Kyle and Alex work together every day and never question if their wives keep in touch. It doesn't even occur to Kyle to invite me tonight.

"Sure," I say, because what else is there to say. "Cody and I will order sushi," I murmur, rubbing my son's thigh with one hand. Another night in. The long hours of this day stretches before me. My chest tightens. Before-Brynn looked forward to the occasional night home alone. I'd order my favorite spicy tuna roll, pop open a bottle of white wine, and get lost in a bad movie. The prospect doesn't hold the same allure.

If Kyle notices my hesitation, he doesn't let on. He blows me a kiss. "Love you, baby," he says. "Give Code-man a hug for me when he wakes up."

"Tell Alex I say congrats," I call out, but he doesn't hear me. The door closes with a final thud behind him.

Cody's eyes pop open. Demanding. Needing.

★   ★   ★

With a little help from the baby forums, I pack the ulti-mate diaper bag. There's literally anything a baby could ever need or want stuffed inside one of the various pock-ets or pouches in the designer backpack. Along with the bag, I've filled a soft cooler with two bottles, filled with six ounces each of pumped breast milk, and an emer-gency container storing an additional eighteen ounces. More milk than any baby could eat in two hours. If I time it right, he will most likely sleep the entire time I'm gone and won't need even one of the bottles. This is ideal since Cody has still been resistant to a nipple not attached to my person. The only person who's been able to con-vince him to enjoy a different meal is Joy. This is one of the reasons why she's the only one I can ask to watch him while I run a few errands. I refuse to admit the other rea-son: I've no one else to ask.

"Two hours, at most," I tell her again as she welcomes us into her home. The July sun is almost unbearable today, the air so thick it made even the short walk around the corner dreadful. Sweat is still pouring down my back and settling into the spandex of my too-tight sports bra. Two window AC units labor against the humidity, but Joy's house is still too warm. I position myself in front of a floor fan positioned to the right of the doorway, between the kitchen and dining room, and let the cool air swirl around my thighs.

"Freddie says they help keep the air moving," she says, nodding down at another fan across the room. "Not that it's helping much today," she laughs, waving a hand in front of her face for effect. "Even Spot has taken refuge in front of the air conditioner," she says, pointing to the black cat balanced precariously on the small sliver of windowsill not covered. "Believe me, it takes a real heat wave to get that cat off the porch."

Cody chirps happily from the rocker. Before leaving the house, I fed him a few minutes extra on both sides. My goal was to get him full, but not bursting. A satisfied, but not gassy, baby. On the short trip over, I talked to him, refusing to allow him to close his sleepy eyes. I figured it best if he held out on napping until he was safe and secure at Joy's house. So far, my time line is working. Maybe I'm finally getting the hang of this mothering thing. Who knows? Maybe next month I'll be ready to start my own mommy influencer account, dedicated to efficiency and planning as it relates to infants. *As if.*

"You're *sure* you don't mind?" I ask for the fifth time, even though I know the answer is the same. I'm so sure of her response that I've already begun emptying the essentials from the diaper bag and lining them up on her worn kitchen table. Binky. Burp rag. Diapers and wipes. Check, check, check.

"You better not be changing your mind on me now," Joy quips back between making kissy faces at a delighted Cody. "He's mine for the afternoon, whether you like it or not."

Relieved, I unzip the cooler bag. "I'll put the milk in the fridge," I say, tugging the door open. My concern that there wouldn't be space on the shelves was for nothing. Joy has some milk and a loaf of bread next to a pitcher of lemonade, but not much else. A few sad vegetables are wilting in a drawer. A stab of worry courses through me.

Catching my gaze, she straightens up. "Grocery day is tomorrow," she says, watching as I place the extra bottles inside and shut the door. "I hate to see things go to waste," she adds, cheerfully. My worry passes. Mostly.

"He ate right before we came over," I start, wondering if I should write a list or a schedule. A feeding timetable might be useful. I always like to see things written down. "He should be good for a few hours."

Joy laughs. "Honey, you left enough milk to last me until tomorrow morning. You aren't planning on ditching us for a sleepover, are you?" she kids. "Not that I'd mind. I don't sleep much anyway."

My cheeks grow hot, but I know her joke is all in good fun. "Not planning on ditching you. I can't imagine Freddie would appreciate a screaming baby keeping him up all night."

Joy's smile fades as she turns to Cody again. His eyelids are looking mighty heavy. Sleep is almost here. "Oh, he wouldn't mind either," she murmurs. She clears her throat. "You better scoot now," she insists, waving both hands to shoo me from the room. "Cody and I will be perfectly fine. You can't get anything done in two hours so why don't you come back at four thirty?"

I bite my lip. That's almost four hours away. It *would* be nice to have the extra time to myself, but I don't want to take advantage of Joy. Despite how spry she comes off, she could be Cody's *great*-grandma.

Sensing my trepidation, she continues. "Come back when you're done doing what needs to be done. How about that?"

I nod. At least I know she has enough milk to last. "Sounds perfect," I admit. I feel lighter with every second I get closer to a little alone time, a whole stretch of day with no responsibility except to myself. "Joy . . ."

"Oh, shush. Get out of here," she says. "You can thank me later, but you know how much I love spending time with this little guy."

Gratitude for this angel of a woman almost brings me to tears. I turn on my heels before I break down. Before I get down the steps, I stop in my tracks, remembering the most important thing of all. "My cell!" I exclaim, unsure how I could forget something so basic. My mind begins spiraling down all the disastrous paths forgetting to leave a contact number could take.

Joy slides in my direction a spiral notebook with *The McGregors* scrawled across the top and a small pen attached by a string. I jot my number down and exhale loudly, closing my eyes. What else might I be forgetting?

"Brynn," Joy says, looking at me with some concern. "Don't worry. It's only a few hours. I promise to call if I need anything." She picks up the notebook and places it beside her old-fashioned landline. At least I don't have to worry about bad reception.

Afraid I'll change my mind if I linger, I bend and kiss Cody on the cheek, his gummy smile both rewarding and guilt inducing. *Don't leave me mommy,* his big blue eyes say. If he cries, I know I will stay. My lip trembles.

"Hey there little guy," Joy whispers, reaching to scoop my son up from his seat. He instantly brightens, his sadness at seeing me go forgotten. "He's okay," she promises. "Everything is going to be okay."

Joy is constantly saving me from myself, quieting the fears I'm too scared to voice. Somehow, she always knows exactly what to say, and because of this, I know she's right. Cody will be fine with Joy this afternoon—more than fine. There's no doubt in my mind.

★   ★   ★

The quiet in the house is unnerving. I can't recall the last time I'd been so completely alone, without a baby or husband in the next room over, someone waiting for me to finish my shower or hurry up and pee. It's a strange sensation, this *not* being needed. The legs of the barstool screech loudly across the tile, and instinctively I wince, sure I've awoken the beast. Then I remember: I'm all alone. There's no one here to wake up. A lightness passes through me. Liberation.

"Hey, Google, turn on Matchbox 20," I say into the silent kitchen. Instantly, one of my favorite songs blasts from the surround sound stereo system Kyle installed the year we moved into the house. Back when we used to entertain, we used the system all the time. Our house has been music-free for months now. "Hey, Google, turn it up," I call out over the chorus, and the room pulsates with the beat.

Settling on the stool, I push aside my pumping paraphernalia. When I first came home from the hospital, I put it away after each use. Now I don't bother. Seemed like a waste of precious minutes pulling it out from the lower cabinets every three hours.

A list. Obviously, I need a list. It's 11:48 AM now. I have about four hours to get all my errands done. Channeling Before-Brynn, I begin mentally sorting the various tasks I need to accomplish, rating them in order of importance and time needed for completion. Standard planning practices.

I reach for the pen and paper always situated on the edge of the island. It's been a while since I've written this type of list. Most mornings a frantic reel of everything I need to achieve runs wildly through my sleep-addled mind. The time line is always hazy, my brain unable to account for all the variables: nap length, quantity of poopy diapers, number of outfit changes because of spit-up or blowouts. Today's list is all for me. Today's list is a Before-Brynn schedule with the potential to be executed, each item checked off with satisfaction.

My pen hovers above the page. Placing the felt tip to the paper, I wait for inspiration to strike. And wait. But instead of inspiration coursing through my veins, there's only dread. All the demons that have been creeping beneath the depths rise at once, fighting for space, digging for purchase.

> *Mani/Pedi*
> *Haircut and color*
> *Massage*
> *Run on the elliptical 30 min*
> *Organize my closet*
> *Organize Cody's closet*
> *Laundry*
> *Vacuum*
> *Grocery Shopping . . . Costco?*
> *Organize baby photos and book*
> *Send thank-you cards*
> *Mop the floor*
> *Pump*
> *Read a book . . . catch up on the news . . . meditate . . .*
>   *take a bath*

I stop writing, the last line hardly more than an angry scrawl against the pretty pale blue stationary. Even though the list stops, it doesn't end. There are so many more things I *want* to do but so many more things that I *need* to do. All the things I intend to do each day, but can't find the time or energy to do after caring for Cody's every need, come barreling at me, demanding my attention. *No excuse now!* they scream. It's the truth. I've no reason not to deep-clean the house from top to bottom or get through the endless pile of burp rags and sheets souring in the hamper. I've no reason not to hit the grocery store and Costco before we *actually* run out of toilet paper. But then I won't have any time to do anything for me. How can I possibly balance my wants with all the household needs? The answer is: I can't.

"Fuck," I mutter. My right hand has gone rogue, and the list is destroyed. The pen has a mind of its own, rendering the words illegible. Angry tornados of ink replace the bullets. With the back of my forearm, I swipe everything off the island. The notebook and a tattered copy of a novel I accidentally grabbed from Joy's house tumble to the floor.

What would Monty do? Clear her mind, take a "me-moment," she'd say. Historically, whenever I got stuck in my own head, it helped to get the wind on my face and the blood pumping extra hard through my veins. Since I haven't run in forever, a walk will have to do. The summer breeze in my hair will have to suffice.

★ ★ ★

I walk through the front door without bothering to lock it behind me. A fifteen-minute stroll around the block—away from Joy's house—is all I need. I start to walk.

And keep walking.

• 20 •

JOY

July 8

*The sigh of all the seas breaking in measure round the isles
soothed them; the night wrapped them; nothing broke their
sleep, until, the birds beginning and the dawn weaving their
thin voices in to its whiteness.*
                                        —Virginia Woolf, *To the Lighthouse*

FOUR THIRTY COMES AND goes. Cody went down for a
nap right after Brynn left. For two hours he remained
happily sprawled out on his back, his arms starfished
above his head and his pacifier hanging loosely from his
lips. When he woke up, whining softly for my attention,
I spent thirty minutes feeding him a warmed bottle while
watching my show.

Since then, he's played on his tummy on the rug. He
didn't like this much, so I moved him to the rocker. I read
a few chapters from an old Nancy Drew novel I pulled
from the bookshelf. Most of my kid-friendly books were
packed away and given to grandkids or donated to the
local library. Katherine loved her Nancy Drews, preferring to read them hidden beneath her covers, with
a flashlight, long after bedtime. She thought she was

pulling a fast one on me and Freddie, but we knew she was up. I never minded until the books were replaced by the phone she begged us to install in her room.

Another bottle. He studies me from beneath his pale lashes, those big blue eyes full of curiosity. I imagine he's wondering where his mommy is and why he's eating from this funny plastic contraption. Thankfully, he took the nipple willingly. Brynn was quite worried for nothing.

"She'll be back soon," I promise, angling the bottle a little higher as he reaches the last few ounces.

But we finish the bottle and still no Brynn. I burp him on my shoulder, wiping a bit of spit-up from the corner of his mouth. I keep expecting to hear her customary three knocks, followed by her quiet steps down the hall. She won't wait for me to say come in. Not with Cody inside.

Cody smiles up at me, his belly full, ready to be entertained. What else is there to do? With my free hand, I turn on another episode of my show and position Cody so he can watch along with me. I know a lot of parents nowadays are concerned with too much screentime negatively impacting brain development, but I don't buy it. Freddie thinks it's a genius marketing ploy by toy companies, who vilify the television, so parents are forced to buy the next-best thing for their kids. Generations of children grew up learning from Sesame Street and turned out just fine.

Five o'clock. A nagging worry begins to take shape. Brynn is often sleep-addled and preoccupied, but she doesn't strike me as a woman who runs late for things. Especially to pick up her child. It was difficult for her to agree to leave him for a few hours, so it makes no sense that she'd lose track of time without so much as a call of warning. Cody is heavy in my arms. Asleep again.

Five thirty. My arm aches and I long to move Cody to the bassinet, but I don't want to risk waking him. He looks so peaceful. Behind us, the floorboards creak and I relax. But Brynn doesn't pop her head around the corner. It's only the wind. Worry curls back in, winding up my shoulders and into my chest.

Six. Cody wakes up and I place him in the rocker, my fingers shaking as I strap him in. My arm fell asleep and hangs heavy at my side. Although it's still light outside, the sky has changed. The clouds are dark, ominous. Trepidation tightens in my stomach.

Cody isn't hungry and contents himself swatting at the mobile above his seat. Brynn was due two hours ago. Two hours isn't running late. Two hours means something is wrong.

Her cell phone number is scrawled across the front page of the notebook on the table. Carefully, I punch the numbers into my home phone. It rings and rings until it goes to voicemail. Swallowing my fear, I hang up before immediately redialing. The result is the same, but this time I leave a short message asking her to call me. I hate to worry her, but I don't know what else to do.

Six fifteen. Cody watches the door, as do I. Brynn doesn't appear. The phone doesn't ring.

The sun has shifted to the back side of the house, casting the front yard in shadows. There should be a few more hours of sunlight, but the clouds are thick. A storm is on the horizon.

"How about we go for a little walk?" I say, gathering my strength for what comes next. "Let's go find mommy."

I busy myself with strapping Cody into the stroller. Then I gather the essentials and hastily toss them into the diaper bag. The minutes continue to tick by.

Six thirty. Cody and I turn right out of my driveway. The short walk looms large, my knees already aching. But there's no time to waste. Steadying myself on the handles of the stroller, I push on, one slow step at a time.

★ ★ ★

Brynn's Lexus is in the driveway. A good sign, I think. The front door is unlocked, and I don't bother to knock. The air is heavy, hot with warning, and I'm desperate for AC and a cold glass of water. Every muscle cries for rest. Now that I'm so close, I worry I might collapse with relief on the sight of my friend.

Although it's the first time I've been inside Brynn's house, I can tell it's empty. It has that particular decibel of quiet only attainable in complete emptiness.

"Brynn?" I call out. The kitchen is huge, as big as my entire downstairs. My voice falls flat, lost in the open floor plan. It doesn't matter, she's not here to hear me anyway.

A laundry basket filled to the brim is tipped over in front of the refrigerator. There's a full glass of water next to the sink. The flip-flops she always wears are tucked on either side of a kitchen stool, as if she walked right out of them. By every indication, she was here recently.

At a loss, I rest my weary hips against the edge of the counter. Now that I'm here, I don't know what I expected. On the walk over, I envisioned finding her napping peacefully on the couch, oblivious to the passing of time. I thought she might hear the door open and snap awake, reaching for her phone, only to find she forgot to set an alarm. When she saw me and Cody, she'd apologize, and I'd laugh and assure her everything was fine. She'd look well rested and invite me to stay for supper. All my worrying would be for naught.

I guess I knew this scenario was unlikely the moment I walked through the door. Brynn didn't seem the type to forget to set an alarm. If anything, she seems more likely to set two or three, just in case. Even though she's constantly in need of a nap, she made it clear she intended to run errands and get some things done. If she wanted to nap, she could've done it at my house, like she's done so many times before. No, I knew I wouldn't find her sleeping inside. I knew this, yet I allowed myself to hope.

A desk is built right into the kitchen cabinetry. *So fancy,* I think. Freddie would love this kitchen. We always talked about renovating our old farm kitchen, but spending so much money to fix something that wasn't broken never made sense enough to justify the cost. Our well-loved oak cabinets didn't look as pretty, but they opened just as well. My eyes fall on a crumpled piece of paper next to a small trash can tucked under the desk.

Smoothing the ruined paper with my right hand, I squint to read the messy writing. A list, most of it scratched out. It could be from anytime, but something tells me this was written today. The scope and type of activities Brynn planned are not the sorts of things one can achieve with a baby in tow. It's a week's worth of things to do. No way could she accomplish all these tasks in the few hours I watched Cody.

Confused, I pull the black chair out, the wheels sliding easily on the tile floor. Holding onto the edge of the marble desk, I fall into the seat, my hip joints groaning on the way down. It's good to sit. My body molds to the comfortable chair, and I worry I won't be able to get myself back up from such a place.

"Where are you?" I whisper, fingering the scrap of paper. I glance around the rest of the work area. A sticky note reminds someone to get an oil change. A phone number with no context is scribbled on another. A cell phone is plugged into a charger. With a growing sense of fear, I pick it up and tap the screen. A photo of Cody sleeping pops up on the screen, along with the time: 7:13.

I'm not sure where Brynn is, but I know there aren't many places she'd go without her phone. Breathing deeply, I try to stem the panic threatening to overwhelm me. Every explanation for an unlocked house and phone left behind is worse than the last.

Struggling to stand, I almost lose my balance, the wheels spinning out from beneath me too quickly. I grab the desk, catching myself before something truly terrible happens. *Get yourself together!* Bumbling about like a chicken with its head cut off won't help anybody, certainly not Brynn. Cody needs me to stay calm.

I shuffle to the stroller and find Cody awake but content. But I know he'll be hungry again soon. Always hungry. I'd forgotten how often babies need to eat. Eat, poop, sleep, repeat. This reminds me—I need to change his diaper. It's been too long. I don't want him to get a rash. Richard used to get terrible diaper rash.

But first, I need to check the rest of the house. At first, I hoped to find Brynn safe inside the house. Now, I hope she's safe somewhere else. Because if she's upstairs . . .

I shake my head, refusing to finish the thought. Standing at the bottom of the landing, I take a deep breath and grip the railing. The stairway looks to be about a mile long. Like the walk over, the only way to get there is to get there one step at a time.

This house is massive. I turn right, opening the first door I come to. A linen closet. Another door. The bathroom. A few more steps leads me to an open door, revealing a tastefully decorated guest bedroom, empty.

At the end of the hall is yet another closed door. I knock this time but am not surprised that the only sound I hear is the echo of my fist against the wood.

"Brynn?" I call for what feels like the hundredth time. The door opens without so much as a squeak of the hinges. Gingerly I take a step, the plush carpet cushioning my footsteps. This bedroom is much larger than the other, with a sitting area to one side, complete with its own fireplace. An arched opening leads to an attached bathroom. I spy an antique clawfoot tub that might make me green with envy at another time. Filled with dread, I cross the room to check the rest of the bathroom. No Brynn.

Backing from the room, I finish checking the opposite side of the hall, but to the same end. Brynn isn't here. While I'm relieved I didn't find her unconscious in the shower, the mystery intensifies. If Brynn isn't in this house, it means she's out in the world someplace, without a phone. Considering the contraption is usually glued to her wrist, this is akin to her leaving the house naked. I'm not sure which state leaves her more vulnerable.

The crushing weight of responsibility threatens to overwhelm me. I'm too old for all this. What was I thinking, offering to watch an infant? My body is bone-tired, and my mind is weary from the stress of these last few hours. The prospect of an evening worrying over Brynn's whereabouts and Cody's well-being loom before me. Brynn laughed when she gave me the extra milk earlier, but I'm down to my last bottle. I imagine she has plenty stored in the freezer, but I can't be sure. I'm not sure about anything.

Cody's soft cry spirals up the stairs and winds down the hallway. Although I'm filled with more questions than answers, I know attending to his needs requires my immediate attention. Bracing myself against the wall with my right hand, I begin the long descent back to the kitchen. One step at a time.

★　★　★

Cody finishes his last bottle in record time. For a baby that supposedly hates bottles, he's sure adjusted quickly. Thank goodness for small blessings. The day would have gone much differently had he refused to eat. Perhaps this would have kept Brynn home. Perhaps then she wouldn't be missing.

She's not missing, I tell myself as I rinse the bottle in scalding hot water. *She's just lost track of time*, I insist. But the logical part of my brain is not so sure. There are a million different scenarios, each worse than the last, that might explain Brynn's failure to pick Cody up on time.

While Cody lies on a play mat in the sitting room, I wander aimlessly around the kitchen. I've always done my best thinking while puttering, a habit I learned from Freddie. I should call him. He'd know what to do. He was always so level-headed in a crisis. When Richard choked on a grape handed to him by his older sister, Freddie didn't hesitate before flipping the poor child over on his lap and administering five rapid blows between his small shoulder blades. The perilous fruit soared from Richie's puckered mouth, leaving him gasping for air. All the while I stood watching, frozen with fear. I couldn't move until Richard was coughing and crying, arms stretched in my direction.

I didn't waste any time scolding Katherine and sending her to her room. Looking back, I wonder if she was truly only trying to share. At the time, it seemed purposeful. Now I'm not sure.

Kyle! Brynn's husband should be called. I'm angry at myself for neglecting to come to this obvious conclusion sooner. Here I am, thinking Freddie might be of help, when clearly Brynn's own husband would have a better idea of where his wife is.

I head to the compulsively organized desk and scan the Post-it Notes and papers pinned to the corkboard. Pinned to the far-right corner is a sheet of computer paper with a list of emergency contacts printed neatly in bold font. Below the fire department and police are Kyle's cell and office numbers.

A portable phone rests on the cradle at the back of the desk. When I pick it up, I'm relieved to hear the beautifully familiar sound of a dial tone. I punch in Kyle's cell number, since Brynn said he was at dinner tonight and would be home late. Just before I begin to give up on him answering, it connects.

"Hello?" A deep voice comes across the line. In the background I can hear laughter, the sounds of a busy establishment.

"Kyle?" My hand shakes on the receiver, and I pin it closer to my ear. "It's Joy from around the corner."

A pause. "Who?" The man asks, confusion clear in his tone.

"Your neighbor, Joy? I'm babysitting Cody this afternoon," I say, even though this afternoon has faded into evening and is rapidly approaching night.

Another pause. The background noise fades, and I can hear him breathing harder on the other end of the line, as if he's walking with the phone pressed to his mouth.

"I'm sorry, I couldn't hear you well," he says politely. His voice is low and soothing, matching the face of the man I see staring up at me from the framed photo on the desk. "Did you say you were babysitting?"

The stricture in my chest tightens. "Yes. Brynn asked me to watch Cody while she ran a few errands this afternoon. I live around the corner . . ." I wait for a note of recognition but am rewarded with more awkward silence. "On Pickman Street?" I add.

Kyle clears his throat. "I'm sorry, she didn't mention it," he says. Another pregnant pause.

I sigh, any hopes of Kyle being the missing puzzle piece fading quickly. "Brynn was supposed to pick Cody up at five. When she didn't return, I walked over to your place to check on her, but she's not here. She's left her phone . . ." I close my eyes and swallow. "I'm worried about her."

"She was supposed to be there at *five*?" Kyle stammers, his confusion turning to alarm. "That's three hours ago," he mumbles, as if I couldn't tell him exactly how many minutes I'd been waiting on his wife. "Brynn isn't late," he states.

"I didn't know who else to call," I say, my voice cracking as my fears are confirmed. *Brynn isn't late.*

He mutters under his breath, my hearing not quite sharp enough to tell exactly which curse word this situation warranted, but I'm betting it's a doozy. "I'll be there in an hour."

The line goes dead.

Although not convinced I should no longer be afraid, I am relieved that the burden is no longer mine to bear alone. I head to the cooler bag and take out the last of the milk Brynn left, and pour it into the bottle. Before taking it to Cody, I remove a frozen baggie from the freezer, the date and amount written in Brynn's neat handwriting across a blue label. Running the hot water, I find a bowl to submerge it in. By the time Cody's hungry again, it should be perfectly warmed and ready. Satisfied I've done all I can, I make my way into the den to feed the baby, eager to rest my weary legs and prepare for what comes next.

◆ 21 ◆

BRYNN

July 8

Mom guilt is real this week! Baby Montgomery is craving pretzels and sleep, but baby's big brothers would much prefer mommy hang out and play. Each time I say no to their pleading faces, my heart breaks a little, but I know I have to prioritize taking care of myself so I can be a better mom to all four. The struggle is real!

Talk to me, Mommas. What you do you to alleviate the mom-guilt?

—3BoysMamaMonty

I'VE SAT HERE FOR hours, looking out at where the ocean meets the sky. I lost track of time and never bothered to go find it. At some point the sky began to darken, the pale pink along the eastern horizon turning red and then magenta before fading to near black. (*"Red sky at night . . ."*) The lights on the marina sparkle. People mill about, some taking advantage of the beautiful weather by unmooring for an evening sail, and others floating to the dock, where they tie up and descend to the pier, heading downtown. A couple who I watched motor in have already returned, their laughter mixing with the

loud music blasting from the tiki bar a short distance off
the shore. Kyle and I bought tickets to the ninety-minute
harbor cruise last summer and had a great time. I wonder
if Joy's husband knows the couple who run it. They are
much younger, but Salem's a small town, and I wouldn't
be surprised if all the boaters knew each other. I'll have
to ask her when I get back.

Whenever *that* may be. I should've picked up Cody
hours ago. Even though I have a terrible natural sense
of time and depend on my iPhone to keep track of the
day, I'm aware I'm more than a little late. I'm a lot late.
Joy must be worried sick, and Cody is going to run out
of bottles. I keep waiting for the guilt to hit me. Closing my eyes, I anticipate a surge of panic or urgency to
return home to my baby. But it doesn't come. Instead, I
am relieved. I'm at ease for the first time in a long time.

My stomach growls and I remember I haven't eaten
since before leaving the house. Somewhere on my
destroyed to-do list was a bullet point to *eat healthy* and
really kick-start my weight-loss journey by eating more
salads and drinking more water. But like the rest of that
dreadful list, it's not going to happen today. It was the
wishful thinking of a delusional woman.

Currently, I'm craving a cheeseburger and fries with
a large Diet Coke with extra ice and a lemon. The burger
bar on Wharf Street is—*was*—a favorite of ours before
Kyle and I stopped having favorite places. If only I hadn't
left both my phone and wallet at home, I'd head over
now and slide all alone into the corner booth, enjoy a
Texas burger, medium rare.

A city bus squeaks to a stop across the street, the air
brakes hissing angrily. I swivel so I can get a better look
and see a few lone travelers unload from the bus before
being replaced by an equal number of passengers looking

to get away. From my bench, the front panel with the digital destination sign is not readable. This bus could be going anywhere or nowhere. The irrational urge to run across the street and catch that bus comes over me, and I grab the edges of the bench with either hand to cement myself in place. The fingers of my right hand press into the semisoft putty of a recently chewed wad of gum.

Where would I go if I could leave it all behind? My mind wanders as I indulge in this forbidden fantasy. I wonder if all moms feel this overwhelming need to escape or if it's only me. This morning Monty admitted she felt guilty for neglecting her three sons while pregnant with her fourth child. But she has a good excuse for checking out. When I was pregnant, the exhaustion and cravings were all-consuming. I can't imagine managing the morning sickness and swollen ankles while also caring for other babies. While pregnant, I expected to be cared *for*. I milked my condition for all it was worth. Kyle made me ginger tea when I was nauseous and indulged in my every appetite whim, making special trips to Wendy's for a bacon cheeseburger and Frosty or to the grocery store for Cheetos and cream cheese when that is the only thing that would satisfy my urges. He rubbed my feet and helped shave my legs when I could no long bend over. Pregnancy wasn't always the most comfortable experience, but it wasn't all bad. I embraced motherhood so eagerly when Cody was tucked safely inside me. I waited for his arrival with bated breath, sure having him on the outside would be even better. What I wouldn't give to be eight months pregnant again, indigestion and all.

Kyle and Cody deserve better than me. They deserve a wife and a mother who can keep it together, do more than the bare minimum. Every day since Cody was born has been a struggle to survive. Even the simple tasks of eating and sleeping, the most basic of human functions, are nearly impossible. My to-do list gets longer and longer. I'm lucky if I manage to shower twice a week. Grocery shopping is so difficult I've sourced it out. How did I dare to jot down so many trivial and unnecessary things on my list when my house was a disaster and I'd neglected to fill in even one page of Cody's baby book? How selfish am I to prioritize a massage and haircut when I haven't sent a single thank-you card or taken Cody to meet any other babies at one of those Mommy and Me playgroups everyone talks about? The poor kid will have no social skills, will turn into a hermit like his mother. Cody deserves a mom who will celebrate his milestones and has enough wherewithal to share them with friends and family. Kyle's mom is constantly messaging me to post more pictures, but who has the time for that? Other mothers, that's who. Better mothers.

The bus pulls out into traffic. The man behind the wheel of an orange sports car lays on the horn, announcing its abrupt departure from the curb. Unperturbed, it slowly shifts into gear, in no rush to make way for an impatient commuter. If I run, I could catch it. I used to be a fast runner, but my speed is one of the many things I've lost. My gaze follows the taillights as they fade into the distance, heading west out of town, into another life.

Standing, I lift my arms above my head and stretch my stiff limbs. This is the longest I've sat in quite some time. My arms are so light without my thirteen-pound load weighing them down. I debate my options and find I only have two.

I begin walking east. Slowly, at first, but with every step my pace quickens. I don't have far to go.

♦ 22 ♦

JOY

July 8

About here, she thought, dabbling her fingers in the water, a ship had sunk, and she muttered, dreamily half asleep, how we perished, each alone.

—Virginia Woolf, *To the Lighthouse*

KYLE PEELS INTO THE driveway forty-eight minutes later. Unable to work the fancy remote control, I've been forced to watch the clock above the couch instead of the television. Although, I don't think even *Grace and Frankie* could've distracted me from the agonizing passing of time, each minute Brynn didn't walk through the door was one more minute she might be out there alone, in distress.

"Hello?" Kyle calls into the kitchen, his footsteps hurried and loud on the tile as he approaches. "Brynn?" I recognize the tone in his voice. Hopeful desperation. The same tenor as when I beckoned her earlier.

Cody sleeps soundly in my arms. I meant to transfer him to one of the various places I've spotted in the room: the bassinet, some pillow contraption, a swing. But he was so peaceful I didn't want to risk waking him. His weight in my arms reminded me I needed to stay awake. Remain diligent. Holding him close, his small body served as a talisman against the ever-increasing fear running through my veins.

"Brynn?" he repeats, rounding the corner and catching sight of me sitting on the couch. His shoulders sag. I'm not his beautiful wife, home safe and sound with his sleeping son. I'm nothing more than a stranger to this man.

"I'm Joy," I say as way of introduction. "Sorry we have to meet under these conditions."

Kyle nods, his brow furrowing. He opens his mouth, but nothing comes out. The poor man is stunned silent. It's not every day you're called home because your wife is missing. *Missing.* The word sends chills down my spine. *Late.* I correct. Brynn is late, not missing.

"Cody's been a doll," I whisper, snuggling him a little closer to my chest. "He had a bottle right after I got off the phone with you, and promptly fell asleep on finishing it." If nothing else, I can assure Kyle that his son is safe. I can do that much.

Kyle runs a hand through his sandy-blond hair, the same color I imagine Cody's will turn once the pale fuzz starts to grow out. He meets my gaze, his eyes laser-focused. In an instant, I know that if anyone can find Brynn, it's this man. That is the stare of a man on a mission.

"Thank you," he says, smiling down at Cody. But the smile is short-lived. "Tell me everything."

I do as he asks, but there isn't much to tell. After our phone call, I gathered Brynn hadn't told Kyle I was watching Cody. Before, this didn't concern me. I truly believed she intended to run some errands and come back in plenty of time—no need to bother her husband with the details. But after I finish telling Kyle the whole story,

I realize he knows very little about me in general. When he expresses confusion as to why Brynn would walk to my house, I begin to understand the truth: Kyle has no idea who I am. The look of shock on his handsome face when I tell him Brynn visits my house several times a week is almost comical.

"I knew she was spending time with friends from the neighborhood," he mumbles, biting the tip of his thumbnail. "Tracy? And the other two she always talks about. Abby . . ."

"Avery and Monty," I correct, wondering exactly what Brynn told him. "She talks about them sometimes," I start. It seems my suspicions surrounding Brynn's mom friends may be grounded in truth. However, I'm hesitant to reveal the details of our private conversations. Brynn trusts me with her secrets, and I'd hate to betray her unless absolutely necessary. I might just be the old lady from around the corner to Kyle, but in my heart I know I'm Brynn's friend. Possibly her only true friend right now.

He shakes his head. "Do you think she's with one of them?" he asks, exuding such boyish innocence that I long to hug him. It's something my son might say in this situation, unable to decipher the subtext in the fact that his wife has been lying to him about her whereabouts for months. Or at least omitting some of the truth. I've found men often need to be clobbered over the head with the details before they see the picture clearly.

"I don't think so," I say. "It doesn't seem to me like they have that type of relationship," I add, treading lightly. In reality, I don't think they have much of a relationship at all. But at this point, I'm ready to bang on every door in the neighborhood to find these mom friends if it might lead to Brynn.

"They meet at the park with the kids. Maybe she went there?" he mutters. He holds Brynn's cell in his right hand and punches in a few different number combinations, trying to unlock the stubborn machine. He growls in frustration each time it buzzes at him, refusing him entry. "Fuck," he mumbles. He glances up at me and blushes, endearing him to me. At least his mother taught him good manners. "Sorry. It's locked," he explains, tossing the phone on the couch.

Agatha Christie is one of my favorite authors, and over the years I've read all her books, a few more than once. I close my eyes and think of all the clues Brynn has laid out, inadvertently and on purpose. There aren't many, but this wouldn't stop Hercule Poirot.

"I don't think she'd go to the park," I say, thinking out loud. "But you're on to something. Her car is here, and she left the door unlocked and her phone on the desk," I babble, repeating things we've noted multiple times. "Her purse!" I exclaim, my eyes popping open. "Is it here?"

Kyle leaps from the edge of the ottoman to search the kitchen. A moment later, he returns with a Coach tote bag in one hand and the familiar diaper bag in the other, the same one Brynn brings with her in the stroller each time she visits. The same one she left at my house, only for me to lug it back here.

"Both are here," he says, clearly frustrated.

I hold up a finger. "No, it's okay. This just tells us she doesn't have any money with her, unless she has some cash in her pocket . . ."

"Brynn never uses cash," he says instantly.

"Okay. Good to know. That means she didn't leave here with the intention of buying anything, so that knocks a lot of destinations off the list."

Kyle brightens, warming to the idea of finding Brynn by process of elimination. "Right. Good call," he says, biting his lip. His face falls. "But she's been gone for *hours*," he whispers. "If she doesn't have any money, that means she's just out there. If she were okay, wouldn't she have come home by now?"

The same thought has been crossing my mind all night, no matter how hard I try to replace it with other explanations. Instead of answering, I search the room, scanning for clues. Brynn was here at some point. She must have left something behind that might lead us to her.

Next to the love seat there's a small side table, almost hidden by the large arms of the chair. Lying open, with its tattered old spine up, is my copy of *To the Lighthouse*, the one I've been searching my house up and down for.

"I know where she is."

★　★　★

Kyle pulls into an empty spot alongside the entrance to the wharf. His seat belt is off before he shifts the BMW into park. He insisted I come with him, tucked into the backseat beside Cody, who sucks on his Binky, oblivious to the adult drama transpiring around him. I didn't argue with him as he ushered me to the door, politely walking two steps behind me and helping me to fold my old limbs into the low frame of his sedan, even though I'm sure he wished I would move faster, every second wasted one more second Brynn was missing.

"Here?" he asks, one hand on the door handle and the other gripping the wheel so tightly I can see all the veins in his hand. When I told him where I thought Brynn might be, he looked puzzled but didn't bother to question me. Kyle and my relationship has been forged

by our shared worry over Brynn. There was no room—
or time—for doubt. Later he might wonder why he
so blindly trusted a woman he'd never met before, but
tonight I'm the only window into his wife's true life.
Maybe it's faith, maybe it's fate, but something compels
him to follow my lead.

I nod once. "Yes. The lighthouse." We both look out
the passenger windows to the dimly lit structure at the
end of the wharf. After a blazing hot day, a cold front is
supposed to move down from the north, and the water
is cast in an eerie summer fog, the velvet curtain of the
sky so thick only a handful of stars are bright enough
to twinkle through. The purple haze wraps the Derby
Wharf Lighthouse in its embrace, only it's sharp beacon
of hope shines forth into the harbor.

Kyle takes a deep breath, steeling himself for whatever he might find. I'm not sure which would be worse:
finding Brynn or not finding Brynn. I settle back against
the cool leather seat and rest my hand on the edge of
Cody's car seat. He wraps his fingers around my thumb,
smiling at me. Biting back tears, I smile in return and
close my eyes. We wait.

★   ★   ★

Minutes pass, it might be five or ten, maybe less. It begins
to rain, heavy droplets splattering on the hood of the
car, the windshield. The front door opens and my eyes
blink open. Kyle holds Brynn in his arms like a child, her
own arms wrapped loosely around his neck. Her eyes are
closed but tears glisten down either cheek, sparkling in
the soft glow of the streetlamp.

Kyle lowers her onto the passenger seat, reaching
across her belly to secure the belt. She turns her head
toward the window, her forehead resting against the cool

glass. Kyle looks over the seat at me, and our eyes lock, the fear and concern I feel mirrored back to me.

He rushes around to his side and starts the car without a word. We head down the main road toward their house, the rain falling faster, his wipers unable to keep up with the steady stream. He passes their house.

"Pickman, you said," he says, his voice hoarse and shaky in the heavy silence.

Clearing my throat, I take my hand back from Cody. He's fallen asleep on the short drive. "Yes. The yellow house on the right."

As fast and furious as the storm swept in, it passed just as quick. Two minutes later I'm standing in my driveway, watching the car reverse into the street and speed away. Relief roots me in place. I long to fall to my knees and pray, something I haven't done in ages, not since I was a little girl who believed in miracles. But I left my cane at Brynn's and there's no way I can get myself up and down without it, so I remain standing.

Watching the quiet street, I cross my arms over my chest. The rain swept away the warmth, and there's a chill in the air. Sighing, I head toward the stairs.

The porch light is bright and welcoming. A few moths dance in the beams, reveling in the new temperature. Spot's silhouette is black against the curtain, and I watch as he stretches and meows when he hears the first floorboard creak, eager to meet me at the door. He must be starving. Somewhere in the back of the house the television blares, the volume all the way up. I kick Freddie's boots out of the way and push open the door, unlocked, glad to be home.

◆ 23 ◆

BRYNN

Two months later

*1 in 7 mothers experience depression or anxiety during
pregnancy or postpartum. Since many mothers suffer in silence,
the number could be much higher. You are not alone.*
　　　　—Mothers of Salem Postpartum Support Group

I'M NOT PERFECT AND no one expects me to be. No one is
perfect. Not even Montana Montgomery or the Lulu-
lemon moms at the park. My mother was flawed, and her
mother before her. We are all doing our best to navigate
the seemingly impossible responsibility of motherhood.

If only I could blame my postpartum depression
for all my issues. But if my therapy sessions had taught
me anything, it's that certain traits and habits develop
over a lifetime. The unique nature of a woman's fourth
trimester—that not-often-spoken-about period after she
gives birth—served to heighten the anxieties I already
had. For most of my life I managed my fear of failure
by working harder in school, preparing more than the
next person, being hyper organized. My fear of not
being loved and needed was conquered by being a people pleaser, by always being exactly what the object of

my love needed and wanted. The disconnection I felt with my own mother increased my desire to be the perfect parent. Not once did I consider putting myself in her shoes, trying to understand what her own issues with motherhood might be. I only saw her shortcomings from the position of the forgotten daughter.

Looking at my parents through the lens of my own journey as a parent has changed my perspective. Perception is reality, and my reality has shifted seismically in the last six months. Motherhood has shaken me to the core, my plates permanently altered. I'm no longer the same woman I once was.

My therapist assures me this is all normal. When I dreamed of becoming a mom, I knew things would change. But I wasn't prepared for the magnitude of this transformation. I envisioned Before-Brynn, only with an adorable little sidekick. I imagined a child as the sum of our parts, a simple math equation: Kyle + Brynn = Cody. Turns out, our family is a complicated calculus equation involving infinite variables I'm still figuring out, one problem set at a time. Maybe it's an unsolvable problem that isn't a problem at all, but rather a challenge. A challenge I'll spend a lifetime computing, balancing the scales, forever solving for X and redefining Y.

"Hey babe," Kyle says, striding into the kitchen, holding Cody in his right arm and an empty bottle in his left. "Chugged this sucker," he laughs, tossing it into the sink before kissing me on the cheek. "Any left?" he asks, nodding toward the coffee machine.

"Plenty," I answer, setting two mugs on the counter and busying myself making us each a cup, mine with hazelnut creamer and Kyle's with heavy cream and no sugar. I curb my initial instinct to grab Cody from his arms, to assert my role as sole caretaker. My heart begins to race, so I focus on my breathing, inhaling deeply through my mouth and slowly exhaling through my nose. I pour the coffee, savoring the strong smell of the freshly ground beans. The dark liquid swirls and blends with the cream. Perfection.

Kyle buckles Cody into the highchair. The straps are too loose, but before I can say anything, Kyle fixes them all on his own. Though Cody's not quite old enough to start on solid food yet, he seems to enjoy sitting upright at the kitchen island. Everyday my little boy gets stronger and stronger, his personality shining through. I pull a wooden spoon from the utensil caddy and hand it to him. He promptly lifts it to his mouth and gnaws on the handle. Yesterday he rolled from his tummy onto his back while playing on his activity mat. Kyle and I marveled at his dexterity, videoing his failed attempts to roll back onto his stomach. A strong part of me wanted to google whether he was rising above or falling behind on his monthly milestones. Instead, I watched him coo and explore the world around him, and realized it didn't matter. Cody was exactly where he was supposed to be, and if I spent every moment measuring him against something else, I'd miss what was right in front of me. *Progress.*

"Should we go get brunch somewhere?" Kyle asks. His phone rests facedown on the island, out of reach. I'm not the only one who's trying harder to be present. We've both been struggling, even if it's been in different ways.

Immediately the list of things I'll need to do to prepare Cody and me to leave the house for brunch threatens to overwhelm me. Dr. Harper's steady voice comes to mind, reminding me to take each challenge one step at a time.

If you told me a year ago I'd need a professional to tell me something I once believed was so inherently part of my persona, my DNA, I would have laughed. But I've found comfort in hearing the words coming from someone else's mouth. She's been teaching me methods to alter the way I tackle my lists. Where I once attacked the list, success measured by how quickly and efficiently I could conquer the entire thing, I now set more attainable goals, with the understanding that babies are unpredictable. Therefore, if something needs to be skipped or changed, the list isn't null and void. My lists are no longer set in stone. I write them in pencil rather than pen.

"If you pick the outfit, I'll get him dressed," Kyle offers, smiling in the way that makes turning him down next to impossible. This is a look he's perfected over the years. I chuckle, envisioning Cody using this same expression on me someday. Then on his own girlfriend. A wife.

"Deal," I say, always a sucker for a mimosa and omelet.

At his last checkup, the doctor diagnosed Cody with a lactose intolerance that was contributing to his bouts of colic. Since the appointment, I'd made a few adjustments to both our diets. Giving up cheese has been a sacrifice I feared I couldn't commit to, but it's been life changing. Suddenly my fussy baby didn't struggle to burp after every feeding. The doctor suggested supplementing my breast milk with a special formula. At first, I resisted the idea, but Kyle convinced me to give it a shot. Now I wish I hadn't been so stubbornly proud, brainwashed that *breast is best*. Cody's thriving, gaining weight a little faster and sleeping longer stretches throughout the night. Now that I don't have to pump every three hours to maintain my frozen supply, I see just how time consuming and draining that process has been on both my body and soul. Kyle's even taken over a few of the bottle feedings during the night. I was so worried Cody would have nipple confusion, but now that he's a little older he greedily slurps down every meal, breast or bottle, formula or breastmilk. My baby is adjusting to the changes, and I am too. I've even lost three pounds since giving up cheese. *Progress.*

Sipping the last of my coffee, I prepare myself to pack the diaper bag and start on my list. Kyle grabs my hand and pulls me onto his lap, wrapping his arms around the small of my back. I tense, my internal clock ticking down the minutes since Cody last ate, my brain doing mental gymnastics as it tries to figure out when he next needs to eat and if this will coincide with us sitting down to order brunch.

"Sit," Kyle murmurs, holding me a little tighter. His blue eyes implore my own. "For one more minute."

Diapers, wipes, pacifier, extra bottle, burp rag . . .

He lifts his hand and cradles my face, his fingers warm against my cool skin. Blinking, I force the thoughts to quiet, to be in the moment.

"I love you," he whispers, rubbing his thumb along my lip.

I nod because I know he loves me. For a while, I forgot this. I forgot what his love looked like, so lost in the fog I couldn't see what was right in front of me all along.

"Love you more," I say, because that's what we say to each other. This is us. I lean into his embrace and press my mouth to his, breathing him in. My skin tingles as he runs his right hand up my shirt, gently rubbing my lower back. A wave of desire courses through me, and I want to cry with relief. My desire might have been lost for some time, but not forgotten.

Kyle pulls away first, his cheeks flushed and eyes wild. He glances at Cody who watches us curiously. Laughing, he kisses my forehead. "I mean, we could skip brunch and 'nap' while the baby naps if you want . . ."

I shove him playfully away, letting my hand linger on his chest a beat. "I think we should walk to town, eat some food and tire this guy out so he takes an *extra-long* nap this afternoon."

Kyle smiles and pushes away from the island. "A nice, long afternoon nap sounds absolutely delightful," he agrees. "You get the clothes; I'll pack the stroller."

Before-Brynn would insist on doing it all. But this Brynn, the only Brynn that matters, embraces sharing the load. I head upstairs, the perfect outfit for Cody already picked out in my head. First, I need to change my own clothes, more specifically what I'm wearing *under* my clothes.

★ ★ ★

Cody blessed us with an unusually long afternoon nap. He was a perfect gentleman throughout brunch, sitting quietly in his stroller while his mommy and daddy enjoyed two drinks each, Bloody Mary's for Kyle and mimosas for me. He fell asleep on the short walk back from town and didn't flinch when Kyle transferred him to the crib, even when his Binky fell from his mouth. I watched over the monitor, convinced his eyes would pop open.

My body quickly remembered what to do when Kyle laid me back on the bed. The blinds were closed, but the bright summer sunshine peeked inside, zebra stripes of light fanning across the sheets. Self-conscious, I wanted to slide beneath the covers, protect my stretch marks and dimples. His mouth lingered at my bellybutton and I tensed up, embarrassed at the extra skin where it was once tanned and taut. But as he gently reconnected with every part of me, I relaxed, allowing myself to enjoy the pleasure of each touch without worrying about what was. I could tell by the way he kissed me that Kyle didn't notice any of these things. As he moved above me, I'm sure he wasn't comparing my current body to what it looked like a year ago, or five or ten. It was all in my head and until I got myself out of that prison, I'd never be free.

Now we sit on our back deck, blissfully satisfied and content to enjoy the easy last days of summer. Cody bounces in his rocker, happily pressing the colorful buttons that produce sounds and lights on demand. Kyle holds the Sunday *Globe* open before him but only skims the pages. Reading the paper takes him all day, as he prefers to start on the front page and read straight through to the back.

Yawning, I lift my sunglasses to rest on top of my head. The brush in our backyard is thick behind the wooden fence, and I must squint to see past the tree line. This time of year, everything is still thick and green, the leaves heavy with life, sucking up the last of the humid summer air. Despite the thicket, I'm able to glimpse the fading yellow paint peeling from the back of Joy's house. I see the porch light, turned off now, anchored beside the door.

"I should visit Joy," I murmur, turning to face Kyle. He lifts his gaze from the sports section long enough to look in the direction of our neighbor's property. "It's been too long."

Since *that* night, I've only spoken to Joy twice and both times over the phone. It's not because I don't want to see her—I do. But I haven't been ready. I'm still so ashamed of everything that transpired, and I'm not sure I'll ever get over the guilt of leaving her in such an impossible situation. Looking back, I'm horrified by my actions. Although I know Joy's too kind to hold a grudge, I'm not sure how to even start asking for her forgiveness. I left my infant son with her and gave her no way of contacting me. The stress I caused her is unimaginable. This is bad enough. But on top of this, she also found out I'd been keeping her a secret from my husband and essentially lying about my entire life. Joy was my lifeline after I had Cody, and I treated her terribly. I'm not sure how I can ever come back from that.

Kyle frowns. "Are you ready to see her?" he asks. After he found me barely responsive at the lighthouse, Kyle had a lot of questions. Most of them revolved around my relationship with Joy. Though he claims to understand why I found such solace in the time I spent with her, I know he can't fully appreciate our connection. Sometimes I'm not even sure how or why we found each other. All I know is that I needed Joy in my life, and then when I didn't, I abandoned her. This truth fills me with even more guilt.

"Yes . . ." I sigh, dropping my glasses onto my face again. "No . . . I don't know." I sigh again. "I owe her an explanation," I admit. When we last spoke, I told her I felt better and Cody was doing great, but we didn't go into much detail beyond that. I doubt she even believed me. We may not have known each other very long, but I think we saw each other pretty well.

Kyle nods, folding the paper into thirds before leaning forward to rest his hands on his knees. "Do you want me to come with you?"

I shake my head. Using Kyle as a buffer would be the coward's way out, hardly better than my pathetic attempt to apologize over the phone. Joy deserves better. She deserves the truth. "No, I should go alone," I say. "Maybe I'll bring Cody. Joy won't be able to stay angry at me if Cody's there."

Mustering up my courage, I push myself up from the deep seat of the Adirondack chair. Kyle looks to me, alarmed. "You're going now?"

I shrug. "No time like the present," I kid, my voice as weak as my knees. If he asks me to stay, I will. One word beckoning me to enjoy this beautiful afternoon rather than confronting the one person who witnessed me at my breaking point is all it will take. I hold my breath, wishing he'd both force me to go and beg me to stay.

He searches my face, and I hope he can find my true desire written there, since I certainly don't know it. He hesitates and my chest swells. I wait. But he nods, doesn't beseech me to sit with him a while longer.

Disappointment and apprehension root me in place. Cody is content in his seat, and I hate to disrupt his schedule by packing him up in his stroller. Checking my phone, I see it's almost time for his evening meal. Then it's bath time, story time, and one last feeding before bed. Kyle notices me staring at the screen.

"Babe, I've got him," he reassures me. "You've gone over the nightly list a million times, and if I've forgotten anything, you've also written it down on just about every surface I can think of. I can handle giving the little dude his tub, I promise."

The color rises to my face. Kyle can read me like a book. "I know," I say. "Just looking for any excuse to avoid this hard conversation," I admit. Heaving a sigh, I force a smile. "Wish me luck," I say before bending to kiss the crown of his head.

As I turn to leave, he calls to me over his shoulder. "The cane!"

Confused, I pause in the doorway. "Sorry?"

"She left her cane here when she babysat Cody," he explains. "I put it in the coat closet so it wouldn't get misplaced."

A deep sadness settles across my shoulders, shoving the guilt and shame aside long enough for it to coil its way into my heart so there's no room for anything but the heavy weight of my sorrow. I'd taken so much from Joy: her wisdom, her kindness, her sweet lemonade, and her endless stories. I'd even taken her cane. It's time I return her many favors. Grabbing the mahogany cane from the closet on my way out, I walk briskly to the house around the corner, my olive branch firmly in hand.

♦ 24 ♦

JOY

Mid-September

Friendships, even the best of them, are frail things. One drifts apart.

—Virginia Woolf, *To the Lighthouse*

"MAYBE IF THE BOY got some proper punishment when he was a child, he wouldn't have grown up into the type of man who'd walk out on his family when things got tough," I stammer, unable to hide the accusatory tone in my voice. This wasn't a new argument, but it's been a while since we've actively fought over the matter. "Maybe if you weren't out on the water every damn weekend, he would've had a male role model around to show him the importance of family," I hiss.

Once again, it all comes back to Freddie's mistress: the Ocean. How many ball games did he sneak into late or completely miss because the fish were biting or tourists were throwing money down, demanding to be taken out on holiday weekends, Friday nights. "At least Richard never used to miss Johnny's games," I note, thankful my son was at least wise enough to remember the hurt he felt every time he looked out into the stands and saw the empty seat on the bleachers beside me. "Although, it seems even that might be changing."

Freddie's favorite rebuttal to this argument (all arguments, really) has and always will be silence. Over the years, he's explained in length how his job keeps food on the table and a roof over our head. A few missed games and family dinners was surely worth the stability it afforded us, he maintained. When I became sick of hearing this irritating truth, I contradicted him, even though I knew my logic was irrational. I told him we'd rather be poor and together than rich and alone. Usually, he'd roll his eyes at me since it was never this simple: never this way or that. Eventually, he stopped arguing and let me yell. He'd cancel the next trip, and we'd all make a big fuss as though things had really changed. Then it was back to business as usual a week later. But I won't let him off the hook this time.

"No, you do not get to leave me to handle this all alone," I cry out, close to tears. "What's your excuse now? You're his *father*. Our boy needs you."

Sarah called this morning, the catalyst for all that followed. After texting back and forth a bunch, I finally worked up the nerve to call my dear daughter-in-law, even though I had the sneaking suspicion I wasn't going to like what she had to say. My instincts were correct. Her words didn't surprise me, but they still upset me to the core.

Always pleasant, Sarah wished me good health and was quick to give me an update on the boys. Tyler was excited for school to start after a month spent at a special science-themed camp. Johnny, on the other hand, was dreading his senior year. From the sound of it, my oldest grandson is shaping up to be the same type of student his father once was, more excited about football games and girls than his studies. Sarah expressed anxiety over his college applications and indicated that might not be the path Johnny followed. Back when I was parenting, college or trade school seemed the only options. Apparently, the modern world affords young adults more alternatives, even if Sarah didn't specifically name them.

Once the small talk was finished, a heavy pause filled the space between us. Both of us waited for the other to address the elephant on the line. Politeness is for younger women, I decided.

"What's going on with you and Richard?" I asked. Even still, my question caught her off guard, an audible gasp escaping her throat. "If it's none of my business you can tell me to buzz off," I say, hoping she doesn't do as much. She remains silent. "But I know my Richard, and I can tell something's wrong between you two, and I'm sure he's to blame." I'm not ashamed to admit I've already taken sides on a battle I know nothing about.

After another beat, Sarah laughed, and I laughed along with her. For twenty years she's been like a daughter to me, sometimes more so than my Katherine. We might not share blood ourselves, but we share more than enough blood to bind us. My thick-headed son isn't going to destroy his beautiful family so carelessly, not if I have anything to say about it.

"Don't be shy," I continued, settling back into Freddie's recliner. "What has my son gone and done?"

For the next thirty minutes I listened as Sarah revealed to me how Richard suddenly decided he wanted more from life. One day he was happy enough to be a father to two teenage boys, a loving husband, and a hard-working insurance salesman. The next, he declared this was no longer enough. He wasn't satisfied at work, he complained. He'd never liked his job but felt compelled to stay on to provide for Sarah and the boys, he explained. I heard the quiver in Sarah's voice when she told me Richard was no longer in love with her. According to my son, the boys consumed all of Sarah's energy, and he felt neglected, like their relationship had grown stale over the years. As far as she knew, there wasn't another woman, but she wasn't sure.

"He's been staying at his office," she said finally, her voice heavy with regret. "He has the kitchen and the pull-out bed. It's not ideal, but he seemed very serious about needing to get out of the house to *find himself.*"

I couldn't help but snort. "So, my son is having a very ordinary midlife crisis," I said, shaking my head with disappointment. "How very unoriginal of him."

This made Sarah laugh again, but there was a painful edge to the sound. "I guess you could call it that," she mumbled. "The boys aren't stupid. They've already started planning where they will spend Christmas and summers. I'm pretty sure this is part of the reason why Johnny's so unmotivated about college."

"Have you talked about divorce?" I asked, the last word hardly more than a whisper. I know divorce is more common than a cold nowadays, but it still holds the stigma of shame in my mind. My generation fought to keep their family together, through thick and thin. It wasn't something you outgrew or discarded simply because you were unhappy with yourself. Richard should know better. *Shouldn't he? Does he?*

Sarah sighs. "No, we haven't formally discussed much of anything of substance lately. It's like nothing's changed, but at the same time everything's changed. He doesn't live at home, but he still brings over pizza on Friday nights like everything is hunky-dory. We still sit together at Johnny's games, and he fixed the dishwasher when it started leaking last week," she said, each word punctuated with defeat. "I don't know what's going on, Joy. But I can't live like this much longer."

I resisted my urge to beg her to forgive him. My instinct was to plead with her to be patient, to make excuses for his wayward actions, and justify his poor behavior by confessing my own failures as a mother. Easier for her to blame my shortcomings than those of her idiot husband. But it wouldn't change anything. It might delay the inevitable and alleviate some of my guilt, but Richard will be spared once again and only for a short while. It's time for my son to shoulder his own responsibilities. Whether this ends in his family being saved or not is still to be determined. But no matter how much Sarah and I discuss the problem, there will never be a solution if Richard isn't brought into the fold.

After I hung up the phone, Freddie bore the brunt of my anger. What was our shared culpability as parents of such a weak man? Richard might be an adult now, but it was our duty to teach him better, to set the proper example. Somewhere along the way we'd let him down. I unleashed my shame and fury on the only other person who might understand the burden I bore, and Freddie let me rage without a word of reproach.

"I'm going to text him right now and demand he come over and talk with us," I say, fumbling for my cell phone. "He hasn't been to dinner here in ages. He's due a visit."

Wishing for my reading glasses, I squint to make out the letters on the keyboard. Slowly, I begin typing a message to Richard, hoping to strike a balance between stern and loving. *Motherly.*

> *Good afternoon, my Darling. It's been too long since I've seen you for dinner, and I miss you! I know it's late notice, but if you are available tonight I'll ma–*

But before I can finish offering to make his favorite dish, shepherd's pie with biscuits, the front steps creak and groan. I lift my head from my phone and accidentally hit "Send."

"Shoot," I mutter, unsure if there's some way to rescind the message before it gets to Richard. But the text pops up on the screen, having traveled through the ether in the space of a second and connecting us by ways of my incomplete invitation.

For a brief moment I wonder if it's possible Richard's at the door now, my desire to see him so great he felt the call somewhere deep within himself and decided to surprise me with an unannounced visit. I shake my head. As lovely as that idea may be, there's about the same chance of there being two Wednesdays in a week as Richard standing on my porch.

Someone knocks on the door three times. It's a pattern I haven't heard in weeks. Afraid to get my hopes up, I struggle to lift myself from the chair, wishing my cane was within reach.

"Joy?" Brynn's soft voice calls from behind the closed door.

I struggle to move faster, willing my legs to cooperate and using the wall for support. "Coming, dear," I call back, hoping I don't sound as out of breath as I feel.

Before I can reach the handle, the door pushes open and Brynn enters the foyer. Her brown hair is lighter than the last time I saw her and it's not the only thing that's changed.

"Sorry to drop by unexpectedly," she stammers, blushing. "I mean, I know I always drop by unexpectedly, but . . . you know . . ." the sentence lingers between us.

I'm tempted to ask, *What do I know?* I'm tempted to demand she explain herself, enlighten me to why she hasn't been by even once to see me since that fateful night. I'm tempted to scold her for being rude and selfish. But mostly I want to pull her in close for a hug, ensure that she's really here, standing in front of me. So many times I've imagined this moment.

Studying her face, all the subtle differences come into focus. She's wearing a light pink lip stain and a rosy blush on the apples of either cheek. Her lashes are coated in a layer of black mascara and lined with a dark kohl, causing her eyes to appear bigger and the whites even brighter. The honey highlights in her hair sparkle in the bright sunlight peeking through the curtains. She looks healthy, vibrant. Seeing this version of Brynn is almost shocking. A startling revelation comes to mind: *she was not well this spring.* It's something I always suspected on some level, but since I only knew her the one way, I had nothing to compare it against.

"You look lovely, dear," I say, deciding to repress my urge to take out my frustrations on Brynn, even if she does deserve a piece of my mind. She's been through enough trauma. And even though I thought we were friends, she doesn't owe me anything.

She smiles, tucking a piece of hair behind her ears. I notice a pair of diamond studs glittering in either lobe. Even her clothes are different. Though she was never unkempt, aside from some dried spit up or milk stains, she was never completely put together either. Today she's immaculate. Her silk tank top is tucked into a pair of jeans. Her tan sandals match her belt.

"Thanks," she whispers, the color still high on both cheeks. She lifts her eyes to meet my own. "I'm sorry," she moans, her face crumpling as the words spill out. "I'm so, so sorry," she repeats, her eyes watering.

When Katherine was little, she was constantly apologizing. For everything, big and small. As she got older, I refused to let her get off the hook simply by saying *I'm sorry*. I told her it was the easy way out. So many girls are taught to apologize for everything, for *existing*, it sometimes seems. Because of this, the words have been cheapened by overuse. I taught Katherine to own her mistakes and to never do something that she'd feel the need to be sorry for later. At the time, I thought I was empowering her, making her a stronger woman. I fear I was wrong. Not only is it important to be able to say those two words, but it's just as important to be able to accept them.

Instead of saying anything, I hold my arms out and Brynn eagerly steps into my embrace. We remain this way for a minute before she finally pulls away, wiping her eyes.

"I'm sorry," she mutters again, but this time I hear a slight chuckle beneath the words. "Seems like you're constantly comforting me for one thing or another."

I shrug, waving my hand at her. "Oh, nonsense. We comfort each other," I say, although I'm not as sure anymore. Our dynamic has shifted, and I can't put my finger on how. I peer behind her toward the porch. "Where's Cody?" I ask, worry tightening around my heart.

Brynn sighs and bites her lip. "He was playing with Kyle at home when I left," she says quietly. "I thought we could talk. Just you and me?"

I swallow back the lump in my throat, afraid that by speaking I might unleash all the sadness festering in my chest. So much has changed in the last few weeks, and Brynn's outfit choice is proving to be the smallest of the lot. She waits for me to answer, but I can't look her in the eye. I turn and take a step toward the kitchen before risking my voice. "I'll get us some lemonade," I offer, sounding much stronger than I feel. "Go sit in the living room. I'll be there in a jiffy."

Without waiting for a response, I busy myself setting a tray with two glasses filled with ice. I place the pitcher in the center and add a few homemade oatmeal raisin cookies to a plate.

"Don't you look at me like that," I sigh, refusing to meet his stare. "We're not through talking about Richard." He lifts his brow at me, and I struggle to lift the tray, wishing I'd asked Brynn to help carry it back. Before I can utter one last word at Freddie, he's slipped away.

"Who were you talking to?" Brynn asks as I place the tray on the table, almost tipping the whole thing over in the process.

Smiling, I fall into the armchair facing the couch. "Oh, just a few words with Freddie," I say, shaking my head.

"Oh! I'd love to meet him," she says, glancing down the hallway. "Is he still here?"

I pick up a cookie and take a nibble. Still soft and chewy, even though I made them a few days ago. "Sorry, dear," I say, swallowing and wishing for a glass of milk. "He's likely off cooling his head. He's never been one to stick around too long after an argument."

A look of distress crosses her face, and I almost feel bad. "Don't worry—he'll have forgotten why he was even upset in the first place by the time we go to bed," I joke. Brynn smiles. "Tell me, what did you want to talk about?"

She takes a long sip before clearing her throat and looking up at me from beneath her lashes. "I need to explain what happened at the lighthouse," she begins, her voice trembling. She pauses and I'm afraid she's lost her nerve, but then she closes her eyes. "But to do that, I think I need to go back to the beginning . . ."

★   ★   ★

By the time Brynn is finished talking about the blistering love suffering she experienced, we've both exhausted our tears and drunk an entire pitcher of lemonade. The sun has faded from the sky, and a low rumble of thunder threatens a storm in the distance.

"I should get going before the rain starts," she says, wiping her cheek with one hand and checking her phone with the other. "I can't believe we've been talking for two hours."

The time passed in the flash, and I wouldn't mind listening to her speak for another two. So much is clearer now. But I know she needs to get home to her baby and husband, even though it seems like they are doing okay without her.

"Thank you for sharing this with me," I say, reaching out for her hands and clasping them in my own. "Please, don't be a stranger." I wish it didn't sound like I was begging, but I can't keep the desperation out of my voice. "Maybe you can bring Cody around next time?"

A shadow crosses Brynn's face. I can't tell if it's a trick of the light or my imagination, or if it was really there. When she speaks, it's gone, and she's the same open book I've grown to love these last few months. "Of course," she says, squeezing my hand once before standing. "I'll never forget what you've done for me and my family," she says, the words sounding more final than a simple goodbye, knocking me off balance again.

"It was nothing," I stammer, unable to hide my apprehension. "It's what family does for one another."

Brynn's smile fades as she heads down the hall, and I struggle to keep pace. "Take care of yourself," she says, turning to face me and giving me a fierce hug. "You have my number, right?"

Perplexed at the trajectory of this conversation, I nod. "Yes, dear. I have it."

She steps down into the porch. The wind has begun to pick up, but the rain has yet to start. Soon it will be here. The air smells like salt and wet grass, the perfume of a summer squall. I predict this storm will wipe out this solstice season, Autumn raising her head and claiming her rightful space in time.

"Goodnight," Brynn says, waving quickly before setting down the driveway in an easy jog, eager to escape the weather.

I wave back before folding my arms across my chest, rubbing my forearms against the sudden chill. "Goodnight," I whisper into the darkness.

Standing in the doorway, I wait until I imagine she's rounded the corner and made it to her own house. If she'd kept up her clip, she'd be pushing open her front door right about now. Then she'd be across her kitchen and picking Cody up, ready to relieve Kyle from his watch. As I click the door shut, the rain starts. A few heavy drops splatter on the edge of the stairs, a slow start that is followed by a steady stream from the heavens. With a crack of thunder, the sky really lets loose.

My phone pings from the other room and I hurry back to see who it's from. Maybe Brynn, ensuring she made it home safe.

Everything OK? Did you mean to send that?

Richard. Irritated, I debate what to write back. Luckily, everything *is* okay. If he were really worried, he would not have waited two hours to ask. A more considerate son would've picked up the phone and called to check in, rather than sending a useless text. I chalk this up to yet another parenting failure.

> *Everything's fine. Please let me know if you can come visit this week. We are long overdue for a dinner. XO Mom*

I wait. Those three little dots appear and disappear four times before clearing for good. My granddaughter told me that meant the other person was writing. No response. Disappointed, I drop the phone onto the table and turn on Netflix. As I hit "Play" for my show, the text alert pings again, renewing my faith in my son a tiny bit.

> *It was so nice catching up tonight. I promise to bring Cody by soon. Take care of yourself. <3 We should plan dinner with Freddie and Kyle sometime soon!*

I stare at the screen, trying to decipher the hidden meaning between the letters of this text. Brynn has never texted me before. Our relationship has always been purely in person. It's my favorite thing about our bond. Everything she revealed to me today about her anxiety and depression after giving birth made complete sense. I always knew Brynn was suffering from something more than your typical baby blues. Her confession was truthful. But something about the politeness of this text message rings false. There's no doubt my neighbor looked brighter today than I've seen her. There was a renewed sparkle everywhere from her eyes to her new clothes. Even though I now know she was lying to me about her make-believe friends and pretending to be happy despite the pain she felt inside, I still think *that* Brynn was more honest with me then the girl who showed up today.

♦ 25 ♦

BRYNN

Early October

With the coming arrival of Baby Girl Montgomery, I've decided to shift the focus of my Instagram. My #momtribe has been like an extended family to me, and I want to give back even more. Although I will continue to share pictures of my growing family, I'm expanding my content to focus more on YOU, my tribe. I may be a Mama to four, but you are all my SISTERS in motherhood. I'm looking forward to the next stage of this journey.
   #SisterMamas
   follow me on TikTok @Monty4Mamas

IT TAKES A VILLAGE Party Consulting is still in its infant stage. Scratch that. More like newborn stage. Actually, let's be real. It's still in the expectant stage of things. In my sessions with Dr. Harper, I'd expressed my overwhelming urge to go back to work. Rather than encouraging me to jump right back into what I was doing pre-baby, she urged me to reflect on what specifically about work was calling to me.

   At first, I thought this was a dumb question. Sitting across from her on the soft leather couch, I listed all the obvious reasons: I missed feeling productive, I longed for structure, I craved adult interaction. Most of all, I wanted—needed—to feel accomplished at something. She nodded along and let me finish. When I was done, she told me to go home and consider these desires and what they meant to me now as opposed to *before*.

Lying in bed, Cody sleeping soundly in the bassinet beside me, I try to break down the homework assignment. Working as a party planner always felt like my calling. It was something I was exceptionally good at and brought me joy. I think being the best at something made it all the *more* joyous. Planning beautiful parties that brought happiness to my clients was a special responsibility that fulfilled my creativity and desire to please people. I also loved the control owning my own business lent me, since I often felt control was something I lacked in other aspects of my life. This revelation gives me pause. Maybe Dr. Harper was onto something.

After I gave birth to Cody I was untethered, my identity so shaken I no longer felt like myself. I was unsure of everything and ultimately felt like I was nothing at all. I'd assumed motherhood would shape my new identity, but in the weeks and then months that followed this monumental event, I didn't recognize myself anymore. Now I realize this might be because I'd never been as sure of myself as I once believed.

Before-Brynn was a people pleaser. From a young age, I never thought I fit in. As a result, I created a persona for myself that could perfectly blend in everywhere. Never the life of the party, I literally brought parties to life for other people. Unable to define exactly what I wanted, I got pleasure giving other people exactly what *they* wanted. My social media presence was built around a very specific image that I considered ideal because it is what I assumed other people liked. I was no better or worse than the Montys of the world, curating my brand and only showing the world the piece of myself that had been polished until it shone.

Parties with Brynn was the culmination of all my insecurities, wrapped up in a pretty bow that I labeled my passion.

I leave Cody and Kyle snoring in unison and tiptoe down the stairs. Grabbing my hand-dandy notebook from the counter, I begin outlining what I need, what I want. Work is calling to me, just as I told Dr. Harper. But, like with everything else in my life, it's time for me to take charge and own my desires. I'm beginning to realize I'll never be Before-Brynn again, and this is okay. Just like 3BoysMamaMonty can rebrand herself to Monty4Mamas, I'll be something new and improved. Better. I'll be a mom and a businesswoman. I'll be a wife and a good friend. I'll be all the things.

In the dim glow of the microwave light, I fill my notebook with all my ideas, my hopes and dreams. It Takes a Village was conceived.

★ ★ ★

"Coffee or smoothies?" Ming ponders aloud, her oversized sunglasses making her expression unreadable. We walk side by side, the sidewalk here extra wide. When we get closer to town, we'll have to go single file or risk getting tangled in a dog leash or trampled by a runner.

Wishing for my own sunglasses, I squint against the glare. The heat rises in waves from the pavement. Last week I was convinced we'd have an early winter. This recent hot front has proven me wrong. I pull the brim of my Red Sox cap a little lower on my head. Better than nothing.

"Iced coffees," I answer, the prospect of a creamy iced drink from the Wharf Coffeehouse makes walking in this sweltering heat almost worth it. "And maybe a chocolate éclair," I add.

Ming nods. "Buttered croissant for me," she quips. "They make the best croissants." She sighs, glancing down at the pink Apple watch on her wrist before tapping the screen a few times. "Yes, a pastry is allowed," she says, looking at me and smiling, her bright white teeth stark against the dark stain of her lip gloss. "We've already walked two miles, so we've earned those calories."

I laugh, shaking my head. Ming is constantly counting calories, a leftover habit from a childhood of tagging along with her mother to Weight Watcher's meetings and finding Slim Fasts tucked into her school lunch box. "Shut up," I say, rolling my eyes. "You look fantastic," I reassure her. Looking at her lean body and slim hips, it seems impossible she gave birth to her little girl less than three months ago.

"Old habits die hard," she admits, shrugging.

We walk on in companionable silence, both babies in that state that isn't quite sleeping, but just about. By the time we get to the coffee shop to meet Taylor they will both be out cold.

Ming slows as we round the corner of Pickman. Although she's taking extended maternity leave, she's eager to return to her role as a real estate agent and thoroughly enjoys scouting out the properties with "For Sale" signs popping out of the lawn when we take our weekly walks.

"Yikes. That's very pink," she says, nodding at the big Victorian with a new sign near the mailbox. It's listed with Ming's rival agency. "Huge house with a ton of original details," she comments, sighing. "They are listing it super high, I hear. God knows, they might get it in this crazy market." She turns to me. "Do you know the owners?"

"We never met," I admit, my ears burning red. When the young couple moved in over a year ago, Kyle and I kept meaning to stop by and welcome them to the neighborhood. Although we never got around to it, we know their story. News travels fast in a small town like Salem. "It's so terrible," I whisper, even though the driveway is empty of any cars and the U-Haul filled with their stuff drove away weeks ago. "He was so young."

Ming swallows. "It's awful," she agrees. She clucks her tongue. "Those vultures at Old Salem Realty swooped in before the poor girl could even bury him, I heard," she says, her tone dripping with disgust and maybe a little envy. Sometimes it's hard to tell with Ming. I'm still learning her tones.

She pushes her glasses onto her head, using them to keep her jet-black hair out of her eyes. "Is there a homeowner's association in this neighborhood?" she asks, stopping the stroller and glancing around as if someone might pop out of the bushes to answer her question.

We are parked in front of Joy's house and my heart tugs me in the comforting direction of her front porch. "I don't think so?" I say, but I'm not entirely sure. "We don't have one on Pleasant." I watch her grimace in the direction of the old yellow cape, and I follow her gaze.

"Well, someone should say something to these owners," she says, pointing at my old friend's house.

Frowning, I open my mouth to defend Joy, but bite it closed. Looking at the yard through my new friend's eyes, I see a modest house with a patchy front yard in a sea of gigantic mansions with manicured lawns. The summer wasn't kind to the place. The chipped paint once seemed quirky. Now it looks unkempt and tired. Even

Joy's flower boxes are in sad shape, the roses she took such pride in, overgrown and bedraggled. The grass is in desperate need of a mow in places but then sparse and burnt in the spots where the sun shines brightest. Freddie's truck has a flat tire, and the license plate is missing a screw, the old green letters hanging at a sharp angle.

Apprehension settles in my empty stomach. *When did they let it get this bad?* I wonder. Surely it hadn't looked like this when I'd visited last month. I'm positive the grass was still green, and the front door was not skewed on the hinges. The paint was chipping in places, not peeling and falling off in faded yellow ribbons.

"Brynn?" Ming says again, lifting her brows. "You okay?" she asks, her pretty face lined with concern.

I force a smile but my gut is churning. "Sorry," I sputter, a pathetic laugh escaping my throat. "I know the couple who lives here," I say. Ming blanches and raises a hand to her chest, clearly eager to walk back her earlier criticism. Before she can open her mouth, I wave her off. "No, it's okay," I say. "They are older and have lived here forever."

"That makes sense," she says, clearly relieved. "Maybe we should see if we can help them clean the place up," she says, dropping her sunglasses back into place. "It's a huge property to keep up with," she muses. Even though I don't know her that well yet, I imagine she's already computing how much value Joy's little cape adds or deletes from the neighborhood. If only she knew my friend, she'd know that home and whom it belongs to are priceless.

The house where I spent so many of my lost afternoons calls to me, and I wonder why Joy isn't out on the porch, enjoying the renewed summer with a glass of lemonade. I hope she's inside watching one of her shows, cooling off in front of the old window AC. Maybe Freddie is simply waiting to do a fall cleanup when it's cooler out. This hot weather can't be healthy for an older man. This must be the reason for the weary exterior of the place. Once the hot spell breaks, I'm sure Freddie will mow up the lawn, and Joy will be back in the garden, tending her beautiful flowers. This rationalization eases my mind, but I make a note to check back in later.

"Ready?" Ming asks, already a few steps ahead of me.

I spare one last look at Joy's house and swear I see the curtains move. Staring at the window, I wait for Joy's face to fill the space. But I don't see Joy's smile and she doesn't wave at us. Nothing moves at all, and I wonder if it was a mirage, my eyes playing tricks on me in the heat, willing me to see something I so desperately wish to see.

"Yes," I say, my voice too loud in my attempt to ignore my misgivings. Ming doesn't notice, bounding forward toward town and our expensive iced coffees and decadent pastries. It would be so easy to push my worries to the back of my mind and push forward into this new life I'm creating with my new mom friends, an amazing group of women I met at the postpartum support group held at the local yoga studio. So easy, that it's exactly what I do.

The farther we stroll from Pickman Street, the lighter I feel. As we pass into the village, I tell myself the yard didn't look as bad as I thought. As the bells on the coffeeshop door jingle and we hug Taylor before ordering, I have convinced myself Joy and Freddie are perfectly fine. They've been living in that house so long, they don't need nosy neighbors stepping in and making them feel helpless. As I sip my coffee, I tell myself I'll visit Joy later this week. Or maybe a call. Something to let her know I'm thinking about her.

✦ 26 ✦

JOY

October 16

She could not say it . . . as she looked at him she began to smile, for though she had not said a word, he knew, of course, he knew, that she loved him. He could not deny it. And smiling she looked out of the window and said (thinking to herself, Nothing on earth can equal this happiness)—"Yes, you were right. It's going to be wet tomorrow. You won't be able to go." And she looked at him smiling. For she had triumphed again. She had not said it: yet he knew.
—Virginia Woolf, *To the Lighthouse*

FALL IS FREDDIE'S FAVORITE time to fish. As the water temperatures cool with the change in seasons, he sets out later in the day, claiming the afternoon and early evening is the best time to catch anything. After the sun is directly overhead a few hours, the water gets more comfortable near the surface, and the fish start biting. I suppose it makes sense. Fifty years married to a fisherman, and I still can't tell you whether fish like cold water or warm, rain or shine. Maybe it depends on the fish. Mostly I think it depends on my husband. It seems as though his favorite weather to fish in is whatever weather we happen to wake up to.

Our first fall in Salem was hard. Not only was Mother Nature intent on ushering in an early winter, but the bills were piling up. First the boiler was on the fritz. We knew it was due to be replaced when we bought the place, but we thought we could eke out one more winter with the old tank. No such luck. It might have been okay except it was a colder than average October, the temperatures dipping below freezing most nights. More than once I threatened to pack the babies up and drive straight back to Maine unless he called a repairman. I think seeing poor Richard dressed in a snowsuit instead of pajamas is what finally kicked Freddie into gear.

On top of all this, the boat needed this, that, and the other thing. *An investment in our future,* Freddie promised as I watched our bank balance dwindle. Thankfully he was right, and in the spring the money he put into the old girl came back twofold.

But that fall I was pinching together two pennies to keep food on the table, and wearing wool sweaters to sleep, the two babies snuggled underneath four quilts between us in bed to stay warm.

Brady Thompson, the local weatherman back then, predicted snow squalls to begin around five in the afternoon. The forecast called for high winds and rough waves. A weather system was brewing in the west, and the barometer was plummeting. Even I knew this was bad news. The real doozy, according to the handsome young Brady, was a storm traveling our way from the east. If the two systems collided, the coast would be hit hard. All these dire predictions directly conflicted with the bright sunshine and cloudless sky outside our windows. The only indication something might be brewing was the early morning red sky and the way the wind whipped through the last scattering of leaves on the trees, flipping them upside down and sending them tumbling to the ground with their fallen brothers. Freddie and Jim were chasing a school of bluefish and stripers that had eluded them the last few days. They feared the fish would head out of the area soon, and were desperate to cast their reels before they missed the opportunity.

I begged him to stay. (Is this the same story as before? Or am I always begging Freddie to stay. The storms all blend together. The reasons all blur.) Like so many other times, he laughed and assured me there was nothing to worry about. This time he made fun of me for listening to the local news, claiming a man who combed his hair with that much gel couldn't know a thing about the sea.

"I know you fancy that young bloke, but I don't trust him to tell me which way the winds are blowing," Freddie snorted, even as he packed an extra raincoat and wool socks in his bag. "By the look of 'im, I'd say he ain't one to brave the elements that often. A gentle breeze might knock a few of those slicked down hairs outta place, and he'd call it a hurricane."

I know it was irrational, but his flippant manner and general disregard for my opinion (even if my opinion was based on a sometimes unreliable weatherman) sent me into a tailspin. As he packed his bag that morning, I raged on and on. I yelled until I was blue in the face, cursing him for caring so little about his family and risking his life for a few silly fish (fish this time, charters and clients another, but always the same: the Ocean.) When he settled his bag by the door like he always did, I grabbed it and ripped the clothes from inside, sent them flying around the foyer. Calmly, he retrieved his items and put them back in place. He zippered the duffel and tossed it onto the front lawn, out of reach.

I'm ashamed to admit I held the children hostage in front of him (not the first time, I'm ashamed of each and every one.) When he tried to kiss Katherine and Richard goodbye, I pulled them to my side and forbid Kathy from speaking to him. She looked up at me with such confusion in her eyes—the look still haunts me. But it was all I could do. The kids were my bargaining chip. Freddie stood in the entrance, his anger at me palpable. He was too good of a father to unleash his fury in their presence (this never stopped me; let them see hell hath no fury like a woman scorned.) My temper was never in my command. With one last long look, his shoulders sagged, and he shook his head at me.

"I love you all the most," he said, staring me in the eye. I looked away, buried my face in Richard's curls. Kathy whimpered at my side, and I gripped her shoulder (too hard.) Richard was clueless to the drama and tugged on strands of my hair, putting a few pieces in his mouth.

Freddie turned and walked out. With my free hand I grasped my mother's antique vase from the side table and heaved it after him (or was it the ashtray? A dinner plate?) It shattered against the closed door. Moments later, his truck roared to life, and tires crunched over the gravel driveway as he drove away.

"How could you leave us then?" I mumble, swallowing back the memories bubbling to the surface.

Sitting in the living room, I can see the table in the foyer. After a few years, I stopped leaving anything breakable on its expanse.

Time slips away again. One moment I'm a young woman standing stubbornly at the door, fierce in the belief that I was right. The next I'm an old lady, filled with regret. Hindsight proves to be more painful than I care to admit.

I almost left that day. Ironically, only the weather stopped me. Although I had my license, I hated to drive, especially at night. The skies were dark and cloudy by three PM, and there was a layer of fog over the roads, the cool air hitting the sun-warmed blacktop.

The rain began around five, starting slow and steady but building until I could hear the hail pellets hitting the tin roof of the little shed off the side of the house. The kids and I ate macaroni and cheese and watched a movie before bed (*The Wizard of Oz*). I locked the front door so I'd hear him when he got home

In bed, I tried not to watch the clock on the wall, but there was nothing else to do. Sleep would not come. At ten past ten I heard keys in the lock, followed by the click of the heavy front door closing. My initial relief was replaced by anger in an instant. I removed my arm from beneath Richard who was nuzzled against my shoulder, his thumb in his mouth. Kathy snored on his other side. I tiptoed down the stairs, sidestepping the creaky step near the landing. I shiver against the damp cold that's settled into the house.

Freddie sits at the dining room table, his back to me. His shoulders shake and water drips off the rain slicker he neglected to remove. Water drops stain my hardwood floor. I hover in the doorway, thankful he's home safe but torn, in equal parts, between my desire to embrace him and slap him.

He lifts his head and sees me in the reflection of the window. We make eye contact.

"I'm sorry," he says, his voice raspy. "I should've listened to you." He drops his head before turning to face me. Tears stream down his cheeks. "I won't do it again."

Biting back my own tears, I nod and cross the three steps from the doorway to the table. I kneel in front of him and rest my cheek against his knee, not caring that he's freezing cold and soaked to the bone. He folds over me, pulling me tight against him. After he cries his piece, I lead him up the stairs to the hallway bathroom. I run a hot shower and help him peel off his wet clothes. Our tears mingle with the water and spiral down the drain. He kisses me deeply, his pain and regret softening the edges of my fury.

After we've dried off and dressed, we tuck ourselves in on either side of the kids, our meager queen-sized mattress barely big enough for the four of us. Freddie is asleep instantly, his breathing deep and rhythmic a moment after his head hits the pillow. I don't succumb as easily. His promise lingers (he's made this promise before), and though I want to believe he's a man of his word, I know he can't resist the lure of the sea. This won't be his last time apologizing for something he's sworn to never do again (it's not.)

"And I was right to worry," I whisper, staring across the foyer to the dining room, the image of Freddie crying into his hands as clear as day. Spot jumps into my lap, and the image dissipates, the table empty again. Time shuffles.

Kathy insists global warming is to blame for the never-ending summers we've had these last few years. August fades into September, which lingers into October. The leaves take longer to color and then they fall all at once, as if autumn is the forgotten child, summer and winter taking Mother Nature's favor.

Today the sun shines as brightly as in July and nearly as hot. The good weather calls Freddie to the boat more than it should. He worries his time on the sea is coming to an end, and he needs to take advantage of the mild temperatures while he still can. On the one hand, I agree. The years have taken the edge off some of my resentment. I'm glad my husband has a passion as we enter our twilight years. My friend Gayle complains about what a bitter man her husband has become after he retired, devoid of hobbies. But Freddie's blood pressure is too high, and he refuses to slow down or change his hab-its, even when the kids and I warn him of what might happen. My stubborn husband waves us off, calls himself the picture of health. But he's nearing eighty-five, and though he acts like a young man sometimes, he's starting to show his age.

This last time, the anger came back with a vengeance. It ignited within my chest, where it had been latent for years, a slow fire smoldering and waiting for a spark. The forecast is clear: sunshine and light winds for the next three days. Freddie promised it was only a short trip, one night at most. It was Freddie and a few buddies looking to chase any striper lingering outside the bay.

I'm not sure what lit the flame. Something loomed on the horizon, a fog of dread worse than the red sky of morning all sailors fear. I begged for him to stay home with me (again), pretending I needed help in the garden. When that failed, I threatened him. I told him if he walked out that door, he shouldn't bother coming back. I didn't have the kids to wield as a weapon, but I hoped maybe I was enough (never enough.)

Like so many times before, he told me he loved me the most and walked out the door. Jim was in the drive-way, waiting to pick him up. They were going out on some fancy new schooner belonging to Jim's son.

The sun passes over the house, leaving the living room in shadows but I don't move to turn on a light. I wait, petting Spot and reliving the first fight (or the sec-ond or twelfth or fiftieth), wondering who was right and who was wrong and if it even mattered, now or then or ever before.

♦ 27 ♦

BRYNN

October 16

Check in on your friends. Motherhood is hard and impossible to do alone. They always say it takes a village to raise a baby, but where is the village? If you need some help—whether you want to plan a first birthday party for your babe or need someone to help with the groceries and housework, It Takes A Village Consulting can help you with all your motherhood needs. We're here for you.

—ItTakesAVillage Instagram account

I WISH I'D SOUGHT help sooner. So intent on pretending to be the perfect mother, I tricked myself into believing I was fine, even though every fiber of my being was screaming for help. Things were on their way to becoming much, much worse.

"Why do you think you put so much pressure on yourself to be such a perfect mother?" the group leader asks of no one in particular. Most of the questions she asks apply to us all, a room full of women struggling with postpartum anxiety and depression. Désirée herself struggled with the condition after experiencing a stillbirth at thirty-nine weeks, followed by a subsequent healthy pregnancy. Once her rainbow baby was born, she was terrified something awful would happen to him. These intrusive thoughts, a common symptom of PPD, made her a prisoner in her own home. She was terrified for the safety of her entire family and often believed she was a danger to herself and all those around her. She's very open about her battle to get well, and her transparency makes everyone in the room more comfortable sharing their own stories, myself included.

Tentatively, I raise my hand. Désirée has told me more than once that we could all speak freely, no need to raise our hands like in school. But I can't help it. It's instinctual, residual good-girl behavior that I'm exploring with Dr. Harper. She nods at me, smiling. "At first, I thought it was because I've always been a perfectionist in everything . . . school, work . . . life in general," I start, chuckling to myself. "Based on this, I wasn't surprised that I expected to be a perfect mom." Looking around the room at the dozen other ladies, I see myself mirrored in their faces, in the eager ways they listen to my story, desperate for connection. It gives me the strength to continue. "Of course, I'm also obsessed with social media and seeing account after account filled with baby pictures and the beauty of motherhood only made me want that type of life even more." I admit. "You know, the Insta-perfect life."

Désirée nods. "Social media can be both a blessing and a curse. I remember being so jealous of the moms I followed who seemed so put together all the time. I was envious of them, but I didn't hate them. I wanted to be them."

Murmurs of agreement around the circle as we all exchange knowing glances. I don't think a single person could say they were immune to the effects these perfectly curated lives have on us, for better or worse.

"Now that I've had some time to think about things, I'm not sure this is the entire reason," I continue. Biting my lip, I wonder how much to divulge and weigh whether telling the whole truth will endear me to these women or separate me further. I realize it doesn't matter. I'm through with telling lies. "I've started going to therapy and taking an antidepressant, which helps immensely. This group has been like a lifeline throughout this. I don't know what I'd do without you all," I say, blinking back tears that seem always ready to fall.

"I've come to realize I was overcompensating. After I got married, it seemed like the next thing to do was to have kids. I mean, I've always liked kids. But I didn't have that primal urge to have children. I wasn't sure if I was too young or too old or when the right time for kids would be," I admit, looking down at my hands. I know a few people in the group struggled with infertility and loss, and I don't want them to think I'm ungrateful for my blessings. It's a fine line women walk. Sharing our story puts us at risk of alienating ourselves from some and binding us to others. "Then I got pregnant, and it seemed like the universe had decided for me. I was thrilled, of course. But I wonder how much of my excitement was over the details: the pregnancy announcement and the baby shower and all the attention you get while pregnant, instead of excitement over the baby itself."

Ming nods at me, smiling her encouragement. I forge ahead, hoping I'm not babbling incoherently. I do have a point somewhere. "When Cody came along, I didn't feel that instant spark everyone promised me, and this destroyed me. It didn't help that nothing went according to plan when he was born. If you know me, then you know I love a good plan," I say, laughing at myself, along with a few chuckles from my friends in the circle. "It seemed like I was already failing before I'd even started. I wasn't used to failure, and I'm terrible at asking for help. So I used a phrase my mom always tossed about: *"Fake it until you make it."* Unfortunately, you can't fake being a mom." A new member of the group nods in my direction, and we lock eyes. *She gets it.*

"Anyway, I was terrified all the time and thought if only I believed hard enough, I could force myself into being okay. Turns out, I wasn't okay."

My hands shake on my lap, and I tighten them into fists, burying them between my legs. Despite the amazing progress I've had in therapy and these group sessions, talking about my depression isn't any easier. Admitting something is hard will never be easy for me.

The newest mother to the group raises her hand, and I smile. Another type-A, Goody Two-Shoes. Désirée spirals in her direction, nodding for her to speak up.

"I'm Judy," she starts, her voice lower than expected. Her halo of bouncy red curls and the scattering of freckles on her cheeks make her look preternaturally young. The hoarse baritone of her speaking voice takes me by surprise. "I gave birth in January, so my little guy is ten months." Only a little older than Cody, I'm delighted to learn. Visions of playdates in the park dance in my head already. "I'm struggling," she cries, her lip trembling. "I'm not married, and I live here alone. I've tried to make some friends, but it's so hard," she murmurs. "Whenever I try and talk to the other moms, I'm pretty sure they think I'm the nanny or the big sister." She shrugs, laughing bitterly. "I'm afraid I made a huge mistake moving here."

I notice a few of the other moms in the group looking sheepishly down at their hands, their purses, anywhere but at the young woman sitting before them pouring her heart out. Clearly, I wasn't the only who judged her as being *too young* the moment she sat in our circle. This didn't make me want to exclude her, but it influenced my perception of her. I don't know why I assumed being younger would make anything easier for her.

Désirée clears her throat. "You made exactly the right choice moving here," she says, the wrinkles in the corner of her eyes deepening. "You wouldn't have found us if you hadn't."

Judy smiles at this, sniffling. "How did you all manage before you made it to this group?" she asks, scanning the circle.

A few of the women pipe in immediately, stating family helped them cope. Ming tells us her husband was her rock throughout everything. Taylor jokes that wine and chocolate were the secret to her coping, causing the whole group to laugh. Judy sights in on me, her face a question that only has one answer from me.

"My friend Joy saved me," I confess. Ming cocks her head in my direction as she tries to discern whether I'd ever said the name. "Sometimes we find help in the most unlikely of places. Mine happened to live in the house behind me."

Satisfied, Judy looks to Désirée again, and the conversation turns toward planning a Halloween get-together with all our babies. Taylor suggests dressing up and trick-or-treating together. Everyone begins to chatter over one another as ideas take shape and opinions are shared. But even the prospect of throwing myself into planning a party isn't enough to take my mind off the one thing I've been purposefully ignoring.

As my new friends busy themselves with future details, I think back to the past, to where I was only a few short months ago. I'm sitting here today because of the one person I've been avoiding at all costs.

★   ★   ★

Kyle rests his fork on the edge of his plate, his brows lifted expectantly.

"What?" I ask, swallowing the last of my dinner. Since Kyle began working remotely a few days a week, our nightly meals have dramatically improved. Apparently, Kyle loves cooking. Go figure. Now that he doesn't spend two hours a day commuting, he has time to hone his skills. Tonight, it's herb-roasted chicken and roasted root vegetables with quinoa.

He frowns at me. "Talk to me," he says seriously. "You've been super distracted since you got home from your meeting."

A few months ago, he would've been content with a simple answer. I would've told him I was tired from being up all night, and he'd offer to watch Cody for a bit while I lay down. That would be that. That doesn't fly anymore. Kyle might've been content to play pretend longer, but we've vowed to be more honest with each other, even when it's hard. Most of the time I think it's made our marriage stronger. But there are days I wish he wouldn't be so insistent I share each and every one of my feelings. Maybe one day we can set some boundaries. For now, this open book mentality is the only way for us to recover what was lost.

The topic of Joy and my friendship with our neighbor is still complicated. Kyle's hurt I never told him about my visits. I worry a part of him is even jealous of the time I spent with Joy. For most of our time together, Kyle was the person I leaned on. It's hard for him to come to terms with the fact that when I needed him the most, I turned elsewhere.

"I'm worried about Joy," I say. I note the slight pinch in his smile when he hears her name. If only Kyle had meet her under different circumstances, I know he would love her. Now her name is a reminder of what little joy I felt after the birth of my son.

He sighs and glances at the rocker where Cody is sleeping. "You said she was doing well last you checked in on her," he reminds me. "Did something happen?"

I shake my head, afraid of to disclose my fears. "No . . . yes. I don't know. Ming and I walked by her house the other day, and it looked pretty bad," I say, biting my lip. "The yard is a mess, and her husband's truck has a flat."

Kyle stares at me as if I have two heads. Confused, I urge him to speak. "Babe, that truck hasn't moved in as long as I can remember," he says slowly. "I don't go that way often, but the house looks the same as it ever did."

My mouth goes dry as I hear the words spoken aloud, my suspicions confirmed. Closing my eyes, I think back to the spring when I first pushed my stroller up the rough gravel driveway, my vision clouded by a haze of tears. So wrapped up in my own emotional distress, I failed to take note of what was directly in front of me. The little details I observed over all the subsequent visits never added up to the full picture. Lost in the brush, the entire forest disappeared around me.

"No," I mutter, shaking my head furiously. "That can't be right," I say, even though my mind has begun replaying every second of every visit, a mental flip-book of clues I'd been too self-involved to recognize. Unwilling to recall the painful truth, I try to fill in the blanks. The truck had surely moved during the time I visited. I'm sure of it. I think. The tires weren't flat in June, of that I'm certain. Almost certain. The door was fixed squarely on the hinges last month. Joy's roses were in full bloom and thriving not long ago. She kept a pretty vase of them in her living room. Or was it the foyer? No, nothing in the front room. That was always bare. Her home smelled of roses and lemonade and freshly baked cookies. The little yellow house wasn't falling apart, it was charming and lived in. *Loved* in.

Kyle fixes me with a concerned smile. "Babe, I'm sure there's nothing to be worried about," he says, his voice confident. "They're an older couple. It makes sense things might fall by the wayside." He takes a sip of his beer, a little froth sticking to the edges of the beard he's begun to grow out while working from home. "Hell, if we didn't have the lawn service come every week, our house wouldn't look much better," he kids.

Relaxing a bit, I nod. Kyle makes sense. His confidence is contagious, I've always said. It's what makes him so successful. You can't help but trust the words coming out of his mouth. But something nags at the corner of my conscience, and I know I won't be satisfied until I figure out what's bothering me. "You're right," I concede, lifting my glass of wine to my lips. The sweet pink liquid is sour in my mouth, burns instead of refreshes.

Sensing I'm not going to let this go easily, Kyle takes my hand in his and squeezes. "It's the fall," he says, stating the obvious without any hint of irony. "Fall cleanups are a big job for everyone," he continues. "How about this: I'll call our guys tomorrow and ask them to add the McGregors to their rotation? This way, Joy and her husband don't have to worry about raking up all the leaves or anything else, for that matter," he offers. "Then sometime this week, you and I can stop over and check on them. I don't want to send anyone to fix the truck and offend the poor guy," he says, chuckling. "You know how those older guys can be. Seems like he might be the type who insists on doing it himself."

I smile, something akin to relief settling over me. With a plan of action in place, I immediately feel better. Kyle's assumption about Freddie tracks with all the stories Joy's told me. Although I haven't met the man, he sounds stubbornly steadfast in his ways, and I imagine he thinks he can fix his own truck, even if he must be getting on eighty-five.

"That sounds perfect," I say, wrapping both arms around his neck and drawing him close, gently kissing him on the lips. As I pull away, I'm reminded of one of my early conversations with Joy. "Oh my God!" I exclaim, a reasonable explanation for everything dawning on me. "I think they are away!"

Kyle lifts his brow and waits for me to elaborate. "Joy asked me months ago if I wouldn't mind taking care of her plants and cat while she went on vacation for their anniversary," I say, my words tripping over one another as they rush to come out. "She must've found someone else to help," I mumble, disappointed I wasn't the one Joy called on to help her. Shaking my head, I look at Kyle. "That explains her flowers looking that way," I say, eager to latch on to this excuse.

Kyle shrugs, happy enough to move on to another conversation. "Well, there you have it," he agrees, finishing his beer. "Either way, I'll still call the guys for that cleanup," he says, pushing his stool back from the island. "We owe them one."

We owe them more than one, but this is a good start. Topping off my wineglass, I watch Kyle head toward the den and readjust the blanket draped over Cody's legs. He plops onto the couch and pats the seat beside him. Pre-Cody, we had a few TV series we watched together before bed. Our ritual fell by the wayside for a while, but it's been fun binging to catch back up.

Eager to join him, I hold up a finger. I've one last thing I need to do before I can allow myself off the hook for the night. "One minute," I call. "Let me run up and change quick." Not a complete lie, since I do need to change out of the tight jeans I'm wearing and into some sweats. But it's not the complete truth. I hear him clicking through some trailers on Netflix as I scurry up the stairs, my phone tucked in my back pocket.

I sit on the edge of our bed and dial Joy's landline. It rings four times and I'm about ready to hang up, content to declare no one home. The line connects, the familiar crackle of a handset being jostled and the hushed sound of someone breathing on the other end before an abrupt silence. Whoever picked up the phone at Joy's house hung up. Bile rises in my throat as my mind races to rationalize this turn of events. I struggle to respond, holding the silent phone to my ear. With a growing sense of unease, I redial her number. Immediately, I'm greeted with the buzz of a busy signal, a sound I thought no longer existed in the time of cell phones.

I hang up and let the phone fall to the bed. As if in a dream, I kick off my skinny jeans and pull on my favorite joggers, one leg at a time. Each movement is heavy and slow, my limbs going through the motions on autopilot, my mind elsewhere. Somehow, I end up back down the stairs. I sit next to Kyle, my wineglass already on the end table. I lean against his chest, eyes on the screen. He's changed to HBO and we watch two episodes of a crime drama, pausing midway through the second for me to lift an awake Cody to my breast. My son falls back asleep cuddled between us, Binky in his mouth. Around ten thirty we head upstairs to bed, the soothing sound of ocean waves playing on the noise machine.

Kyle and Cody fall asleep instantly, their snores syncing together, a sweet cacophony of peaceful dreaming.

Lying on my back, I let my eyes flutter closed, but I can't quiet the chaos inside. I count backward from one hundred, hoping to drown out the insistent call of my conscience, begging me to act, to *think*. Nothing works and sleep is elusive.

I give in to the voice inside and lie in wait, watching the clock draw closer to dawn, one slow minute at a time.

★   ★   ★

October 17

The clock on the dresser glares in the darkness. The red numbers taunt me. 6:04 . . . each second drags, my heart racing at lightning speed, willing something to happen as I wait for the minute digit to increase. 6:05.

Standing in front of the window, I stare out across the pitch-black expanse of lawn between Joy's house and my own. It's still dark, the sun still resting before making its first appearance. Confused, I sit on the edge of the bed, careful to perch just enough so I can still see over the edge of the windowsill. 6:06.

I'm almost certain this is when Joy should be flashing the lights. Squeezing my eyes shut, I struggle to remember the very first time I met Joy, eager to find the source of the mystery SOS in my backyard. Although it was only a few months ago, I was a different person then. Sleep-deprived and desperate, I half expected to find out my mind was playing tricks on me, my body and soul so thoroughly wracked by a mess of hormones and unhappiness that I willed the signal into existence. All I remember is the relief I felt at finding out I wasn't going crazy. The lights were real. But what of the actual story . . .?

Dawn. That magical time before the actual sunrise. Joy always flashed the lights at this time. Back in May, it was earlier, if I recall correctly. Back when the world lights up a little earlier and goes to sleep sooner. In a fit of panic, I grab my phone to google "dawn today" and end up down a short rabbit hole. Within two minutes I've discovered *nautical dawn*, the magical time Joy refers to, and learn it changes slightly with every day. After further scrolling, I realized this makes sense. Sunrise changes with the season, therefore that special moment at dawn would also change. I assumed Joy followed the same pattern. Sunrise isn't until a little after seven AM. Do I wait until then? I set an alarm for seven. I'll go check on her when the sun comes up.

Slipping under the covers, I hold my phone in both hands over my chest but know it's pointless. The next hour will crawl by even slower than the last. Debating whether I should leave Kyle a note, I decide against it. I should be back before they wake up, and if I'm not, I'll deal with it later. It's not like I won't have my cell phone.

The front door closes silently behind me as I step out into the chilly October air. It finally feels like fall, no trace of the oppressive humidity of the previous week. Relieved to be acting, I push into a light jog down the driveway before turning left. The streetlights are dim overhead, but I don't need their guidance. I could travel this course in the dark. I once did.

★　★　★

The little cape looms in the darkness, looking more dilapidated than ever. Without the cheerful glow of the summer sun, the house looks abandoned. Gathering my courage, I mount the few steps onto the porch. The two rockers are the same as always, pointed in the direction of the street. An empty glass sits on the table, the rim smudged with Joy's pink lipstick.

Suddenly I'm not sure what to do next. If I knock on the door and the McGregors are home, I'm as likely to scare them half to death as anything else. I'm not sure what I will say to them to explain why I'm on their doorstep at dawn, aside from admitting I'm worried, and I'll risk embarrassing us both. For a moment, I contemplate turning on my heel and running home. I can check on them later this morning, like a normal person.

As I'm about to leave, something claws at the window to the right of the front door. The hairs on the back of my neck rise as I spin to face the sound. Stifling the scream perilously close to escaping my throat, I see Spot's bright green eyes glowing in the darkness. He meows loudly, rubbing his black body against the window before using his front paw to scratch the windowpane over and over.

My heart flutters in my chest as I struggle to catch my breath. Spot meows louder, his pleas setting off alarms in my head. I glance to the ground beside the door and see his food bowl pushing against the side of the porch railing, empty. My eyes wander to the welcome mat where a pair of LL Bean boots are resting, as if the occupant had simply walked out of them, leaving them as they stood. Figments of past visits come to the surface: Joy tripping over these same boots, complaining Freddie never put them away. Yet they were always here, right in the doorway. Freddie never put them away, but neither did Joy. No one ever moved them.

Spot jumps from his perch, and I hear him scratching at the door in front of me. My flight instinct screams for me to run home, but the better part of me is rooted in place, no longer willing to close my eyes to what is right in front of me. "Joy?" I call, lifting my fist to the door. I knock three times. Nothing. "Joy!" I call louder, followed by three more pounds against the door, each harder than the last, until the whole frame is rattling. I test the doorknob. It twists without hesitation, unlocked.

Spot immediately crowds my legs as I enter the foyer. Twisting his lithe body around my ankles, he rubs against my calves, purring loudly as he stares up at me. On the dining room table there are a few cans of wet food scattered in every direction. Clearly Spot's been busy trying to find his own food. The house remains silent.

"Here," I whisper, snapping open a can and putting it on the floor beside the staircase. Spot meows gratefully and rushes to eat, his slurping the only sound in the darkness.

"Joy?" I call out, standing at the bottom of the steps and looking upstairs. Not surprisingly, there's no answer.

Taking the stairs two at a time, I reach the top and open the first door, only to find a bathroom. The next door is a linen closet. Frustrated, I shoulder open another.

The soft glow from the streetlamps reaches through the windows, casting the bed in a halo of light. On the near side of the bed, Joy is curled on her side beneath a quilt, her back to the door. The far side of the bed is empty, the covers tucked in tight beside her. Her shoulders are shaking, her sobs barely audible.

"Joy?" I whisper, tiptoeing across the space between us.

A rustle under the covers. She sniffles back tears and slowly rolls to face me. She clutches a jean jacket in her arms.

"Fred?" she murmurs, blinking into the darkness. "Is that you?"

Falling to my knees beside the bed, I wrap my arms around her, burrowing my cheek into the pillow beside her. "It's me," I say, choking back my own tears. "It's Brynn."

Joy sighs, a low moan escaping her mouth as she collapses against me, her forehead now resting against my own. "I knew you'd come back," she cries, her slight frame convulsing beneath my embrace. I'm not sure who she's talking to, but I hold her close, shushing into her hair.

After a minute or ten, or maybe only a few seconds, she lifts her cheek from the pillow and wipes her eyes with shaky hands. Slowly she slides toward the center of the bed, and without another word I fold myself in beside her. Her glasses are on the bedside table, and her hair is loose around her face. She looks both older and younger than the last time I saw her. Lost in time.

"Tell me about him," I whisper. My eyes are finally open to all the minutiae I'd missed: a book facedown on the nightstand on the far side, an ace of spades tucked into a page; men's pajamas folded over the chair in the corner, a pair of slippers tucked beneath the legs. Everything left in waiting, it's all still there.

Joy lets out a deep breath, settles deeper against my shoulder before clearing her throat. It's a sound I've heard her make so many times before. Her storytelling sound.

"Freddie had a favorite poem," she starts, her strong voice betraying the tremor I feel in her body as I hold her close. "When we first visited a lighthouse together, we were looking out over the sound, and the sea was covered in a fog so thick we could barely see our outstretched hands," she says, lifting a frail hand toward the ceiling. "Fred wrapped his arms around me from behind and told me to close my eyes. So I did. We reached our arms out toward the water, and he slipped a diamond ring onto my finger. Of course, I was desperate to open my eyes and declare my love, but he held a finger to my lips," she says, her voice hushed as she falls backward through the years. "Then he recited his favorite line in my ear, his mouth so close I can still feel the goose bumps like it was yesterday. *"When the fog lifts, everything's still there,"* he whispered to me." She chuckles, wipes a tear from her cheek. "He told me to open my eyes and, like he could charm Mother Nature herself, the fog dissipated. Then he got down on one knee and properly asked for my hand. The ring was already there, as if he knew I'd never be able to say no to him," she laughs again. "That was Freddie for you, so confident. I thought that man was magic."

We lie in silence a moment, and I fear she's fallen asleep. Sighing deeply, she turns her face up to me, and we lock stares. Her blue eyes are no longer cloudy with tears or age but shining brightly up at me. "I've been waiting for Fred to lift the fog," she says, shaking her head. "But I fear I have to do it all by myself this time."

I wait for her to elaborate, but she rests her head back against the pillow, and we stare up at the ceiling, the minutes until dawn ticking away.

28

JOY

October 17

The fog is an illusion—
A master of disguise,
Which hides the tangible,
Before our very eyes.

But when the fog has lifted,
Everything's still there,
And the tangible,
Only seemed to've disappeared.

I KNEW IT WAS Brynn the moment I heard those first three knocks. The harsh pounding of the following three was a bit alarming, but not altogether surprising. When the phone rang last night, I suspected it might be my young neighbor, some latent motherly intuition sneaking across our connection, binding us together. But neither of us spoke into the void, both too frightened of the truth to address the words aloud. I saved her the trouble by leaving the phone off the cradle. A busy signal seemed less scary than a message that the line had been disconnected.

Never in my wildest imagination did I envision this would be the way it all happened. Not only the fact that I lay crying into the arms of a young woman not my daughter, but everything at all. My life. This was not the way it was supposed to go.

It all comes pouring out. The truth, the lies, the in-betweens. I'm talking to Freddie. To my children. To myself, this version and the others. Brynn listens, her arm around my heaving shoulders. She's not the one who should be here, but she's also exactly who should be here. Everything is wrong, yet right. Nothing is here, but everything's still there. In the darkness before dawn, it's easy to let the secrets escape, the black abyss the perfect place to hold the forbidden thoughts. So, I let the words rush from my mouth, eager to empty myself of their burden before the sun peeks over the horizon and steals the courage from my soul and shines its light on the parts I'd rather left hidden in shadow.

"When you're married for as long as us, there comes a point when you stop finding new things to fight about. Instead, you carry on with the same old fights, year after year. Even when I thought I was finally over something, it turned out the old resentments would still creep in and coil around my heart, same as before," I say, replaying battle after battle. Always the same, always a little different. Freddie leaving when I wanted him to stay. Me using the children as leverage. His sad smile when he walked out the door. Loving us most. The vase, the picture frame, the can of spaghetti, the insults and threats, all hurled at the door, a window, his head, his heart. The fights blend with the years, mingling and mixing so I'm uncertain which trip is which. Was Katherine a teenager when I broke the window, or was Richard still a toddler, scared of the sound? Were the kids in school when I packed them up and took them to my mother's house or was it summer vacation? I can't recall the exact details anymore. Only the hurt remains.

"He always came home," I say, staring at the ceiling. The overhead fan is still, a layer of dust and cobwebs reminding me of yet another chore I'd been neglecting. "Even when I forbid him from walking through those doors, he always came back, and I always forgave him. I even believed him when he promised not to do it again," I mutter. "Never did I really think our turbulent good-byes would be something permanent. As angry as I could get, in my heart I knew it wasn't real."

I sigh. I see his face at thirty, tanned and movie-star handsome. At fifty, the hair at his temples starting to gray, the whiskers in his beard more red than blond. Sixty-five, his shoulders beginning to stoop but still as strong and solid as the day I met him. *When did we get so old?* I wonder. We celebrated our eightieth birthdays, the wrinkles on our faces betraying the youth we felt inside. Freddie refused to slow down. He saw the young man in the mirror still, despite the high blood pressure and the little skin cancer scare from a decade prior. Freddie believed he was invincible and had me convinced of the same.

Brynn is staring at me, and I've no idea if I've been speaking out loud. Maybe this is all in my head. I blink, but she's beside me on the bed. I haven't completely lost my marbles.

"When he didn't come home that evening, I didn't worry. The boys would often grab an early dinner near the wharf," I begin, trying to pick up where I left off, but unsure where I lost the thread. A year ago, one might argue. I'd been clinging to loose spools since then. "The phone rang right after the clock struck six." I was standing in the kitchen, wrapping up the leftover chicken from dinner. I intended on using it to make chicken salad for lunch the next day, Freddie's favorite. "Something about the way the phone rang was different," I claim, knowing this sounds like the musings of a crazy old lady. "It rang five times, but when the answering machine clicked on, the person on the other end hung up. Not two seconds later, my cell phone rang," I say, recalling the exact way the screen lit up, the ring tone too loud and the little square vibrating across the counter in time with each ring. "No one ever called my home line first and then my cell," I ramble. "The other way around, sure. My kids always tried my cell, and when I didn't pick up, they went to the landline. Even though they knew I hated that cell phone."

I let the cell ring, frozen in place. If I didn't look at the messages, it wasn't happening. I continued to layer the chicken breasts into the Tupperware container. I scooped the extra broccoli into the garbage, not wanting to stink up the fridge. Nothing worse than old broccoli. I set the dishes to soak in the sink. I left the cell on the counter and took my glass of lemonade into the den. I settled into Freddie's chair with a book, but I couldn't concentrate. I kept waiting for the phone to ring again.

"But it didn't ring," I mutter. The sound that broke the silence was so much worse. "A car spun into the driveway, so fast I could hear gravel flying from the back side of the house. The driver didn't even bother to cut the engine before I heard a car door slam, a pair of boots stomping up the steps. I met them at the door, opening it before the assailant could even knock."

Jim's son, now a grown man whom I hadn't seen since he was a teenager a few years below Richard in school, stood on the porch. When he saw me, he swiped the ball cap off his head.

"I knew before he could open his mouth," I whisper, wishing I could stop the flood of memories, that I could use my clicker and hit "Pause," like I do on my shows when I need a break. "Calmly, I listened to the man and followed him down the stairs. He helped me into his car, and then he ran back up the steps for my purse, which I'd left in the foyer. I stared out the window and watched all the familiar houses pass by in a whiz as we raced to the hospital, going much too fast and probably running all the yellow lights."

But we didn't have to rush. Freddie was already gone. He passed away on that fancy new fishing boat from a heart attack that took him blessedly fast. The doctor informed me he felt no pain. I should've taken some comfort in the fact that he died doing what he loved, but it was a bitter pill to swallow. Freddie died in the arms of his mistress after I sent him off with a string of angry words I'd never be able to take back.

"I left the hospital in the jacket he was wearing when he died, still smelling of his aftershave and the sea," I say, said jacket currently bunched under the covers beside me. Sometimes I think I can still smell him on the collar, but his scent is so intertwined with my own now, it's hard to tell. "It was a year ago today," I whisper, unable to choke back the tears any longer. "He died a year ago, and I'm still so goddamned angry at that man," I admit, my jaw clenching against the sobs. "If only he'd listened to me and stayed home," I moan, envisioning another life where it's Freddie lying beside me, sleeping in because he's no longer a fisherman who needs to chase the tides. "He'd still be here," I mutter. "You'd still be here!" I cry into the darkness, my anger exploding. "You promised me you'd come back," I weep, my rage exhausted. Regret fills the hole in my chest. "You always came back."

Brynn pulls me closer to her shoulder and rests her chin on the crown of my head. I want to yell, to scream, to kick my legs out from the blankets and storm the house, unleashing my fury like I did so many times as a young woman. But I'm so tired. I'm so tired of being mad. All I want is for Freddie to walk through the front door so we can forgive each other, close the loop on our cycle, as predictable as the tides.

Instead, I take solace in Brynn's arms. In a different version of this story, Katherine and I had already cried into each other's shoulders, mourning the loss of her father. But the reality was, rather than connecting in our shared grief for Freddie, Katherine brought the family up from Connecticut for the funeral and stayed only one night, and not in her childhood home, but at a local hotel. She handled all the arrangements with her characteristic efficiency and even cried dutifully in the front pew as they ushered the coffin away. But when her tears dried up, she left town, happy to escape the sadness that surrounded me. I think Kathy cried all her real tears for her father as she watched him sail away again and again. I'm sure it came as no surprise to my pragmatic daughter that, in the end, he didn't come home.

I cry now for my daughter, for my failures as a mother, as a wife. I close my eyes and wish to drown in the salty waters of my sorrow. But Brynn shifts beneath me, a buoy bobbing to the surface.

"It's almost dawn," she says, looking out the window.

Peeking through half-closed lids, I see the hint of brightness edging over the houses across the street. Not a hint of red to be seen.

"Let's call him home," she says, her own voice thick with emotion.

I shake my head, clutching the sheets on either side. I've no desire to keep up the ritual any longer, to play pretend. Look what good it did me.

"Joy," she says, taking my hand. "Please," she begs, something in her tone belying the turmoil I feel inside.

"I can't," I mumble, my strength gone. The thought of rising from this bed and creeping down the stairs is too much, more than I can bear. "Please."

Brynn studies me and nods once. Gently, she removes her arm from beneath my shoulders and tucks the quilt up to my neck. Smoothing back the hair from my forehead, she bends and kisses me lightly on the cheek.

"Rest," she says, standing tall beside the bed. "I'll be back in a few minutes."

She backs from the room and is out the door before I can stop her. My eyes flutter closed, the exhaustion from telling my story overcoming me all at once. I give in to sleep, certain that Brynn will watch over me and be here when I wake.

◆ 29 ◆

BRYNN

October 17

We are the village.

—ItTakesAVillage Instagram account

I TAKE THE STAIRS two at a time, knowing I only have a minute to spare before the clock strikes 7:07, the official sunrise. Weaving through the dining room, I stub my toe against the leg of a chair and am thankful for my sneakers. I stumble the rest of the way to the kitchen, holding my arms out in front of me so I don't knock anything over.

Spot waits by the window and looks at me with knowing eyes when I enter the room. It's as though he's been waiting for me. Clearly, Joy isn't the only one who values this morning ritual.

"Let's bring him home," I whisper, earning myself another pointed look from the cat before he starts licking his paws.

Flash flash flash. I count to six. *Flash flash flash* before counting back to six once more. *Flash flash flash.*

I stare out into the backyard, my house plainly visible now that the trees have begun shedding their leaves.

A light is on in my bedroom. Cody must've woken up early, a prospect I only briefly considered before creeping from the house earlier. I whip out my phone and shoot Kyle a quick text, hoping to catch him before he worries when he doesn't find me sipping coffee in the kitchen or running on the treadmill in the basement.

> *Hey. I'm over at Joy's. Everything is fine, but I need to stay here for a bit. There's a bottle in the fridge. Sorry if I worried you, I didn't want to wake you guys. I love you the most. Xoxo*

I wait, imagining Kyle reading this message as he fumbles to change Cody's diaper, a task he's only begun to master. He'll be wondering whether he should lift him from the bassinet or try to settle him back to sleep. These questions were once mine alone. Even though we now share the burden, I still feel the tug of responsibility just the same. I'm guessing it will take me a lifetime of mothering before I'm confident enough to divide the tasks without guilt, always feeling like it's *my* job, not Kyle's, no matter how many times I'm reminded otherwise. The weight of parenthood always skews a little heavier on the maternal side. Thank the patriarchy, Ming might say. A text alert pings back almost immediately, startling me from my short reverie.

> *Take all the time you need. Code-man and I are fine. Take care of your friend. Love you back.*

Smiling at the screen, I can't help but feel a bit surprised. Obviously, I don't give Kyle the credit he deserves. I'm glad there are still things left for us to learn about each other.

With a renewed sense of purpose, I lift the kettle from the stovetop and fill it with water from the tap. While it boils, I raid the fridge and pantry. If Joy neglected to feed Spot, I'm sure she hasn't eaten anything herself. I slice an apple and cut up some pieces of cheddar from a block wrapped in Saran Wrap. In the cupboard, I find some crackers and the almond biscotti I love and add them to the plate. On the counter there's half a chocolate bar, and I toss it into the mix. A little morning chocolate never hurt anyone.

The kettle whistles and I pour the steaming water over two cups of lavender tea. I place the white ceramic saucer filled with sugar beside the mugs. On the sideboard, I find the tray Joy always uses to carry her lemonade to the porch. I carry everything upstairs.

Joy opens her eyes as I enter the room, the sunlight spilling across the sheets. Setting the tray on the dresser, I take a seat next to the bed as Joy pushes herself up so she's resting on a collection of pillows. She slides her glasses on and smiles at me.

Instantly, I'm reminded of every time this woman sat back in her rocking chair and listened to me while I fretted over Cody and worried about being a bad mom. She offered me lemonade and cookies while I told her made-up tales about pretend friends in the park. Joy watched over Cody and me while one or the other of us napped. She found me when I was lost in the darkness. She did all this without judgment and without expecting anything in return. She did this because we were more than neighbors—we were friends. When I needed a village, she was my village.

"Tell me about Freddie," I say, folding my hands in my lap, returning her many favors not because I need to, but because I want to. "Tell me the whole story."

EPILOGUE

One Year Later

A FTER TWO DAYS OF rain, they awaken to a morning so bright it's as if the skies had opened wider to reveal the heavens, glorious rays of golden sun cascading on the rolling hills surrounding the castle-turned-hotel they were staying in. Dew sparkles on the grass, the blades so green they look almost fake, a child's Crayola portrait of what Ireland should look like.

Outside the window, the birds chirp and chatter among themselves, reveling in the delightful weather and beckoning the women to the outdoors. Brynn had to resist the urge to post a picture to her Instagram, even though she had the perfect caption in mind. She'd been serious when she swore off all social media for the trip.

To distract themselves from the inclement weather, Brynn and Joy had enjoyed a tour of the best ale houses in the area. The kindly woman who managed the castle gave them a very specific list of places to eat and drink. She went as far as to tell them exactly what to order at each establishment. This suited Brynn's love of schedules and order. Joy only laughed and told her she planned on ordering the chef's special wherever they went. Together they relished a little bit of everything, sharing plates and indulging in at least two desserts at every meal. *Vacation calories don't count,* Brynn said whenever she felt a twinge of guilt for over imbibing. Joy promised they'd walk off the calories when they were finally able to tour the surrounding castles.

Today would be the day they visited Fanad Head Lighthouse. It was obvious the moment they woke up to the glorious sky. They didn't even need to discuss the day's plans, they were so in tune with each other. After a big breakfast of eggs, sausage, and baked beans, served with the host's famous orange marmalade on sour dough, Brynn and Joy packed a light backpack full of snacks and waters, eager to set out on the task that had brought them to this very special part of the world.

By ten AM, the pair had secured a ride to the Fanad peninsula, a mere thirteen miles away. They were both impressed by the hospitality of the locals, everyone eager to be of assistance and keen to aid the women with whatever they needed. Today's driver would also be their tour guide of the lighthouse, a special arrangement made by their host when she found out the reason for their stay. The kindness of strangers never ceased to amaze Brynn and Joy, who were both accustomed to the American habit of minding your own business.

It had taken a fair bit of planning for this trip to manifest and become reality. Although Joy had nothing but time on her hands, as she was always quick to remind Brynn, there were still the minor details of securing her first passport at the age of eighty-three and making sure she was cleared to fly at her advanced age, a factor Brynn seemed much more concerned about than Joy herself, who insisted she didn't feel a day over seventy.

Brynn had a bit more to organize on her end. Kyle was more than happy to stay home with Cody for the week, enlisting the help of his mother, who was eager to visit with the grandson she didn't see often enough. Her new business partners, Désirée and Judy, promised to hold down the fort at their fledgling endeavor. It Takes a Village had expanded from a simple party-planning company to encompass a variety of roles. While still available to plan parties, they also offered a mother's helper service, with aids ready to assist with every possible scenario a new or experienced mom might encounter: grocery shopping, babysitting, or helping get the kids dressed for daycare—it was all covered. You name it, and It Takes a Village could help with it.

Lately they expanded to make their service available to older residents in the community. They hired Earl, Joy's favorite taxi driver, full-time, to assist those who needed a ride to run errands. They also ran support groups, the goal of the company to promote community and make life less lonely. So far, they'd exceeded all of their expectations. They were up for a Best of Salem business award, an honor Brynn didn't dare get her hopes up for but secretly knew they'd win.

The stars aligned and the trip was booked and extensively planned, thanks to Brynn's meticulous care. This lighthouse tour was the highlight of the trip, made even more exceptional by the help of the Fanad locals, who insisted they get a private showing for their special ceremony.

Standing at the top of the tower jutting out from the Donegal Gaeltacht on the wild and windswept Fanad peninsula, the two women hold hands, each staring out across the vast expanse of the sea. Below them, the waves crash against the rocks, the white froth reminding them both of turbulent times not that long ago. Their tour guide, Cian, gave them a brief history on the view before them before excusing himself, giving the women a bit of privacy for their final act.

Brynn releases Joy's hand and removes an urn from the backpack, the ceramic a beautiful swirl of blues and greens, reminiscent of the water below them. Wordlessly, she hands it to Joy, who clutches it in both hands against her chest.

"We made it," Joy says, looking out into the ocean, past the horizon, to the other side.

Brynn nods, even though she knows Joy is talking not as much to her as to the memory of the man she promised to visit this lighthouse with.

The view from the tower is crystal clear, hardly a cloud in sight. A ship could see for miles in all directions today. But these women know that as quick as the skies cleared after the recent storm, they could darken twice as fast. When stuck in the fog, sometimes it took the brightest light to lead you home.

"Everything's still there," Joy whispers. "Wherever you are, my love, you don't need to worry. Everything's still there."

Brynn settles a hand on her friend's shoulder, a tear falling down her cheek. Joy opens the urn and solemnly hands her the top. Joy is smiling, tears sparkling in the corner of either eye, tears made up of everything: sadness and hope, happiness and regret, finality and new beginnings.

Holding both arms out over the edge of the tower, Joy tips the urn in the direction of the wind, and the women watch the remains swirl in the breeze before spiraling downward to meet the waves, drifting away in the current, taking Freddie home.

ACKNOWLEDGMENTS

THANK YOU TO MY wonderful editor, Tara Gavin. Your belief in this novel has made it what it is today. Your guidance and wisdom gave me the confidence to bring *Everything's Still There* into the world.

Thank you to the amazing team at Alcove Press. Rebecca Nelson and Dulce Botello—thank you for always answering my questions and never making me feel like a nuisance (even when I'm sure I was!). Your assistance and support throughout this process will not be forgotten.

To Jill Pellarin, my fantastic copy editor: if only you could sit by my side while I write and fix all my tense and comma issues! My book is better because of you. To Sandra Chiu, my cover designer: you created a beautiful reflection of this book—it's perfect.

Thank you to the members of the Women's Fiction Writers Association. I learned so much from all of you, and your encouragement kept me going when times got tough.

To Kenny: thank you for reading early drafts of the book. You have no idea how much it meant to me for you to even read it, and your comments and advice were invaluable. I mean it when I say you should pursue a career in the publishing industry!

Thank you to all the mothers who shared their stories with me. I see you. I hope this book makes you feel heard:

I thank my family and friends for their endless support. Since my first novel came out into the world, everyone has been so excited for book two. This gave me the courage to claim my title as author and share another piece of my heart in novel form. I'm blessed to have such an extensive network of amazing people surrounding me.

To Kevin and my girls: You are the reason I keep writing. After *What We Carry* came out, it would have been easy to end there. That was a deeply personal story that I needed to tell. But I have more stories in me, born of personal experience and out of my curiosity of other people's experiences. Book two is a mixture of these, and the love and support of my husband and children is the only way these little nuggets of ideas come to fruition in book form. Kevin, without you I wouldn't have had the time or resolve to finish. You're an incredible husband and partner, and your belief in me was absolute—even when I didn't believe in myself. Hayden and Hunter, you keep me on my toes, but thankfully you both like to sleep and grant mommy the time to type away at this keyboard. Everything I do, I do for you three.